Praise for *Man of Shadow and Mist*

Near the atmospheric ruir [illegible] ırarian Rosa Edwards meets an unexp[illegible] l mysterious Sir James Morgan—who [illegible] s the secrets darkening his soul. As the two are drawn together, local superstitions—and enemies—conspire to keep them apart. Filled with vivid writing, romance, danger, and faith, this novel is not to be missed.

—Julie Klassen, bestselling author of *Shadows of Swanford Abbey*

Man of Shadow and Mist is another fabulous tale from Michelle Griep taking us into the depths of Draculan lore and the heights of romantic hope. As a reader, first and foremost, I look for the dark and the Gothic. This is why I grab every novel by Griep, and this one is one you can certainly sink your teeth into!

—Jaime Jo Wright, author of *The Vanishing at Castle Moreau* and Christy Award-winning, *The House on Foster Hill*

What a Gothic delight! In her newest, a novel that is delightfully eerie, Michelle Griep weaves Dracula and Bram Stoker into a delectable romance between a bookish heroine and her brooding hero. Readers will adore this unusual hero, his sacrificial and tragic nature, and the intelligent and resourceful woman who loves him. Griep's brilliant writing brings to life a passionate couple, a family curse, and an entire town of interesting people. *Man of Shadow and Mist* is sure to captivate fans of Bram Stoker and all gothic literature.

—Joanna Davidson Politano, author of *The Lost Melody* and other Victorian novels

Yet another excellent work by Michelle Griep. Beautifully researched, excellently written. One thing I admire about Michelle is that she is so fearless, never sparing her characters, taking them so deep into trouble that you think all hope of happiness must be lost. But every time, Michelle crafts an ending both satisfying to the heart and serving the story well. The homage to Bram Stoker in this story is a bonus treat.

—Erica Vetsch, author of *Millstone of Doubt*

How can Griep manage to be so heartrending and yet heartwarming at the same time? She writes some of the most mesmerizing stories, and this one is no exception! Another "monster" tale, this time with echoes of *Dracula*, with light and shadow blended seamlessly into a stunning portrait of God's grace.

—Shannon McNear, 2014 RITA® nominee,
2021 SELAH winner, and author of *The Blue Cloak*
and the Daughters of the Lost Colony series

Ms. Griep has outdone herself yet again in this Gothic tale of Dracula that had my emotions leaping all over the place, from fear to sorrow to finally tears of joy. Dare I admit that the deliciously handsome, dark, and mysterious hero made my heart skip a beat? And the spunky heroine was a delight. The story was full of everything a reader could want right up to the last extremely satisfying page.

—MaryLu Tyndall, author of the bestselling
series Protectors of the Spear

Another stunning novel by Michelle Griep. She paints characters with earnest longings, pain, and pathos against a backdrop of vibrant settings. Themes of hope and redemption shine among the honest depiction of suffering, injustice, and human frailty. Don't miss this one!

—Sharon Hinck, Christy Award–winning
author of *Hidden Current*

Known for her literary artistry, Michelle Griep has done it again! Brimming with memorable characters and rich history, *Man of Shadow and Mist* will thrill Griep fans. I loved this book and didn't want it to end.

—Ane Mulligan, award-winning author
of the Georgia Magnolias series

With her trademark style of intrigue, romance, and gripping power, Michelle Griep once again delivers a stirring tale of loss and redemption. *Man of Shadow and Mist* left me turning pages far into the night, and James and Rosa left an indelible mark on my heart.

—Tara Johnson, author of *Engraved on the Heart*,
Where Dandelions Bloom, and *All Through the Night*

MAN OF SHADOW & MIST

MAN OF SHADOW & MIST

MICHELLE GRIEP

BARBOUR
PUBLISHING

Print ISBN 978-1-63609-565-3

Adobe Digital Edition (.epub) 978-1-63609-566-0

All scripture quotations are taken from the King James Version of the Bible.

This book is a work of fiction. Names, characters, places, and incidents are either products of the author's imagination or used fictitiously. Any similarity to actual people, organizations, and/or events is purely coincidental.

Cover Design: Kirk DouPonce, DogEared Design

Published in association with the Books & Such Literary Management, 52 Mission Circle, Suite 122, PMB 170, Santa Rosa, CA 95409-5370, www.booksandsuch.com.

Published by Barbour Publishing, 1810 Barbour Drive, Uhrichsville, Ohio 44683, www.barbourbooks.com

Our mission is to inspire the world with the life-changing message of the Bible.

Printed in the United States of America.

DEDICATION

To Ada Clare,
who took away a bit of the darkness
in this world,
and, as always, to Jesus,
the true and only Light evermore

"... the world seems full of good men—
even if there are monsters in it."

Bram Stoker, *Dracula*

ONE

I do believe that under God's Providence I have made a discovery.

Transylvania, 1890

Books are joy. And blight. Day and night. A bane, a strain, the rain that washes a soul caked with mud.

And in this moment, books were strewn everywhere about the library.

James Morgan scowled at the mess of titles cast askew over his massive desk. He was close, by Jove. A hair's breadth away. But to what? Another defeat? Or—*God, please*—a victory?

It wasn't so much a prayer as a desperate exhale.

Rising from his chair, he sidestepped a tower of leather-bound tomes leaning against the coal scuttle, then bypassed a sofa so thickly covered with medical journals that even if by some great miracle a caller wished to converse with him, there was no place to sit. He pulled down the last book on the highest shelf he could reach without using the ladder.

Philonium pharmaceuticum et chirurgicum, de medendis omnibus, cum internis, tum externis humani corporis affectibus.

He tapped the spine, thinking hard. This could be it.

"Would you like a pot of tea before you retire, my lord?"

He clutched the book and faced Sala, his butler, steward, everything but cook and housemaid. And—somewhat pathetically—his sole companion in the world. James frowned. What a heartless lot he'd drawn in life, with none but a tightly buttoned servant who wore a perpetual scowl to claim as his exclusive confidant. Though truly, Sala's fate wasn't much better, locked into a position handed down by previous generations, serving a family rumoured to be vampires—not that James did anything to extinguish such poppycock. Solitude was a small price to pay to pursue his research in peace.

"No need for refreshment, Sala. Though, with any luck, I shall not be retiring." He waved the book through the air.

"As you wish, my lord." Sala's face was lost to the lamplight while he dipped his head and backed from the room.

As soon as he disappeared, James thudded the book on his desk and flipped open the cover. He should have thought of looking through these pages long before tonight. Skimming past the first several chapters, he ran his finger down one column of information, then another and another, until finally he stopped and narrowed his eyes. Glucose? Could it be? Sugar was far too simple an ingredient, but one he'd not tried in combination with his current solution. Absently, he rubbed the side of his throat. Perhaps he'd been a fool for overlooking the ordinary.

"God, please." This time the words groaned out of him audibly.

He slammed the book shut and fled the room. Air cold as a crypt slipped in through the front of his gaping banyan, lifting gooseflesh on his bare chest. Even in August, castles were notoriously chilly. His mother's family fortress was no different.

Wall sconces flickered against all manner of ancient weapons adorning the walls, blurring them into a streak as he strode across the great hall—which wasn't so great anymore. Far too many decades of misuse had collected like cobwebs. When had these stone walls last heard laughter? Well, they would tonight, if his instinct was correct.

With a renewed spring in his step, he entered the study-turned-laboratory, grateful to see the tea tray he'd abandoned hours ago had not yet been removed. He grabbed the sugar bowl and set to work.

Twenty minutes later he held a syringe up to eye level and studied the clear liquid inside, just as he had countless times before this night. Would this truly be any different? His gaze drifted to the rabbits nosing about the food trough in their cage. He really ought to test the solution on them first to make sure the ingredients were safe. But he felt so sure, so right about this remedy.

And he was running out of time.

He plunged the thick needle into the side of his neck.

A burning sensation spread like wildfire through his veins, leaving a trail of hope. Sugar poultices to treat burns had been around forever, but he'd never thought of injecting the substance. It made sense, though. If glucose helped heal blisters on the skin, why couldn't it serve to protect against those very welts before they were formed? Judging by the unique feel coursing through his body, this might be exactly what he'd been searching for.

Practically giddy, he extracted the syringe, a drip of warm blood trickling down his neck. The mark would take days to heal, but it mattered naught. This *was* it! It had to be. He'd stake his life on it. . .and more importantly, his mother's.

The needle landed with a clatter on the silver tray as he rushed to the bell pull and yanked the velvet cord. Before Sala appeared in the doorway, he poured the rest of the solution into a brown glass bottle, corked it, and put it in his pocket.

"You rang, my lord? Oh, you are bleeding." Without so much as a lift of his brow, Sala produced a crisp white handkerchief.

James stifled a smile. Nothing caught this man by surprise. Were the entire world to blow up, Sala would remain, a broom in one hand and dustpan in the other, ready to tidy up the chaos with his usual competence.

James pressed the cloth to his neck. "Have my horse readied, then pack my bags and send them posthaste to Bistrița. I sail on the next ship to England."

"Yes, master, but…" Sala's dark gaze shot to the blackness outside the window.

James patted the man on his shoulder. "You fret like a *bunica*. Fear not. If I ride hard, I will make it before the sun rises. Now, off with you."

"It shall be done, my lord." Sala left as silently as he'd come.

James picked up the needle one last time, a rare smile growing. Things would be different now. A chance for him and his mother to lead normal lives.

For as surely as there was a God in heaven, he was certain this would outsmart death.

TWO

To add to the difficulties and dangers of the time, masses of sea-fog came drifting inland—white, wet clouds, which swept by in ghostly fashion, so dank and damp and cold that it needed but little effort of imagination to think that the spirits of those lost at sea were touching their living brethren with the clammy hands of death, and many a one shuddered as the wreaths of sea-mist swept by.

Whitby, England

Another cup of tea is always a good idea—except when it's not. Rosa Edwards gripped her bicycle handles tighter, regretting her decision to linger at Mrs. Hawkins's house that afternoon. Nay, nearly evening, now. The front tyre slipped over the dangerously slick cobbles, dampened from an influx of sea fog. The mist was so thick she could barely see six feet in front of her. Perhaps Mrs. Hawkins had been right.

"Sich a foulish fog is comely for wraiths and vampires, not young lasses such as tha. Nip on 'ooam, Miss Edwards, 'n be sharp abaht it."

Bah! What was she thinking? She pedaled all the harder. Stuff and nonsense, the lot of it, the very superstitions she'd been trying to eradicate. Fishermen's yarns and old maids' tales were for those who didn't know any better. This ride through the fog would have a happy ending. She'd make sure of it.

Blinking away the moisture collecting on her eyelashes, she readjusted her grip. As much as she despised irrational claptrap, there was nothing make-believe about the dank-smelling fog. She'd seen it billow in earlier, chasing the last ship to moor before a thick gloom had choked the entire town. Doubtless, others had marked its eerie appearance as well, which would cause a spate of ghost ship rumours at the public houses tonight. May God bless the poor souls who disembarked from that vessel. They'd get nothing but the evil eye for days—if not forever—for such a suspect arrival.

Carefully maintaining control of the library's delivery bicycle, she turned onto the narrow seawall path. Thankfully this stretch was short, for the heavy books in the front basket made steering a treacherous task. One wrong move could hurtle her past the stone barricade and plunge her into the grey abyss. Though it be summer, the cold arms of the North Sea would drag her down into blackness.

Indeed, that second cup of tea *had* been a bad idea.

Her foot slipped. The bicycle wobbled. Rosa leaned towards the landward side of the path as she replanted her shoe on the pedal. Perspiration added to the beads of mist on her brow. That'd been close. If she made it back to the library in one piece, Father would be sure to blister her ears for taking such a risk.

She turned another corner, where the narrow path connected with a wide road. A grateful sigh whooshed from her mouth. Here businesses lined one side of Pier Road while on the other a higher seawall kept pedestrians from toppling into the waves. Relief tasted sweet. The rest of the way home would be easy compared to what she'd just—

The front tyre stopped.

She didn't.

Rosa flew over the handlebars. Flailing, she broke her fall with her hands, the rough cobbles jarring her bones and scraping her flesh as she landed. Sharp pain stabbed her left wrist as she pushed up to sit. Dreadful. All of it. Books lay on the wet street, as did her bicycle, the front wheel stone-cold dead against the rock she'd hit.

"Are you hurt?" A deep voice—one with a slight accent—cut through the mist. A man dressed all in black swooped towards her, a huge cape billowing like bat wings with each powerful stride of his long legs.

"I—" She swallowed. Words—ever her companions—fled like rats from a ship as the big man dropped beside her. Oh, but he was striking. Raven hair thick with droplets curled past the brim of his hat. Wide cheekbones, full mouth, eyes so deeply brown that the accompanying golden flecks startled. But none of that was the cause of the sudden loss of her words, for she'd certainly seen handsome men before. In fact, she'd been courted by several.

This man was different. An odd mix of light and dark, both alluring and repellant at the same time. Instinct warned he was not a man to be trifled with. He was a general, a king, an immortal used to getting his own way. One who might not only match her strength of determination but exceed it.

She inched away from him.

He held out his hand, staring into her very soul. "Allow me to help you to your feet. It will do neither of us any good should a carriage happen by in this dreadful fog."

A truth undeniable. Still, she hesitated—foolish, for he was simply acting the part of a gentleman. Which, judging by the fine cut of his garments and air of authority, he was.

"Pardon me, but clearly the shock of the fall has bewitched you." There it was again, a faint yet very real foreign accent, one she couldn't quite place. Without further permission, he collected her hand.

They sucked in a collective breath, her from his electric touch, him no doubt from the bloody mess the cobbles had made of her palm.

"You are hurt." His grip slid to her arm, and he led her to the side of the road. Pulling out a handkerchief, he wrapped it tightly around her hand.

He smelled of the sea, this man. Of distant shores and foreign places. A whiff of cinnamon. A dash of something earthy, like freshly turned dirt. And something more metallic. Perhaps patinaed copper or. . .blood.

She shivered, then immediately warmed when his dark gaze bored into hers.

"Th–thank you," she stammered. Botheration! At six and twenty, she was well beyond such a schoolgirl response. Apparently that fall really had shaken her. "What I mean to say is, I do not wish to hold you up, sir. I shall be fine."

Truly, she would have been had he not ignored her dismissal and reached for her other hand. Again, that touch, gentle yet firm, jolted a current clear down to her toes.

"There is nothing fine about this," his deep voice rumbled. Without releasing his hold, he fumbled with his cravat and removed it, then wrapped the fine silk around her scraped skin.

And that's when she noticed. Truly, it was rude of her to stare, but he was too busy tending her injury to take note of her gaze fixed on the perfectly round wound on his neck. Small yet jarring.

"There now." The man tucked in the end of the cloth and dropped her hand. "Wait here."

He snatched up a nearby book, but before he could grab another, she joined him, heart breaking over the water damage already swelling the pages.

The stranger righted her bicycle then helped her stack the books into the basket, his dark eyes seeking hers. "This is quite a great load for one so slender, especially dangerous in this sort of weather. Perhaps I ought to see you home, make sure no more mishaps befall you."

She reached for the handlebars, hiding a wince when the hard metal pressed against her abrasions. "Thank you for your concern, but there is no need to trouble yourself further." She flashed him a smile. "I am certain I can manage."

His brow drew into a line, mocking her resolve. "Can you?"

Now there was a challenge. She lifted her chin, her earlier shyness fleeing. "I have no doubt whatsoever, sir."

His dark eyes widened. "You seem very sure of yourself, considering I found you splayed in the middle of the road not five minutes ago in a deadly fog."

"And believe me, I am grateful for your help, but I assure you, I do not intend to do so again." Taking care with her sodden skirt, she hefted her leg over the bicycle frame.

The man flicked water from the brim of his hat as he retreated a step. "Well then, seeing you will not be persuaded, good day, Miss...?"

"Edwards." She set one foot on a pedal, the other yet anchoring her to the road. "Rosa Edwards. And you are?"

His gaze drifted away, giving the distinct impression his mind did as well. A beat later, those all-knowing eyes shot back to hers. "Does it matter?"

"I should say so. I would like to know who to thank."

"All thanks be to God above. As for me, none is required." His tone was matter-of-fact, too flippant to be a clergyman, too genuine to be a lie.

"My, but you are a mysterious one." She spoke before she thought, a bad habit of which Mother frequently reminded her.

He tipped his hat, an amused quirk to one of his eyebrows. "Good day, Miss Edwards."

He wheeled about, his great cape arcing out in a black swirl. She really ought to pedal onward and get back to the library, but there was such raw power in the way he moved that it mesmerized her like little else she had known. She watched his tall form until shadows and mist swallowed him whole, leaving her entirely unsettled.

THREE

For life be, after all, only a waitin' for somethin'
else than what we're doin'; and death be
all that we can rightly depend on.

The familiar scents of the library greeted Rosa like a long-lost friend as she slipped in through the back door. Rich aromas filled the air—leather, ink, and the piercing tang of camphor oil. She was back in familiar territory.

But that didn't mean she ought not remain vigilant.

She eased the door shut then peeked around the corner of the half wall separating the makeshift office from the rental and sales area. Thankfully, Father stood near the front of the store, rearranging bottles of her mother's famed medicinals the library sold along with newspapers and stationery. An off-tune rendition of "Spanish Ladies" whistled past his lips.

Whirling about, Rosa hid the bundle of waterstained books in the nook between the supply shelves and the dust bin, then set the broom in front of them. Hopefully Father wouldn't notice before she had a chance to salvage the damaged goods. Maybe she could close the shop alone tonight, and then she'd coax the dampness from the pages with dry rags.

That settled, she padded over to the water pitcher while peeling off the wraps on her hands. No more blood oozed from her scrapes, but the fine fabric was stained. She'd have to wash and return the man's cloths later—if she could find him. For now, she put the dirtied items in a basin and doused the material with water. A good soaking would go a long way towards removing the stains. Now for her hair, which hung like seaweed past her shoulders.

Wincing, she worked out the pins and finger-combed what she could of the snarls, mind roaming back to the mystical man in black. Those all-knowing eyes. That faint yet distinct accent. He was like a dream, unreal but vivid, one she'd not easily forget—which was new and perplexing. She never gave any man a second thought.

"Please tell me the bicycle is in a better state than you."

Rosa faced her father with a gasp. "How did you manage to creep in as silently as the fog?"

"Easy enough. Your body may be here, but apparently your mind was in a distant land." Lamplight reflected off his spectacles, making her blink. His mouth pinched in disapproval as his gaze landed on her muddied hem. "What happened?"

"I took a little tumble, that's all." She inched her hands behind her back and pasted on a smile. "But I am happy to report that aside from needing a good washdown, the bicycle is in tiptop shape."

Eyes the colour of weak tea narrowed on her. "What of the books?"

She swung back her wet hair with a quick flick of her head. "Don't worry, Father. I delivered the new primers to the headmaster before my fall, so they arrived without a scuff." Which was true.

"I am happy to hear it, but I shouldn't have thought it would take you all of two hours for such a simple task." He directed a pointed glance at the wall clock. "Where else did you go?"

She licked her lips, stalling. She couldn't very well tell him she'd delivered a free load of books to Mrs. Hawkins, especially after their last row about such a service. Not that she didn't understand his strict business ethics. She just didn't agree with them, leastwise not when it came to providing the poor with the same access to education that the middle and upper classes enjoyed.

"Oh, you know." She forced a shy smile, hopefully adding just the right touch of meekness. "A girl likes to dawdle in front of shop windows."

A twinge of guilt nipped her heart, but it wasn't exactly a lie. She had fallen in front of the millinery's front window and tarried there for quite some time with the man who still refused to leave her thoughts.

Father retrieved his pipe off the desk then pulled a bag of tobacco from his pocket. A single brow arched above his wire-rimmed spectacles as he tamped some of the brown leaves into the bowl. "You were window shopping in this weather?"

Oh my. That did sound rather unbelievable. She inhaled deeply, debating how to answer, and came up woefully short. There was nothing for it, then, but to tell the truth—at least some of it.

"I also took a cup of tea with Mrs. Hawkins. Two, actually. I know I shouldn't have stayed so long, leaving you here to manage on your own."

"No, you should not have, not with such weather settling in."

She dipped her head. "I am sorry, Father."

"Hmm." He tucked away his tobacco pouch and struck a match, taking several pulls on his pipe before continuing. "Mrs. Hawkins lives nowhere near Cholmley Grammar School. Whatever possessed you to travel that far in such dangerous conditions?"

She poured a cup of water—anything but face what was turning into the Spanish Inquisition. "Her husband only recently passed away. The poor dear is lonely. I thought it a mercy to keep company with her."

"Yes, well, perhaps next time you ought to keep your socializing to sunny days and not on library time, mind."

The sweet fragrance of cherry tobacco filled the room. Taking care to hold the mug loosely lest she grimace from pain, Rosa sat on the worn settee, more than ready to change the subject. "So, did anything happen while I was out and about?"

"Mrs. Quincey stopped by for her copy of *The Castle of Udolpho*. Why she reads such gothic rubbish is beyond me, and this is her third time through it, no less!" He blew a perfect ring of smoke as he leaned against the desk. "At any rate, she was in quite a lather about a particularly bloody killing on her brother's farm. Several sheep were found today with their throats torn out."

"How disconcerting." Rosa sipped her water, holding at bay the horrid image of mangled animals.

"Indeed. Were a predator to blame, more than the throat would be missing."

A chill shivered across her shoulders. The sooner she changed out of this damp gown, the better. "So"—she shifted on the cushion—"what do you think happened?"

"Far be it from me to say, but rumour has it 'tis the workings of a bargheust hound."

She nearly snorted out her mouthful of water. This was the sort of inane talk she'd been trying to eliminate by delivering free books. Apparently she'd have to increase her efforts. "That is utterly ridiculous. There is no such thing. Just more superstitious drivel, if you ask me."

Father peered over his glasses at her. "I believe it was you who posed the question. All the same, until the cause is found, I'd prefer if you would keep your morning walks inside city limits."

"What?" A mischievous smile quirked her lips. "And miss all the danger?"

"Rosa, I mean it."

She rolled her eyes. "Please do not tell me you believe such blather."

"You cannot explain everything." He aimed the tip of his pipe at her, adding emphasis. "Still, what I believe on the matter is neither here nor there. The fact remains, something killed those sheep in an unnatural fashion. I will not have you harmed before your mother can marry you off."

She hid a smirk. If only he could see her palms right now. "Very well, Father. I shall mind where I walk."

"Capital. Oh! I nearly forgot. A package arrived for you." Setting down his pipe, he rounded the desk. A paper-wrapped parcel appeared, and he handed it over. "There you are."

"Thank you." A smile lifted her lips as she read the return address. *York School of Business and Commercial Enterprise.* Just as she'd expected, but the usual thrill of receiving the next lesson in her correspondence course vanished within seconds. Until she could purchase a typewriter, this would be her last tutorial, putting her dream on an indefinite hold. How long would she have to wait to finally begin her life? She stared at the packet as if she were a starving man holding his last bite of bread.

"Not the giddy response I was expecting." Father picked up his pipe, once more pulling on it and puffing out a smoke ring. "Dare I hope this means you are ready to give up your fantasy of becoming some grand secretary in a fancy York office?"

She clutched the package to her chest and returned the mug to the stand. "While I hate to dash your hopes, Father, I still endeavor to do everything in my power to rearrange society's expectations. I *will* be a secretary, and a successful one at that."

Father shook his head. "You already have a suitable position here at the library. Not to mention your mother would never allow you to cheat her of the opportunity for grandchildren."

"Lucy has already provided her with two, so I see no need for my future to include the restraints of marriage and family or even—as much as I dearly love books—this library. I want to be more, Father. I want to *see* more. A job as a well-paid secretary can provide that opportunity."

"Well. . ." He tipped his pipe over and dumped the unused tobacco onto a tin dish. "I suppose ultimately we shall all have to trust God for your future instead of our own designs, though I daresay your mother will have none of that sentiment tonight."

Rosa clutched the package all the tighter. "Please, don't tell me."

"No need, for I see you've already surmised what this evening has in store. Clean yourself up and put on a fresh gown. And were I you, I'd do so without your mother catching sight of you." He winked. "Now, make haste."

Oh dear. This wouldn't do. If Father chanced upon those swollen books, she'd have to come clean about her secret mission to educate the poor at no cost. "No, Father. It was I who abandoned you this afternoon. Why don't you leave early, and I will close up shop?"

"It was a slow afternoon. I have already reshelved the returns and pulled requests for tomorrow, so no need to stay. I shall see you at dinner." He strode from the room, whistling a rather flat rendering of "The Coasts of High Barbary."

Rosa tossed a sidelong glance at the corner. Should she drag the books home and spread them open around her room? No. A good pressing might work better. Quickly, she laid a cloth atop the stack then lugged over the coal scuttle and balanced it on top. If Father noticed, so be it. She'd rather face the consequences than leave the books to ruination.

That settled, she removed the mystery man's cloths from the basin, wrung them out, and tucked them into a handbasket to bring home.

Those she would lay out for drying in her room. My, what an afternoon. She headed to the door. As if tumbling from her bicycle hadn't been bad enough, now she had to endure yet another matchmaking dinner with some dolt who'd been hoodwinked into believing he could snag her hand. Definitely not a happy ending to the day.

She heaved a deep sigh. Too bad her mother hadn't invited the mysterious stranger who'd cared for her scraped palms, for at least then the evening would be intriguing.

Coming home ought to be like shrugging one's arms into a well-loved coat, one that molds to the body from so much use. Familiar. Warm. An embrace that set to rights an overly harsh world. James peered out the carriage window at his childhood home, a hulking black fortress that blended in with the night, and a smirk twisted his lips. Morgrave Manor was as pleasant as a cold slap to the cheek.

The front door opened. A black skeleton emerged, backlit by the lamplight glowing inside. Snatching his small leather bag off the seat, James alighted before old Renfield could hobble all the way down the stairs.

"That be you, Sir James?" The old butler squinted into the dark.

"In the flesh."

"Praise be, and none too soon. Come quickly, sir." He shuffled towards the door.

James beat him to it, and once inside the vestibule, he removed his cape and hat before Renfield shambled in. If he allowed the man to lead him all the way to his mother's room, the trek could take well into the wee hours of the night. "How about you see to my things? I can make it to Mother's room on my own. Is the doctor here?"

"He has already been and gone, sir."

Gnarled hands reached for the items. James frowned at the man's walnut-sized knuckles and tightened his grip on his medical bag. He would have to set about devising some sort of salve to reduce that swelling.

Renfield's pale gaze sought his. "Dr. Seward says there is nothing more he can do that Nurse Bilder cannot."

He snorted. Agatha Bilder had been threatening to leave his employ since the day he'd hired her. "*If* she stays."

"She's remained thus far."

"I was merely jest—"

The wail of a wounded animal cut him off. An awful sound, throaty and blood-chilling, cutting straight to James's heart. He jerked his head towards the pitiful cry. "Thank you, Renfield. That will be all."

"Very good, sir."

James took the stairs two at a time. Much had changed here, more so than what he'd expected. A fine layer of dust covered everything. The vase stands at the top of the stairs were empty. He glanced into the open door of his father's room as he passed by. White sheets draped the furniture like a gathering of ghosts, untended and forgotten. Naturally the maid couldn't keep up with everything, not with having to sit in for the nurse when she required an absence. But could not Renfield have found another serving girl? At the very least, the man should have made him aware of the dire condition of the manor. James sighed. Just one more task to which he must attend.

Annoyed, he rapped his knuckles against his mother's door, then entered without waiting for a bidding. Just past the threshold, he froze. Heaven above! What sort of madness was this?

His mother writhed on the massive four-poster bed, knotting up the white linens beneath her, her hair—nearly all white now—tangled and frizzed like an unholy halo about her head. When was the last time it had been combed? Her eyes were scrunched shut. The skin of her arms where her sleeves had bunched up was parchment thin and bluish. White foam bubbled at the sides of her mouth, and if that weren't horrifying enough, her wrists and ankles had been tied to each corner of the bed. No wonder she wailed so woefully.

James dropped his bag and darted to her side. "Mother?" He entwined his fingers through hers, despising the restraints pinning her to the bed like a beast. "I am here now. I have returned home."

No answer. No eye contact. Even so, she stilled.

He squeezed her hand. "Can you hear me?"

"No use trying. She don't hear a blessed thing. Not in this state." Nurse Agatha Bilder faced him across the bed, her collar as starched as her insensitive words. "Won't be long now, though I doubt I'll stay till the end, not with ye bein' about."

James gritted his teeth. For all her irritating bluster, the nurse truly had been a faithful caregiver. "Thank you, Nurse. If you do not mind, I should like a moment alone."

"As ye wish. Might be all ye get."

Her heavy step thudded towards the door.

"Oh, and Nurse?" He glanced her way. "When you return, please bring a fresh basin of warm water and a towel. I should like my mother's hair properly attended to."

She clicked her tongue. "Lady Dorina prefers it as is."

Her skirts swished out the door, and he turned back to his mother—then sucked in a breath. Electric blue eyes stared at him.

"Mother?" he whispered.

A single tear leaked onto her cheek.

This was not to be borne. Not by him. He fumbled with the knot securing her wrist and untied it, then pressed a kiss to the paper skin of her palm. "Mother, your son is here."

"You?" Her voice was a rusted hinge.

"It is James."

She blinked.

Then smacked him hard across the face.

"I have no son," she bellowed. "You hear? *Nici un fiu! Nici un fiu!* Filthy dog."

He captured her flailing hand, recanting of untying her restraint. His stinging cheek was nothing compared to what she might do to herself in such a frenzy. "Mother, calm yourself. Please!"

She thrashed all the more, her strength surprising. "Liar. Murderer! You drank his blood. *Dragostea mea. Dragostea mea! Oh, my love!*"

Memories reared like bucking horses. Such vile indictments were nothing new. She'd been accusing him of repulsive deeds since he was a child. Shortly after his father's death, her disease spiraled downward in a noticeable and uncontrollable spin. At first it had been sporadic and she was always repentant of her vicious words. But those bouts eventually increased, wounding him with each outbreak and causing most of the staff to flee. Porphyria was a debilitating disease, stripping the body of humanity and leaving it nothing but a bag of skin and madness.

In a trice, James reknotted the soft rope at his mother's wrist, then dashed to his medical bag. He'd felt revitalized since injecting the new medicine into his own neck. Would that it might work a miracle for his mother. He flicked the air bubbles out of the syringe as he closed in upon her.

"No!" She thrashed. "Nooooo."

Though he hated to do so, he forced her against the mattress. He searched her arms for a probable injection site, but like him, those veins had been ruined long ago with overuse. Blast! Could nothing come easy? He'd been willing to take the risk of infection and abscess himself, but to inflict such hazard upon his mother twisted his gut. Still, it was either that or certain death. He heaved a sigh.

Then jabbed her in the neck.

Her spine arched. An ear-splitting shriek ripped past her lips. A breath later, her eyes rolled back in her head, and she collapsed.

James's own heart stopped beating. By all that was holy! Had she been right? Was he a murderer?

He pressed his ear to her chest, hoping, willing, *needing* to hear a steady beat. A faint—very faint—*lub-dub*, *lub-dub* met his ear.

Clutching the syringe, he retreated to the nurse's chair and sank, weary from travel. Weary of life. He scrubbed his hand over his face, his fingers coming away with sweat.

Oh God, this time please heal her. Heal me.

He dropped the syringe onto a small table, wondering if this latest remedy would save his mother.

Or was she—and he—doomed to a gruesome death?

FOUR

The whole scene was an unutterable mixture of comedy and pathos.

Of all the men ever seated across from her at the table—and thanks to her mother, there were more than Rosa could remember—Albin Mallow was by far the dandiest popinjay ever to grace their dining room. Even their serving girl Mary had stared with a gaping jaw when bringing the soup to the table. And no wonder. From the lace-trimmed collar of Mr. Mallow's shirt to the golden embroidery on his waistcoat, there was no doubt he was a man of means. How Mother had managed to land this prize fish spoke volumes of her determination to get Rosa married off. She should probably be impressed.

Instead, she chased a roasted potato around her plate, looking at anything but the soft-cheeked fellow. To be fair, he seemed nice enough. Polite. Well-spoken. Willing to overlook her mother's many breaches of etiquette. But Rosa didn't want to give him any delusions she might consider him as a potential husband. Not that she had to. Her mother was doing a stellar job on that score.

"—agree, Rosa?" Her mother's voice sharpened. "Rosa?"

Drat. Caught in the act, and though she tried to deduce the subject, she had no idea onto which lane the conversation had veered. "Forgive me. What were you—?"

A razor-sharp look from Mother carved off the end of her question. "I said you are most attentive to your sister's little ones, that your motherly instinct runs deep and true."

Of all the topics to bring up at the dinner table! This was a new low, even for her mother. Rosa laid her fork and knife across her plate, what little appetite she'd had now completely vanished. "I hardly think Mr. Mallow is considering children at the moment, Mother."

"On the contrary, Miss Edwards." Mr. Mallow smiled, his teeth surprisingly white against his pale skin—quite the contrast to the swarthy man who'd come to her rescue earlier that day. "My uncle says it is high time the Mallow name was handed down to the next generation. I fancy I am ready to settle in with the right woman."

She met his gaze directly. "Then I wish you all the best in finding that woman, and I look forward to meeting her."

Father coughed into his napkin.

Mother warbled a laugh. "Many a wife has been found without having to look any farther than across a table."

Good heavens. Her mother couldn't be any more obvious if she tried. Rosa peeked at her father, pleading for intervention.

Oblivious, he picked the last bite of meat off the chicken bones then wiped his lips with a napkin.

Crooking her finger, Mother ordered Mary to refill Mr. Mallow's wineglass.

He sipped his drink, his gaze wandering. "This is quite the quaint little house. Very cozy."

"Yes, well—" Her mother dabbed her lips with her napkin. "I daresay our modest home is nothing to compare with your uncle's estate, Mr. Mallow, but even so, Rosa has had the best domestic education. She will be an asset to any household, big or small."

Rosa pressed her lips tight to keep from smirking. She barely knew how to make tea without scorching the kettle.

Mr. Mallow appraised her with an arched brow, a gleam of appreciation deepening the brown of his eyes. "As heir to my uncle's dynasty, I am happy to hear you might be able to manage a large manor house."

She opened her mouth, but once again Mother beat her to it.

"And that's not all. My daughter has many other skills." Mother glanced at Father. "Does she not, husband? Is Rosa not able to manage accounts and. . .well. . .attend to whatever it is you do in the library?"

Father peered at her over the rim of his spectacles. "Pray tell, my dear, what is it that you think we do?"

"Oh, you know. Books and. . .well, the sale of my medicinals, of course." She swirled her hand in the air. "But that is not the point. What matters is that Rosa is an invaluable help to you and will be to her future husband." She smiled at Albin with a grin more saccharin than a debutante's.

Rosa balled her napkin into a wad as tight as her nerves. She'd rather die than sit here a moment more, yet if she dared leave the table, that wish would come true. Mother *would* kill her. So, how to get out of this gracefully? Feign a headache? Accidentally tip her glass and spill the rest of her wine onto her lap? Shoot to her feet with a feral cry and claim momentary insanity?

"It's just a matter of time, really," Mother blathered on. "A short time, I suspect. Nearly all the eligible bachelors in Whitby have already asked for her hand, but Rosa hasn't chosen one yet. Isn't that right, darling?"

She creased the life out of her napkin and laid it to rest next to her plate. "I am sure that Mr. Mallow has no interest in hearing of past suitors."

He tipped his head at her. "My uncle always says knowledge is power, and your mother has been a fount of information tonight."

Pleasure deepened Mother's cheeks to a rosy hue. "Why, thank you, Mr. Mallow. My family does not always appreciate my intellect."

"Oh, for pity's sake," Rosa huffed under her breath.

Mother cut her a scathing glance. "What was that?"

She bit her lip. Twice caught in the act. Perhaps that fall earlier today had taken more out of her than she'd cared to admit. "Nothing of consequence."

"I say, dearest"—Father shoved away his plate—"why not retire with Rosa and let us men get on with our brandy and cigars?"

"Yes, I suppose it is that time. But don't keep Mr. Mallow to yourself for long." Beneath her pleasant tone ran an undercurrent of threat. If Father did regale the man with one too many stories, he might end up sleeping on the sofa tonight.

Rosa hurried from the room. Pity that her pace couldn't speed time as well, for she was more than finished with this farce. The only one interested in a match between her and Mr. Mallow was her mother, for surely after such an awkward dinner, the man could have no desire to attach himself to this family.

The empty sitting room—a calming atmosphere with its glow of golden lamplight and scent of lemon wax—eased some of the tension in her shoulders. A relief short lived, for her mother stormed in a few breaths later.

"You have really outdone yourself tonight, Rosa." With a great scowl, Mother aimed a finger at her. "Staring at your plate. Mumbling beneath your breath. Not once did you smile at the man, flutter your eyelashes, or anything else that could be even remotely construed as interest in the fellow."

"Because I am most emphatically *not* interested."

"Well, you should be, for you've turned down the bulk of the men in this town already." Mother sulked onto the sofa, smoothing her skirts as if she'd been the one on the selling block tonight. "Albin Mallow is a fine catch. The best one we've entertained thus far. He is heir to his uncle's prosperous shipbuilding business and quite a good looker. What can you possibly have against him?"

Silently, Rosa fiddled with the hems of her sleeves, for the fact of the matter was her mother was right. Mr. Mallow was an eligible bachelor, one whom many a girl would swoon over.

But she'd never been like other girls. Too bookish. Too dogmatic. Too cynical. A long sigh leaked out of her. "It is not about him, Mother. It is me, which you would know if you ever really listened."

"Go on." Mother folded her hands in her lap, for once her blue eyes focused—*truly* focused—on Rosa instead of glazed over with her latest scheme to marry her off. "I am listening now."

Rosa's breath hitched. This was new. Dare she bare her heart? Then again, would she ever get another chance to share her hopes with a mother who usually had no time because she was too busy matchmaking? "Very well, Mother. I have a dream. Several, actually."

Where to begin? Gathering her thoughts, she sank on the cushion next to her mother. "First, I want to help rid this town of its superstitious ways. Mr. Mallow was right about one thing. Knowledge *is* power, and I wish to spread knowledge to those in need of it most, those who cannot afford a library subscription. I believe once people are educated, they cannot help but to advance in their lives, in their careers. Why, Father would have a whole new population of subscribers in no time."

"Mercy, such thoughts you have." Mother's brows dipped, making her small eyes even smaller. "Is that all? *That's* what is keeping you from wedding a nice young man?"

"No, not entirely." She shifted uncomfortably on the sofa. Mother knew of her correspondence course but not her goal of leaving Whitby when finished. Rising, Rosa paced the rug, concentrating on the green threads in the carpet. "I want to move to York, Mother. I long to be a secretary just like Miss Mavery, a bold woman who is paving the way for females to work outside the home. Who knows? I might even work my way up to a London position, see what the world has to offer, be more than a nameless wife and mother tucked away in a nowhere town. I want more than that, don't you see?" She stopped and faced her mother. "My happily-ever-after is not here in Whitby. It is being a secretary in a high-paced office, making things happen, hobnobbing with important people. . .making a difference in this world."

"Oh Rosa." Her mother's shoulders shook with laughter, the sound more degrading than any insult. "You have read one too many library books, my darling. Your father never should have allowed you entrance into a man's world to begin with. I blame him for such outlandish whimsies—which is what they are, you know. Had I not set aside my girlish fancies and married your father, I wouldn't even be having this conversation for you wouldn't be here. My granny was a thriving herbalist, keen to hand over her business to me. But the duty of a young woman is the rearing of the next generation for the greater good of mankind. Surely you can see my sacrifice was worth the death of my own dreams."

Mother rose like a cloud on the horizon, swooping in close to pinch colour into Rosa's cheeks. For a final touch, she licked her thumb and smoothed her eyebrows. It took everything in Rosa not to wrench away and scream at the top of her lungs. Could her mother never treat her or her father like anything but mistakes in need of improvement?

"There now." She finished her ministrations with a tap to Rosa's nose. "Be sensible, Daughter, and make the most of tonight's opportunity. Lord only knows if you'll get another." She spun towards the door.

Rosa clenched her fists to keep from swiping away the moisture on her eyebrows. "Where are you going?"

"To occupy your father so you and Mr. Mallow may have time alone."

Alone? She gaped. "But that is highly improper."

"You can thank me later." Her fluttering fingers were the last to leave the room.

Rosa blinked. Unchaperoned time alone with a man? Her mother really was desperate. Though without her mother censoring her words, she could speak plainly with Mr. Mallow and have him out of here in record-breaking time.

Heartened, she prodded the poker into the few coals. Unbidden memories flared to life, as real and red as the glowing embers. Here in front of the hearth, she'd turned down Thomas Harker and Grayson Billings, the first two men Mother had foisted upon her several years ago.

She jammed the poker into the holder and crossed to the window, but that was no good, either. Right here by the blue draperies, she'd refused Jonathan Harper and George Witherspoon.

Whirling, she advanced to the overstuffed wingback, then stopped cold. Victor Whiting had knelt there on the carpet and professed his undying love for her. Of course, it wasn't her he truly loved. More like the idea of her, a delicate spun-glass idea held up to an incandescent light of embellishment cast by her mother. All these men, every last one of them, had fallen in love with the picture her mother painted of her, not the real her.

"Pardon, Miss Edwards, but your mother said to let you know she's feeling rather faint. Your father is seeing to her now."

Startled, she faced Mr. Mallow, suddenly sorry for the man who'd been told impossibilities. "Well"—she smiled—"in that case I think it best to call it an evening." She headed towards the door.

He sidestepped her, blocking her route. "No need. Your mother assured me it is nothing serious and entreated me to stay as long as I wish."

Oh Mother. Rosa couldn't help but sigh. "Please do not feel obligated, sir. I apologize for my mother's behaviour tonight. She can be a mite. . .intense and forceful in the management of people's lives."

"So can my uncle." He strode past her, leaving the scent of his spicy—and very expensive—shaving tonic lingering on the air. Stopping near the mantel, he turned to her with a smile. "It seems we are both beholden to headstrong influences in our lives, but that does not have to be a bad thing. I have learned to appreciate plain speaking, for therein one never need wonder what is at stake."

Hmm. There was an interesting thought. Perhaps there was more to Albin Mallow than she credited.

He closed in on her, standing so near she now noticed the faint ivory flowers and vines woven into the fabric of his cravat. "I should like to see you again, Miss Edwards. Perhaps you'd like to take a turn about town in my new ralli cart? It's a real looker, with a ride as smooth as ice. Does tomorrow afternoon suit, say three o'clock? The library is so close to the shipyard, it's no trouble at all to swing by."

And here it was, time to perform her usual speech.

She squared her shoulders. "Mr. Mallow, being that you value plain speaking, allow me to be frank. While I appreciate your attention, I am not interested in pursuing any sort of relationship with you other than a polite acquaintance. You are a fine man, but I am not the woman for you or anyone else. Simply put, I am not marriageable material. And on that note, I shall see you to the door."

She retreated before he could respond, leading the way to the coat tree and offering his hat with a smile. "Good evening, sir."

He held the felt brim loosely in his hands. "Come now, say we at least part as friends."

Rosa hesitated, nibbling her lower lip. She didn't want to encourage any delusions that might yet linger in the man's mind, yet it would not do to upset one of Father's best subscribers. "I am afraid I must insist that is all we can be."

"Then I look forward to nurturing our friendship." He winked as he donned his hat. "Meanwhile, I bid you a very good evening." He dipped a bow and disappeared into the night.

Rosa shut the door, pressing her forehead against the cool wood. How many more of these evenings would she have to endure before she moved to York or her mother gave her up as a lost cause?

"I cannot believe you let that one get away!"

She turned, facing the angry pucker of her mother's mouth. So much for sharing her dreams aloud. "Oh, Mother, did you hear nothing I said tonight? I am not interested in marriage."

"Twenty years from now you will be, when Father and I are six feet under and you're a drudge in your sister's household. And then your remorse will be too late." She jabbed her finger into Rosa's collarbone. "Mark my words, young lady. If you do not mend your ways, there will be no happy ending for you."

Rosa Edwards was trouble. Albin had no doubt about that. A headstrong woman if there ever was one. But she was a pert little thing with that adorable upturn to her nose. Scrappy. Hardly the Virgin Mary her mother made her out to be. Albin hung up his hat and lit the lamp on the foyer table just inside his uncle's home, a smile curving his lips. He'd made great strides in winning her already. After all, he'd secured what no man before him had acquired—her friendship. It would only be a matter of time to cultivate that into something more.

He grabbed the lamp and strode into the hall.

"You are home early. How did it go?"

His uncle's voice drifted out of the parlour, and Albin turned toward the sound. No lights shone in the dark room save for the red glow of a cigarette.

"Bad. . .and good." Albin lit several other lamps, the glow bouncing off the Egyptian artifacts his uncle kept behind glass. The place was a veritable museum. "The food was abysmal, though I shouldn't have been surprised. It's not like the Edwardses are the wealthiest family in town."

"True, but they do own the library, and a very pretty piece of real estate it is. If your head weren't so filled with the latest trends and fashions, you'd remember I told you I've been trying to purchase the place from Edwards to expand our business. The location is perfect. . .which, unfortunately, he claims as well for the distribution of his infernal books. It's a prime little piece of property, and he knows it. Central to everything." Uncle Preston took another drag on his cigarette, the inhale sucking the life from his already sunken cheeks. "So, what of the girl? The elusive Miss Edwards?"

"As elusive as ever." Albin retrieved his own smoke from the gilded box on the table. "She told me in no uncertain terms that despite what her mother says, she is not marriageable material."

"Then you have much in common."

"How so?" Furrowing his brows, Albin rolled the cigarette between his fingers, then sniffed it from one end to the other. "I am a fine catch. Any woman would be proud to have me bestow the Mallow name upon her."

"Yes, but you did not start out that way." Uncle rose like a spectre from a grave. "Tell me, Albin, who was that rotund little boy deposited onto my doorstep twenty years ago? The roly-poly crybaby who took a good bullying during those early years at school?"

Albin stiffened, fighting a flinch as his uncle grabbed him by the shoulders and marched him to the great mirror over the mantel. "But look at you now. Thanks to my molding, you are a man to be reckoned with. Wealthy. Powerful. Heir to a prosperous shipbuilding dynasty. Do not be so uncertain about Miss Edwards. People can—and will—change. All it takes is the determination to reshape them into the image you wish them to be."

He stared at his reflection, at the aquiline nose just a little off center, one that would make a Roman proud. It was a Mallow trademark, a herald of success, so Uncle Preston always said.

He met his uncle's gaze in the mirror. "You are right, as usual."

"Of course I am." His fingers dug into Albin's shoulders just a little too hard. "So, what do you say? Are you going to let a snippet of a skirt get the best of you by turning you away?"

"I think not." He wheeled about to face his uncle. "In fact, I rather like it this way. The thrill of the chase and all. Have no doubt, Uncle. I vow I shall be the man to catch Miss Rosa Edwards."

"A worthy pursuit." The approval in his uncle's eyes hardened to blue steel. "See that you do not fail this time. She is the bargaining chip we need. Once she marries into the Mallow family, her father will have no choice but to cede me that land."

FIVE

All we have to go upon are traditions and superstitions.

By the next morning, the mist had sailed off to some far corner of the North Sea, leaving behind a mouldy stink and leaden skies. A brisk constitutional was just the thing to warm one in body and spirit—and Rosa wasn't the only one who thought so, for ahead, two white-haired ladies stood in her path, peering over the railing of the swing bridge at something below. The closer Rosa drew, the easier she could hear their words.

"It were an ill wind a'blew in 'ere yesterday, bringing all manner o' evil with it."

"Aye. Poor soul."

Curious, Rosa stopped next to the woman in a green coat so tightly buttoned there was no telling if she even had a neck. She followed the woman's gaze down to the River Esk, where a limp bridal bouquet swirled in the current, stuck between the bank and a rock. A shiver spidered across her shoulders. Those flowers should be clutched in the hand of a beaming bride, not half-drowned in the murky flow of black waters. A surprising sorrow closed her throat.

Taken aback by such depth of emotion, Rosa lifted her face to the ladies. "What happened?"

The woman next to her shrugged. The other answered, her hooked nose bobbing as she spoke. "T' lady in white, no doubt abhat that."

Rosa frowned. The old tale of a wandering ghost lady who mourned the loss of her sailor was one she'd heard hundreds of times, but all the same it grieved her. The people of Whitby lived in such needless fear. She flashed a smile, hoping to lighten their moods. "I am sure there is a more logical explanation."

The green coat lady shook her head. "No lass willingly tosses away sich a love token. This were devil work—an' I hear tell that devil is 'ere ta stay."

Both ladies' heads swiveled towards the abbey ruins up on the hill, though it was hard to tell if they indicated the abbey itself or the dark hulk of Morgrave Manor next to it.

"What devil?" Rosa asked.

"Hisst!" The green coat lady swung back to her. "Best not ta speak his name, child. Might conjure 'im up." She crossed herself.

The other lady followed suit. "Like ol' Moll 'ere says, it were an ill wind a'blew in yesterday."

Oh dear. They really believed such morbid fancies. Rosa pulled out a library calling card, printed with her name and the hours of operation. She pressed it into Moll's hand. "If you ladies would like to stop by the library this afternoon, I should be happy to find you a book about wind. I am sure it will set your minds at ease to learn its function is neither good nor evil."

The lady shoved the card back at her. "Thou is too young ta know there's more to a North Sea mist than can be explained wi' ink and paper." She hooked arms with her friend, and they tipped their heads at her in dismissal. "Good day to ye, miss."

"Good day, ladies," Rosa called after them as they bypassed her. "I hope to see you again sometime."

She continued on her way into town, though this time her steps were heavier. Why could people not see that such supernatural fears were unnecessary? Even more, such fears were harmful. Why, if—

She stopped, her train of thought completely derailed by a shiny black dream in the window of Guffy's Emporium. Facing the glass, she pressed her hand to her chest, longing tingling in her fingertips. Oh, how she'd love to purchase the new typewriter sitting atop the wooden pedestal. That was her ticket out of this town. . .and a very expensive ticket it was. Though she faithfully saved part of her weekly wages, the money in her hope jar at home was still woefully short.

"Oh God," she whispered, "please provide the means to buy this typewriter, and if it is all the same to You, gracious Father, sooner would be better than later."

She reached her gloved fingers to the display, then pulled away and set off once again. No sense waiting around for coins to fall from the sky, for then she'd be no better than the ladies who expected a devil to appear merely by the mention of a name.

Two blocks later, her pace slowed in front of the milliner's window. She'd intended to ask if the shopkeeper had seen or known the man who'd helped her yesterday, but she hadn't intended to experience the same tingle that'd traveled up her arm when he'd wrapped her hands so tenderly. Pausing, she closed her eyes. Sure enough, the man's penetrating gaze flashed so real in her mind, she could feel his warm breath against her cheek. And was that a hint of cinnamon in the air? Gasping, she popped open her eyes, fully expecting him to be inches from her.

The street was empty—save for an old man with a broom across the road, who stared at her as if she were daft. Maybe she was.

She patted the bulge in her pocket to make sure the mystery man's cleaned handkerchief and cravat were still folded inside. Satisfied, she approached the millinery door but then pulled back, thinking better of it. Even if the clerk had caught a glimpse of him, how was a hatmaker to know the identity of a foreign man? It's not like the fellow would have been shopping for a frilly bonnet, especially in yesterday's weather. No, if he'd arrived on the last ship to moor, he'd likely have stopped at the White Horse & Griffin to rent transportation or maybe even stay the night.

So that's where she went next.

It smelled of vinegar and overcooked beans inside the small front hall of the coaching inn. Could be their cook was having a bad morning, or might the odd scent be coming from the spindly fellow behind the desk? His suitcoat looked as if it could use a good scrubbing. Should he not be out back with the ostlers instead of greeting the public?

He set down his pen as she approached. "How can I help you, miss?"

"I should like to know if a man stopped in here yesterday to rent a room or maybe hire a horse or carriage?"

"There were several." He rubbed his knuckles along his jaw. "The *Demeter* carried more than one passenger looking for accommodations."

"I see." Truly, she should have known there'd have been more than one man seeking shelter. This was, after all, a port town.

But the clerk overlooked her absurd inquiry as he pulled a ledger off a nearby shelf. "I was on duty at the time. Perhaps a description of the fellow would help."

Oh dear. It didn't take much to envision the striking face of the man who'd visited her last night in her dreams. Cheeks suddenly warm, she straightened her lace gloves. "He has black hair, a matching moustache, brown eyes, and is more olive of complexion than fair. His black cape and hat are of the finest quality, so clearly he is a man of means. Oh, and he is tall." She narrowed her eyes at the clerk, calculating his height. "An inch or two taller than you, I would say. His speech carries a slight accent, one I cannot quite place. All in all, he is definitely a man not easily forgotten."

The clerk's nostrils flared. "You're sure of all that, miss?"

"Yes." She angled her head. "Do you remember him?"

A lump traveled his skinny throat as he audibly swallowed. "I do, but if he's the one I'm thinking of, it's best you forget him."

"Why? Who is he?"

He tugged at his neck, loosening the knot of his tie. "Elsewhere—Transylvania, I believe—he is known as the Count of Umbră Castle, but here he's called Sir James Morgan, the baronet of Morgrave Manor. He came in on the mist, the fog following him right through that door." The clerk aimed a bony finger at the inn's entrance. "He rented a wagon for his trunks—to be delivered today, for none had been readily available—and he secured a carriage for himself."

Rosa glanced at the open ledger, hoping to spy verification of his words, but the page was empty. "He is the master of Morgrave Manor?"

The clerk nodded sharply. "One and the same, miss."

She studied him, expecting any moment to see humour twinkling in his eyes. Everyone knew the baronet had passed on long ago, leaving his widow alone in that drafty old manor house on the hill. She arched her brow at the clerk. Did everyone in this town spout nothing but superstitions? "Are you suggesting that the old baronet rose from the grave and crept in on a swirl of shadow and mist?"

"Pish! None of it, miss." He eyed her as if she were the mad one. "It was his son."

She sucked in a breath. "Oh! I did not think. . .I mean, I. . . Never mind." She sputtered to a stop. Perhaps she was mad. After all, it was highly unlikely a baronet would have so gallantly braved yesterday's weather to scrape her off the wet cobbles, and after that, offer to see her home. "Perhaps we are both wrong. Who else rented yesterday?"

"Let's see." The clerk flipped back the ledger's page and ran his finger down a column. Rosa leaned closer, following the action.

"Mr. Timothy Borgo let a room for three nights. Anthony Constata stayed just the evening and left on a rented horse." The clerk squinted at the next entry. "Humph. Should have written this one with a steadier hand. Looks like a Mr. Robert Pruth needed no quarter but required a small donkey cart and should return it later today." He flipped back to today's blank page and looked up. "There you have it. May I ask why you are so interested in finding this particular man?"

"I have something of his to return."

"Ahh. Would you like to leave it here and I could ask Mr. Pruth or Mr. Borgo if the item belongs to them?"

Hmm. That would take care of the problem, but then she wouldn't get to see the mysterious man again. A rogue desire, really. One she probably ought not give into, and yet she lifted her chin and smiled. "Thank you for your offer, but I should like to return it with a personal message."

"Very good, miss." He dipped a nod. "Will there be anything else?"

"No, thank you. You have been very helpful. Good day."

She stepped outside and dug into her pocket. Bypassing the thicker folds of the cravat, she pulled out the handkerchief. Gently, she rubbed her finger over the finely embroidered letters stitched into one corner.

JM

James Morgan. Could it be? She looked beyond the row of businesses, past St. Mary's Church and the jagged ruins of the abbey atop the hill, to fix her gaze on the dark blight neighbouring it. Morgrave Manor. The baronet's home.

A place rumoured to house a family with a bloodline of vampires.

Death crouched in this room, biding its time, waiting, sullen and strong. James could feel it. The beast would eventually pounce. The question was when. . .a question he thought he'd banished once and for all. Apparently not. He stood in silent rage at the foot of his mother's bed, clenching his hands into fists so tight his arms shook. He'd been certain his latest physic would help. Abysmally certain. Yet when he'd checked on Mother this morning, she lay still as an alabaster statue, her skin every bit as cold, her heart barely fluttering.

It had nearly broken him.

"Well, Doctor?" He fixed his gaze on the blue coat leaning over his mother. "Your prognosis is. . . ?"

Dr. Seward pulled the stethoscope from his neck and faced him. "I am sorry, Sir James. As I told your butler last week, there is nothing more traditional medicine can do for your mother."

The words landed like thrown bricks. "There must be something."

"I—and you—have done all we can. Her next attack will likely be her last, assuming, that is, she survives the lingering effects of this one." He began tucking away his tools into his leather bag. "I recommend you move her to York County Hospital. It's a teaching institution where methods beyond us might be employed."

James snorted. It was either that or curse. "Despite her pallor, look at the colour of my mother's skin and then tell me you expect every measure will be taken to spare her life. She is not your average English woman. She is not English at all."

Dr. Seward's sharp blue eyes—keenly intelligent despite his seventy-plus years—met his gaze. "Not all men are prejudiced. Have I not faithfully served your mother?"

"Yes, because I pay you well to do so." Bitterness left a rancid taste in his mouth. Were it not for a fat purse placed in the doctor's hand every month, no doubt the man wouldn't trek all the way out here quite so faithfully. Or quietly. Similar purses kept every servant's mouth shut.

"You have been very generous, Sir James, and for that I thank you. But I assure you that you will find good Christian doctors at York County, those who will overlook Lady Dorina's Romanian heritage and treat her as well as I have."

Bah! James pounded over to the water decanter and poured himself a glass, barely able to swallow for the fury tightening his throat. He would show no mercy to the punching bag today once the doctor left. "Do not speak to me of good Christians, Doctor. Those who claim to be so are the most brutal fiends with whom I have ever had the misfortune to cross paths. Arrogance. Pride. Cruelty. These are the marks of the church, so forgive me if I refuse to subject my mother to the scorn of those who would see her as nothing but a stain upon humanity."

The doctor's bushy eyebrows rose. "I am sorry to hear you feel that way. I fear such vitriol may blind you to the good that is yet to be found in God's people."

James plowed his fingers through his hair, the fight in him draining. Dr. Seward didn't deserve his wrath. "Perhaps," he murmured. "Though I suspect I shall remain firm in my resolution to trust in God and not in man."

"Then for your sake and your mother's, I sincerely hope such a misguided sentiment will change. You must learn to trust others, Sir James, for often such are the conduits of God's ministrations."

Sitting lightly at the side of his mother's bed, James brushed back her silvery hair—locks that used to be thick and dark, the envy and mockery of the women in Whitby. She was nothing but skin stretched across bones now, but at least in this moment, she was at peace. "Are there no more avenues of aid I might access here in town?"

"None I can personally recommend, though some claim to have had success with the tonics made by Mrs. Edwards that are sold at the Whitby Public Lending Library. I'm skeptical, however, that a simple tonic will be of benefit." He snapped the clasp on his bag. "I wish you and your mother all the best, Sir James, and with that I bid you not only good day but goodbye."

"Thank you, Doctor."

James turned back to the shell of what had been his mother, his hope fading as surely as the doctor's footsteps. He'd failed her. Failed himself.

Just as his father had predicted.

SIX

Oh, what a strange meeting, and how it all makes my head whirl round! I feel like one in a dream.

Rosa sulked out the library window at the brooding sky. Would the gloom of these days never end? August should be sunny, sparkling like a handful of diamonds cast over the expanse of the North Sea. But *should be*s didn't always come true, and such was the case for this summer's weather. Ever since the queer mist two days ago, not once had the sun peeked out. It was hard enough on her, but what of the poor tourists who'd come to the seaside town on holiday?

She pulled out last month's invoices Father had asked her to sort before he returned from the post office. She had plenty of time for the task. He and Postmaster Hillingham could gossip more than all the women in the Ladies Aid Society combined.

The bell above the front door jingled. In strode a man wearing a dark suit, a well-trimmed beard, and the look of a stoat who'd just peeked his head above ground, highly alert and—judging by the clip of his steps—somewhat irritated.

Rosa set aside the invoices as he approached the desk. "May I help you, sir?"

"Indeed, I hope so." His voice boomed, the sort that might be heard from a stage. "I am looking for a particular book."

"Then I shall do my best to locate it for you." She nodded towards the card catalogue. "What is the title?"

"*The Accounts of Principalities of Wallachia and Moldavia* by William Wilkinson."

"Very well. Give me a moment." She opened the first drawer and fingered through all the titles beginning with *Ac*. Hmm. No such title. . .unless the card had been misplaced. On the chance the book had been filed under the author's name, she searched the *W* drawer before facing the man once again. "I am afraid we don't carry it."

"That's odd." He scratched behind his ear then smoothed back the hair he'd ruffled. "An acquaintance of mine informed me you did."

"In that case, there is one more place I could check." From the shelf below the counter, she pulled out the leather-bound catalogue that listed the library's expensive titles, then paged through it.

"Mystery solved." She closed the cover with a smile. "It seems your friend has good taste, for it is a rare publication. I cannot allow you to check out such a costly book, but you are welcome to read it here."

He nodded sharply. "Then let us be about it."

"Very well." She retrieved the patron ledger and pointed to the next available blank line. "If you would sign here, please."

He flourished his name on the paper, each stroke shouting his impatience. Interesting. That book must be quite the intriguing read. She determined then and there to delve into the requested title as soon as he left.

"Right this way"—she glanced at his name while rounding to the front of the counter—"Mr. Stoker."

He followed her to the corner nook, where she gestured for him to sit at a small table. Pulling out her set of keys, she unlocked the wooden cabinet containing the library's most valuable books. The requested title wasn't a very large edition, but it was gorgeous with its gilt-ruled spine and black Morocco label. She ran her finger over the marbled front board, admiring the colours. No wonder Father kept this one locked up.

Mr. Stoker's small eyes brightened as she set the beauty in front of him. He pulled out a notepad with relish and produced a pencil to go along with it. Apparently he might be here awhile.

She settled on a nearby stool, debating if she ought to retrieve the invoices and sort through them while the man worked, when once again the bell jangled. Her gaze slid to the door.

And her breath caught.

Eyes dark as black treacle stared into her soul. It was him. The count. The baronet. The man who'd visited her dreams these past two nights. And judging by the flash of recognition in his eyes, he knew her as well.

She slid off the stool and straightened her skirt. "Pardon me, Mr. Stoker."

"Mmm-hmm," he mumbled, engrossed in a flurry of notetaking. He wouldn't even know she was gone.

She stopped at the front desk and pulled out the small package in which she'd wrapped the man's cravat and handkerchief, then approached him where he stood near her mother's medicinals. He was dressed head to toe in black, from the top of his silk hat to his leather gloves and on down to the tips of his shoes—very expensive shoes, if she didn't miss her mark. In the midst of all her scurrying, not once did his gaze stray from her. She inhaled a deep breath. The intensity of the man was nearly too much to bear.

She held out the package and forced confidence into her voice—which was new. She'd never been so nervous around a patron before. "How fortuitous you have stopped by. I have been meaning to return these to you."

"No return was expected, though I thank you." He tucked the parcel inside his coat pocket then turned her hands palm up without so much as a "May I?" or a "Pardon." His breath was warm against her skin as he studied the remains of her abrasions.

Tingles ran up her arms. Could he feel the gallop of her pulse beating in her wrists where his thumbs gently rested? How indecent of the man! How bold. And secretly. . .how deliciously delightful.

She pulled away, unsure what to do with those very same hands that suddenly missed his touch. Lacing her fingers behind her back, she retreated a step.

One of his dark eyebrows rose, as if he knew—and relished—the effect he had on her. "It appears you are healing quite nicely."

"Yes, I. . ." She licked her lips, mouth abysmally dry. This was absurd. No man was worth this amount of giddiness. She tossed back her shoulders and met his gaze head-on. "May I find a book for you?"

"No, I came here to see the medicinals." He tipped his head at the nearest shelves lined with bottles.

Finally, familiar ground. She knew as much as her mother when it came to the tonics. "Then please allow me to help you. Is there any particular symptom you are hoping to ease?"

A shadow crossed his face. "None I wish to discuss."

She whirled towards the shelves, cheeks aflame. She should have known better than to ask such a personal question. "Forgive me."

"I take no offense. The tonic is not for me." His deep voice rumbled behind her, as captivating as an August twilight.

"Regardless"—she faced him—"it is none of my business. I shall leave you to it." With a dip of her head, she stepped away.

The touch of his hand to her arm held her back. "Stay."

She shouldn't. She couldn't, not with Mr. Stoker alone with one of the library's rarest books. And yet she stood spellbound by the man in black, who pulled down one of Mother's amber bottles.

"This one." He tapped the glass. "Would there be a problem in acquiring more should the need arise?"

"No." She shook her head. "My mother often accommodates such requests."

"And this one." He reached for another elixir and shook it, sloshing tiny waves inside the glass. "Why is it only half full?"

She smiled at the common question. "That product contains saffron, an ingredient most folks cannot afford, hence the smaller volume or no one would be able to purchase it."

"Mmm. Thoughtful."

And entirely a moot point with this man. He could afford to buy a case of those bottles, should he choose. "I suppose I should admit I know you are Sir James Morgan, the recently returned baronet of Morgrave Manor."

He stilled, his dark gaze seeking hers. "I wonder that you found time to check up on me when you are so occupied working for your father here at the library and helping your mother with her medicinals."

Her mouth dropped. Surely she must look like a landed perch, but it was not to be helped. "How do you know so much about me?"

"Both were assumptions. . .until now."

Well, that was a little off-putting. She lifted her chin, gathering what dignity she could find. "What else do you assume about me?"

Silently he drew close, the weight of his penetrating gaze pressing in on her, stealing what little breath she had left in her lungs.

For a long time he said nothing, just stood there, toe to toe, assessing her far too intimately with his eyes.

"You are an intelligent woman," he said slowly, his gaze diving deep into hers. "Keenly so, I think. You like to write, though not in the usual sense. More. . .driven, I should say. You hope for a happy ending in all things, and sweets, namely sugared biscuits, are your downfall."

She blinked, grateful for the shelving at her back. If she swooned, at least she'd not sprawl on the floor like a dumped load of laundry. "How could you possibly know so much?"

He shrugged, completely unfazed. "You work in a library, hence the intelligence, for no doubt you read the titles that come and go. When I studied your hand, I noticed a callous on the inside of your middle finger caused by overuse, the crown of it indelibly smudged with ink, so there is no question you are familiar with a pen." He pointed at the tonics. "Perhaps these very labels are composed by your own hand. As I have already assessed, you read a great deal, evidenced by the fine lines creased at the edges of your eyes, and what bookish female does not hope for a happy ending after having devoured so many stories? Lastly, there are a few biscuit crumbs on your collar, leftover from lunch no doubt."

Her knees weakened, and she shored herself up with a hand to the shelving. No one—not one single suitor—had ever paid her that much attention.

"So, you see, Miss Edwards, I am no diviner. I daresay you could do the same." He angled his head, the challenge unmistakable.

Her competitive spirit every bit as undeniable.

"All right, let me give it a go." She brushed away the crumbs on her collar, heart beating hard. Yet remarkably, the longer she examined him, the more her angst faded, pushed away by a rising pity.

"You are weary, sir," she said softly. "There are shadows beneath your eyes. You spend your nights worrying, hoping—else you would not be here seeking a medicinal."

He dipped his head, and for a moment she wondered if he'd put a stop to this game, but then he murmured, "Go on."

Her gaze roamed his face, from his strong nose to the high cut of his cheekbones. Permanent creases lined his brow, bowing beneath a great weight. "You are lonely, I think, for clearly you hide yourself away. While your skin is darker than most Englishmen, it lacks the luster of sunshine."

She leaned back on her heels, taking in the whole of the man. "And lastly, you are accustomed to having your own way, as evidenced by bidding me to stay here with you rather than asking, and yet your power grieves you, for it is a wall of separation—and you dearly long to share your life with someone you love."

His jaw clenched, his voice a lion's low growl. "What makes you say such things?"

She swallowed. Had she gone too far? He was, after all, a man of status and means, unused to those of lower standing speaking their mind. "I beg your pardon, Sir James."

"I would hear your answer, Miss Edwards, not another apology."

"I. . ." She drew in a fortifying breath. He had asked for this, had he not? "Well, clearly you are fretting over the possibility of losing a loved one, for you said the tonic you seek is not for you. Therefore, it must be for someone you care about—someone who currently shares your life."

A warm light of admiration deepened the brown in his eyes. "Well done."

The words. The look. His heady scent of earth after a rain was all too much. She looked away, checking on Mr. Stoker across the room. Though he appeared to be engrossed in his book, she should be over there supervising instead of bantering in this corner with a foreign baronet.

She turned back to Sir James, determined to break the spell he'd cast upon her. "Is there anything more I can help you with?"

"You seem uneasy, Miss Edwards." His gaze flicked to Mr. Stoker then back to her. "Is that gentleman bothering you?"

"Nothing of the sort. It is just that he is reading one of our most valuable titles, and I should be overseeing him."

"Then by all means, do not let me keep you. I can manage—"

Footsteps pounded, but before she could turn, Mr. Stoker dashed past them both and flung open the front door. "Good day and thank you!"

No.

Oh no.

Rosa whirled, eyes locked on the desk. If Mr. Stoker had stolen that book, Father would have her head.

Owning a shiny yellow ralli cart was complicated—a fact Albin Mallow hadn't counted on. First there were the stares. Ogles, really. Not that he minded. It was a duty of his to show off such a beautiful carriage, especially for the price he paid. But he hadn't counted on the distress twisting his gut whenever a wheel hit a rut. Would the springs be weakened? The axle damaged? And God forbid a piece of gravel might nick the paint! Thankfully the Whitby Public Lending Library wasn't far from the front gates of the Mallow Shipyard.

As he alighted outside the library, a new fear cropped up. Dare he leave such a fine piece of workmanship unattended on this dirty seaside street? He ran his hand along the smooth splash guard. Who knew if some grubby-handed tradesmen might suffer a fit of envy and try to make off with it? Perhaps he ought to return home and fetch a groom to hold the horse's head.

Glancing at the library's front window, he scrapped the idea. The beguiling Rosa Edwards stood close—far too close—to a tall man dressed in black, staring at his face in a much too familiar fashion. This would never do. Such a gaze ought to be directed at him.

Straightening his hat, Albin strode to the door—and was immediately bowled backwards by the crush of a man hell-bent on charging through it.

"I say!" Albin flailed his arms to keep from toppling to the ground.

"Beg your pardon, sir." The bearded fellow tipped his hat at him without slowing a step. "I must be off. The words, you see. I must capture them. Oh! What a name. What a blessedly perfect name!"

Albin sneered. What an ill-bred chuff and mad as a hatter. A gentleman ought to be able to walk the streets of Whitby without such an assault. The board of commissioners would hear of this, especially since he was a member.

Smoothing away the wrinkles on his sleeves, he strode inside. Rosa—for yes, he really ought to be on a first-name basis with her—now stood near a table in the corner. So did the dark-coated man. When they glanced up at his entrance, neither looked pleased at his intrusion.

Albin pursed his lips, unsure what to make of the situation. "Am I interrupting something?"

Rosa flashed a smile. "No, Mr. Mallow. I just had a fright." She picked up a book and cradled it. "I thought this may have been stolen, but here it is, safe and sound."

"Well." He closed the distance between them, anchoring himself at Rosa's side. "I am here now, so calm yourself." He glanced at the man in black, annoyed that he must tip his chin to do so. The man was abominably tall. "There is no need to trouble yourself any further on behalf of Miss Edwards, Mr. . . ?"

"Sir." The title was a well-aimed arrow. "Sir James Morgan. And you are?"

A baronet? Of all the unfortunate luck to be outranked. . .nothing he couldn't—and shouldn't—overcome, though. After all, his uncle hadn't invested so much time and money into him that he didn't deserve to be of equal status. He inhaled deeply, broadening his chest. "I am Mr. Albin Mallow, operating president of Mallow Shipyard and Marine Supply."

The man's dark gaze flicked over him as if he were naught but a barnacle to be scraped off and discarded. He turned to Rosa. "I wonder if I might purchase those medicinals we spoke of?"

"Of course. Excuse me, Mr. Mallow." She dipped her head at him as she set off.

Sir James followed.

For a moment, Albin studied the two at the front counter. The baronet watched her every movement, a hawk to the prey, far too consuming for a casual acquaintance. Rosa didn't seem to mind and, in fact, blushed beneath his perusal. Was she so taken by the man or by his title? Either way, she must be made to see that a Mallow was the better choice.

He approached the counter, eyeing Sir James and his purchases. No books, surprisingly. Bottles, several of them. Why would a baronet buy such provincial remedies when surely he could afford better?

"Have you need of a referral for a physician, Sir James? My uncle and I keep the finest doctor in Yorkshire on retainer." He paused so Rosa might register the privilege. "I could ask if he has any space in his diary to pay you a visit."

A winter wind couldn't have been any colder than the contempt in the baronet's dark eyes. "Thank you, but that will not be necessary."

Rosa peeked up as she wrapped each bottle in brown paper. "How can I help you, Mr. Mallow?"

"No aid required. I was merely driving by and thought I would stop in."

She handed the bottles to Sir James. "There you are. I hope this helps."

"Hope is a precious commodity." He tipped his head at them both then stalked out the door.

Albin narrowed his eyes. "What a strange fellow."

"Yes, he is."

The words were breathy, which vexed him. The sooner he turned her head back to him, the better. "Rosa—"

Her face snapped towards him, fire in her eyes. "You are very familiar with me, sir."

"Your mother gave me leave to use your Christian name." He smiled, employing the charm that'd worked on many a serving girl. "I was wondering if you might reconsider taking a drive with me. My carriage is just outside."

Shoving aside the twine she'd used to secure the wrapped bottles, she tapped a stack of papers on the counter. "I have work to do, Mr. Mallow, and besides, I believe I made it clear there cannot be anything between us."

"One friend cannot take another for a ride?"

"Well. . ." She shifted, her face softening.

"I could come by after your work is done. Just name the time."

A half-smile quirked her lips, which he would have considered a success—if he hadn't just witnessed her interaction with the baronet. "You are persistent, sir. I will give you that."

A necessary survival trait, one he'd learned well from Uncle. And yet if he could not win Rosa Edwards by singing his merits, perhaps playing a dirge against the baronet was in order. "I cannot help but wonder,

Miss Edwards, that if Sir James asked you for a drive, would you turn him down as well?"

"Do not be silly." A rosy hue painted her cheeks. "He would never ask the likes of me."

"Are you sure? Perhaps it is me, but he strikes me as a man used to getting his way, one who would not give second thought to plucking any flower that catches his fancy." He leaned over the counter, wrinkling his brow with what he hoped was the right amount of amicable concern. "All I ask from you, as your friend, is to be careful around him. *Very* careful."

"You are overly troubled, Mr. Mallow. Sir James came looking for medicinals. I find nothing to malign in the baronet's character."

He cocked his head. "You are quick to defend him."

She held the papers to her chest as a shield. "I neither defend nor sing the man's praises. Sir James purchased tonics I supplied, and that is the end of it."

"I hope so," he said under his breath. It would be hard enough swaying this woman to his side without contending with a rich and powerful baronet. By all that was right and true, he was just as distinguished as Sir James, but wouldn't it be just like a self-important gent to try to steal Rosa right out from under his nose by flaunting his wealth and status? Albin sniffed. He wouldn't stand for it. Besides, if he failed in successfully wooing the elusive Rosa Edwards, he'd disappoint Uncle Preston, and he knew exactly what would happen if he did that.

He bore the scars to prove it.

SEVEN

I stood in silence where I was, for I did not know what to do.

After four days of gloom, the sun staggered in like a rogue who'd been out carousing all night. Rosa glanced back to make sure Father was still at his desk, then braced her hands on the reshelve cart and leaned into a brilliant beam of sunshine streaming through the window. Warmth bathed her face, seeping deeply into her cheeks. She tucked the feeling away, storing it for when the inevitable bluster of fall came calling. She really ought to be working, but oh what a glorious break.

The bell jangled, breaking the sanctity of the moment. An errant desire welled to see the dark form of the baronet stride through the door, but it was only crook-backed Mrs. Godalming, a scarf on her head and a basket of books on her arm. Oh dear. This would never do.

Rosa rushed to the woman, blocking her from delving any farther into the library. If Father witnessed the return of books that never should have been lent in the first place, there'd be a price to pay.

"Good morning, Mrs. Godalming." She kept her voice low. "There must have been some miscommunication. I will bring your new titles tomorrow, as I said."

A few spare whiskers stuck out of the older lady's chin like pins in a cushion. "Ah come to town for market and thowt I'd save thee a trip." She held up the basket.

"I see." Rosa plucked out the books, casting several glances over her shoulder towards the office, then nudged the woman towards the door.

"I shall bring those other titles tomorrow."

Mrs. Godalming planted her feet. "But I'm 'ere now. Besides, 'tis not safe for thee ta travel all the way ta my cottage. There's bin more sheep killed. Throats ripped out. There's a bargheust about an' make no doobt about it."

The woman's accent ran as thick as the fear in her eyes. There'd be no putting her off, not in this state.

"Very well. Wait here." Rosa set the books on the counter then flitted from shelf to shelf, collecting three more titles to tide the woman over until her next visit. All the while she kept a keen eye on the back room, pulse racing. Thankfully, Father was too busy whistling the rousing sea shanty "Ben Backstay" to notice.

She placed the titles in Mrs. Godalming's basket. "Here you are. I appreciate you taking the time to stop by, but it is truly easier if I bring the books to you in the future. Paperwork and all, you understand." She winked.

"Awk! Ah don't mean ta be breakin' rules."

"None of it. You were just being thoughtful." Rosa patted her arm while herding her to the door. "Good day to you, Mrs. Godalming. I shall see you next Thursday."

"A reeight gran' day ta thee, Miss Rosa." The older lady grinned, a few teeth missing, then looked past Rosa's shoulder. "An a gran' day ta thee too, Mr. Edwards."

Rosa froze as the door slapped shut.

"Rosa?" Father's voice boomed.

She winced, then pasted on a smile and faced him. "Yes, Father?"

He stood at the counter, the ledger open in front of him. "Why was Mrs. Godalming leaving with a basket of books when I do not see her name or her payment registered?" He tapped the paper with a thick finger.

"I. . .em. . ." Her throat closed. *Think. Think!*

"Well?"

And just like that, she was four years old again, toeing the carpet, knowing she must confess it was she who'd broken the flower vase and not her sister. "The truth is I gave Mrs. Godalming the books, but I made sure they were old copies. Quite worn, actually. I highly doubt anyone will request them before their return."

"You *gave* them to her." The words were calm, a total contradiction to the vein popping out just above his collar. "At no cost?"

"She could not afford to pay."

"I suppose this explains the other missing titles."

Now there was a direct hit. She tucked her chin, focusing on the buttons of Father's waistcoat instead of the fire in his eyes. "You noticed?"

"It is my business to notice because books are my business."

She cringed. She'd been so careful to cover her tracks. Apparently a career as a spy was out of the question.

"Rosa." He pinched the bridge of his nose, likely counting to ten before he continued. "We have been over this before. People cannot check out books unless they pay for them."

She glanced up. If only he would see what a benefit this was to those who couldn't afford subscriptions. "But Father—"

"I mean it, Daughter." He tapped his finger against the register. "While I appreciate your compassion, this is our livelihood, not a charity. Would you take food off your mother's plate?"

"No, but—"

He flung up his hand, staving her off. "This is not a debate. Not one more book is to pass from our door without its subscription fee paid in full. Am I clear?"

He was more than clear, but that didn't mean she agreed. She tugged down her bodice. "Education should not be for only those with pennies in their pockets. It is a mercy, Father, to lend to the poor, leastwise those who can read. It enriches their lives and—"

"Rosa!"

She stiffened.

"The only thing I want to hear coming out of your mouth right now is 'Yes, sir.'"

She hung her head, defeat tasting bitter on her tongue. "Yes, sir."

"And if I should discover one more book leaving this library without a payment, you are finished here. These books—this business—is too important. Is that understood?"

"Understood, Father."

"Good." He softened his tone as he pushed the small pile she'd lent to Mrs. Godalming across the countertop. "Then see to filing away these returns."

Rosa collected them, tears burning in her eyes. What was she to do, other than to pray and ask God to provide? Yet wasn't expecting miraculous funding to drop from the sky nothing but supernatural whimsy? Why, she may as well also believe in faeries or bargheust hounds.

She wedged one of the books onto a shelf with a huff. No, God helped those who helped themselves. She was sure of that. It said so in the Old Testament, didn't it? But she couldn't purchase herself a typewriter, let alone begin to cover subscription fees. If she didn't have the funds and God didn't supply them, then from where would the money come?

Once again her gaze strayed to the door, her mind wandering back to yesterday, when the dark-coated baronet had strode in.

And then she knew. Sir James. He would have the money. But would he agree to become a patron for the poor?

"—will you, sir?"

James startled awake to see the skeletal frame of Renfield bending over his bed. Digging his elbows into the mattress, James half rose. "What has happened? Is it Mother?"

"No, sir. As I said, there's a Miss Edwards at the door. Did you not hear me?"

No, he most certainly had not heard that. Rubbing the sleep from his eyes, he shifted his gaze to the ribbon-like gap where his bedroom draperies did not quite meet. Daylight ruptured the shadows in a thin line.

He frowned at Renfield. "I believe I made myself very clear that no one is to be admitted to this household—especially when I am asleep."

"Indeed." The butler nodded, pale skin stretched tight over his cheeks. The old fellow was nearly as decrepit as James's mother, but were James to let him go, how would the man survive? "There has been no breach, sir. I left the lady standing on the doorstep."

"You—" James bit back a retort. It wouldn't do any good to lecture Renfield on proper etiquette when the blunder was by his own orders.

"Never mind." He scrubbed his hand over his face, stubble rough against his fingers. "Find out what she wants then send her on her way."

"She wants you, sir."

His mouth dropped. "What the deuce could she possibly want with me?"

"I don't know, sir, but she was quite adamant."

Of course she was—and the thought was oddly pleasing.

Renfield retreated a step, his knees cracking with the movement. "Shall I see her into the parlour, sir?"

James arched a brow. "Do you really think we should allow strangers into the house when my mother might succumb to another fit at any time?"

"I beg your pardon, sir. My error. How would you like me to handle the matter?"

Flinging back the counterpane, he rose. "Leave it to me."

Renfield's jaw unhinged. "But it's not yet nightfall, sir. You cannot go outside, for the sun is shining brightly."

"Do not fret so, man. I will remain inside the foyer. Now, help me dress—and quickly."

But he should have known better than to make that request. By the time his old butler managed to pull his frock coat from the wardrobe and brush off any offending pieces of lint, James had already put on his shirt, trousers, waistcoat, stockings, *and* shoes. His hair was as wild as the moors, doubly frazzled by his long-legged trek to the front hall, but so be it. He'd already kept the woman waiting long enough.

He yanked open the door, then inhaled deeply. It wasn't every day an alluring woman stood on his stoop, and stars above, Rosa Edwards was an uncommon beauty. Wide-eyed with a button of a mouth, and cheekbones that begged the touch of a finger along the curve. Beneath her bonnet, stray auburn curls gleamed in the sun. He leaned against the doorframe, taking care to remain in the shadows of the great old mansion while memorizing her face. "Miss Edwards?"

She blinked several times before answering. "Yes, I–I. . . Forgive me. I assumed your butler would open the door."

"I understood it was I you wished to see."

"Indeed." She nodded but said no more.

"Well, here I am," he prodded.

"Yes, here you are." Her brilliant smile matched the afternoon sunshine out on the lawn. "Shall we—?" She looked past his shoulder, clearly expecting to be invited inside.

A pity he must deny her. He folded his arms, unyielding.

"I. . ." She pressed her lips tight and a charming little dimple he'd not noticed before appeared in the cleft of her chin. "I suppose we can conduct business as well out here as in your parlour."

He cocked his head, more curious than piqued. "Have you business with me, Miss Edwards?"

"I do. I mean, I hope to."

"Intriguing. What do you propose?"

A breeze rolled in off the highland, pushing a strand of hair onto her forehead. She tucked it back then straightened her shoulders. "As you know, I help my father run the local subscription library. There are those in town who are unable to afford the user fee, and being that you are a gentleman of standing, I wondered if you would consider becoming a benefactor to those less fortunate."

His brows shot to the sky. "You think me a gentleman of standing?"

"Are you not?"

A laugh burst out of him, foreign, dusty, like a long-awaited drink of water in a desert land. "Oh Miss Edwards. Clearly you have not heard the dark tales of the Morgan family."

Her lips pulled into a pretty pout. "I make it a point to disregard hearsay."

A woman who didn't partake in gossip? He didn't know such a thing existed. "My, but you are a singular creature."

Her pert little nose lifted. A peahen couldn't look more ruffled. "I shall take that as a compliment."

"Good, for I meant it as such."

Her cheeks pinked—instantly sobering him. What was he doing? He had no business trifling with this woman. He tugged at his waistcoat with a grimace. "So, this patronage, what have you in mind?"

"Currently I have eight people in need, so two pounds ought to cover a month for them all. Unless"—she dared a step closer—"you would like to donate more. I can always think of others who would benefit from such a service."

His lips twitched, a smile threatening to break. If nothing else, her persistence was amusing. "Very shrewd. I see now why your father employs you. If I agree to such a commitment, could it be on an anonymous basis?"

"Yes. No one need know but you and me."

A secret between him and Rosa Edwards seemed a delicacy to be savored, though he doubted very much she'd see it that way. "Is your Mr. Mallow donating as well?"

The pretty pink on her cheeks blanched. "He is not mine, and no, I did not ask him. I do not intend to ask anyone else, actually."

Now that was interesting. He rubbed the back of his neck, contemplating the strange truth. "Why am I the favoured sponsor?"

"Because, well. . ." She shrugged and looked away. "Perhaps this was a rash idea."

"Perhaps it was." He allowed his gaze to linger on the saucy upturn of her nose. Rash or not, the idea could be profitable for them both. "But I rather like it, as long as I may add to our agreement."

Her brown eyes snapped back to his face. "In what way?"

"I should like a daily delivery of books myself, along with the newspaper."

She grinned. "That should not be a problem. Tom Barker passes this way to and from town every day. He could—"

"No." The word came out sharper than intended, sending a few sparrows to flight from a nearby boxwood.

Miss Edward's brow wrinkled. "But it would not trouble Tom at all."

Wrong. He knew exactly what kind of trouble would show up on his doorstep—the kind that traveled with pitchforks and torches. No, he'd learned long ago to limit relationships. Ana-Maria had taught him that much. He speared Miss Edwards with a direct look. "You will make the deliveries or there is no agreement between us."

"As you wish, but only on days when the library is open. To do so at other times would raise eyebrows."

"Oh, I assure you. Coming here at any time will raise eyebrows." Just then the sun disappeared behind a cloud, leaching colour from the world. "Are you up for the challenge, Miss Edwards?"

"As far as I am concerned, the only challenge is crossing the Spital

Beck bridge to get here—but it has held up this long. I doubt I shall cave it in."

"Excellent. I should like to begin with exhausting whatever resources you have on haematology. Shall I let Renfield know to expect you here tomorrow at the same time?"

Holding one hand to her bonnet lest the breeze blow it away, she glanced over her shoulder towards town. "If you do not mind, I should like to come early. Say, around sunrise?"

Once again his brows raised. "Are you not afraid to wander this far when night shadows might still be about?"

"Are you?"

Another chuckle rose in his throat, but this time he pushed it down. He liked the woman's spunk, yet it would not do either of them any good for him to get used to it. "I suppose you have reasons of which I need not be privy."

"Thank you." She shot out her hand. "Shall we shake on our agreement?"

He complied, though he should have known better, especially after their last contact. The same jolt ran up his arm and lodged deep in his belly, paralyzing him completely. He stood silent, unwilling to let go, unable to stop searching her eyes—where the same flare he felt burned like a fire in her gaze. That he felt it was one thing, but her? What was he to do with that?

She wrenched from his touch. "Good day, Sir James."

Turning, she fled down the walk, skirts swaying in a crazed pendulum with each hurried step.

James released a long, slow breath. What had he done by agreeing to allow Rosa Edwards here every day? Those visits might very well prove to be his undoing.

And he prayed to God it would not be hers as well.

EIGHT

Never did tombs look so ghastly white; never did cypress, or yew or juniper so seem the embodiment of funereal gloom; never did tree or grass wave or rustle so ominously; never did bough creak so mysteriously; and never did the far-away howling of dogs send such a woeful presage through the night.

The rise of an early moon cast a sickly pallor over St. Mary's graveyard, bleaching the rows of tombstones to an eerie fluorescence. Flipping up his collar, James strolled past a slab sporting a skull and crossbones. Had the corpse beneath ever imagined he'd bear such a foreboding mark for eternity? What a legacy.

Then again, what sort of legacy would he leave behind? A few empty houses and some ugly rumours? No one would mourn him, save for Sala and—perhaps—old Renfield. Loneliness, his old familiar companion, draped a heavy weight on his shoulders.

Bah! He kicked at a small rock, sending it skittering through the grass. This nighttime outing was anything but the peaceful reprieve for which he'd hoped. Neither had a particularly strenuous session in his makeshift gymnasium given him any release. He glanced back at Morgrave Manor, tempted to turn about, but to what end? Another eternal night alternating between his dying mother and medical journals he'd already read scores of times?

A chill breeze whipped over the cliffs, lashing his coat hem against his legs. He jammed his hat on tighter and pressed onward.

Rounding the corner of St. Mary's Church, he stopped before he bowled over a man kneeling in front of a headstone. The man jerked his head towards him, the wild flicker of his lantern on the ground casting eerie shadows on his face—the same face James had seen last week at the library. Was the fellow in mourning, then?

James fingered his hat brim with a stiff nod. "My pardon. I did not mean to intrude."

"No intrusion whatsoever. I don't actually know the poor soul who resides here"—he tipped his head towards the gravestone—"but I intend to make him famous." He rose and offered his hand. "Bram Stoker."

James glanced at the man's fingers. Either he wasn't from around here or he had no qualms about shaking hands with a vampire.

"James Morgan." He shook Mr. Stoker's hand.

Stoker squinted at him, searching his face. "I'm sorry, but have we met before?"

"We crossed paths at the circulating library, or rather you crossed mine."

The man stroked his beard for a moment, then lifted a finger in the air. "Aha, yes." He chuckled. "Why, you must think me mad, dashing out of there like a lunatic, and now to find me kneeling before the tombstone of a man I don't know. But you see, sir"—he waved a small notebook in the air—"I am writing a novel, and inspiration strikes in the strangest of places. This has been the most fortuitous of holidays, for I've already found several character names I intend to use."

James glanced around the shadowy landscape, from the great wind-pocked walls of the church to the black waters of the North Sea. So much darkness. So much death. "It must be quite the gothic tale."

"It is, actually." Stoker tucked away his notes, then readjusted his glasses. "Pardon my noticing, but I detect an accent. Romanian?"

James reared back. "What makes you say so?"

"Oh, I mean no offense. It's simply that I have immersed myself the past year or so in Romanian history, culture, and language. Might I ask where you are from?"

Leery, James scrutinized the man. He'd been fooled before by wolves in sheep's clothing, but by all appearances, the stoat-faced fellow seemed to be in earnest. "I am from here, Whitby. In my younger years, at any rate. Of late, though, I hail from Transylvania."

Stoker let out a whoop that could wake the dead. Hopefully it wouldn't.

"You don't say! Capital. Capital! You're just the sort of fellow I've been looking for." The man bounced on his toes. "Transylvania is where my story opens. Tell, me, sir, would you mind looking over my first few scenes to see if I've captured the full flavor of the place? I'd travel there, but business and family, you know."

An immediate denial rose to his tongue, but James kept his mouth shut. Had he not just been lamenting his solitary life? Perhaps some human interaction with a man who'd obviously not yet been tainted by local folklore would be just the thing...though it wouldn't hurt to be cautious.

"If you will leave your manuscript with Miss Edwards at the library, she will see that I get it."

"Excellent! Then I am off to polish it up." He swiped up his lantern and called over his shoulder as he darted along the walkway. "I bid you goodnight, sir."

What an odd fellow. Crouching, James squinted at the letters on the headstone. Swale. William Swale. What was so inspirational about that name?

He straightened just as the nearby church door opened. Out stepped a stubble-headed man in a clergy collar.

"Who's there?" He held his lantern at arm's length, spying James. "Is there a problem?"

"No, merely an enthusiastic visitor." He gestured towards Stoker's bobbing light, which was growing smaller at the edge of the graveyard.

The fellow craned a look past James's shoulder. "At this time of night?"

"The dead have no notion of time."

"Well said." He chuckled. "I am Mr. Austen, rector of St. Mary's. Will I see you on Sunday morning?"

Not likely. He hadn't stepped foot in a church in years, and why should he? He knew the sort that attended. Hypocrites, all, with their barely concealed looks of disdain. "I think not."

"Oh, on holiday are you?"

"I am not."

The man stepped closer, holding his lantern high and squinting.

James stiffened as the man's gaze burrowed into the sacred spaces in his heart. It was a violation, but one he'd come to expect from a clergyman.

"I see," Mr. Austen drawled as he lowered his lamp. "I shall pray for your soul, then, sir."

James bristled. The man could have no idea of the state of his eternity. "My soul is at peace with the One who created it, so do not trouble yourself."

"I am happy to hear it, but inside the fold or out, we all need prayer, my son." He winked and disappeared back into the church.

Dogs howled in the distance, sounding much like his mother's nighttime baying. James snugged his collar tighter and strode off through the tombstones towards the dark hulk of Morgrave Manor.

Perhaps Austen was right. He did need prayer—and lots of it.

Every time the wind gusted, a draft leaked through the window, unseasonably chilly for August. Albin shifted on his chair, turning his back to it. Annoying, but not nearly as irritating as losing a game of chess to his uncle. He moved one of his pawns.

Uncle Preston immediately knocked it over with a rook and deposited it onto his ever-growing pile of white pieces.

Blast!

Albin snagged a kipper on toast from a tray and popped the small snack into his mouth. While he chewed, a chorus of howls invaded the night, traveling all the way into the sitting room. He licked his fingers. "Sounds like more sheep will be killed tonight."

"On the contrary. The culprit was shot earlier today. A rabid dog, apparently."

"Then why the howling?" He grabbed another toast.

"Who knows? There must be something in the area they don't like. Maybe they've cornered a badger or a fox or some such." His uncle stared at the morsel in Albin's hand with a sneer. "Now, are you going to play or yammer on about nothing?"

Albin shoved the bite into his mouth, refocusing on the game and. . .there. He captured Uncle Preston's bishop with his knight, smiling as he dropped the black piece onto his side with a flourish.

Uncle merely humphed—then immediately seized Albin's knight with his queen. "Not that I don't appreciate a night of sport, but why are you here playing with your old uncle instead of courting that tasty morsel Miss Edwards on this moonlit eve?"

Albin hid a wince at the slur, but his uncle was right. He should be out with the lovely Rosa instead of eating smoked fish and losing abysmally at chess. He met his uncle's gaze. "She has not yet accepted my invitation for a ride."

"What is her hesitation?"

"I merely asked at an inopportune time."

"Tell me about it." Uncle Preston added the knight to his pile, the sleeve of his smoking jacket nearly toppling the great heap.

"I stopped in at the library, but she was preoccupied with another man."

"Hmm. Do you know this fellow?"

"I do now." He pushed one of his last pawns forward. "Sir James Morgan."

A low whistle slid past his uncle's lips.

"You know him?"

"I knew his father." Uncle's blue eyes iced over, his gaze straying to the ceiling as if the man himself were a ghost come to haunt him. "The Morgans are to be avoided at all costs," he murmured.

Had he known the Morgan name would be such a distraction, he would've mentioned it earlier in the game. Albin slipped one of Uncle's rooks into his pile while the man wasn't looking. "Why is that?"

Uncle Preston's gaze snapped back to him. Gads! Had he seen the move?

"How have you lived in Whitby these past twenty years and not heard the tales?" Disgust curled Uncle's upper lip.

But disgust was better than rage at being found cheating. Albin waved his hand in the air. "I can hardly be expected to keep up with all the blather that goes on around here."

Uncle Preston grunted, then took Albin's queen with a pawn.

A pawn of all things!

Rot! Better to keep his uncle on the topic of the Morgans than die a quick death on the chessboard. "So, what exactly is the story of this baronet and his family?"

"Infamy has riddled Morgrave Manor for centuries. One Morgan was burned at the stake for witchcraft. Another hanged for piracy. But all that pales in comparison to the current Lady Morgan." Uncle strode to the liquor cart and poured a glass of Irish whisky.

The perfect opportunity to steal one of his knights while advancing his own bishop. "Why?"

"Sir Jonathan—the father of the current baronet—took a foreign wife." Uncle resumed his seat and stared directly into Albin's eyes. "A Romanian."

Clearly he was driving home some sort of point, but what? "And?"

Uncle huffed a curse. "You really are brainless, you know that? Must I educate you on everything?" Once again his queen attacked, defeating Albin's bishop. "Romania is a vile place, known for black magic and blood-sucking creatures."

Albin grinned. Surely his uncle didn't think he'd fall for a ghost story. "So, the former baronet wed a vampire."

"He did." Not a shred of humour lightened his uncle's deadpan tone.

Albin's grin faded as he moved his last remaining rook. "Oh."

"It's said she bewitched him to her bed then slowly over the years drained him dry."

"Dear me." Albin grabbed his goblet and downed his wine in a great gulp.

Uncle Preston burst out laughing. "But I know better. It was the baronet who did the bewitching and the draining, the old conniver. Lady Dorina came from a very wealthy family. Their union was a much-needed infusion of funds for his gambling problem."

"So, the stories are not true?"

"That's the thing about fisherfolk tales. There's always some truth to them." Uncle Preston pushed his queen forcefully into Albin's king, sending it flying with a hearty "Checkmate." He stood, victory gleaming like lightning in his eyes. "But knowing that the spawn of Sir Jonathan

Morgan is in town, a few deeds in the dark and some carefully placed gossip could remove him from the picture. I'll see what can be done. And the sooner you win Miss Edwards's hand, the better."

NINE

. . .the ravings of the sick were the secrets of God, and that if a nurse through her vocation should hear them, she should respect her trust.

Miserable. That about summed it up. First crossing the rickety old Spital Beck bridge and now a persistent rain, but there was no sense in turning back, not when she'd come this far. Rosa tucked her head deeper into her hood as she steered her bicycle onto Morgrave Manor's front drive, inwardly cursing the dampness soaking through her light cloak.

She rose to the pedals as the bicycle dipped into a rut. An inconvenience but not a danger. At least she hadn't had to look over her shoulder all the way here to see if a killer were about to rip out her throat. Thank God the mad dog sheep slayer had been put down yesterday.

Pressing lightly on the brakes, she stopped near the manor's front steps and dismounted, then removed her basket from the handlebars. Good thing she'd thought to cover the top with a waxed piece of sailcloth. With her free hand, she heaved her sodden hem higher as she slogged up the flagstone steps and rang the bell.

The only answer was the loud pattering of raindrops against her hood.

She rang again.

And again.

Moisture seeped through the seam at her neck, skittering a shiver across her shoulders. Had she or the baronet gotten the day wrong?

As she reached to ring one last time, the door swung open to the stick figure butler draped in black, the colour a stark contrast to the bleached parchment of his face.

Rosa dipped her head in greeting. "Good morning. I am here to see Sir James."

A spark of colour lit his pale blue eyes. "Miss Edwards."

She smiled. The baronet hadn't forgotten after all.

"I shall take your delivery and thank you." He held out an arm so thin, she feared the weight of her basket would snap it like a dead branch.

She clutched the handle all the tighter. "I would like the payment first, please."

"I wasn't told of any payment, but I am certain the master will make good on his word." His arm didn't waver.

Neither did she. She needed that money today if she were to bring Mrs. Hawkins and Mrs. Godalming their next order of books—and she was oh so close to ridding them of their superstitious thoughts, particularly when it came to bargheust hounds. She shook her head. "I am afraid I cannot hand over these books without compensation."

The man's thin lips pressed tight, pulling the skin taut over his cheekbones. He remained silent for some time before finally saying, "Very well. Wait here."

"But it is raining!"

He glanced past her. "So it is."

He shut the door—or tried to. Rosa shoved her foot in the gap. "I should like to wait inside, if you please."

Lines creased his brow. "I have been instructed by my master to allow no one entrance."

"I understand you may not go against his wishes, but I assure you I am expected to meet with him. We agreed so yesterday right here at this very door. He may simply have forgotten to tell you, and if such is the case, I am certain you would not want to disappoint him."

"Hmm. Sir James did say you were coming. . ." At last he stepped aside. "But perhaps you are right. He has much on his mind of late. Do come in."

She shook off her hood before entering. Despite the scent of rain following her into the room, the shadowy foyer had a dampness all its own. Perhaps it hailed from all the medieval furnishings—old as dirt themselves—or perhaps from the draperies that looked as if they'd not been opened in centuries. No wonder Sir James smelled of freshly turned soil.

The elderly butler passed around a massive pedestal table. Rosa hesitated. Sitting at center was a hideous statue of a winged gargoyle. Warts covered its body, along with spikes on its spine and fangs the size of bear claws. A shiver tingled along her shoulders. What sort of greeting was that for a guest? Giving the awful thing a wide berth, she quickened her pace to catch up with the butler.

The man stopped at the next open door, gesturing inside with one of his gnarly fingers. "Settle yourself in here, Miss Edwards. I will summon the master."

"Thank you." She entered a room shrouded in gloom. Heavy red draperies shut out the world. A thick red carpet muffled her steps. And all she could think of was blood.

She set her basket on a long, narrow sofa in front of a cold hearth. How cheerless. No wonder the baronet had such a melancholic air about him. She would too if she lived here.

Absently, she strolled the room while waiting, from curio shelves holding an odd collection of mortars and pestles to a bank of windows where it sounded as if something scratched against the glass. She bent closer, listening hard.

Tap-tap-tap-tap-tap. Tap-tap-tap-tap-tap.

Fingernails? Swallowing down an insane rise of fear, she yanked back the draperies. Then chuckled to herself. What a ninny. It was nothing but a branch caught beneath a steady cascade of water, causing it to click against the glass. She was no better than the fishwives who spun their ghastly tales.

Crash!

Her gaze shot to the ceiling. Something had fallen up there. Hard. Thank God the plaster held.

A moan followed. Or was it her imagination? She straightened and angled her ear upwards.

Sure enough, another muffled moan followed. Someone was clearly hurt. Had the butler fallen and broken one of his frail bones?

She darted out the door, arcing wide around the gargoyle, and stopped at the bottom of the great stairway. "Hello?" she called out. "Do you need help?"

"No need for alarm, Miss Edwards."

She whirled towards the deep voice. The baronet loomed over her, so close she could see the stubble on his chin. Where had he come from? She'd swear to a magistrate she'd not seen him as she'd run to the stairs.

"Sir James, I—" She caught her breath, calming her heart rate. "I thought I heard someone in distress. Your butler, perhaps? He seems somewhat feeble. I do hope he is all right."

His dark eyes bored into her, mesmerizing. Almost hypnotizing. "I assure you there is nothing wrong with Renfield. What you heard is the creaking and moaning of a house that is centuries old."

"But. . ." Her objection languished on her tongue. Perhaps he was right. Her imagination had been getting the best of her ever since she'd arrived.

Sir James held out an envelope. "Renfield tells me you wish for your payment in advance."

"Yes, thank you." She collected his offering. "Father is quite adamant about such things."

"Entirely my oversight." He stepped closer, his hint of cinnamon intoxicating. "You will forgive me?"

Mouth suddenly dry, she licked her lips. She knew better than most not to judge a book by its cover, but stars above! This man was striking. Eyes that consumed. A mouth that could as well.

"There is nothing to forgive," she breathed out, cheeks burning at the intimate sound of her voice.

A hint of a smile wavered on his lips. "Allow me to see you to the door."

As if in a trance, she followed him—then snapped out of it when they passed the sitting room and she spied her basket on the sofa. "Pardon, Sir James, but I need my basket."

He pivoted, his face unreadable. "After you, then."

She crossed to the sofa and began unloading the books. "I pulled the few titles we have on the study of blood and circulation. I also took the liberty of adding one I thought you might like." Book in hand, she turned, surprised to find that once again he'd drawn close without so much as a sound.

"*The British and Foreign Medio-Chirurgical Review*," he murmured as he read, then snapped his gaze to hers. Undeniable admiration lit the golden flecks in his eyes. "Very astute of you."

Ahh, how easy it would be to get used to basking in this man's praise. How addicting to wish to earn it.

Pah! What was she thinking? Sir James was a patron of the library, nothing else. She shrugged. "I am a librarian, after all."

"I think you are much more than that, Miss Edwards."

She turned back to the basket lest he see the heat once again flushing her face. For such a drafty old house, Morgrave Manor was entirely too hot. Irritated with herself, she yanked out the newspaper. "Here is the *Gazette*." She set it with the rest of the books, fiddling around with straightening the pile—anything to avoid the spell of the baronet's gaze. "What shall I bring you tomorrow?"

"Is what I choose a matter of public record?"

"No, only my father and I are privy to our patron's records."

"I see." He stared at the book in his hand, clearly lost in thought, and judging by the slump of his shoulders, those thoughts weighed heavy. Was he so concerned with privacy?

"If you like"—she flipped on her hood, preparing for the trek back to the library—"I need not share your requests with my father. You can trust me to be discreet."

He narrowed his eyes. "Why are you so accommodating?"

She blinked. Had the man never experienced such a simple kindness? "Everyone needs a trustworthy friend, even a baronet."

He drew close, his puff of breath warm against her cheek. "Are you offering for the position?"

"Yes." The word slipped out effortlessly, surprising her.

Surprising him as well, if the rise of his brow were any indication. Then just as quickly the look disappeared, replaced by something dangerous glittering in his eyes. "Be careful what you agree to, Miss Edwards."

He wheeled about and strode to the mantel, frock coat stretching tight across his shoulders.

She collected her basket, unsure how to navigate the sudden silence.

"Well, I. . .I bid you good day, Sir James."

The steady click of the branch against the windowpane accompanied her all the way to the door, where she paused and glanced over her shoulder. He hadn't moved a whit, just stood there, lost in thoughts she couldn't begin to comprehend. Then again, who was she to try to decipher the eccentricities of a baronet?

Readjusting the basket on her arm, she headed for the front door. Just before she stepped foot outside, a shriek winged out like a bat from a cave. Skin prickling, she fled to her bicycle.

That was definitely not the moaning of an old house.

Cursing himself, James watched the swirl of Miss Edwards' skirt swish out the sitting room door. Brick by brick the woman was tearing down his wall of self-protection, and he didn't like it. Not at all. He'd devoted too many years to building that defense, and there was no doubt the more time he spent with the woman, the more vulnerable he would become. Worse, the more danger to her. He'd witnessed the death of innocence in Ana-Maria's eyes. He would not willingly see the same thing happen to Miss Rosa Edwards.

A shriek rang out directly overhead, and he clenched his jaw. Had Miss Edwards heard?

He stalked to the window. Parting the drapery with one finger, he heaved a sigh of relief. She was already grasping the handlebars of her bicycle, thank God.

Retrieving the stack of books, he trotted up the stairs to his mother's bedchamber. Inside, she crouched on the floor, cowering with her arms over her head. Nurse Agatha's chair sat empty in the corner. Of all the untimely moments for the woman to take a break.

He set down his burden, then herded his mother back to bed with a gentle touch and even gentler words. "Shhh, now. There is nothing here to harm you. I am here. You are safe."

She struck so fast he barely had time to register the move before the metallic taste of blood welled in his mouth. A sailor couldn't have damned him more thoroughly than the blasphemous oaths spewing from her lips. Hurtful but understandable, for such was the madness before death.

Licking his split lip, he dashed to the medicine table and sprinkled a rag with chloroform. Before she caused any more damage, he pressed the cloth to her nose. After one great inhale, her body sank to the mattress like a discarded rag doll.

Just then Nurse Agatha bustled into the room. "Pardon, Sir James. Nature were a'callin.' Couldn't be helped."

Irritated—yet understanding the need—he rose. "I lay no blame against you, but in the future, I should like you to call for Renfield or the maid to sit in for you. My mother is not to be left alone under any circumstance."

"Aye." Her chin waggled as she bobbed her head, the fleshy folds brushing against her starched white collar. "But you ought to find someone else for my position, for like as not, I'll be quittin' my post any day."

He stifled a snort as he collected his books. "I shall take that to heart, Nurse."

"Well ye should."

Her words followed him out the door, as did a growing dread that his mother was not long for this world. He slammed the books onto the desk in his study, and shrugging out of his frock coat, he yawned. Normally he'd be closing his own eyes about now, accustomed as he was to sleeping through the bulk of daylight hours, but too much was at stake. He rolled up his sleeves and sank to the chair, flipping open the cover of the first thick book.

Hours later his eyes burned. But so did a flare of hope. Slowly he massaged his left temple, contemplating what he'd just read. Soy leghemoglobin. Now there was something he hadn't tried. . .and also didn't have amongst his many bottles and jars. A trip to the apothecary would be in order.

He glanced at the clock, surprised to find he'd missed not only luncheon but dinner as well. Turning in his seat, he spied two trays on the trestle near the door. He must've acknowledged Renfield when the food had appeared, but he surely did not remember doing so.

Rising on stiff legs, he shook out his hands, cramped from taking copious notes. It was too late now to send Renfield to town. Yet who was he kidding? The old butler would take a day and a half for such an outing, and he needed that ingredient as soon as possible.

Sighing, he pinched the bridge of his nose. He could send Nurse Agatha and sit with Mother himself, but the nurse would bray like a stuck donkey. For all her bluster of leaving off to her sister's in Robin Hood's Bay, she never left the house. He might charge the maid with the task, but once Betty went into town, it would take her hours. The woman was a devoted window shopper and wouldn't be satisfied until she'd taken an assessment of each shop on every street. No, that wouldn't do. He rubbed the back of his neck. He could ask Miss Edwards, but he ought not get her any more entangled in his life than she already was.

He slammed the book shut. There was nothing for it, then. He would have to go into town himself as soon as the apothecary opened.

And pray all the while that the sun would not touch his skin.

TEN

. . .there are strange and terrible days before us.

The higher the sun rose, the more it burned off the ghostly fog, lifting Rosa's spirits. She'd suffered another dismal trek to Morgrave Manor earlier that morn, her route plagued by drifts of mist, only to be met by a grim baronet who'd seemed almost morbidly distracted as she swapped books with him. Whatever troubled him surely weighed heavy, and at the rate he'd devoured those medical texts, she suspected it had something to do with someone's health. A member of his household must be suffering from some sort of ailment, for such would explain the moaning she'd heard yesterday. But who exactly? And why be so secretive about it? Either way, how sad—and how gallant that he took it upon himself to ease such evidently serious distress.

Still, it was none of her concern, or so Mother would scold if she knew the turn of her thoughts. But her mother had hardly come up for breath on this entire stroll to the apothecary, chattering about the most inane things possible as they passed storefront after storefront. She hadn't so much as glanced at Rosa for the past seven shops.

"Your sister has invited us all to dinner next week. Oh, look at those pastries!" She pointed at a basket loaded with tea cakes inside the baker's great glass window. "Perhaps we should purchase some of those fat rascals on our way home. You know your father cannot get enough of them, and I am not inclined to suffer the heat of an oven today."

Rosa arched a brow, ignoring the pastry portion of her mother's dialogue. "All? You mean someone other than you and father and I has been invited to Lucy's?"

"Yes." Mother fiddled with her bonnet ribbons. "Mr. Mallow has been kind enough to accept."

Aha. More than a coverup. This was skullduggery of a severe matrimonial degree. "Mother, I do not wish to—"

"Enough, Rosa!" She whisper-chided while dipping her head sweetly to the passing Mrs. Graves. "I've spoken with your father, and we have agreed Albin Mallow is your best prospect. He is a man of standing with ample wealth to provide for you. He stopped by the library yesterday to speak of such to your father. When the time comes—pray God it is next Wednesday at your sister's—you will accept his suit."

Rosa gripped her shopping basket. Mother and Father had joined forces? This was new. She'd have to stand stronger than ever to weather this matchmaking storm. "Mother, I am not interested in Mr. Mallow, nor will I—"

"Hsst! Here comes the man and his uncle now."

A garish yellow carriage rolled their way. Rosa upped her pace, hoping to scurry inside the apothecary shop before the Mallows made eye contact. Too late. Albin pulled on the reins, stopping the red-wheeled monstrosity at the kerb. And if that weren't enough, Mother clutched her arm, rooting Rosa in place just steps away from the apothecary's door.

"Good morning, ladies." Both Mallows tipped their hats.

Rosa dipped a small curtsey, noting that several pedestrians stopped to admire the shiny new ralli cart. Capable of going as fast as a horse would take it, this newfangled carriage was the height of self-indulgence, leastwise according to her. The money spent on such a gawdy piece of transportation could buy books galore for the library.

Mother stood a full inch taller, clearly proud that the Mallows had chosen to publicly acknowledge them. "Why, we were just speaking of you, Mr. Mallow."

A smile lifted a mole at the corner of Albin's lips. "All good conversation, I should hope?"

"The best, I assure you." Mother's elbow dug into Rosa's side, coercing her to agree.

"Of course, sir." She forced a smile.

Preston Mallow eyed her like a fish to be purchased, his scrutiny traveling from bonnet to hem and back again. His murky blue gaze was direct, the sort that could unnerve a rock-solid saint, calculating her worth with a wisp of a smile. "My nephew looks forward to your engagement, Miss Edwards."

Her blood drained to her toes, leaving her cold in the August sunshine. "Engagement?"

Another few pedestrians joined the others, heads cocked like vultures to a kill.

Albin sat taller, obviously pleased at the attention. No wonder Mother adored this man so much. He was just like her. "I have already written down the engagement for dinner at your sister's home in my diary."

She let out a breath, relief weakening her knees. "Oh."

"Naturally," Mother said, stepping forward and dragging Rosa along for the ride, "one does hope a more permanent engagement is not far off."

Rosa planted her feet, fighting a gag reflex that threatened to toss her accounts on the street.

"I see no reason why that cannot be arranged." Preston swiveled his head at Albin. "Do you, Nephew?"

An indecent smile spread on Albin's face. "None at all, Uncle."

Whispers swirled around the pavement from the onlookers.

"Hear that? Looks ta be a marriage in t'making."

"Finally. Bin a long time coming for that 'un."

"Guess she won't end up a spinster after all."

Rosa pulled from her mother's grasp. Three more steps, maybe four, and she'd make it inside the safety of the apothecary shop.

Once again Mother hooked her arm through Rosa's, ending her flight. "Autumn weddings are so enchanting, don't you think so, Rosa?"

Oh Mother, do stop talking. She pressed her lips flat lest the retort slip out. Quarreling with her mother would not only attract more onlookers but earn her a sound tongue-lashing once they got home.

"My thoughts exactly, Mrs. Edwards." Albin jumped down from the carriage and held out his hand, the skin soft-looking and with an overlarge golden ring on his pinky finger. "Come, my dear. There is no better time than the present for a turn about town with my uncle and me. We have much to discuss."

She blinked. How had their status as friends changed overnight to something more intimate?

More whispers shooshed around those gathered nearby.

"How romantic."

"Wish he'd ask me."

"What's she waiting for?"

Albin's hand didn't waver, his open palm not only a challenge but somehow a threat.

"I—I cannot." She gave a pointed look to the basket on her arm. "You see, I must help my mother with the morning shopping."

Mother clucked her tongue. "How thoughtful, Daughter, but I can manage on my own."

And that's when it hit her. All her mother's fluttering and muttering as she'd fingered through her medicinals at the library, bemoaning how suddenly short of inventory she'd become and how a visit to the apothecary was of the utmost need. That she'd never be able to carry all the supplies on her own. It made sense now. Clearly Mother and Mr. Mallow had planned this little meeting.

"There you have it." Albin shoved his hand closer to hers, fingers curled to snatch her away the second he made contact.

Mother gave her a little push.

Rosa tucked her hands and her basket behind her back. "I am sorry, Mr. Mallow, but I am afraid my answer is no."

A flush ran up his neck, a startling merlot against the crisp white of his neckcloth and matching the tiny embroidered flowers on his waistcoat. "Why?"

"Yes, Rosa." Mother turned on her, anger as sharp as the set of her jaw. "Tell us why on earth you cannot go for a ride with your future intended."

"Because I. . .I—"

She swallowed, which did nothing to ease the tightness in her throat. There was no possible way out of this quandary without saying something that would publicly shame her mother and Mr. Mallow.

Behind her, the apothecary door opened. Wonderful. Another person to add to the crowd already witnessing this nightmare.

Albin dropped his hand, but stepped closer, the scent of his limey cologne far too cloying. "Don't be shy, Rosa. I may call you Rosa, mayn't I?"

"You may, Mr. Mallow," her mother answered.

"Excellent." He dared a step nearer. One more and he could pull her into his arms. "Come now, Rosa. I don't think you have considered all the benefits of a more permanent agreement between us. As you know, my uncle is one of the town's biggest patrons. Imagine if you were to become a Mallow. Why, that patronage would increase tenfold if not more, for Uncle is ever generous to his own family members."

She gaped. "Are you bribing me, sir?"

"You misunderstand, my dear. I merely speak of my uncle's kindness." His grin disappeared, replaced with a stern lifting of his nose. "Ride with us, Rosa, and get to know the man who would bestow riches on you and your family."

"Go on, Rosa." Mother fluttered her fingers in the air, shooing her away.

Panic welled, tasting sour in her throat. There was no getting out of this. She'd be wedged between two Mallows high up on that blazing yellow carriage, on parade for all of Whitby to see, practically sealing the deal to marry her off to the doughy-skinned man in front of her.

No. She couldn't. She *wouldn't.* Even if she had to stretch the truth into an unrecognizable shape.

"While I appreciate the offer, it would not be fair to you or your uncle to mislead you in any way. The fact is, Mr. Mallow, I am already seeing someone." She was. . .sort of. . .for didn't it count that she'd already gone several times to the baronet's house and *seen* him?

A collective gasp sucked in air all around.

"Who can it be?"

"She's a fool ta choose someone else."

Mother laughed shrilly, drowning out the naysayers. "Don't be absurd, Rosa."

Albin Mallow's hands curled into fists at his side. "Who is this someone else that you're seeing?"

She held her breath. She couldn't very well say the baronet, for it would get back to him. Oh, that the earth would just open up and swallow her whole here and now.

A deep voice rumbled behind her, "She is seeing me."

He'd done hasty things before. Spoken without thinking. Blurted a thought that never should've seen the light of day. But what on earth had possessed him to say such a thing now, right in front of Rosa Edwards and a growing number of Whitby's citizens? James inhaled until his chest hurt, wishing to God he could rewind the hands of time and stop up his mouth. He never should have inserted himself into this mess and wouldn't have had to if not for Mallow acting such a bully to the woman who never seemed to leave his thoughts.

Rosa Edwards turned to him, wide-eyed, surprise adding a luminescent quality to her already lovely face. No doubt his declaration was a shock, but even more so must be his appearance. He'd covered every square inch of his skin save for a thin swath from chin to nose. How ghastly she must think him, but the gloves, the dark glasses, the wide-brimmed hat—all were necessary to avoid the sun.

She didn't shrink from him, though. Didn't so much as wince or grimace. No, the brave girl drew closer, her unblinking eyes staring past the shaded spectacles and into his heart. The same current he'd felt earlier between them once again charged, and he instantly knew why he'd publicly proclaimed this woman as his.

Because he wished it were so.

"Is this true?" Mallow squeezed out the question as if through a clenched fist. He appeared calm on the outside, if not a little pouty with the way his thick lips pursed. Yet underneath that haughty mien and all those expensive garments, James would wager the family silver that a furious fire burned white-hot inside the man.

Miss Edwards closed her eyes, a faint shudder quivering the fabric of her collar. And he didn't blame her, not with being caught between a bully and a monster. For her sake, he must bear the humiliation and retract his claim on her. Now.

He opened his mouth just as Rosa gave a little shake of her head, staying him.

She faced Mallow like a soldier on the front lines. "Yes, Mr. Mallow, it is true."

Whispers whooshed around them like an unholy wind.

"She's gone 'n made a pact with a devil like 'im?

"Stupid lass."

"No good will come o' this."

"I don't understand." A woman with the same upturned nose and button mouth as Miss Edwards scowled at him. "Who are you, and why was I not told of this relationship?"

"Mother, I—"

James held up his palm, stopping the mother and daughter duo as he stepped even with Miss Edwards. She should not have to shoulder the burden of wading through a problem he'd created. He faced her mother. "I am Sir James Morgan, recently returned to Whitby." Murmurs spread from person to person. Some benign, others malignant. "So you see, Mrs. Edwards, there was no time to inform you. This is a new development."

Her face twisted into a question mark as her gaze bounced between him and Mallow, apparently deciding which man was the trump card. Finally, she skewered him with a stare. "But how did you—I mean, when did you meet my daughter?"

"I can tell you that, Mrs. Edwards." Mallow narrowed his eyes at James. "I saw them together in the library, and I admit I wondered at their familiarity."

Mrs. Edwards inhaled sharply, as did several onlookers. Blast. This was going from bad to worse. A few more word grenades launched from Mallow and the situation would explode Miss Edwards's reputation to shreds. Either he needed to shuffle her to safety—which would cause the tongues to wag faster than a spaniel's tail—or he needed to leave.

He tipped his hat at the ladies. "Forgive me, but I am expected back at the manor. Let us table this discussion for a more appropriate time. Good day to you both and good day to you, Mr. Mallow."

Mallow blocked his path, a petulant tip to his chin. "There will be no other time. You have beguiled the girl, and I will not stand for it." He held out his hand to Miss Edwards. "Come, Rosa. I shall see you home."

She edged closer to James, her sweet lilac scent fresh as an April morn. "I'm afraid that is impossible, Mr. Mallow."

Mallow snorted, sweeping his hand towards the onlookers like a ringmaster rousing an audience. "Do you all see this? He has bewitched the girl! That is what vampires do, is it not?"

A collective gasp sucked in all the air, followed by furious crossing motions and several bemoanings of "God help us." The shuffle of feet was unmistakable as the crowd backed away and some outright fled down the pavement.

There it was. Out in the open. A mere week after his arrival. He'd known all along the ugly past would catch up to him; he just hadn't expected it quite so fast.

"Well, Morgan?" The sunken-faced man atop the yellow carriage sneered down at him. "What have you to say to my nephew's accusation?"

He set his jaw, saying nothing—a survival skill learned from past skirmishes with superstitious fools.

Beside him, Miss Edwards fisted her hand on her hip. "That is ridiculous. There is no such thing!"

Her defense warmed him, but she had no idea of his family's past. It was only a matter of time—a very short time—before the same fear that infected her neighbours and friends would smite her as well. Her mother snagged her arm. "The shopping, Rosa." Mrs. Edwards dipped her head at the Mallows and at him. "Good day, gentlemen."

Their skirts swished into the apothecary shop, leaving him with two hateful Mallows and what remained of the morbidly curious pedestrians.

Mallow poked his finger in James's chest. "This isn't over, Morgan."

Wheeling about so abruptly that his coattails slapped against James's legs, Mallow hiked up to the carriage seat. Without another glance, he ordered the horses to walk on.

James turned with a heavy heart. As much as he hated to agree with the man, Mallow was correct. This wouldn't be over until he did the right thing and cut off all relationship with Miss Rosa Edwards.

ELEVEN

For some time after our meeting this morning I could not think. The new phases of things leave my mind in a state of wonder which allows no room for active thought.

Maybe there were things in life that couldn't be explained, but Rosa doubted it. There was always an explanation waiting in the wings, though as she pedaled to Morgrave Manor this cloudy morn, she still couldn't comprehend why Sir James had allowed her mother to believe he was her beau yesterday. Her parents' willingness to accept the baronet could be attributed to the Morgans' bank account, despite the unorthodox way they'd learned of the supposed courtship. But for Sir James. . .what possessed the man to say such a thing?

Fueled by the desire to know, she pedaled all the harder. Taking the old bridge at Spital Beck at such speed raised the hairs at the nape of her neck, but she continued on undaunted. Her front tyre bumped over the gravel, now and then dipping into ruts from all the recent rain—more on the way today, judging by the gunmetal clouds.

She parked in her usual spot, next to the front stairs, just as the man himself came trotting down the steps, books in hand. He was not dressed as severely as yesterday. No dark glasses. No leather gloves or wide-brimmed hat. Even so, she caught her breath. No matter what he wore, the man was an imposing figure, a lion of his lair.

"Sir James." She dipped her head, her previous determination wilting now that he towered over her. This was a man of power, of might, not a simple fisherman to be led about with a wink and a smile. "I—I did not expect you, not out here on the front lawn, I mean."

He shifted the books in the crook of his arm. "It is I who did not expect you, Miss Edwards. I was on my way to return these."

No wonder, there. She hadn't left the house until well after ten o'clock. "I am rather late, and I apologize for it. My mother suffered a megrim that her elixirs could not relieve, so I read to her until she fell asleep."

"Perhaps the events of yesterday were too taxing." He put his load into her basket, his earthy scent filling the space between them. He did not, however, take out the new titles. Instead, he turned towards the front door, calling over his shoulder, "I have just the thing for her if you will allow me to send you off with a parting gift. Come along."

She followed, a twinge of unease in her chest. His words—his very stride—seemed so final, almost as if he couldn't get away from her fast enough. Once again, she gave the gargoyle in the hall a wide berth as she treaded faster to catch up with him. "That is very kind of you, but what do you mean 'parting gift'? Are you leaving Morgrave Manor so soon after you have arrived?"

"No." He stopped at the sitting room door and faced her. "But I think it best we end your daily visits. Oh Renfield." Looking beyond her, he beckoned the butler with a twitch of his finger. "Please bring me the envelope of megrim powder I mixed up yesterday. It is on my desk."

"At once, sir." The old fellow's shuffling steps belied his words.

It was a curious thing that the baronet had such medicine within reach. Were debilitating megrims the ailment he sought to cure? And even more curious, why the curtailing of their previous arrangement for book deliveries if he weren't quitting the country? Unless. . . Her cheeks heated. But of course. He must surely regret his hasty words of yesterday.

Sir James ushered her into the sitting room, indicating the sofa for her while he took the opposite chair.

She smoothed the wrinkles from her skirt, worried about the loss of this man's support for women like Mrs. Hawkins and Mrs. Godalming. How to broach the subject without insulting him or embarrassing herself?

"You are agitated, Miss Edwards." He rose. "If you would rather wait alone, I shall leave you to it and wish you a good day."

She forced her hands flat against her thighs. "No need. Your presence does not disquiet me in the least."

"Then what does?"

Meeting his gaze head-on, she inhaled for courage. "If I may be so bold, Sir James, why must we end our association?"

He sank to the chair cushion. A sigh deflated his chest as he raked his fingers through his hair, leaving behind a jumble of dark waves hanging ragged against his collar. "It was not a good idea to begin with. I should have known better than to allow your good reputation to be tainted by association with me. People will talk, as you witnessed yesterday."

"That is a baseless concern, sir, for I do not care a farthing for what people say."

He studied her so intently her stomach tightened.

"Does Mr. Mallow's accusation against me not frighten you?"

That's what bothered him? She grinned as she relaxed against the sofa cushion. "Vampires do not concern me a whit, for they are not real."

His dark brows lifted somewhat. "You are a very singular woman, Miss Edwards."

"I am not given to superstitious nonsense, sir, and furthermore, I fully intend to continue upholding our agreement. There is no reason to see those less fortunate suffer merely for the sake of preventing wagging tongues."

"So, this is about the less fortunate now, is it?" He crossed one long leg over the other, an amused tilt to his mouth. "If money is what you are worried about, fear not. I will still provide the means you need to deliver books to those who cannot afford a subscription. Consider me a permanent patron if you like."

"You are more than generous, Sir James, but..." She broke eye contact, running her finger along the stripes on the sofa. "It is much more than that, really," she murmured.

"Oh? Such as?"

This was it. Her opening to ask him the question that'd burned in her heart ever since that fateful moment in front of the apothecary shop. So why the sudden wish to run out the door and forget any of it had ever happened?

Before she actually did, she looked the baronet straight in the eyes. "Might I be frank?"

"I should hope so." Interest twinkled in his gaze. "I am not given to trivial offenses, so please speak as bluntly as you like."

Good. Then there was no reason not to dive right into the crux of the matter. "I appreciated your stepping in yesterday, allowing my mother and the Mallows to believe that we are. . .that you and I. . .well, that we have a certain romantic understanding between us. Your declaration put an end—once and for all, I hope—to Mr. Mallow's advances, and yet I cannot help but ask why you said such a thing in the first place."

"He was trying to bully you into something of which you did not wish to take part."

A simple answer, one that made her breath catch. Once again this handsome man had helped her out of a scrape. Sir James was chivalrous to a fault.

"Tell me, Miss Edwards"—his face darkened as he leaned forward in his chair—"has the man harmed you in any way?"

"Other than to sorely try my patience, no." A smirk twitched her lips. "I simply do not wish to pursue a relationship with him or with any other man, for that matter."

"Hmm." Rising, he poured a glass of water, offering her one in the process, which she gratefully accepted. Surely he must think her an odd specimen, for he said nothing as he returned to his seat.

At length, he set down his glass. "What is it you wish, then?"

"As you already know, I desire to spread education to the poor of Whitby, starting with those who can read, but also. . ." She took another gulp of water. Just how transparent should she be with a man she barely knew? Granted, he'd given her no cause to fear a mocking look or unkind words, for he had ever been a gentleman with her.

"Also?" he prompted.

She set her glass on the tea table, still debating if she ought to bare such a personal part of her life, but why not? She had nothing for which to be ashamed. Just because it went against social norms didn't mean it was wrong. "You may think this silly, but someday I hope to become a secretary, move to York, maybe even London. I would like to see more of the world, and in the process help someone's business succeed because I was there to manage the paperwork."

"If this is so, then why are you still here?" His brow furrowed. "What stops you from pursuing this dream right now?"

"Oh, I would love to, but I am not certified yet."

"Because?"

"The next step is learning to type."

At that moment, the butler scuffled in and handed Sir James a small brown envelope. "Your powders, sir."

"Thank you, Renfield. That will be all." The baronet rose, offering her the remedy. "I hope this will be of help to your mother, and I wish you all the best in your secretarial pursuits. You are an intelligent woman. I expect you shall master typing in no time and be well on your way towards achieving your dream."

"I would if I had a typewriter." She stood with a rueful smile. "And thank you for the powders. I am sure my mother will be grateful. I shall retrieve your books at once."

"After you." He swept out his hand.

An unaccountable sadness dogged her steps all the way to her bicycle. As forbidding as Morgrave Manor was, she truly would miss her morning ride here.

But was it the ride she'd miss—or the man?

Bah! Undoubtedly it was the exhilarating ride. She reached for his items at the same time as he, their hands bumping into one another's, skin against skin. She sucked in a breath at the now familiar current that ran up her arm at his touch.

He pulled back, face unreadable as he clutched the books. "I suppose this is goodbye, then."

Goodbye. The word was a slamming door, ending the brief hours of respite she'd had from her mother's endless matchmaking schemes. What a dreary future to think of resuming the continual parade of suitors. The thought churned her stomach, and she pressed a hand to it.

"Are you well, Miss Edwards?"

No. She most certainly was not. Gathering all the courage she yet owned, she peered up at the baronet. "I wonder, Sir James, if I may impose on your good graces for one more thing?"

He leaned back on his heels as if wary of her question. "Such as?"

"I know this is highly unconventional," she blurted before she could change her mind, "but would you mind very much if we, well. . .if we continued to allow everyone to think we are courting? I mean, you would not have to actually court me, just play the part for a while. Attend my sister's dinner next week, since my mother already uninvited Mr. Mallow and is expecting you in his place, and allow me to continue my daily visits here. That should do it."

Perplexed lines furrowed his brow. "What exactly do you hope my role in this farce will accomplish?"

"Remove the noose of threatened matrimony from my neck. You have no idea how persistent my mother can be." She slammed her mouth shut, heat flooding her cheeks. What a squawking mawker she must sound. "Never mind. Please, forget this entire conversation." Hiking her skirts, she settled on the bicycle, prepared to flee. "Once again I thank you for your kindness and wish you all the best. Perhaps I shall see you at the library sometime. Good day, Sir James."

She put her foot on one pedal, but before she could take off, the baronet stayed her with a gentle grip. A faint smile rippled across his lips. "Though you may very well regret your request, I think I can manage one dinner and a daily delivery of books."

Her heart skipped a beat. "Really? Why, you are a godsend!"

Releasing his hold, he shoved back a dark swath of hair. "I have been called many things, Miss Edwards, but *godsend* is a first."

"Well, it is true." She turned her bicycle around then peeked at him over her shoulder, "Good day, Sir James."

He nodded. "Good day to you as well, and oh—perhaps leave off the *sir* if we are to be believed as a couple, leastwise in public."

The heat in her face spread clear to her chest at his suggestion. She'd never called any man by his Christian name, save for old man Joe down at the wharf, whom anyone and everyone called such.

She rode off, pondering how much life could change in the space of a week. Not only did she have an assured source of funding for her book deliveries to those in want, but she'd secured a pseudo-suitor who would prevent her mother from dragging home any more potential husbands. And a baronet, no less! What a boon. What a blessing. The gloom of this cloudy morning could do nothing to shadow the lightness in her spirit. Why, this might just be her best day ever.

With a grin she couldn't stop, she pedaled past the abbey ruins, broken walls rising from the ground like black ghosts from a grave. Shortly past it, though, she slammed on her brakes.

No. Oh no.

At the side of the road lay a sheep. Eyes glassy and staring into eternity. Blood—so much blood—pooled near its head, throat torn out. This was a fresh kill.

The hair at the nape of her neck bristled. She flicked a gaze across the field that ended at the cliffs. Nothing moved there, so she snapped a look behind her. The road wound empty towards the manor. Ever so slowly, she turned to study the ancient walls that remained of the old abbey. A predator might be hiding there, but it couldn't be the mad dog. The men in town had boasted of their victory, going so far as to hang the carcass on a pole at the city's edge.

A shiver spidered down her spine, and she set her feet to her pedals, kicking up gravel as she sped off.

Maybe there were things in life that couldn't be explained.

Completely baffled, James watched the lovely form of Miss Rosa Edwards ride off down the drive. Albin Mallow had been entirely wrong about one thing. It was the woman with the beguiling smile and fresh innocence who'd bewitched him, not the other way around. He'd intended to end things with her today, and yet here he was, committed to the sweet torture of seeing her every day and dining with her family next week. Whatever had possessed him to agree to such a thing?

Heaving a sigh, he strode into the house, depositing the new titles from Miss Edwards onto his desk before taking the stairs to his mother's room. Just before he swung into her doorway, Nurse Agatha sailed out, a battleship on the move in her standard grey skirts.

The smell of lemon balm and sweat wafted about her like a noxious cloud. "I were just about to summon ye, Sir James."

That couldn't be good. His stomach knotted. "About my mother, I assume?"

"Aye." She lifted her stubby fingers towards the door. "Lady Dorina's taken a turn."

He inhaled sharply. Clearly that recent elixir hadn't worked.

"I will see to her at once." He made to pass by, but the woman blocked his way.

"Thought ye should know, sir, that I'll like as not be leaving for my sister's on the morrow."

It was a struggle, but he refrained from rolling his eyes. Now was not the time to revisit Agatha's perennial threat of resignation. "I will take that into consideration, Nurse."

He strode around her, straining to hear any moans or groans leaching from his mother's bedchamber, and his heart turned to ice when nothing but silence emanated from within.

"Mother?" He dashed through the door, steeling himself for what might be his mother's final moments or—God forbid—to discover she'd already drawn her last breath.

Piercing blue eyes stared at him.

His mother sat propped against cushions, white hair upon white pillowcases, a stark contrast to her darker skin.

"Mother!" He dashed to her side and sank next to her on the mattress.

Her slim fingers pressed cool against his cheek. "My son." The words were rusty from disuse. "You have come!"

Though more than thrilled to see her so lucid, concern niggled that she'd not remembered he'd been here for over a week now. He covered her hand with his own. "How do you feel?"

"Weary." She pulled free of his touch, as if the lifting of her arm had drained some of her newfound strength.

Even so, it was a relief to see her so calm instead of the usual mad thrashing contorting her body. "God be praised."

"Pah!" She turned aside and spat.

Nurse Agatha would not be happy to clean that up, nor was he pleased to witness such blasphemy. How it grieved him that she refused to leave behind her dark past.

He pressed a kiss to her brow, her skin cool and somewhat clammy to the touch. "I pray for your soul as much as for your body."

She turned her face from him. "You waste your time. Let us speak of happier things. My land?" She peered back at him. "My home?"

"All in good order and awaiting your return. Sala manages in my absence."

"Mmm." Her eyelids fluttered, her chest rising and falling with shallow breaths.

"Rest now, Mother." He gathered her hand, hoping to soothe. "I will sit with you while you dream."

The words barely passed his lips before she drifted off. How frail she looked, this woman who used to be so robust. So intimidating. If only she would surrender her soul to the Creator of all before she drew her last breath. He closed his own eyes.

Oh God, make it so. Grant Your redemption for my mother who seems so far beyond Your reach. . .and yet, nothing is impossible for You, great King.

His throat tightened. It went without saying that God could act, could snatch his mother's very soul from the precipice of hell. But would He?

"Sir?"

He stiffened at the maid's voice.

Betty entered, holding out a white square of paper in her hand. She was a scrappy little mongrel, a bit patch-haired beneath her mob cap and more bones and sinew than bulk under her apron. "This arrived for you, sir. Renfield bid me to give it to you straightaway."

Rising, he collected the letter then dismissed her, but before Betty disappeared, he added, "Would you see that Nurse returns to tend my mother?"

"Right away, sir." She dipped her head then scuttled off.

With a quick check to see that his mother rested peacefully, James sank onto the chair near the hearth. Before breaking the seal, he tugged off his neckcloth and loosened the top few buttons of his waistcoat, the heat in the room excessive for his tastes. But fully needed. His mother refused to keep tucked beneath her counterpane, and God forbid she should take a chill in her state.

He slid his finger beneath the wax and shook out the paper, happy to see Sala's strong hand in black ink on the page. But the more he read, the more that happiness waned. Funny how just when the world seemed a brighter place, shadows gathered about him. He re-read the last few paragraphs twice over just to make sure he hadn't misinterpreted anything.

I regret to inform you, my lord, that the Baron Vulpe Vicleană has returned to the neighboring manor. He swears that in his absence, you have moved the southern boundary markers and that the water rights of the Bega River belong solely to his lands. Naturally, I informed him otherwise but to no avail. He threatens to take control, move the fencing, and block our livestock from drinking from the river, which, of course, is our only source of water. I needn't tell you such an action would endanger the livelihood of your tenants. Considering the recent drought, water is gold.

For now, I shall endeavor to manage in your stead, but I fear I must ask you to return as soon as you are able. If the baron should take this grievance to court or worse—into his own hands—I have not the means or power to block him.

James let out a long breath. The Vulpe Vicleană family had been a thorn in the side of his mother's family for generations. Of all the times for the feud to flare up, it had to be when he wasn't there to defend his holdings? Or perhaps his absence was the reason why the man had instigated such an outrageous claim in the first place.

Fighting the urge to crumple the paper in his fist, he refolded the missive, then glanced over at the deathly still woman on the bed. By God's grace, his mother had rallied today, but would her condition last long enough to endure an arduous sea voyage to Transylvania? Because the ever-prudent Sala couldn't be more correct.

He must return to Transylvania as soon as possible.

TWELVE

The real God taketh heed lest a sparrow fall; but the god created from human vanity sees no difference between an eagle and a sparrow. Oh, if men only knew!

Albin set his bouquet of red roses lightly on the ground and tightened his neckcloth, aligning the silk just so. Timing may be everything—but so was a crisp cravat knot. Satisfied his appearance was nothing but perfection, he swiped up the flowers and rang the Edwardses' bell.

The moment the door swung open, he dipped a perfect bow for Rosa's mother. "Good afternoon, Mrs. Edwards."

"Why, Mr. Mallow, what an unexpected surprise." There was no pleasure in her voice or in the tightening at the sides of her mouth. Not to worry, though. Soon enough he'd have her begging him to take on her headstrong daughter.

"I thought I'd deliver this bouquet myself." He hefted the package, wafting just the right amount of enticing fragrance. "Is Rosa at home?" He suppressed a smile, already knowing the answer, for he'd peeked in the library window to make sure she was occupied.

"It's very kind of you, but Rosa is not here." Mrs. Edwards's dark little eyes narrowed on the flowers. "But you do know that Sir James has already spoken on behalf of my daughter."

"Oh? Has an engagement been announced?"

"No, not yet." She lifted her chin to a regal air—a commendable pride. "Though I fully expect something more permanent will be arranged shortly."

That stung, but only for a moment, because a permanent arrangement with that man would never come to pass, not if he had anything to say about it. And he had plenty to say. He stepped closer, lowering his voice to a mysterious tone. "I confess, Mrs. Edwards, that while these flowers are meant for Rosa, I had hoped to speak with you about the baronet."

Surprise rippled across her face. "I can't imagine why." She opened the door wider. "But do come in."

That'd been easy. Almost too easy. Perhaps the woman was more malleable than he credited. He followed her midnight-blue skirts, a grin on his lips—one that widened when he spied his previous bouquets dotting the room.

"Do take a seat, Mr. Mallow." She continued on to a tea cart. "Will you have tea?"

"I would." He set the roses on a side table then sank onto the sofa, once again considering timing. Uncle often stressed the art of stringing out one's words like pearls on a necklace. So he waited for Mrs. Edwards to serve him, to refill her cup, and to straighten her skirts on the chair.

Then waited some more.

Mrs. Edwards eyed him over the rim of her cup. "What is it you have come to tell me?"

"Dreadful tidings, I'm afraid." He sipped his tea, enjoying the flare of her nostrils at that dropped gem. Let her think he spoke of the baronet—for in a backhanded way, he did. Finally, he set his cup to the saucer, balancing both on his thigh. "About the recent spate of sheep killings, I mean. Ghastly, is it not? One worries the predator will move on to bigger game. Perhaps a small child, even."

"Goodness!" She put her cup on the table, porcelain rattling. "But surely it's only another dog taken with hydrophobia. Someone is bound to shoot the beast any day now."

He shrugged, taking care not to slosh tea onto his perfectly creased trousers. "Perhaps. Of course, there's the whole matter of the latest reports. A tall man in black was sighted near the Browns' farm. Shortly thereafter, several carcasses were found that had been completely drained of blood."

Mrs. Edwards gasped. "Truly? I hadn't heard."

He shoved down a shudder of his own. He was here to frighten the woman, not himself, but even so, the matter was disconcerting. “I have it on good authority from my uncle, who told me so only this afternoon. He suspects there is something much fouler than a dog behind it all.”

“Dear me. I should hope not.” Rosa’s mother fanned herself for a moment before folding her hands in her lap. “But what has this to do with the baronet?”

“Nothing. . .though it is curious the dead animals started appearing only after he set foot on English soil.” And there it was, seed number one planted.

She frowned. “Mr. Mallow, if you have come here to tell me that Sir James is responsible for murdering sheep, I will have none of it.”

He chuckled. “Not at all, Mrs. Edwards. I merely wondered if you knew the history of the Morgan family, namely, Lady Dorina, Sir James’s mother.”

“I do not fancy myself a gossip, sir.” But she didn’t move so much as a muscle to rise.

The woman was hooked.

“Nor would I label you as such, Mrs. Edwards. I merely thought, being Sir James is to grace your daughter’s house and possibly your other daughter’s life, that you should know what is said.”

“Well, I have heard rumours, but. . .none of us have actually seen Lady Dorina for some time now.” She shifted on the cushion, head cocked like a curious robin. “Still, I suppose since you’ve come all this way, it would be rude of me not to hear you out.”

“You are all graciousness, Mrs. Edwards.” He set the cup aside, biding just the right number of seconds to enhance her interest yet not over-enflame it. “I had a conversation with my uncle last evening, and it is by his wise counsel and permission that I share with you the things he told me. He is well versed in the Morgan family, having had business dealings with Sir James’s father, Sir Jonathan.”

“I had no idea.”

“Yes, well, not that it signifies other than to say he is intimately acquainted with the Morgan family. As such, I am even more convinced my accusation of last week rings true.” He paused a beat for emphasis, preparing to plant seed number two. "Vampire blood runs deep in the Morgans' veins."

The woman's pupils widened. "That is a very serious accusation, Mr. Mallow."

"It is, and I do not make it lightly. I merely wish the best for you and Rosa, for your entire family, really."

She spread her hands. "But what evidence can there be?"

Victory! That was the exact question he'd hoped to fish out of her. Uncle Preston had been right—as usual—to have suggested such a course of action for him to follow here this afternoon.

"As you know"—he crossed his legs, settling deeply in his chair for a good tale telling—"Lady Dorina hails from Transylvania, the historical birthplace of such monsters."

Mrs. Edwards sniffed. "My family roots tie back to Ireland, sir, but that doesn't make me a leprechaun."

He chuckled. What a spry bird she was. "A valid point, Mrs. Edwards, and if that were all there was to it, I'd not be here now. But it has also been verified by several witnesses that when Lady Dorina landed on our fair shores, she brought with her several trunks of her native soil, dirt that reeked of death."

Mrs. Edwards's fingers fluttered to her chest. "Why would a lady travel with such a queer cargo?"

"It is said a vampire cannot rest unless laid upon the earth of his homeland."

She edged forward on the cushion. "I didn't know that."

Rising, he flourished his hand towards the gilt-framed mirror above the hearth. "I suppose you did not know there are no mirrors in Morgrave Manor. Not a one. My uncle bears witness to this, having been there several times in his younger years. I suppose I need not embellish on that matter, for surely you know the implication."

"The undead bear no reflection," she murmured, her face blanching once the words passed her lips. "Still. . ." She straightened, an apparent move to pull herself together. "Even if that is all true, it doesn't mean Sir James is a—I fear to say the word."

"Nor should you." He perched on the edge of the sofa, lowering his voice to just the right mix of conspiracy and alarm. "We wouldn't want to summon anything untoward by the speaking of it."

Her eyes widened to dark buttons of terror.

Satisfied, he leaned back against the cushion. "Did you notice that day in front of the apothecary shop how tightly laced the baronet appeared, to the point of shading his eyes with coloured glasses?"

She thought a moment, then nodded. "Yes."

"I submit he can no longer bear the touch of sunlight against his skin, which is a clear and present mark of a creature of the night."

She drew in a breath as she stared off to an undisclosed point on the ceiling. "Could it be. . . ?"

Perfect. His work here was finished. He rose and patted her on the arm. "Well, I shouldn't keep you any longer. I merely wished you to be informed." And judging by the tense muscles beneath her sleeve, she was more than informed.

"No need to see me out. Give Rosa my regards, and good day, Mrs. Edwards."

He strolled to the front door, content he'd planted just the right amount of doubt in the woman. Time soon to water those seeds but not today. Tomorrow would do very nicely.

Indeed, timing was everything.

There was something about a new book. The crisp pages. The scent of fresh ink. Or perhaps best of all was the promise of an adventure to a world beyond her own. Rosa shelved a particularly handsome cover—one with embossed lettering and swirly vine embellishments at top and bottom—then ran her finger down the gilt lettering on the spine. *The Firm of Girdlestone.* She and Father had been shelving the new inventory for the past hour, but this one was tempting to tuck away in her reading basket. Who could resist a first edition by Arthur Conan Doyle?

Sighing, she returned to the front desk, where her father finished cataloguing the most recent shipment. She'd already snagged two titles, and Father would surely chide her if she grabbed a third. Tempting, though. The more reading material the better, for she'd likely not sleep tonight, not when tomorrow evening would be the baronet's debut as her beau at dinner.

As if her father read her mind, he peered at her over the rim of his spectacles. "This baronet of yours, tell me again exactly how you met?"

Inwardly, she cringed. The baronet wasn't hers, nor could she tell her father the full truth of how she'd taken a tumble with a load of books she ought not have been delivering in the first place. Thankfully she'd been able to successfully dry the pages and return the titles to the shelves.

She grabbed another new release off the pile. "We crossed paths the day he landed. He helped me up when I tumbled off the bicycle."

"Quite the gallant move for a man travel worn and of the upper class. You must have really caught his eye." Her father leaned back on the stool. "Truth be told, your mother and I couldn't have hoped for a better match. Well done, Rosa."

She hugged the book, one of the corners cutting into her collarbone. For once she'd pleased both her parents, but their approval sat like a stone in her belly. The urge to come clean welled up to her throat. But telling him would not only discredit her, it would cast the baronet in an untrustworthy light—and the man already had enough naysayers in town.

Father reached for his pipe from beneath the counter, then pulled a bag of tobacco from his pocket and filled the bowl. "I am surprised your mother didn't think of a daily book delivery to a potential suitor's home before you did. Brilliant move."

"Father, really! You make me sound as if I set out to ensnare the man."

"Whether you meant to or not, you did."

She turned aside, searching for the shelf that would be this book's home while also searching her heart for any shred of legitimacy in her father's words. She hadn't technically snared Sir James. He'd been the one to suggest the frequent visits—and oh, how she'd come to treasure those morning chats. He was as well-read as she, able to converse on just about any topic, and frequently offered insights on humanity she'd never even considered. And above all, he was ever the gentleman.

She returned to the desk, where Father quirked a brow as he puffed on his pipe, clearly amused by something.

"What?" she asked.

He aimed the bowl at her. "I believe you are smitten, Daughter."

She huffed. "Do not be absurd."

"Then tell me"—he leaned over the countertop—"why are you still holding the same book you set out to shelve?"

She glanced down at the volume yet clutched to her breast. Of all the rubbish! She wasn't smitten. It was Father's fault for speaking of snares in the first place. She marched over to the bookcase and slid the title where it belonged, then circled back to swipe up one of the last two. "We are nearly finished, unless there is another crate in the office?"

"No." He gathered his papers, rapping them against the countertop. "This should do it."

The bell above the door jangled. Father looked past her and bellowed, "The library is closed. Come back tomorrow, thank you." Then he lowered his voice for her alone. "I thought I told you to lock that door?"

She shrugged as she whispered, "Sorry, Father, I have been too busy helping you."

"Just dropping off a delivery. Last one o' the day." A man smelling strongly of sardines thwunked a crate the size of a large bread box onto the counter, then pulled out a slip of paper and jammed his index finger on a big X. "I'll need a signature here, if ye please."

Father grabbed his pen.

But the man shoved the paper closer to her, tapping his finger against it for emphasis. "Says here this box is for a Miss Edwards." He glanced from the receipt to her. "I'll be needing your signature, miss."

A package...for her? Other than her correspondence course mailings, she never received any deliveries, least of all one of such a substantial size. A load of books, perhaps, that the publisher had mislabeled, putting down her as the recipient instead of her father?

Father handed her the pen with a curious tilt to his chin. She signed her name and returned the receipt to the fishy fellow. "Thank you."

He tipped his hat. "G'night to ye both."

Rosa faced her father, one hand resting atop the small crate. "Well, this is highly irregular. What do you suppose it is?" She drummed her fingers against the wooden lid.

"Only one way to find out." He retrieved a crowbar from the back room. "Here you are."

She jammed the iron wedge between box and lid, then put all her weight into prying the thing off. Nails screeched. Wood groaned. Slowly—but surely—the lid came off. Hmm. Not books, but a box full of wood shavings. She scooped them out, uncovering yet another box. Father helped her wrestle the thing from its nest, and once again she pried off a lid.

"Oh!" she breathed, fingers trembling as she pulled out the sleek black typewriter from Guffy's Emporium. Reverently, she ran a gentle touch along the hard rubber platen, then curved her fingertips over the keyboard like a prayer. How perfect it was.

"Thank you, Father!" Rising to her tiptoes, she kissed his cheek.

He chuckled. "As much as I appreciate the show of affection, the gift is not from me."

"What?" Her eyes widened. "Are you saying this is from Mother?"

Her father shook his head. "Your mother does not have that kind of pin money. That typewriter is not from us."

But if not her parents, then...

Heat flared in her chest. The only other person she'd told of her dream was Sir James—which begged the question...

Why would a pretend beau give her such an expensive, albeit thoughtful, gift?

THIRTEEN

They are very, very superstitious.

How could time fly and stand still at the same time? If one of the fishwives down at the wharf had told Rosa such a thing were true, she would have refuted the illogical phenomenon with a laugh and a book on the physics of chronology. Yet now. . .

She dabbed her lips with her napkin, nearly finished with her meal, but even so it seemed mere seconds ago that she'd taken her seat next to Sir James in her sister's dining room. Each minute stretched to an hour while also whizzing past. It was an exquisite sort of torment, heightened by a strange awareness of the man at her side. She felt the heat radiating off his body. Could almost hear the strong cut of his jaw working as he chewed. And she must keep her hands busy lest she tuck into place that one dark curl breaking rank in front of his ear, refusing to lay flat with the rest of his slicked back hair. She reached for her glass lest she give in to the urge and embarrass them both.

Across the table, her mother and sister conspired about something with bent heads. At the far end, Robert, Lucy's husband, spoke to his manservant. And just to the right of her, her father mopped up the last drips of mustard sauce with a forkful of roast beef.

With everyone so occupied, she snuck a peek at Sir James—and his brown eyes immediately caught her in the act. Again. Warmth flared in her chest. How did he always know when she sought him out?

She leaned close, trying desperately not to get lost in his earthy, cinnamon scent. "Thank you for coming tonight," she whispered. "And thank you once again for the typewriter."

"There is no need for such continual gratitude." His voice was a summer breeze, dreamy, warm. "Both are trifles, so think nothing of it."

"Oh, but I do, very much." The words flew out too earnest, too intimate, and far too husky.

"Such manners, Rosa." Her mother tapped her finger on the table—as if that weren't a breach of etiquette. "Speak so all may hear you."

She straightened her spine lest her mother launch into a discourse on posture as well. "I was merely thanking Sir James for the typewriter, Mother."

"That was quite the thoughtful gift." Lucy, all pearls and bows and flouncy lace—exactly the sort of feminine beauty Mother admired and Rosa could never compete with—smiled at the baronet. "You should know, Sir James, my mother and I have been despairing of Rosa ever finding her Prince Charming. My sister is a rather particular princess, and we are delighted she has found you. . .or rather, the other way around, as I understand it."

A particular princess? Of all the images. What would Sir James think of her after tonight? She stabbed a piece of Yorkshire pudding, the burn of shame as hard to swallow as the mouthful. To be fair, the baronet's opinion ought not matter so much. It wasn't as if they were really courting. He was doing this as a favour because he was a kind soul, nothing more.

"A basket full of books on wet pavement is a recipe for disaster," he answered her sister, then looked directly at her. "I am glad I was there to help."

Her mouth dried, his gaze so intense it was supernatural. She might easily believe he was an immortal, crafted by God and not meant for this world. And yet here he was, gazing at her, doing strange things to her heart. It wouldn't be a far stretch to imagine a happy ending with him.

"I cannot agree with you more, Sir James." Father stabbed her with a sharp look. "Books on wet pavement *are* a disaster, one of which that Rosa neglected to inform me."

Rosa swallowed hard, and for once was grateful when Mother took up her interrogation of the baronet without missing a beat.

"Is it true you arrived from Transylvania?" Mother signaled for a refill of her glass. "I have heard such—tales of the place."

"Yes." Sir James set down his fork, and Rosa tried—and failed—not to admire the strength in his long fingers.

"My mother's family estate is there," he explained.

Mother speared a roasted carrot, allowing it to hover above her plate. "Did you, by any chance, happen to bring along any unique cargo, say. . .crates of soil, for instance, from your homeland?"

Rosa scrunched her brow. "Mother, what an odd question."

Humour rumbled in Sir James's throat. "I am afraid I brought no such thing. Though horticulture runs in my family, my thumb is anything but green. It is my mother who would have brought her precious gardening soil."

"Ha ha. . .nothing to be ashamed of." Mother ate her bite of carrot with gusto, almost as if she were relieved—but why?

Sir James shifted on his seat, his knee brushing against Rosa's skirt and sending a jolt up her leg. "I am told, Mrs. Edwards, that you are quite the master of all things growing, what with your prolific medicinal industry."

"Well, I. . ." Mother cleared her throat, rosy blooms spreading on her cheeks. "I suppose I do know a thing or two about plants."

Rosa smiled. There was no doubt about it: Sir James was quite the charmer, and she wasn't the only one under his spell. . .for now, at least. Ever since last night, Mother had been a bit out of sorts about hosting the baronet for dinner, but now that angst seemed to be fading fast.

"There are rumours, Sir James—" Robert's voice trumpeted from the head of the table.

Holding her breath, Rosa suppressed a cringe.

Please don't say he's a vampire, Robert. Please, God, don't let him say—

"—that Transylvanian iron ore production is set to take off." Robert tossed his napkin on the table and spread his hand. "Is this something I should invest in?"

Rosa's shoulders sagged, the relief heavenly.

Lucy pressed her fingers against her husband's sleeve. "Please, Robert, can you not save such masculine talk for port and cigars?"

"Hear. Hear." Mother rapped the table. "Let us get to know the man himself, not his view on business ventures."

"You cannot extract the man from his business." Father swiveled his head to Sir James. "Not that you need go into detail, Sir James, but even the gentry have been known to suffer from poor finances. I would hope this is not the case for you. I should like Rosa to be amply provided for in her future."

Oh dear. Was her father seriously asking for a financial accounting from a man who no doubt owned more than anyone at this table had ever dreamed? Rosa placed her cutlery on her plate, appetite completely gone. "Sir James and I have only known each other for a fortnight, Father, so surely it is too early for that sort of conversation." She turned to the baronet. "You do not need to disclose anything you do not wish to."

"I never do." He winked—and her breath caught.

Sir James looked past her to her father. "I assure you, sir, that I am very comfortably settled."

"Oh!" Across the table, Lucy squealed, her long lashes all aflutter. "Will you be throwing any balls, then, Sir James? Any garden parties or the like? I dearly love a good soiree."

Rosa wrang her napkin beneath the table, wishing her whole body could slide under there and disappear. "Lucy, Sir James has hardly had time to settle in, let alone think about organizing a large event."

Her sister lifted a slim shoulder, riffling the lace of her collar. "I merely thought a gathering would be the best time to announce something—that is, if one were to have anything to announce." She smiled sweetly at Sir James. "Say an engagement or the like."

Rosa rolled her eyes and side-whispered to him, "Please forgive my family, Sir James."

"Do not be so quick to discredit them," he whispered back. "They merely wish the best for you."

Her heart warmed. How gracious. How endearingly patient with her family's pokes and prods. She would do well to learn from him and not be so quick to think the worst of her mother and sister.

"Well, daughters"—Mother pushed back her chair—"shall we retire to the sitting room and allow the men their time alone?"

Everyone rose as Mother stood, yet she lingered with a touch to Father's sleeve. "But pray, Husband, do not weary Sir James with too much talk. He is here at Rosa's bequest, and as such should rightfully spend time in her company."

"Don't fret, my dear." Father patted her hand. "Robert and I have already lined up our questions for Sir James, so we ought to fire them off quickly."

Questions? Rosa shoved her chair in towards the table. "He came for dinner, Father, not an interrogation."

Her father laughed. "I think Sir James is man enough to withstand anything we can give him."

She peered at the baronet. Oh yes, he was definitely all man, from the broad width of his shoulders beneath that exquisitely tailored suit, to the strong outline of his thighs.

But just how long would the man be willing to continue this charade without calling it quits?

He hadn't been this amused since Sala had helped Cook chase chickens in the yard on a muddy day. James rubbed his hand along his jaw as he resumed his seat at the table with the men. He was enjoying himself far too much here. Rosa's family was amongst the few—nay, the only—who were willing to set aside rumours and give him a chance. . .though admittedly her mother had been most incisive with her questions, hinting at the nefarious gossip she'd obviously been fed. Still, he'd have been disappointed had she not queried him so pointedly, for a mother bear ought to be protective of her cub.

And what a fine she-cub was Miss Rosa Edwards. He glanced at the door as the hem of her blue gown swayed out. God love the woman, she'd been as protective of him as her mother had been of her, deflecting any questions that probed too deeply. Several times he'd even caught her studying him when she thought he wouldn't notice. But he did. Against his better judgment, he observed every little detail about her.

Which was a mistake. As much as dinner with this family had been a wonderful reprieve from isolation, to believe such a future might be in store for him would only lead to bitterness. Best to drink the port then bid goodnight to the ladies and ride back to the shadows of his own solitary life.

"So, Sir James." Rosa's father handed him a glass of deep red liquid. "When will you be leaving again for Transylvania?"

"Soon, I fear. I have business to attend."

"That could break my sister-in-law's heart." Robert swirled his drink around then took a sip, eyeing him as if he were a criminal. "Unless you intend to bring her along with you?"

"Exactly my question." Mr. Edwards puffed on his cigar before aiming it at him like a canon. "What are your intentions towards my daughter, Sir James?"

James filled his mouth with the sweet wine, stalling. Any man would and should jump at the chance to claim Miss Rosa Edwards as his own, announce a betrothal, marry her, and count himself blessed. But oh, how well he knew that he was not like other men—a truth he'd learned the first time the sun had touched his skin. He had nothing to offer the woman but a future of madness and death. . .and the moment these men learned of his family's curse, he'd be run off.

He met their gazes directly. "I intend nothing but the best for Rosa." Ah, how honeyed the name tasted on his tongue.

Robert narrowed his eyes. "That's quite an opaque answer."

Mr. Edwards slid the box of cigars across the table. James passed it along to Robert without opening the lid. A few sips of wine was indulgence enough for one evening. "As Scripture says, 'for now we see through a glass darkly,' and this is indeed a dark world in which we live. One never knows what the future holds, so I find that prudence is the best policy when speaking of what is to come."

Robert chuckled. "So, you are a religious man, albeit one of a rather morose shade."

"Actually, I avoid religion."

"And what of the tradition of marriage?" Edwards huffed. "Do you avoid that as well?"

The man was dogged, he'd give him that. Something to be admired and feared—as was marriage. Naturally he'd given it some thought on those cold, lonely nights when a companion would've been a blessing. "While I am no expert, I imagine marriage to be like a flower, something to be appreciated and nurtured as one of God's greatest gifts, an image of what is yet to be when we meet our Creator face-to-face."

A slow grin curved Edwards's mouth. "Well said, Sir James. I am happy to hear your high view of the institution."

"How. . .poetic." Robert angled his head. "Now, about that iron ore—"

"Pardon the intrusion, sir." A servant strode in, pausing just past the threshold. "There is a caller at the door who will not be put off."

"At this time of night?" Robert shoved back his chair, rattling the glasses on the table. "Forgive me, gentlemen, while I see to this. I'll meet you in the parlour shortly."

"It is not you who is being requested, sir"—the servant's gaze drifted across the table—"but Sir James Morgan."

"Sir James?"

Mr. Edwards's question echoed his very thoughts. Who would call for him—and so adamantly?

"Yes, sir."

James rose, gut twisting. "Pardon me."

He strode to the door, with each step lifting a prayer that whoever it was had nothing to do with his mother. Hopefully she hadn't taken a turn. . .or worse, a fall. She'd been sleepwalking of late, and a tumble down the stairs when Nurse dozed off could snap her neck.

He heard the buzz of men's voices before he reached the door. Apparently so did Robert and Mr. Edwards, for their footsteps thudded down the corridor after him.

A rush of cool night air greeted him, along with a waft of sweat and hatred. Angry faces sneered at him, torchlight reflecting in the stark whites of their eyes. Some carried clubs. Others crucifixes. A deadly hush came over them all as they fixed their gazes on him.

This would not end well.

James planted his feet on the stoop, calling over his shoulder for the servant to please see his carriage brought 'round with all haste.

And then the dam burst. Shouts, threats, curses.

"There's the devil himself! Mallow was right."

"Run 'im out now, I say. Tie 'im up fer fish bait."

"A pox on ye! God spare us."

James clenched his jaw. He'd heard it all and more, but that didn't make such abuse any easier.

Robert stepped beside him. "Bloofer, what is the meaning of this?"

A ruddy-skinned man the size of a mutant ox and just as ugly advanced, aiming his thick index finger at James's chest. "Ye kilt all ye're goin' to, ye daemon." He flipped over his hand, palm up. "I expect my due now for what ye've taken. Empty yer pockets to satisfy yer debt, or we'll take it from ye."

The only way to deal with a mob was to maintain a calm voice and distance—*much* distance. He shook his head carefully, for any abrupt movement would only incite. "I have no idea of what you speak."

"Liar!" the man roared. "My sheep. Ye drained 'em dry, ye blighter! Not a drop o' blood left in a one o' 'em. And don't be thinkin' o' comin' fer our women or children next, neither."

James glanced beyond the gathering, hoping to spy his carriage rolling into the glow of the streetlamp. Nothing yet. He squared his shoulders, meeting Bloofer's fervour with a deadly even voice. "I have nothing to do with your livestock or your families. I tend to my own, and I suggest you do the same."

Bloofer's face contorted. Cheeks working, he let fly a wad of spit that hit James on the cheek. He swiped away the saliva with the back of his hand, silent. Furious. Frustratingly impotent, for whatever he said would not be heard with open ears, nor could he take on the gathering of ten or so men, not on his own. Where was that blasted carriage?

"Hear, now!" Mr. Edwards glanced from him to Bloofer. "This man has been with us all evening. He has done nothing wrong."

"Ye have no idea the trouble ye bring upon yer head by letting this creature of darkness inside yer home. He's a vampire, he is. A vampire! Taking life. Stealing souls." The man's podgy fingers curled into a fist that he shook at James. "Off wit' ye! Off, I say! And if ye show yer face e're agin' in this town, we'll see ye staked through that black heart o' yers." He glanced at the men surrounding the stairs. "Aye, fellows?"

"Aye!" The chorus belched into the night just as his carriage rolled into view.

"Can it be true?" Mr. Edwards spoke out of the side of his mouth to Robert.

Rosa's brother-in-law fixed James with a cold stare.

While keeping one eye on the mob, James tipped his head at the man and Mr. Edwards. "I think it best I leave now. Please give Miss Edwards my goodbye, and thank you for a fine dinner."

Her father gave him a curt nod, saying nothing.

Bracing himself, James pounded down the few stairs and shouldered his way through the crowd—not an easy feat with all the jostling and shoves. And especially hard when everything in him wanted to strike back, take them on with an elbow to the gut or a few uppercuts to shut their mouths.

He swung up into the driver's seat and with a slap of the reins, urged the horses to a fast pace wholly unsuitable for the narrow, curving lane. Blast! But he should have known better than to have come here tonight. Should have known a normal life was not to be, not for him. Not ever.

If—and it truly was a very big *if*—Rosa had the temerity to deliver his books in the morning, he'd make sure it was her last visit.

FOURTEEN

So far there is much that is strange.

Fatigue draped over Rosa, weighing down her shoulders like a wet woolen mantle. She yawned—again—as she pulled the last book she needed off the shelf and added it to the small pile on the library counter. She'd spent the previous night wrestling with her bedsheets, angry at her mother, the townspeople, the world. The display of ugly accusations and angry men on her sister's doorstep last evening had been beyond the pale, unacceptable and unbelievable. Worse, she'd not had a chance to assure the baronet she didn't believe a word those men had shouted. Unlike her mother. She and Lucy had denounced Sir James with equal fervor, claiming a man like him to be an unfit husband and demanding Rosa never speak to him again.

Fighting another yawn, she double-checked the titles she'd gathered while an off-key rendering of "Boney Was a Warrior" whistled out from the back room. Satisfied she'd pulled the correct books, she collected them in her arms and set off for her morning deliveries.

Father looked up from his desk as she neared the back door, his tune abruptly ending. "Where are you off to?"

Strange, he didn't usually ask about her regular departure. "The daily drop offs."

He set down his pen, furrows digging into his brow. "Sir James Morgan's?"

"Yes, for one. Also, a stop at Cholmley School and Mr. George's."

A rumble vibrated in her father's throat. "Very good. . .but make this your last visit to Morgrave Manor."

She cocked her head. "Whyever for?"

"You heard those men last night. You saw your mother's terror, your sister's alarm." He pushed up from his chair and planted his hands on his desk. "We don't need that kind of trouble, Rosa."

She'd flail her arms were she not cradling books. "But that is preposterous. Sir James obviously had nothing to do with those men or their livestock."

"The people believe otherwise."

"The people are a misguided lot desperately in need of education. I suggest we order a book or two on sheep and their natural predators."

"Which will be a case of too little, too late. You cannot stop a tide from crashing ashore, Daughter, and I will not have this one swamping us." He waggled his finger at her. "I realize you care for the man, and this is no easy thing that I ask of you, but you must understand I have worked hard to keep this library afloat. I don't believe the claptrap about vampires either, but I do believe in the power of public opinion to ruin a business."

She shifted the books to her other arm, a mix of emotions stirring in her heart. She did care for James, and it was kind of her father to acknowledge how hard this would be for her, but that did nothing to lessen the need to see the baronet every morning. She'd grown too accustomed to it—to him.

She approached the desk, her brow folding. "If this truly is a matter of business for you, then have you considered that by stopping the baronet's delivery, you will no doubt stop his subscription fee as well? I have seen what he pays, and it is quite a tidy sum. Other than Preston Mallow, he is our best patron, is he not?"

Her father deflated in his chair with a huge sigh. "Yes, he is." He pinched the bridge of his nose, adding a little shake to his head. "But I don't like it, Rosa. I don't like it at all."

"Neither do I." Likely for very different reasons, however.

"Go, then." Father dropped his hand, fluttering a paper on his desk. "Though it is against my better judgment—and see you do not tarry."

"I shan't be long." She shoved open the door and loaded her books into the basket. Breathing in a waft of fresh air, she pedaled off towards the imposing manor, anxious to let Sir James know he still had a friend despite the ravings of the horrid mob.

With the sun on her face and a light summer breeze fluttering her bonnet ribbons, she eventually gave in to the glorious August morning and enjoyed her bicycle ride. Mostly. Sunshine or not, crossing the rickety bridge at Spital Beck never failed to set her teeth on edge, and passing by the abbey ruins always made her a little melancholy. How grand the place must've been with its towering spires that yet reached towards the heavens. Most people claimed the place was haunted and warned against looking overlong in the gaping top right window lest you catch sight of the ghost of Saint Hilda. But all Rosa ever saw was the quelling of promise, the disparagement of hope. And what did God see, looking down from His great throne, other than the desecration of what had once been a holy center of worship?

These thoughts followed her the rest of the way to Morgrave Manor, right up to the point when Renfield opened the door. His wiry eyebrows lifted clear to his receding hairline. "Miss Edwards?"

Strange that he appeared surprised to see her. The old fellow was slow and riddled with rheumatism but had always seemed sound of mind. She jostled the books in her arm, a visual reminder of why she was there. "I have Sir James's requested titles, as usual."

His mouth pursed into duck lips, thin and purple against his parchment skin. "I do not think he is expecting you, but come in."

"I am a little late this morning. I can find the sitting room myself if you would like to call for him."

He nodded. "As you wish."

The closing of the door shut out air and light. She'd gotten used to the crypt-like essence of the manor, but she would never make peace with the gruesome gargoyle in the hall. Someday she might ask about it. Today she merely skirted the hideous thing and set her books on the table in the sitting room.

She glanced at the ornate sofa hunkered in front of the hearth, tempted to sink onto its thick cushions and close her eyes for a few minutes, for surely it would take Renfield all of that and more to shuffle off and find Sir James.

Stifling yet another yawn, she took to wandering the room and eventually ended up at the drawn drapery, blocking the grand summer morn. Why was it no matter the time of day, the heavy fabric closed out daylight and lamps burned at all hours? Well, leastwise, the early morning hours when she visited. Perhaps the housemaid didn't arrive until later or had other duties to tend first. She reached for the edge of the thick curtains, intending to help the girl out.

"What are you doing here?" The baronet's voice was a thunderclap.

Startled, she whirled. Even more startling, a black glower twisted Sir James's handsome face. He was always imposing, but she'd never been afraid of him.

Until now.

She clenched handfuls of her gown, wholly unable to force out one word.

His long legs ate up the carpet as he stalked towards her. "You did not answer my question, Miss Edwards."

There'd be no refusing him. A shiver of fear settled in her belly, and she retreated a few steps until her back hit the wall. "I—I brought your books."

In one more stride he hemmed her in, pressing his hands against the wall on either side of her shoulders. The whites of his eyes flashed like a stallion's. "Are you not afraid I will try to seduce you and drain your blood? I am a vampire after all."

She swallowed, knees nearly buckling. Clearly he was trying to frighten her, but why? Had those men last night been right?

How ludicrous! What was she thinking? She was no better than the tale-spinning Mrs. Godalming. Gathering every last shred of courage she owned, Rosa lifted her chin. "Nonsense."

"But what if it is true?" He leaned dangerously close, running his finger down her cheek, then lower, caressing her neck. His flesh smelled metallic, as if he'd been grasping a gun or a knife. Smelled of blood. Her skin tingled beneath his touch.

"What if I am a vampire?" he whispered.

Was it a question? A threat? Had he even spoken it aloud or was this all in her head? Hard to think with the warmth of him soaking through the thin fabric of her gown. Fire licked along her bones.

"You are not a vampire," she breathed.

He wrapped his fingers around her chin, bending close, practically nose to nose. Unfathomable mysteries glinted like gold dust in his brown gaze, hinting of other worlds and ancient sins. He tilted her head, baring her neck, his gaze never once leaving hers. "Are you so sure I am not a creature of the night?"

His warm breath feathered against her exposed skin, his mouth a hair's breadth away, and her heart took off at a gallop. Too many desires warred inside. To run. To scream. To give herself up to the intoxication of his touch.

She swallowed, forcing out words that were barely a squeak. "I am certain you are no such thing."

He clenched his jaw as if he'd been dealt a mortal blow. Closing his eyes, he wheeled about, a shudder rippling the fabric across shoulders that suddenly sagged. "Go home, Miss Edwards." There was loss in that tone, a defeat she couldn't begin to understand. "You will sully your reputation by being with me. I release you from our agreement."

"I do not wish to be released." The words flew out before she could stop them, the truth of them stunning her.

He spun back, nostrils flaring. "Why?"

A valid question, one she wasn't sure she could answer. All she knew was that despite the man's brooding mood and frightening manner, she didn't want to say goodbye. Not yet. She smoothed her clammy palms along her gown. "The citizens of Whitby need to see you are not a man to fear."

"Am I not?"

Actually, he was. Sir James towered a good head taller than her, his powerful muscles clearly defined by the dark blue cloth of his suitcoat against the swell of his biceps. Should he wish, he could snap her in half.

Even so, deep in her heart, she knew without a doubt he'd never harm her. He'd never harm anyone. Not willingly. She stepped away from the wall, showing him—showing herself—she trusted him. "I am not afraid of you."

His lips twisted into a smirk. "Maybe you should be."

"Petulance ill becomes you, sir. You are no more a vampire than am I.

Furthermore, I intend to prove you and the whole town wrong."

He sighed, his big hand kneading the muscles at the back of his neck. Dark crescents hung beneath his eyes, as if he'd grappled with his own bedsheets in the long hours of the night. "You are quite unstoppable." He dropped his hand. "Nevertheless, I insist you end your daily delivery here. I will not have you endangered by association with me. Those men last night brought clubs. What do you think they will bring next time?"

"Hopefully there will not be a next time. But even so, dangers abound in this world. You cannot protect me from that which I freely choose. You are not God, sir."

A harsh laugh rumbled in his throat. "How well I know that."

His words came out ragged. Actually, now that she looked closer, everything about him was off. Lamplight carved harsh lines on his face, and his brown eyes were so dark not even the glints of gold could be seen. Clearly some sort of battle raged in this man. What had life dealt him to bring him to such deep waters? If last night's spectacle was any indication, she shuddered at the answer.

She placed her palm lightly against his sleeve, hoping to impart encouragement. God knew everyone could use a kind word in this cruel world. "You are recently returned from distant shores, which is grounds enough to make the residents of Whitby wary. They are a superstitious people, easily influenced by unexplained happenings. Your arrival unfortunately coincided with a spate of livestock killings. It is nothing personal, Sir James. You are not the cause. You are the scapegoat."

He inhaled deeply as if breathing her acquittal into the farthest reaches of his lungs. "Not many would look beyond the consensus to view things so plainly. You are a rarity, Miss Edwards."

"It is kind of you to say so, but I am no rarity, sir. Rather, much like yourself, I am an outsider. I have always seen things differently, and it puts people on edge. Makes them nervous when their long-held beliefs are challenged." She pulled away, a rueful smile lifting her lips. "Maybe you should take a care for your reputation by associating with me."

The barest hint of a smile ghosted his mouth. She'd never seen him grin fully—and suddenly yearned to be the one to put a smile on his face.

"So," he murmured, "we are bad for each other, then?"

"Most definitely." She crossed the thick rug to the table where she'd set the books and patted the small stack with her fingertips. "Here are three titles I think you will find interesting."

He strolled over and rifled through them, obvious interest playing across his face. "Some very astute choices. But I wonder if there can be many more titles of medical interest remaining in your collection that I have not yet read?"

"You have not exhausted our resources, though you are getting close."

He set the books down and stepped toe to toe, peering into her eyes as if she were the only woman on the earth. "Then I shall have to read slower."

The air charged. Her breath caught. "Or I shall have to find more books."

It was indecent the way they stood so close, unmarried, unchaperoned. But it was also life and need, this soaking in of his attention, this craving for more.

"Rosa." Her name on his tongue was shockingly intimate.

And wholly delicious. Unbidden, she leaned towards him, wishing once again to feel his breath against her skin.

A gruff throat clearing sounded at the door.

She immediately backed away, heat singeing her cheeks.

Renfield's bushy brows pulled into a severe line. "Pardon, sir, but there's a matter for you to attend upstairs."

The baronet's jaw hardened. "Thank you. I shall be there after I—"

"An *urgent* matter, sir."

Sir James inhaled sharply.

Rosa glanced between the two of them. She'd never seen the butler so forceful.

"Very good, Renfield. See Miss Edwards out, will you?" Sir James dipped her a curt bow. "Until tomorrow." He skirted around Renfield, the heels of his footsteps hard against the marble tile in the hall.

Rosa drew near the butler, peering at the backside of Sir James as he took the stairs two at a time. "I hope everything is all right," she murmured.

The butler shook his head. "One never knows with these things."

What things? She pressed her lips tight lest the question fly out. He'd never answer a direct enquiry into such personal information about his employer, so she'd have to find a better way to discover the answers she sought.

She followed the old fellow to the door, thinking hard. "Yes, I suppose one does never know." She repeated his words, hopefully putting him at ease by her agreement. "I only pray the books I bring will provide the cure Sir James seeks."

Renfield stopped, hand on the doorknob yet not opening it. "He's told you, then." He turned, his pale eyes sorrowful. "I suspected as much, being you've obviously become confidants. Try not to get too attached, though, my dear, for your own sake. It's only a matter of time before he starts displaying more symptoms."

She sucked in a breath, suddenly wide awake. *Symptoms*? The word was an ugly vagrant, setting up an unwelcome camp in the middle of her chest, settling where it had no right to be. Though she tried to evict it, the horrid thought of Sir James ailing would stay with her whether she wanted it to or not.

Once again she clutched her skirts, giving her hands something to do other than flail helplessly in the air. "Well then, we must pray it is a very long time until such happens, but in the meantime, what specifically must Sir James do to remain healthy?"

"Stay out of the sunlight, obviously." He pulled open the door. "Good day, Miss Edwards."

Leaving behind the gloom of the manor, Rosa stepped into the glorious day, unsure what to believe. The only ailment she knew of that required abstinence from sun against skin was the very thing of which the townspeople had accused Sir James. But surely the baronet's own butler didn't think he was a vampire, or the old man would not remain in service to him.

Then again, the only times she'd seen Sir James when the sun was out, he'd been covered head to toe, face shadowed with a broad-brimmed hat, gloves encasing his hands, and dark glasses protecting his eyes. She grabbed her handlebars and pulled her bicycle upright from where it leaned against the stair pillar. Perhaps there was some truth to the old butler's words.

Settling on the bicycle seat, she took off, pea gravel spraying up behind her. There was no time to waste. She had a lot of reading to do, for if the baronet truly did suffer from such a disease, perhaps she could help him find the cure he needed.

James took the stairs two at a time, cross with himself for not sending Rosa away permanently. At first he'd been surprised by Renfield's announcement that she awaited him in the sitting room, for he'd not expected her to come at all. Yet there she'd been, looking so lovely in her blue lawn gown, her skin aglow from the morning air. A spring violet couldn't have been purer. He should have dismissed her straightaway. Told her in no uncertain terms to leave Morgrave Manor and never return. Whatever had possessed him to try to frighten her off? To act the part of a rogue only made him one. What a cad. What an idiot.

And what a fiercely brave woman she was.

He cleared the top step, mortified afresh at how close he'd been to kissing the woman. Granted, it'd been foolish to draw so near to her in the first place. Oh, what an ill-fated day. And now this—whatever *this* was. It wasn't like Renfield to insist so adamantly he attend his mother. Would to God she'd taken a turn for the better, but as he dashed down the corridor to her room, his gut twisted. Silence poured out her door. Deadly silence. Had she drawn her final breath?

He stalked across the threshold, gaze shooting to her bed. Bedsheets rumpled. A pillow forgotten on the floor. The counterpane sprawled like a drunkard passed out half on and half off the mattress.

Nurse Agatha stood at the footboard, wringing her hands. Her usually starched collar wilted around her neck.

Alarm drove a stake through James's heart. "What's happened?"

"She's gone, sir."

"I can see that," he snapped. "How? Where?"

"She were sound asleep, sir. I swear it. So I stepped out just for a minute to call for Renfield—Betty never hears the bell when she's sorting laundry from the washer woman. I wished him to summon you for the day's instructions. I weren't gone but a minute, and when I returned, the bed was empty as you see it. I've given the room a proper go-over. She's not crawled into the wardrobe, hidden beneath the dust ruffle, or holed up in the water closet. Like I said"—the woman fidgeted nervously—"she's gone, and I thought you should be the first to know. Also, I'll most likely be—"

"Yes, yes! You will be leaving my employ on the morrow." He cut his hand through the air, irritated beyond measure. "If we do not find my mother posthaste, there will be no tomorrow. You shall be relieved of your duties at once. Go now and gather Betty, Cook, the stable boy, Renfield, even the washer woman if she is still here. This house must be searched from cellar to rafter. Move!"

He tore from the room, heedless if the nurse took offense at his brusque manner. If his mother had ventured outside, she'd not be able to withstand the sunlight against her skin, not in her weakened state.

God, please. Guide me to her. Let me find my mother safe and—

Crash!

Glass shattered down the hall. He wheeled about. Paces from him, Nurse Agatha pivoted as well. He raced past to the next door, nearly tripping on the threshold of his father's former chamber—where he stopped so abruptly he staggered. He grasped the doorframe, horrified at the sight.

Blood was everywhere.

Streaked on the walls.

Smeared on the counterpane.

Dripped on the rug in a dotted, crazy pattern all the way to where his mother hunched like a wounded animal in a pile of glass shards. Her white hair hung in strings over her face as she licked one of the many slices on her arm.

James's heart broke as he neared her, glass crunching beneath his heels. "Mother, come, let me get you back to bed."

She jerked up her head, pink-tinged spittle dribbling down her chin. Her eyes flashed wildly blue, the sharp edges of a lightning bolt. When he reached for her, she struck surprisingly fast.

He recoiled, blood now seeping from his own body, oozing out the fresh gash that gaped on his forearm.

"Here, Sir James." The nurse's voice was a foghorn at his back. "There's naught to be done but this when she's in such a way."

With one eye on Mother lest she cut him again, he pivoted somewhat to see Nurse Agatha holding out a syringe.

"Thank you." He gladly took the offering.

"Now, now, my lady," Agatha cooed, drawing his mother's attention. "I've got a seedcake waiting for you." The nurse briefly met his eyes, urging him on.

While she distracted his mother, James edged around the sea of broken glass and came up from behind, stabbing the needle into the fleshy part of his mother's arm. A scream ripped through the air. She swung again—too late. He wrapped his arms about her in a bear hold and lifted her up from the rubble of a crystal vase.

She writhed. He held strong. By the time he carried her back to her bed, she was limp. He laid his mother's still body onto the mattress, brows sinking at the pitiful sight. For all the world, she looked as if she'd been out on a hunt, made a fresh kill, and drank all the poor creature's blood. The picture of a vampire. How ironic.

If the nurse breathed a word of this scene outside the manor, those men from last night would be at his door with pitchforks.

FIFTEEN

There has been so much trouble around my house of late that I could do without any more.

A fortnight was plenty of time to scale a mountain, fall in love, or even start a war, but apparently fourteen days was not enough time to find a cure for the baronet's illness. And it wasn't for lack of trying. Night after night, Rosa burned her lamp long into the witching hours, paging through medical books, journals, and faded *vade-macums* on the off-chance the old physician guides might shed light on whatever it was that ailed Sir James. *If* anything ailed him, that is.

For she was beginning to doubt Renfield's claim.

With a sigh, she shelved the last of the returns then glanced out the library's front window. Instead of gazing upon the cloudy afternoon that cloaked the lane in monotone misery, all she could envision was the vibrant man she met with every morning. Each day for the past two weeks she'd studied everything about the baronet, from the bump on his nose to the tiny triangular scar on his chin. She scanned him repeatedly for any hint of the infirmity that might be affecting him yet came up short every time. The man was a rock. Solid. Strong. Capable in body and mind. And when he'd caught her in the act of staring—which he frequently did—he was annoyingly adept at arching a knowing brow.

She fanned herself with one hand, blaming the perspiration tickling her neck on the humidity in the oppressive air. Another storm brewed. Would that the heavens might simply open and be done with it. She'd seen damp summers before, but this one was an anomaly. Thankfully autumn would soon be here.

Across the street, a man marched towards the library, a paper-wrapped package tucked under one arm. By the time he reached the front door, Rosa recognized the stoat-like downturn of the fellow's mouth and the slit of his narrow eyes.

She met him as he entered. "Mr. Stoker, good to see you again."

"You as well, Miss Edwards." He tipped his brown derby.

"Is there something I can help you find?"

"I found more than enough on my last visit here. That book on Transylvania was just the thing." He patted his package with thick fingers.

Rosa angled her head. "I thought the title you requested was on Wallachia."

"True." He nodded. "But those provinces are neighbours, and the area of most interest to me fluctuates between the two borders. So much political intrigue, you know."

Actually, she hadn't known, which was somewhat embarrassing. "I suppose I should brush up on my geography and foreign politics." A half-smile quirked her lips.

"In the long run, that's probably neither here nor there. Border lines—like politicians—change at the whim of the people. What is of import is that this parcel is put into the hands of Sir James Morgan." He held out a package secured with twine.

Rosa received it with a scrunch to her nose. "If this is for the baronet, why are you bringing it to me at the library? His manor is not that far."

Mr. Stoker sniffed, his moustache rippling. "Sir James suggested you might not mind delivering my manuscript, and so I ask your favour. I'd meant to ask you sooner, but my wife and son have taken more time than I accounted for, and now we must return to London straightaway. The only thing more demanding than my family is the theatre, you see, and I am needed back there immediately."

"Oh, I am sorry your holiday is cut short, though I must admit our northern climate has not been very cooperative with merrymakers this season."

"Even so, the last few weeks were bliss compared to the odiferous bouquet one must endure in the city. Yet all pleasantries eventually come to an end." His big shoulders rounded with a shrug. "Now then, I trust you are a woman who values the written word, more so than a simple delivery boy or a postman. As such, I wonder if you would see Sir James receives that package today." He shot a pointed stare to the bundle in her hands. "Timing is of the utmost importance, for I have a publisher already clamoring to meet with me. Beneath that brown wrapper are the first several chapters of my manuscript. Of course it's not finished yet, but it is a substantial beginning. Being the baronet has spent much of his life in Transylvania, he has agreed to read the text for any errors I may have committed against his homeland."

"How kind of him," she murmured, pulse suddenly racing at the thought of seeing Sir James twice in one day. She inhaled deeply, tamping out the wanton urge, and forced her attention to the barrel-chested man in front of her.

Mr. Stoker fingered his hat. "Sir James appears to be a benevolent man despite the off-colour rumours I've heard whispered of him at the pub."

Rosa's belly tightened. She'd made no headway with extinguishing the ghoulish vampire stories amongst her own family, let alone among the townspeople. It seemed everyone save for herself—and now Mr. Stoker—was bent against him.

She clutched the package to her chest, lifting her chin. "Such gossip is nothing but malicious conjecture. I vouch wholeheartedly that Sir James is not some supernatural ghoul but a compassionate man."

"You are quick to come to his defense." His dark eyes twinkled. "I knew I made the right choice by bringing my manuscript to you. And for your trouble in uniting the baronet with my writings, I shall donate a collection of my short stories to the library."

She smiled. "My father and I would welcome a donation, but please do not feel obligated. I am happy to deliver your work to Sir James."

"Thank you, Miss Edwards." He glanced out the window. "Perhaps make haste. There is a foul feel to the air. I shouldn't like you to be caught in a storm." He reached for the door, then paused with his fingers on the knob. "Oh, and if you're ever in London, look me up at the Lyceum. I'm the manager there and will provide you with tickets for a production."

Her grin grew. What a treat that would be! "I look forward to it. Good day, sir, and safe travels."

"Good day, miss."

Pivoting, Rosa crossed to the counter and set down Mr. Stoker's manuscript, then silently tapped it with her finger, thinking. That book on Transylvania had admittedly been helpful to the man. Would it be as beneficial to Sir James? It was one title he'd not yet read and perhaps might have a nugget of information about his particular ailment.

She snatched the display case key and retrieved *The Accounts of Principalities of Wallachia and Moldavia.*

A quick page-through dashed her hopes. The text appeared to be mostly political but. . .hold on. She narrowed her eyes on a section discussing resources, specifically the mining of natural ores that had been—at least in a time long past—sought after for medicinal purposes. Hmm. Did the baronet know of this? Would it provide him any insight for whatever it was he tried to remedy?

She nibbled on her fingernail, debating what to do. She could bend the rules and simply deliver this book along with Mr. Stoker's manuscript. It wasn't as if Sir James would steal the thing or mar it in any way. But this was a rarity, one Father wouldn't wish to circulate in the general public. She stifled a snort. As if anything about Morgrave Manor was public. As far as she knew, she was the only soul who dared cross its shadowy threshold.

Ouch!

She yanked her finger from her mouth and examined the hangnail she'd just created. A dot of blood welled where the skin had ripped. She rubbed it away with her thumb and stared down at the book, her free hand lingering on the finely embossed title. She might ask Sir James to come here and read it, but then he would risk the censure of the residents who feared him, and Father would definitely not welcome an ugly confrontation at the library. Besides, there really wasn't much difference if she supervised the baronet with this rarity in the solitude of his own sitting room versus here at a table. It wouldn't take him long to digest the information, not at the rate he read, and she'd take great care in handling the valuable book there and back.

She glanced at the old clock on the wall, the bent hands just shy of three, then drifted her gaze out the window at the grey afternoon. Some sort of storm was gathering, one that could be a monster, though it wouldn't hit for several more hours. On such a dismal day, there wouldn't be too many more patrons venturing out for a read. Father would manage just fine. She could pedal up to the manor, allow Sir James to peruse the book for an hour, and still be back by closing time. Besides, waiting until tomorrow might not be such a good idea. If she hoped to keep her word to Mr. Stoker, it had to be now, for if a raging storm did break tonight, it could take out the Spital Beck bridge.

That decided, she made haste in wrapping Mr. Stoker's manuscript and the rare title in a waxed canvas bag while Father whistled a rousing—if discordant—version of "Nancy Dawson." She took extra care in sealing the package, so if the rain did break on her trek, then neither would be ruined.

"I have an errand to run, Father." She pecked him on the cheek on her way to the back door. A nip of guilt bit her conscience, and for a moment she nearly turned around to put the book back in the glass case.

Father lowered his spectacles to the tip of his nose, peering up at her from his desk. "There's a storm brewing. Is your errand truly necessary?"

"It is. I promised one of our patrons I would deliver this today." She indicated the parcel. "And you know how storms go around here. It is not even thundering yet. I have plenty of time, but even so, I shall try not to tarry."

"See that you don't." Her father's lips twisted as he dropped his gaze back to the pile of paperwork. "Your mother will not thank either of us if the clouds loosen and you return home a drowned rat."

She pushed the door open to a world that smelled like a dank cellar. Rosa loaded the package into her basket, nose curling at the off-putting scent, and set off, pedaling as fast as she dared on the narrow streets. The effort, combined with the thick air, made her gown cling to her skin. She glanced at the sky at regular intervals. The grey clouds held steady, though it finally let loose a few low-pitched grumbles to the west. With any luck, she ought to make it home without a drop of rain.

But what would the baronet think of her showing up on his doorstep twice in one day? To be sure, she'd been glad when Mr. Stoker had asked the favour of her, but now that she pedaled along the gravelly lane to Sir James's home, she started to doubt the wisdom of giving in so quickly. She could have as easily delivered the package tomorrow at her usual time. Perhaps she should have.

Slamming on her brakes, she stopped just shy of the Spital Beck bridge, debating if she ought to turn around. Ahead, the old wood creaked like an ancient's bones, the water below rushing fast and high—much higher than usual, nearly lapping over the warped decking. With so much rain lately, it was hardly a wonder. And after one more great storm, she wouldn't be surprised at all if the thing finally gave up its ghost and laid down for an eternal rest.

The thought squeezed her chest. No bridge meant no way to get from Whitby to Morgrave, putting an end to her daily banter with a certain brown-eyed enigma. Oh, how she'd come to cherish her mornings discussing what the baronet had read the night before. He owned a keen mind, one that fascinated her—one that looked upon her intelligence as an equal instead of the frivolous rantings of a woman who ought not stick her nose in a man's world.

She glanced again at the sky. It was dark, but not so much as a mist dampened her face. Just a jaunt across the bridge and in no time she'd sail straight through the baronet's gate. Wrapping her fingers tight around the handlebars, she set her feet to the pedals. The sooner she finished this errand, the better.

By the time she made it halfway across the bridge, the planks groaned louder than ever beneath her wheels. Wood cracked behind her like a gunshot. She flinched as she pumped her legs all the harder, afraid to look back.

Another crack. Closer this time. Then the horizon tipped.

No, the bridge did.

Rosa leaned into the bicycle, hunched like a jockey atop a racehorse. *Move. Move!* She strained against the pedals. Felt the first fat drop of rain against her brow. Or was it sweat? No matter, her front tyre made purchase on solid ground.

The back tyre did not.

Solid ground gave way. Slipping far. Slipping fast. Fear choked her, but not enough to stop a terrified scream.

There was something about the eerie void before a storm that never failed to lure James outside. He was a moth to such a dark flame, relishing the electric charge in the air, the hollow sound of his heels crushing grass and weed alike as he followed the footpath along Spital Beck. The promise of rain meant hope for greener things to come, and oh how desperately he clung to such a hope for his mother. Hope was all he had, really. She'd worsened, the madness methodically eating her mind bite by bite. Twice now she'd slipped past the nurse and wandered through the manor, a danger to herself and others. As volatile as his relationship had been with her over the years, he did not want to have to restrain her to the bed, tying her down like some wild animal. It just seemed wrong.

Then again, everything was wrong as of late.

Sighing, he tipped his face to the sky. "I am at a loss, Lord, to heal my mother or myself. Perhaps I have been a fool for trying, for are You not the great healer? And so here—now—I surrender at last to Your will. Heal or not, either way I shall continue to trust in You, for it is You alone who numbers our days. Not me. Not medicine. Not even the cursed disease that haunts our family. Give me the wisdom to create a cure or give me peace, for I cannot live like this anymore. Bring to me what I need, Lord, to carry out Your will."

He stopped and closed his eyes. Desperation always birthed the most earnest times of need and fulfillment. Tentatively, he held out his hands to receive something—anything—that the Creator alone could provide. A warm sense of peace, perhaps. Maybe the flash of a new ingredient to try as a remedy.

What he got was a scream.

He sprinted towards the sound, the holy moment morphing into one of horror as he rounded a bend in the path.

The bridge—what was left of it—clung as frantically to the river's bank as did Rosa. Rushing water submerged the rear wheel of her bicycle and the hem of her skirt. Blood leaked from a gash on her brow. His gut cinched. If he didn't snag her soon, she'd be washed away.

In three great strides, he shored up his right foot against a rock and leaned precariously over the embankment, arm outstretched. "Grab hold!"

"I cannot," she wailed. "I will lose the bicycle."

"Blast it, woman! I will buy you a new one." He lunged, grabbing hold of her arm.

"The books. We must save—ooph!"

His back hit the ground. Rosa whumped atop him. Their gazes locked, an unaccountable despair welling in her eyes. Why such misery when he'd just saved her life?

"No!" She wriggled away and shot to her feet. "Oh no!"

He shoved off the ground, batting away gravel from the seat of his trousers. Rosa faced the raging waters, hugging herself.

"Rosa?" Gently, he turned her to him, his gaze drifting from the cut on her forehead to the bruise on her chin. Her pupils were wide circles. How much damage had that head injury caused?

"You do not understand." Her tears broke.

So did the rain.

He yanked out his handkerchief and pressed it to her brow, then swung her up into his arms. "You are hurt. Let me get you to the manor before you take a chill as well."

She struggled. "I can walk."

He held her all the tighter, bending to shelter her from the worst of the downpour. "It is faster this way. I will not have you taking another tumble."

Like an overtired tot, she rested her head against his chest just as the dark hulk of the manor came into view. How well she fit against him. How right. Would to God that the circumstances were different. The story of his life, really. His lips twisted as he shoved open the front door.

"Renfield!" he bellowed. "Come quickly."

Surprisingly, the old butler showed up on the sitting room threshold just as he propped Rosa against the sofa cushions.

"Sir?" Renfield's wiry eyebrows lifted.

And no wonder. What a sight, him hovering closely over a bloodied woman.

"Some towels and my robe, immediately," he ordered.

Rosa shook her head. "Please, do not trouble yourself. I shan't be here long."

"Go!" he thundered.

Rosa frowned, then winced when the action surely stung a wound that needed to be cleaned. "I appreciate the effort, but truly, I must go home."

"Even were it possible, I could not allow you out in this storm." A crack of thunder echoed his words. "You saw the bridge. There is no way for you to get back to Whitby."

She pushed away from the cushions. "But I cannot stay here! Not overnight."

He inhaled until his lungs hurt. She couldn't be more right. Mother was always most restless in the darkest hours. He strode to the tea cart and doused a napkin in water, thinking hard—and coming up short. Drawing in a shaky breath, he returned to Rosa's side, trying not to breathe in her lilac scent. What he was about to say was already hard enough.

"I am afraid there is no other option at present. You will remain as my guest tonight."

SIXTEEN

One of the greatest and suddenest storms on record has just been experienced here, with results both strange and unique.

How could life go from bad to worse in less than a quarter of an hour? Rosa strangled the sofa cushions with her fingers, seeking some sort of stability now that the world had been yanked from beneath her feet. She'd lost the library's bicycle, Mr. Stoker's manuscript, and a costly rare book that would take her years to repay. But the one thing she'd never be able to restore was the loss of her reputation—and that's exactly what she'd forfeit by staying the night in the house of an unmarried man. . .and an alleged vampire at that.

She winced as the baronet dabbed a cloth against the wound on her brow. "Sir James, please, can you think of no other way for me to get home?"

His breath warmed her cheek, the tangy scent of rain and earth radiating off him in a way that ought not be so enticing. "I am sorry to disappoint, but I am a mere mortal, not given to calming storms."

She stared at the hollow of the baronet's throat, shivering from both the memory of how he'd cradled her against his chest and the thought of facing her father and mother when this was all over.

"You tremble." Sir James eyed her closely. "You do know you have nothing to fear from me, do you not?"

Did she? Not completely. The man was a danger, inspiring all sorts of rogue thoughts she ought not entertain.

"I am merely cold." The excuse sounded hollow even in her own ears.

He shrugged out of his rain-dampened coat and wrapped it around her shoulders, tucking it tight at her neck. "It is wet, but it will have to do until Renfield returns."

The heat from his body lingered on the fabric. Though it was only an embrace by proxy, her pulse soared.

He returned to the tea cart, mesmerizing her with the way his shirt sleeves clung to the swell of his muscles—a sight she had no business admiring.

Having retrieved another square of fine white linen, Sir James again dropped to one knee and pressed the fabric against her brow. "There now. Thank God it is not a deep laceration. No stitches required."

"For which I am grateful, but please see to your own needs. I can manage." She lifted her hand to apply pressure to the cloth. Too quickly, though. Her fingers bumped against his, the familiar jolt of his touch tingling up her arm.

A knowing gleam flashed in his eyes as he shoved back a hank of his dark hair. "What were you about, anyway, riding up here so late when clearly the skies were about to open?"

She nibbled her lower lip. What would he say if she told him she'd risked everything simply to see him twice in one day? "Mr. Stoker asked me to deliver his manuscript to you posthaste."

"Hmm." It was a growl, really, the next boom of thunder making it all the more ominous. "Why did you not simply add the manuscript to your daily delivery and bring it tomorrow?" He glanced towards the closed drapery, where a flash of lightning outlined the edges of the fabric.

"Mr. Stoker was quite adamant his writings be delivered today," she explained. "He said it was of the utmost importance because there is a publisher interested in his work. Besides, I suspected the storm would take out the bridge. I just did not count on it washing away before the clouds broke."

The baronet's gaze shot back to hers, a muscle on the side of his neck stiff as an iron rod. "The man never should have endangered you, publisher or not."

She sucked in a breath. My, how she'd hate to be on the receiving end of such a dark look. "I am sure Mr. Stoker did not mean any harm. In fact, he encouraged me not to tarry so I would make it back before the storm hit. He could have had no idea the bridge to your home was so rickety."

Sir James tilted his head, the set of his jaw—now familiar—an indication his mind was processing something at whirlwind speed. "But *you* knew the condition of the bridge. Why would you take such a risk for a casual acquaintance?"

Because I wanted to see you again.

She pressed her lips tight lest the thought fly out.

"Clearly I am missing something." Sir James peered at her closely, the deepening brown in his gaze hunting for secrets. "Is there something more between you and Mr. Stoker that I do not know about?"

"Posh! Mr. Stoker is a married man. He told me so himself." Frustrated with James, with herself, with the whole situation, she yanked the cloth from her wound. If more blood leaked out, so be it. "Besides, there was more in my basket than his manuscript. I found a book—a rare book—I thought might help you find your cure."

The baronet's sharp inhale competed with the hiss of the blaze in the hearth. "What makes you think I seek such a thing?"

Footsteps tapped just outside the sitting room, drawing their eyes to the door. Renfield entered, a white towel and a deep green robe draped over one arm. The colour contrast was startling against his black livery and ashen skin. "Here you are, sir."

Sir James rose at once. "Thank you. Please have Betty set a fire in the guest room. Miss Edwards will be staying the night."

A shadow darkened the old butler's face, adding an unnatural hue. "Do you think that wise, sir?"

"Would you send a woman into this storm?" Sir James flung out his hand as the next peal of thunder cracked. "And the bridge is out."

For a moment, Renfield said nothing, then slowly dipped his head. "As you wish, sir."

Though the old fellow acquiesced in word, Rosa didn't miss his stiffened spine and stilted stride as he exited.

But Sir James was already turning to her, holding out the robe and towel. "This is the best I can offer until your garments are dried—which should not take long once Cook gets hold of them. She keeps the kitchen to a hellfire temperature that could leach the moisture from your very bones. Shall I call the maid to assist you?"

Rosa collected his offering, holding it at arm's length lest the moisture from her garments seep into the dry fabric. "No need. I can manage if you will simply direct me where to change."

"There is no time to waste, not in these drafty halls. Change here. I shall wait outside and show you to your chamber when you are ready." He wheeled about, waving a hand in the air as he strode from the room.

And with that she stood alone in the sitting room of a man she admired, in a house she had no business being in, expected to strip down to nary but what God had given her.

Rosa scurried to the far side of the room, debating if she ought to somehow rig up the curtains as a sort of shield should Sir James—or anyone else, for that matter—stroll through the door before she finished, but eventually abandoned the idea. Cold was seeping into her skin, and it would not do to take a chill.

After much shimmying and peeling off of wet fabric, she finally buffed away the dampness on her skin and shoved her arms into the fine garment belonging to Sir James. Before cinching the robe tight at the waist, she gathered the wide lapels and breathed in his musky scent. Sweet heavens, if her mother saw her now, she'd faint dead away—and likely still would when Rosa returned home with the tale of where she'd been.

She padded to the door. Sir James paced like a lion on the prowl. Evidently he was completely lost in thought, for he didn't pause or even look her way.

Rosa cleared her throat. "I am ready."

He turned, his gaze brushing warm over her from head to toe, a distinct gleam of interest flashing in his eyes. "So you are." The words came out husky. Intimate. And why not? She stood there in naught but his banyan.

A fire spread from her belly to her cheeks.

"This way." He set off down a corridor so quickly she was left alone with the horrible gargoyle.

She dashed to catch up, nearly tripping on the thick carpeting. "That statue, Sir James, may I ask why such an imposing figure is the first thing to greet your guests?"

"Morgrave Manor is not accustomed to hosting guests."

"But still, it is a rather fearsome ornament even for you to face every day."

"There are more fearsome things in this world than a lifeless bit of carved rock." He turned left, then cut her a sideways look. "But since you ask, that statue is an ornament my mother brought over when she first married my father, a little something to remind her of her home, taken from the roof of Umbră Castle."

She blinked. She'd known he possessed wealth, but so much? "You have a castle in Transylvania?"

"I do—or rather, my family does."

"Is that why you do not usually live here?"

He hefted a deep sigh and upped his pace. "Among other reasons, yes."

"Such as?" Hiking the long hem of his robe, she scurried to gain his side.

"You have seen for yourself how England greets me."

True. The reception of her fellow neighbours had been as chill as the cool air licking against her bare calves. "Are you accepted much more in Transylvania?"

An acrid smile twitched his lips. "No, not really, but at least I am respected."

"As well you should be. I find no fault in you."

He stopped abruptly, his dark gaze staring deep into her soul—a look that frightened and captivated with equal ferocity. "You are light and air," he murmured. "I wonder if you know that?"

"I—" She swallowed, unsure how to respond.

Reaching past her, he pushed open the door at her back. "Here is your room."

She entered a faery tale. A canopied bed graced one wall, the bedclothes sprigged with honeysuckles and grapevines. Layers of gauzy curtains hung on the windows like free-floating clouds come down from heaven. An ornate dressing table adorned one corner and a white washstand the other, the entire area being lit by a cheery fire on the grate and merry wall sconces. She turned back, surprised to find Sir James standing so closely behind her.

"It is lovely." She smiled.

"As are you."

Her heart skipped a beat. And another. Suddenly it was hard to breathe, and even harder to understand the depth of intense feeling furrowing his brow. She could get lost in that look of appreciation, dive into his arms and once again feel cherished and protected.

He retreated a step, abruptly ending the moment she wanted to live in. "I shall send the maid with your gown once it is dry, then Renfield will retrieve you for a late dinner with me, for I expect you will be famished at that point. Until then." He bowed his head deeply then wheeled about, shutting the door softly behind him.

Rosa hugged herself, unsure of what to do with all the peculiar feelings fluttering in her belly. What a strange evening this would be. And a late one, no doubt. It would take several hours to thoroughly dry her wet garments. Yawning, she settled atop the bed. It wouldn't hurt to close her eyes for a moment or two.

Minutes later, knuckles rapped against the door. She stirred, still groggy, then jolted awake as her gaze landed on the mantel clock. Ten? How had she slept so soundly for nearly six hours?

"Miss Edwards?" the old butler's voice filtered through the wood. "Are you all right?"

She scurried to the door. "I am fine, just sluggish, I suppose."

"The maid was worried when she could not rouse you." He held out her garments. "All is dry, now. If you please, I shall wait in the corridor until you are ready, then escort you to the dining room where Sir James awaits."

"Thank you, Renfield."

It was an unaccountable loss, this taking off of Sir James's garment and slipping back into her gown. She folded his banyan into a neat square before joining the butler in the passage.

"This way." Without another word, the old fellow led her to the dining room.

And what a surprisingly grand room it was. Mahogany paneling glowed almost amber in the lamplight. White linen draped over a table at center, set with gleaming silver and crystal goblets. Oil paintings, large and in ornate frames, hung at intervals. Why were the guest room and dining hall so grandiose compared to the rest of the manor?

But no time to ponder that now, for all the elegance in the room paled in comparison to the dark-haired man in a smart black suit who strode her way. Sir James had tamed his hair, relegating the wildly curling ends to the back of his collar. He'd tidied up his moustache and the patch of whiskers on his chin as well, emanating a masculinity that weakened her knees. Or perhaps she wavered on her feet because he stopped so close to her. She breathed in a lungful of his shaving tonic, spicy and foreign.

He tilted her head with a gentle touch to her jaw, eyes narrowing as he studied her brow. "I wondered if you would feel up to joining me. How are you?"

La! She'd been fine until he'd cast such a spell upon her.

She licked her lips, mouth dry beyond reason. "Much better after a lie-down, thank you."

"Well"—he brushed his thumb along the curve of her cheek as he pulled away—"I am happy to hear it."

In two steps, he held out her chair and signaled for Renfield to remove the covers from the dishes. "I should warn you the fare here is not what you may expect from a manor home, not to mention it is late, which warrants a lighter meal."

The rich scent of beef broth curled up from a tureen, next to which sat a platter of thickly sliced bread and cheeses.

"It is perfect." She smiled.

"Very good." Sir James shook out his napkin. "I have instructed my stable hand to assess what may be done to bridge the gap across the river tomorrow morn—assuming, that is, the storm lets up by then. It quieted for a while but seems to be regaining strength."

Sure enough, the glass panes rattled from a gust of wind.

Rosa sipped her consommé, hardly tasting the soup. "My mother must be frantic."

"Hopefully your family will assume you reached my home before the worst of the weather."

She shook her head. "Neither of them knew I was coming here."

"Oh?" His gaze sharpened. "Why would you not tell them?"

Absently, she stirred the liquid in her bowl, saddened to think of the malicious things her mother and sister had said about Sir James. "While my father allows my daily delivery, I am afraid my family has given ear to the town gossip."

He eyed her over the rim of his goblet. "So I am to understand that you not only go against what your neighbours think of me, but your parents as well? Why?"

Because I'm falling in love with you, James.

Her spoon clattered to the table, instant heat flushing her cheeks. What a thought!

"P–pardon me." She inhaled deeply.

Pull yourself together, girl. You're dining alone with a handsome man. Surely that's all there is to it.

She reached for the platter of cheese and speared a thick piece with a fork before gaining enough courage to face the man. "I have told you before that I do not believe in silly superstitions. No matter what my family or others may say, you are not a supernatural fiend."

"True." He savored his own bite of soup before setting down his spoon. "But that does not logically rule out the supernatural at large. There is always some seed of truth to the tales people tell."

"Do not tell me you put stock in ghosts and ghouls?"

"Not specifically, but I do believe things happen which cannot be explained by man." He shoved away his empty bowl and reached for a slice of bread, then chewed a mouthful before continuing. "God is not so limited that He cannot act outside the boundaries of physical law, for it is He alone who decides where those boundaries lie. Think of it. . .turning water into wine, feeding a multitude with naught but a few fish and some loaves. And what of the disembodied handwriting on the wall at Belshazzar's feast or the walking dead at Christ's death?" He held up his glass in a salute. "God is bigger than you credit, I think."

She blinked. "I had no idea you were a man of such deep faith."

"Faith in God, yes. It is His creatures who do not inspire my confidence."

Plate now empty, she placed her napkin on the table. "Well, I hope you know you can trust me, Sir James."

"I hope so too." He spoke so quietly she nearly missed it.

But there was no missing the enigmatic look washing over his face.

He cleared his throat. "Now then, if you are finished, I will see you to your room."

And just like that, their perfectly lovely dinner ended.

They wove their way through the corridors. For a long while he said nothing, leaving her to wonder if she'd somehow offended him, but honestly it wasn't him she ought to be worrying about offending. She'd gone and lost Mr. Stoker's precious manuscript. That man would be outright furious and rightly so.

The baronet's brown eyes sought hers in the shadows, pulling her from her failure for the moment. "How are your studies coming along? Is York to gain a new secretary in the near future?"

"I have finished the shorthand portion of the course, but I confess I struggle with the typewriter. It is so. . .mechanical, I suppose. I am forever hitting the wrong letters, and sometimes I type too fast, which makes the keys get all locked up. I am afraid patience is not one of my virtues."

A low chuckle rumbled in his chest. "Nor mine." He opened her door. "And here we are. Ring the bell if you require anything. I have instructed Renfield to enlist the help of the housemaid to see to your needs. She and Cook are stranded here as well, thanks to the weather."

"Thank you. Truly. If only others knew how kind you are."

"It is enough that you think it." The brown in his eyes softened to velvet. "Goodnight, Rosa."

Her name on his lips was a caress, a dream, the very essence of promises and happily-ever-afters—and her heart swelled with the fullness of it. "Goodnight. . .James."

His lips parted as he sucked in a breath. His fingers brushed lightly against her face, outlining the shape, sending a tingle down to her toes. She couldn't help but lean into it.

Nostrils flaring, he pulled away and stalked off—then abruptly turned back with a stern look. "Oh, one more thing. For your own safety, I must ask you to remain in your room all night. The key is there. Lock the door and do not venture forth until Renfield calls for you in the morning. Am I quite clear?"

"Yes."

"Good." He strode away, leaving behind a chill that shivered across her shoulders.

She entered her room and pressed the door shut, puzzled by how his moods could change like the spring weather. Not that she had any intention of roaming Morgrave Manor in the darkest hours of the night, but why such a warning?

He'd never dined alone with a woman. Never had his robe cling to a lady's skin. And not once had any female—other than his mother and the servants—slept beneath his roof. James marveled at the strange turn of events wrought by the storm as he stalked through the shadowy corridors. Oh, how easily he could get used to living with Rosa, to cherishing every smile she shared and delighting in her conversation into the wee hours of the night. Though it troubled him that her family must certainly be worried to distraction, he wasn't sorry she was here. . .as long as she stayed far away from Mother.

Or more like Mother stayed far away from her.

He plowed his fingers through his hair as he entered his study-turned-laboratory. It wouldn't hurt to supply Nurse Agatha with an extra sleeping draught for his mother until Rosa traveled safely back to her home.

"Sir?"

Renfield's monotone voice stabbed him in the back before he reached his desk. James turned with a frown. "I thought you would be abed by now."

"I would have been, but when I removed my suitcoat and emptied the pockets, I realized I'd forgotten that a letter arrived for you earlier today. I meant to give it to you when you got back from your walk, but then there was the whole ordeal with Miss Edwards." The old butler held out a battered envelope, and James was pleased to see the swelling of the man's knuckles somewhat lessened. That salve must be working.

"I do beg your pardon for such neglect, sir."

Frowning, James took the missive, knowing full well he ought to pension off the old fellow. Such defects in the man's service were becoming more and more frequent. But without a purpose, Renfield would wither away. He had no family. No friends. Nothing but a lifetime of servitude to a family shunned by society.

"Thank you, Renfield. That will be all."

As the butler shuffled off, James broke the seal of a letter he didn't want to read.

> *My Lord,*
>
> *Would that this salutation were anything but what I must tell you. No number of threats or cajoling on my part has diverted the baron from beginning the construction of new fencing to keep your livestock from reaching the river. For now, your tenants are managing to drive the herds around the impediment, but such a reroute won't last. Naturally I have filed several legal complaints on your behalf, but as you know, the wheels of law grind at a painfully sluggish pace. I fear it is imperative you return at once.*
>
> *Ever your humble servant,*
>
> *Sala*

Blast. James crumpled the letter into a tight wad and flung it into the coals on the hearth, then watched with a cancerous eye as the paper flamed into a fiery ball. Horrible timing for such a squabble—and well did the baron know it. Even if arrangements were made to leave as soon as the bridge was fixed, he'd likely not make it back here before his mother drew her last breath. And the thought of leaving Rosa behind punched him in the gut, though it shouldn't. He had no business whatsoever caring for her the way he did.

With a growl, James snatched several sleeping draughts from his desk and stomped out of the room. Would that God might perform one of the miracles James had spoken of so freely to Rosa at dinner and solve this dilemma.

He took the stairs two at a time, listening hard and dreading to hear any mournful wails or eerie shrieks coming from his mother's room. Surprisingly, nothing but gusts of wind and deep thunder rattled the bones of the manor.

Easing open the door, he exhaled relief. On the far side of the room, Nurse Agatha dozed in her chair, head against the wall, mouth open. Mother lay equally a'slumber, eyes closed, breaths lifting her chest in a steady rhythm. She'd lost weight since he'd been here, her cheekbones pushing hard against nearly transparent skin. But she slept, thank God, and peacefully at that.

Even so, James padded silently across the rug and shook the nurse's shoulder. "Shhh," he warned, as her eyes fluttered open.

Her gaze immediately shot to the bed, then back up to him. "Something amiss, sir?" she whispered gruffly.

"I merely wish to give you these." He handed over the packet of sleeping draughts. "See that my mother rests quietly for the next day or two."

The nurse's lips pinched. "She is quiet and has been all afternoon. I should let you know, though, that I'll most likely be leaving tomorrow and ye'll have to find another nurse."

"I would expect nothing less, and with that I bid you goodnight." The threat didn't annoy him in the least. What did it matter when his mother slept so sweetly? He left the room lighter than when he'd arrived.

Thank God this would be a good night.

SEVENTEEN

What I saw appalled me. I felt my hair rise like bristles on the back of my neck, and my heart seemed to stand still.

The earth exploded—a sharp-edged shattering that cut to the bone. Rosa shot up in bed, clutching the counterpane to her neck. Heart racing. Terrified.

Hardly a foot from her mattress lay a huge tree limb, branches grabbing for her. Wind howled through the broken window, whipping the curtains like a gathering of ghosts. The thunder had stopped, but not the rain. Merciless liquid pellets lashed in horizontally with each succeeding gust, dousing the rug and the bedclothes, lowering the temperature in the room by at least ten degrees.

Rosa crawled from bed, taking the counterpane along with her and donning it like a cape over her thin shift. The acrid scent of chimney ash blended with the dampness, and she scrunched her nose, debating what to do. There'd be no staying here, that much was obvious. And once again her gown was soaked, the chair she'd laid it over crushed beneath the rude intruder across the room. Yet despite her state of undress and Sir James's implicit command that she not leave her chamber, there was no other choice. The servant's bell had been completely ripped from the wall, snagged by one of the thick branches.

Stepping carefully to avoid the shards of glass littering the carpet, she grabbed an oil lamp and lit the wick with shaky fingers, then replaced the globe. After a final look at the sorry mess, she fled the room in hopes of waking Renfield for some assistance—though she dreaded having to search for him in the upper regions of the servants' quarters. Her palms turned clammy at the thought. Wandering alone through a dark manor in the middle of the night was the stuff of nightmares. Hopefully, due to the old butler's advanced age, he'd been given a small room at the back of the house on this same level.

She wound her way from one corridor to another, not really sure which direction she traveled. Every nerve stood on a cliff's edge. My, how different it was to tread these passageways without the broad-shouldered baronet at her side. Shadows sprang like monsters from the darkness. Old family portraits eyed her with ill intent. A loose floorboard creaked like a gunshot, and she nearly jumped out of her skin. In this creepy atmosphere, belief in the supernatural didn't seem quite so silly.

Turning another corner, she heaved a sigh of relief at seeing the glow of lamplight spilling out beneath a door. Perhaps this was the old butler's room and he wasn't yet asleep.

"Hello?" She rapped on wood. "Renfield?"

No one answered.

"Renfield?" She called louder this time—and again, no reply.

"Pardon my intrusion"—she nudged the door open as she spoke—"but—"

She blinked. This was no bedroom. Bookshelves lined three of the walls. A cozy chair in front of one of them had a lamp burning on a small table just beside it. On top was an empty cup and a pair of spectacles glinting in the light, waiting for the owner to return. Against the fourth wall stood a large desk with all manner of beakers, burners, jars of powders and tubes of blood.

And the baronet's distinct scent of earth and cinnamon lingered on the air.

This was his lair?

Shivering, she took a step closer to the desk, her gaze homing in on a black swath of cloth with an alarming array of hypodermic needles spread across it. By all that was holy, what sort of madness was this?

She backed out of the room. Renfield had said his master was afflicted with a skin malady, but she'd not seen one shred of evidence Sir James suffered from anything at all. Surely such drastic measures were not needed, which begged the question. . .what was the baronet concocting in this dark corner of the house? Was this why he'd warned her to stay in her room?

She upped her pace. Broken window or not, the baronet wouldn't thank her for nosing into his personal affairs. Perhaps she ought to simply try to find the sitting room and curl up on the sofa for the rest of the night. He could have no quarrel with such a choice. She'd have to pass that gruesome gargoyle to get there, but what else was she to do?

Measuring each step by the loud beat of her heart, she dug deep for courage. It was only a silly piece of lifeless rock. Nothing to fear. The baronet himself said it was just a memento that had reminded his mother of her homeland, something which clearly brought the woman comfort. Rosa held her lamp a little higher while clutching the counterpane tighter at her neck. She could do this. She *would* do this! Squaring her shoulders, she entered the front hall.

Wind moaned against the front door like a ghoul begging entrance. The eerie sound buffeted her nerves but did not alter her step. Boldly, she fixed her gaze on the devilish effigy looming large on its pedestal, determined to conquer her fear.

"I'm not afraid of you," she whispered as she edged around it, never once pulling her eyes off the horrid creature. "Do you hear me? I'm not afraid of—"

A screech wailed behind her. Something sharp raked across her back.

Rosa whirled, her lamp crashing to the tile.

In front of her swayed a wild-haired ghost, skin as white as a death shroud. Blood crawled out of the figure's nose in two dark streams below eyes that were sunken black holes. A hair-raising cackle punctured the night. Flames arose from the dropped lamp, painting the hideous spectre in a hellish light.

Rosa swayed.

Then swooned into blessed blackness.

A hot pot of fresh tea was just what such a late hour called for. Weariness draped over James's shoulders, yet sleep would not come, not with knowing the fair Rosa Edwards rested sweetly beneath his roof. If his head hit the pillow now, he'd only lay awake, gazing upon the image of her that was burned in his mind. How lovely she'd been at dinner. How beautiful a rose in this tomb of a manor. A smirk twisted his mouth. Since when had he become such a lovelorn poet?

His step slowed as he neared his study. Lamplight spilled out in a thin line from a crack in the door. Hmm. He'd pulled the thing shut when he'd left, a practice he never forsook.

Listening intently, he pushed the door open and scanned the entire room. Nothing appeared out of the ordinary. He set the teapot on the small table near the chair then strode to the desk and double-checked the instruments. Everything was as it should be. What was he thinking? The way the wind and rain pummeled the old house this night, it was likely only an errant draft that'd worked the door open. All was well.

Until it wasn't.

A shriek blasphemed the stillness, instantly chilling his blood.

Mother.

James snatched a needle from the collection and tore from the room. Blast that nurse! She had one task—*one*! How had she let his mother escape yet again?

Screeching laughter hit him full in the face as he dashed into the front hall. Mother teetered a crazed dance in front of a flaming blanket lying at the base of the gargoyle. First broken glass and now fire?

He darted ahead, but the closer he drew, the more his gut cinched. That was no mere blanket. At one end of it, locks of amber hair spread over the tile.

Rosa.

His heart stopped.

"Mother, step back!" He bolted between the two, snatching the counterpane and whumping the fabric against the tile again and again. He didn't stop until nothing but the stink of burnt material remained.

"What—?" Rosa pushed up from the floor, shoving hair from her face. "What is happening?"

An enormous question, that. One he could barely comprehend. He swung around and swiped for his mother. She struggled with lunatic strength until he jabbed the needle into her arm. Two breaths later, she collapsed against him.

"I thought..." Rosa's voice curled over his shoulder, hardly a whisper. "I thought she was a spirit."

"No," he murmured as he swung his mother's slight body into his arms. Her nose was bloodied. That was an alarming concern—as was the woman shivering at his side in naught but a shift. He blew out a lungful of air. "Go to bed, Rosa."

"I cannot. A tree crashed into my room."

Bitter laughter burned up his throat at the news. This manor truly was cursed. Still, dwelling on all the misfortunes of the night wouldn't make the situation any better.

"Go to the sitting room, then. A coal scuttle sits by the hearth and there should be banked embers." He eyed the counterpane lying in a lump then glanced back at her. "You will find a fresh blanket in the closet just off the hall from there. Warm yourself until I rejoin you."

He set off before the questions in Rosa's gaze slipped to her lips. He had too many of his own to deal with—namely, how and why the nurse had allowed his mother to roam the halls of Morgrave. The woman wouldn't have to threaten to quit this time. He'd dismiss her on the spot.

The door to Mother's room stood open. Across the room, Nurse Agatha moaned on a bunched-up rug, clutching her ankle. A bump purpled her forehead. Broken glass littered the floor near a pool of liquid. James laid his mother on the bed, trying to make sense of the scene.

"What happened?" he asked as he helped Nurse up to the chair.

"Tch! 'Tis a foul evenin' and that's for sure. I'll be quittin' this place come morn. Oof!" She landed on the chair and immediately pressed her fingers to her head.

James grabbed a footstool and propped up the woman's foot. Her ankle swelled hard against her stocking. That would need some tending. He rang for Renfield before circling back to the nurse, taking care to straighten the rug on his way. "Do not tell me my frail mother overcame you."

"No, sir. She did stir, though, and being you wished her kept quiet, I thought to give her the medication you gave me right away. Must've tripped on the rug and hit my head on the footboard." She pressed two fingers against her temple. "Your mother were gone when I come to, but my ankle wouldn't bear no weight, sir."

The censure he'd intended dried on his tongue. The woman could hardly be blamed for carrying out his instructions and taking a tumble in the process.

By the time he'd wrung out a cool cloth for Nurse's head, bolstered her foot even higher with a cushion, and cleaned the mess from his mother's nosebleed, Renfield shuffled in the door, white hair an explosion of dandelion fluff atop his head.

"You called, sir?"

"I am afraid I must ask you to tend to my mother and Nurse Agatha. Both have had an eventful evening."

The old butler dipped a nod, running a hand through his crazed hair. "It will be as you wish, sir."

James bypassed him, heels pounding the floor in frustration. What a night. And it likely wouldn't get any better with all of Rosa's questions.

Soft lamplight glowed inside the sitting room as he entered. Rosa curled on the sofa, feet tucked beneath a woolen blanket, eyelashes feathered shut—a sight so lovely it ached deep in his chest. Artists would beg to paint such an angelic portrait.

He padded back to the door, the tension in his shoulders easing. Perhaps by an act of providence, Rosa would sleep the rest of the night and think her encounter with his mother had been naught but a nightmare.

"Sir James?"

He paused on the threshold, holding his breath. His name had been wispy enough that he might've imagined it.

But then the sofa creaked and fabric shushed against fabric. "What happened? Who was that?"

He turned. Rosa sat upright now, hair spilling over her shoulders in waves, glinting amber in the lamplight. The scuff on her brow from earlier was still red. So much had happened to her today. With how much more ought he burden her?

He trudged over to the hearth and poked at the coals. Though she'd asked, he'd dearly hoped to keep from telling anyone else about his mother. Dr. Seward had been a necessity, same for Nurse and Renfield.

The maid and Cook were aware of her presence as well, though both were paid handsomely to say nothing of his mother outside the manor. He could bear all the gossip the town might heap upon him, but if Mother were somehow added to the mix, things would get ugly. His father had died fighting just such a battle, trying to defend her name and killing himself in the process.

"If you would rather not answer," she said, her voice soft, tentative, like the padding of cat's feet, "I understand."

No, you don't.

He jammed the poker into the coals. Such an innocent couldn't begin to understand the snarled mess of his family. And yet here she was, offering him a way out, kinder than anyone had ever been other than Sala. In truth, Rosa had given him no reason not to trust her. And yet. . .he'd stood on the edge of this cliff before. Plummeted over the edge and landed hard on jagged rocks. If he opened up to her, would this time be different?

Oh God, please let it be different.

He set the poker in the stand then sank onto the sofa next to her—a dangerous position yet necessary to read her face, judge her honesty, try to keep from getting burned this time around.

"You said I could trust you." He stared deeply into Rosa's eyes, searching for truth. "Do I have your word?"

She pressed her lips tight, her adorable dimple making an appearance on her chin. Ever so slowly, she nodded. "Clearly you have been hurt before, but I would not betray you. I would *never* betray you." Sorrow thickened her voice—or was it pity?

Rising, he paced to the tea cart—empty now save for a carafe of water and two glasses. He filled one then another, giving his hands something to do other than to clench into helpless fists. "There was a girl I once knew," he began as he turned back to Rosa. "One I took compassion on when I first arrived in Transylvania. Ana-Maria was a simple-minded young woman, and if that weren't bad enough, she bore a hideous scar that ran from cheek to chin. The combination made her the scorn of the village boys."

"How sad." Rosa took the offered glass but held it in her lap, too much sympathy pinching her mouth.

"Indeed. However, I was well acquainted with managing the cosmetics of scars, and so I offered to treat the girl with a regiment of salves I had created. It worked. Ana-Maria transformed into quite the beauty." He tossed back his drink, remembering with regret the innocent butterfly he'd helped metamorphose. "Her father was happy, as was she. We formed a friendship, a bond. I trusted them. They trusted me."

"So. . ." Rosa peered up at him, gaze suddenly guarded. "You cared for her, this Ana-Maria?"

"I did, but not in the way your tone suggests. I saw her as a younger sister, one who needed protection, and yet—" He studied the leftover drips inside his glass, the same old feelings of feebleness and fury running roughshod through his veins. "Funny, is it not, how the protector can suddenly become the prey?"

Without so much as a sip, Rosa set down her glass. "What happened?"

He closed his eyes, unable to stop a grimace from clenching his jaw. "Some blackguards took advantage of her." Wheeling about, he slammed his fist onto the cart, rattling the glassware. Behind him, Rosa gasped, no doubt horrified. So be it. He would never get over the horror of what happened to Ana-Maria.

He clutched the edge of the cart, holding on for dear life—for there was naught else to do when telling a tale of death. "When it became apparent she was with child, the girl's father blamed me. Me! The man who had done nothing but help him and his family. Worse, when the babe was born with a blood-red stain on its face, the villagers—all churchgoers, supposedly holy to the core—said it was the mark of a vampire. They killed the infant, drove Ana-Maria and her father from the village, then came after me. That is when I learned it was better to live a solitary life inside the castle than to venture out."

"But what they did was so wrong!"

He spun back, his own sense of justice white hot in his chest. "We live in a world of wrongs, Rosa! The sooner you learn that the better."

His ragged words silenced them both. Even the wind outside quieted.

He collapsed in a wingback chair, scrubbing his hand over his face. Oh, for the blessed rest the grave would bring.

"I am grieved by your tale." Rosa's voice was a shiver on the night air. "Yet I cannot help but ask what it has to do with what I witnessed tonight?"

Speaking of Ana-Maria had been hard enough. This question cut to the bone. He dropped his hand, feeling leagues older than his thirty-two years. "That tale—as you call it—is the reason I do not easily trust. And so, if I am to answer your question, I must be certain what I say will remain in the strictest of confidence. Do you understand?"

"James."

He startled at his name on her lips, startled even more when she knelt at his side, blanket billowing around her. She collected his hand, her small fingers soft and warm against his skin. "I am not one of those villagers of which you spoke. I would never willingly hurt you. I am your friend, and ever more shall be. Of that you can be confident."

He breathed in so deeply his lungs ached. He wanted to believe. *Needed* to believe. But would doing so bring freedom or bondage?

Rosa brushed her thumb across his palm, over and over, maddeningly soothing.

He wrapped his fingers tight around the action. Let her hear the whole story and then see if she still wished to hold hands with such a spawn of darkness. "Years ago, when I was first sent to school and I daresay you were naught but a child in swaddling, my mother was involved in a quarrel with Elmira Mallow."

Rosa's nose scrunched. "Preston's mother?"

"Yes. But the woman painted the row with a bloody brush, spreading awful rumours about my mother. I am sure you have heard them, for the taint of that dark gossip never went away, and in fact has only resurfaced against me upon my return." He released her hand and gripped the arm of the chair instead.

"You must mean the whole vampire narrative."

"I do. My father tried to tamp it down, going so far as to call a town meeting in my mother's defense. What he should have done was call it off, though. Stubborn man."

"What happened?"

"There was a storm that night, much like the one that seems to be dying off now." His gaze drifted to the draperies, the glass no longer rattling in the frame. "My father took a chill from which he never recovered."

"I vaguely remember that." She tapped her lips, trying to recall everything about the tragedy. "And your mother?"

"She became embittered, to the point of frothing up the rumours, taking delight in frightening the locals whenever she ventured into town. She wanted to leave all of them shaking by the time she boarded the ship back to her homeland." He shook his head. Oh, how well he understood her lashing out, for how many times had he wished to do so?

"It all blew up in her face, though." His lips twisted at the memory. "Before my mother could travel to Transylvania, she became ill, a devious ailment that only added to the fearsome persona she had created. She became the monster her own words created. . .a disease of which you witnessed the final stages tonight."

Rosa's eyes widened. "*That* was your mother?"

He nodded.

"So that is the remedy you seek. Something to cure her."

"It is, but I am running out of time. You have seen the state she is in. She has not got much longer to live." And neither would he once the same vicious disease finally embedded its claws into him.

"But surely something can be done." Rosa stood and paced in a small circle. "I have known Doctor Seward to work miracles. Have you tried him?"

"I have tried everything, even the good doctor. He has washed his hands of it, I am afraid, leaving her in the care of Nurse Bilder. . .who will now require some care herself. The reason you crossed paths with my mother tonight is because Nurse twisted her ankle and was incapacitated."

"I see." Rosa's face folded. "So many troubles beset you, my friend, that mine pale in comparison."

He pushed to his feet, a smirk twitching his lips as he rose. "I suppose standing next to a Job has a way of putting things into perspective, eh?"

"If there is anything I can do to help, anything at all"—she pressed her fingers against his sleeve as if driving home her offer—"please let me know."

"I appreciate that more than you can guess. But my mother is my burden alone."

"Well, then." She pulled away, lifting her chin with her usual determined—and charming—resilience. "Rest assured all you have told me tonight shall remain with me. You and your mother have suffered enough rabid hearsay. I pray that ultimately your search for a remedy ends in success."

"As do I."

And pray he would, but believing in a timely answer would be near to impossible. . .after seeing the telltale blood leaking from his mother's nostrils.

EIGHTEEN

There will be pain for us all; but it will not all be pain, nor will this pain be the last.

There were two things Albin couldn't abide in life—no, make that three. He hated cloudy days, and this summer had been abhorrent. Today's sullen sky was no different. Neither did he like it when Cook overheated the eggs, leaving a hard, greyish yolk sitting atop his toast, as had been served at breakfast. He was still cross about that. But most of all, he couldn't abide anything other than being the first to set a trend in this town. It was important to stand out as a man of position, especially when he was up against a baronet.

Bringing the newspaper closer to his nose, Albin stared at the elegant gent in the advertisement for a new men's cologne. *Fougere Royale. A sophisticated scent for a discriminating man.* Which meant he must have it. It was practically tailor-made for him.

He pulled open the top drawer of his desk, frowning as he withdrew his purse. The kidskin pouch was far too light. He fished around with his finger, jingling the few coins. Enough for a tasty luncheon with a fine red wine, but definitely not enough for an exotic cologne. There was nothing for it, then. He shoved his purse back into the drawer and strode from the room.

The corridors of Mallow Shipyard and Marine Supply were a rat's maze, the original building having been expanded one time too many over the past century. Floors bucked and canted like the deck of a ship at sea. At one point, he had to turn sideways to allow a burly mechanic to pass by where the passage narrowed into a thin throat. He'd never appreciated the fact that Uncle had relegated him to the office farthest from his own. Yes, Uncle Preston had explained it was so that he learned to operate without having his hand held every step of the way. But hang it all! He'd worked here eight. . .no, nine years now. Ought he not have a front room with a wide bank of windows overlooking the massive shipyard? Maybe not quite as nice as the one where he now rapped his knuckles against the door, but surely as the operating president of such a prestigious company he'd earned a better view.

Inside, Uncle grunted. Not an encouraging welcome, but it would do.

Albin entered a room smelling of horehound from his uncle's ungodly ritual of chewing the hard drops while he worked. Uncle Preston's jaws worked on a candy as he ran a finger down a ledger column.

"Good morning, Uncle." Albin pasted on a cheerful smile as he flipped out his coattails and sat on one of the leather high backs in front of Uncle's desk. "I missed you at the breakfast table."

"Hmm?" Uncle Preston lifted his face, eyes narrowing on him. "Shouldn't you be seeing to that shipment of hemp?"

"Already ordered." Albin huffed a moist breath onto his fingernails then buffed them on his waistcoat. For once he was ahead of his uncle. "It will be here a week from Tuesday."

"Good." Uncle dipped his head, once again losing himself in numbers. Whatever those figures were, they couldn't be good, for hardly a second later Uncle grumbled an unsavory oath beneath his breath.

Pooh. In this focused of a mood, asking for money would be like baiting a bear—and he never wagered on a bear fight. Too many variables.

Albin shifted on the seat, leather creaking. He'd have to tread very lightly, but what to say? Something relevant to the man. Something businesslike. *Think. Think!* But oh, how hard it was to think when all that filled his mind was leaving a waft of Fougere Royale in his wake just like the newspaper advertisement had promised. . . . *Newspaper?* That was it! What else had he read in today's news?

He flicked a piece of lint off his sleeve as he perused the headlines in his mind's eye. "I see that your stock in Granger's is on the up, Uncle."

"Mmm." The man didn't so much as glance at him.

But that wouldn't stop him. "And I noticed the price of iron has dropped considerably. Now might be a good time to secure a cache of it. Could save you in the long run."

Uncle Preston slammed the ledger shut, his lips crimped as he faced Albin. "What do you want?"

Throat tight, he smoothed his hands along his trousers to keep from loosening his cravat. Appearing weak was a mortal sin in front of this man. "I merely thought you might be interested in what the newspaper had to say, and while reading, I also noticed a certain cologne—"

"Pardon!" The door burst open and Morris, Uncle's right-hand man, dashed in, waving a paper. "Sorry for the intrusion, sir, but this telegram just arrived. It's the one you've been waiting for."

"Very good." Uncle Preston snatched the yellow sheet from his hand.

Morris tipped his head at Albin as he strode from the room. The door barely shut behind him when a tiger's growl ripped out of Uncle's mouth.

"Blast that Van Helsing! Cutthroat son of a blackguard!" Uncle Preston whirled about, hands fisted at his side as he stared out over the shipyard.

Albin hid a smirk. Though family loyalty required he wear the same mantle of disdain for the Van Helsings, he couldn't help but admire the grit of old Abraham, Uncle Preston's number-one competitor in the shipbuilding business.

"What's the ol' jackal up to now?" he asked.

"Snatching the very bread from our table, that's what!" Uncle's voice rattled the glass panes. "I should have gotten that contract from Woodhouse, but no! That snake in the grass Van Helsing beat my proposal by six weeks. Six! Had I the extra space, I would have built that ship faster than the cully could wipe the sweat from his brow."

Uncle Preston slumped into his chair, finger tapping like gunshots against the desktop. "And none of this would be an issue if that bullheaded Edwards would sell me his library, the briny old goat. I need that property, and I need it now!" His black eyes bored into Albin. "The Edwards girl is the key. We get to her, and we get to the father. Tell me she's within your grasp."

This time Albin did tug his cravat, the silk cool against his heated fingers. One wrong word and he might as well hang himself with the fabric. "Soon, Uncle. Very soon."

"What is the holdup?" Uncle Preston's tone chilled the entire room.

"Well, you see. . ." He fumbled with the fabric.

"For pity's sake!" Uncle Preston rounded the desk and retied the cravat. Tight. "What keeps the girl from accepting your suit?"

Albin struggled for air yet didn't dare loosen the tie. "Rosa is not quite willing to consider anyone at the present. She's too busy sticking her nose in a book or visiting that villainous baronet every day. I need to turn her head back to me, show her I'm the better man than Sir James."

"Bah!" Uncle scrubbed his knuckles across his chin as he stared at the ceiling. "It appears the baronet shall have to be removed from the equation."

"Removed?" The word was barely a squeak, so hard was it to breathe.

Uncle pounded his knuckles against his chin a few times before dropping his hand. "Time will tell." Leaving his desk, he squatted in front of a small safe in the corner, then threw a money bag across the room.

Albin caught it single-handedly, mouth dropping. "How did you know I wanted—?"

Uncle Preston glowered as he yanked open the door. "Go away."

He didn't have to be told twice. Albin fled. The second the door slammed behind him, he ripped off his neckcloth and filled his lungs with air. Thank God that was over. But at least he now had funding for the cologne, a sure leg up on Sir James.

Sir James. Tush! The name rankled him as he settled into his ralli cart and followed the dirt track by the river leading to the road. The man was hardly a match for him. Albin dressed better. Soon he'd smell better. Besides that, he drove a far more stylish carriage and enjoyed all the delights society had to offer. What did Rosa see in that cheerless hermit?

Just before he turned onto the main road, a flash of red caught at the corner of his eye. He swiveled his head—then stopped the horse. What in the world?

He hopped down and picked his way towards a bend in the river, taking care lest he muddy the hem of his trousers. The rear wheel of a bicycle was caught on a log that was half in and half out of the water. The fine hairs at the nape of his neck prickled to attention. It was Rosa's, if he didn't miss his mark—and for once, he dearly wished he were wrong. She'd not have survived such an accident. His pulse pounded erratically. He'd be in serious trouble with Uncle Preston if something bad had happened to her.

He paused, unwilling to take another step. What if he came upon the woman, face bloated beneath the stream, eyes staring at him like a dead fish? Oh, how he hated to think of that lovely young lady caught beneath the water. What a horrid way to remember such a beauty! He shuddered as he pressed the back of his hand to his mouth. Perhaps he ought to simply alert the authorities. Yes. That was it. Better to leave this to the professionals who dealt with this sort of thing.

Mind made up, he turned, then whipped back around. Something was in the front basket. A carefully wrapped package. Trying hard not to look any further than that, he worked free a sealskin pouch and scooted back up to his carriage. He sank onto the plush seat with a sigh. My, that had been taxing.

He unwound the leather lace binding the package shut, then unwrapped several layers of waxed paper. Whatever she'd been transporting must've been of the utmost importance to have protected it so fully.

Turned out it wasn't just one item, but two. First, he pulled out an old book, scuffed on one corner and emitting a mouldy sort of stink. Eew. Setting it down, he reached for the other book. Or maybe it wasn't a book at all. Hard to tell since it was covered in paper. He ripped off the wrapping only to find an entire sheaf of papers tied with twine. A note was tucked beneath the cord—a note addressed in elegant handwriting to Sir James Morgan. Air hissed through Albin's teeth. Now this was a find! Immediately he unfolded the missive.

Salutations Sir James,

I am in your debt for your knowledge and insight on these writings of your homeland. I dearly hope I've done justice with the story. Any haste in editing on your part would be greatly appreciated.

Sincerely,
Bram Stoker

Albin flipped through the pages, scanning the text as he did so. Transylvania. Dreary castle. A blood-sucking creature of the night. Was this fiction or fact?

Absently, he laid the note in his lap. Either way, Uncle was right again. Time *did* tell. Turning in his seat, Albin glanced across the river, up past the cliffs and beyond the abbey to where the baronet's mansion sat dark and gloomy. He could use this letter and the incriminating manuscript of horror as proof positive Sir James was a vampire. The man wouldn't even see it coming. And once Sir James was gone, Rosa would be his at last—*if* she hadn't met the same terrible fate as her bicycle.

For despite his dreadful imaginings, he refused to believe it until there was evidence otherwise.

"Would you like to go home now?"

Rosa looked up from her book as Sir James strode into the sitting room. Naturally she should wish to go home—and she did, if only to remove the angst her parents must surely be suffering. Yet hidden in a secret space in her heart was an unreasonable yearning to stay here with this enigmatic man. James seemed as much a part of her as the very air she breathed. He was a necessity, one she couldn't imagine living without.

But she couldn't very well tell him that. Her cheeks heated at the mere thought.

She set the book on the tea table, purposely avoiding an answer. "I assume your stable hand has worked a miracle?"

"The bridge was easier to manage a quick fix with than the guest room. The window and the wall will need to be repaired. But for now, your horse awaits. Come." He swept his hand towards the door. "I will see you to the new makeshift bridge."

She fell into step beside him, and for the first time since she'd set foot in Morgrave Manor, the horrid gargoyle on the pedestal seemed a little less frightening. "How is your mother faring since you checked on her after breakfast?"

"She rests quietly, and for that I am grateful. The nurse's ankle has deflated to a normal size as well. And once you are safely across the river, most of yesterday's wrongs shall be made right. I think you will find Belle to be a delight to ride."

"Truly, Sir James, I do not need a horse. You have done so much already by sheltering me the night, and it is not so far that I cannot walk to town."

He held open the front door, allowing her to pass. "I insist. Belle is more surefooted than either of us and will get you safely across the wooden planks. They are only temporary and not fastened to anything."

Rosa's lips parted as she spied a black mare tethered to a post near the bottom of the stairs. "Oh, she is beautiful!"

Gathering her hem, Rosa sped down the steps then slowed as she approached the animal. Belle whickered a greeting, her head bobbing merrily, and they were instant friends. Rosa stroked the beauty's neck before turning to Sir James and was once again surprised at how close he'd drawn without her awareness, for he stood hardly a pace away.

"I am happy to see Belle has your approval—and apparently you have hers."

Rosa couldn't help but pat the horse one more time. "She is a fine animal, but I insist on returning her once I am safely across the river."

"At least you concede to trusting her that far. You might just change your mind, you know, once she has worked her magic on you." He winked.

Rosa's knees weakened, traitorous things.

"Come now, I shall have to give you a lift. I wish I had a sidesaddle for you, but Mother was never given to riding. Bend your left leg, and I will assist you as much as possible."

Easy enough, at the moment. The trick was not bending them both—especially when he edged behind her and his warm breath feathered against her ear. He crouched then, with one of his hands underneath her knee and his other on her ankle. Though his touch was through fabric, her heart galloped nearly out of her chest.

"On three," he commanded. "One, two, three."

He lifted. She flew, instinctively flinging her leg over the animal's back. Belle, sweet horse that she was, didn't flinch beneath the flurry of skirts when Rosa landed atop her. That had been exhilarating!

She smiled down at James. "Thank you."

"Entirely my pleasure."

The words were husky, followed by a half-smile that nearly unseated her. She was glad when he turned his back to her—for surely her cheeks must be a flaming crimson by now.

He untied Belle then led off with sure steps. For a long while she admired how his muscles moved beneath his clothes, how his long legs effortlessly ate up the ground as he strode along the drive. She could watch this fine display of man for hours, and no doubt would have done all the way to the river if a nearby titmouse hadn't chirped an incriminating *shame-on-you, shame-on-you.*

She patted Belle's neck, the hair smooth beneath her touch. "Such a good girl."

Sir James peered over his shoulder, amusement in the arch of his brow. "Having second thoughts about her already?"

"No." She smiled. "Though it is a generous offer, I actually have one of my own to make. I'd like to help you with your mother. I would be happy to pick up anything you might need from the apothecary and deliver it along with your new books. It would save you a trip into town and, well. . .you know." Her smile fled. It wasn't right the way the people of Whitby treated him. The ugly looks. The scathing remarks.

James shook his head, his amusement replaced with a solemn set to his jaw. "I will not have you risk your pretty neck for the likes of me. I am afraid your daily visits will have to be put on hold for now. This is no sturdy bridge for you to cross alone."

He stopped in front of two thick planks set side by side across the gap of Spital Beck. The river slithered like a dark snake beneath it, much lower than yesterday. And by tomorrow it would be lower still.

Rosa shifted in the saddle. "It is no risk at all, for I am certain you will make those boards safe if you know I am to cross it again tomorrow."

He narrowed his eyes. "You think you know me so well?"

"No," she admitted, then added under her breath, "not nearly enough."

A hint of a smile curved his lips. Oh dear. Had he heard?

He moved to the horse's side and patted Belle's flank. "You forget that your bicycle is lost."

Would that she could forget. Though Father did tend to dote on her, even he would frown upon the loss of the library's only vehicle and a rare book as well.

"That is true." She nibbled her lower lip then met James's gaze. "But as I said, the walk is not so overwhelming. Besides, I fancy a morning stroll, though I daresay I will not bring as many books as usual."

"Have I mentioned before how stubborn you are?"

"Several times."

"Well, it's true." He sighed. "Hold tight, now."

Taking up slack in the lead, James stepped onto the planks, leading Belle with a steady stream of soothing words. Despite the groan of the wood and rush of water below, the horse seemed perfectly content to follow her master's voice, sensing—as did Rosa—that this man would allow no harm to either of them.

Once across, he stopped Belle with an "easy now," and a scratch behind her ear, then gazed up at Rosa. "For the last time, are you quite sure you would not like to ride Belle home? I can send my man after her. It will be no inconvenience to me."

"I appreciate the offer, but explaining to my parents where I have been will be hard enough without prancing in on this fine horse."

He angled his head, brows creasing. "Would it make things easier if I come along to verify you suffered no harm save for that scuff on your head?"

Her heart warmed at his offer to bear the scorn that would surely be hurled at him by the people of Whitby. "I think not, but I thank you."

"You are consistent in your tenacity, I will give you that. Off with you, then." He reached up his hand.

The moment his fingers wrapped around hers, a now-familiar zing ran up her arm. Using his strength, she leaned forward and swung back her leg—just as Belle shuffled aside, catching her off-balance. Rosa fell sideways.

Strong arms caught her up, setting her right. Righting her entire world, actually, with the way James held her and didn't let go. She was more than aware of how his body fit against hers, unleashing all sorts of new and confusing sensations.

"I suspect Belle did that on purpose." Humour flashed in his eyes.

"To what end?"

"This." He nuzzled his cheek against hers, the touch like a lover's kiss. "Though I know you must leave, my home will not be the same without you."

"I am not the same since we have met," she whispered.

"Nor am I."

Warmth rushed through her from head to toe. She could barely breathe for the fierce emotion glinting in James's eyes. She ought to look away, save him the embarrassment for such an unguarded show of feeling. Save herself the mortification of the love that must surely be written on her face.

She gasped. *Love?* Was that the irresistible pull that bound her to this man?

"James?" She leaned into him, seeking, wanting, *needing* an answer to the question.

"Rosa, I—"

Belle snorted and stamped a hoof, ending the enchantment.

James backed away and grabbed hold of the lead with a ghostly smile she'd never before witnessed. "I suppose I should see Belle home. Goodbye, Rosa."

"Until tomorrow, you mean."

And then he did grin, in full, white teeth flashing. "Until tomorrow."

He swung with ease into the saddle and urged Belle back to the planks. Rosa set off down the road, her feet hardly touching the ground, so light did she feel. He'd smiled—he'd smiled *at her*. She fairly floated with the satisfaction of it all the way back to town, though by the time she reached the city limits, a blister on the back of her heel brought her quite nicely back to reality. Either she'd have to choose a more sensible pair of shoes or find a shortcut to Morgrave Manor if she was to hoof it there every day.

She turned onto Newton Street, deciding to try the library before going home. It would be far easier to explain her mishap to Father than to face Mother, who by now was no doubt squawking about the house like a wet hen. Besides, if she took the back routes, she wasn't likely to cross anyone's path and have to explain the scrape on her brow.

Reaching the library's rear door, she tried the knob, but the silly thing didn't give. "Father?" She rapped on the wood. No answer. Odd, that. Stranger still, when she went around to the front, a closed sign hung in the window even though it couldn't be much past noon. Had Father gone out for lunch? Guilt twanged her belly. If she'd been here, there would have been no need to close up shop.

Resetting her hat, Rosa once again stuck to the less frequented lanes to make her way home. Not only did she avoid contact with any of the town gossips—which was good, because now she'd resorted to pulling off her shoes and going stocking-footed—but it gave her time to pray Mother would be in good humour despite her prolonged absence. That would take a miracle, though, one on par with what Sir James had spoken of the night before, enough to make her reconsider her stance on the supernatural.

Her step hitched as she closed in on her house, where a hive of activity buzzed. She ducked behind a shrub to put on her shoes, then peeked past the green leaves. Several carriages were parked outside the white-stone building, one of them a police wagon. Her sister Lucy's children played tag in the front yard, and a few women carrying covered food dishes stood chattering near the door.

Oh dear. She shrank behind the greenery, mind whirling. Surely that hubbub wasn't because of her, but what else might have happened during her absence?

Sucking in a breath for courage, Rosa charged ahead, giving her niece and nephews a quick wave and a tight smile to the women, who gasped at her approach—which rained down a fury of questions and comments as she passed.

"Where have you been, child?"

"Were you abducted?"

"Ach! Look there! She's marked on th' head. Be tha' the work o' th' vampire?"

Ignoring them all, she pushed open the front door. "Father? Mother?"

Chatter spilled out of the sitting room, then immediately stopped when she crossed the threshold. Time suspended in a queer sort of way as five sets of eyes blinked at her.

And then all was shattered when her mother let out a shriek and collapsed onto the sofa. Lucy immediately dropped beside her, fanning Mother with a lace handkerchief. Father broke away from the two men he huddled next to and wrapped her in a strong-armed embrace.

"Oh, my girl," Father murmured as he pulled back and held her face between his hands. His gaze strayed to the scuff on her forehead. "Are you quite all right?"

"I am, Father." She smiled. "Just a scratch, nothing more."

Relief uncreased the deepest lines that'd furrowed his brow—lines put there by her. So, all the hubbub *was* on account of her. The delicious cup of tea and milk she'd taken at the manor curdled in her belly.

"I assume the lost has been found, eh?" the man in a constable uniform rumbled.

"Indeed." Father faced the men. "Thank you, gentlemen, but it appears I won't be needing your services after all."

The fellow in a dark blue suit tucked a small notebook into his coat pocket. "Easiest case I've had all year. I am glad to see a happy ending for once."

Before Rosa could say anything, her sister tugged her over to the sofa, where their mother reclined against the cushions, one hand pressed to her brow.

"Do you see what you have done?" The censure in Lucy's voice was enough to freeze water. "Our mother has suffered such pains on your account." Once again her sister took to flapping her handkerchief, fanning air against Mother's splotchy face. "Where have you been?"

Mother batted away Lucy's hand, wafting gardenia toilette water in the process. "Yes, Daughter, where *have* you been?" Her sister's voice may have been cold, but Mother's was an arctic blast.

Rosa clasped her hands in front of her, holding on for dear life for what was sure to be a most unpleasant exchange. "One of our patrons, a Mr. Stoker, asked me to deliver a manuscript to Morgrave Manor for him posthaste. He made it clear it was of the utmost importance, and being I had finished my work for the day, I thought I would deliver it before the storm hit. I would have easily been home within the hour if the Spital Beck bridge had not collapsed once I crossed it. There was no way for me to return or even send word until the baronet had his man rig up some planking. As soon as some boards were safely secured, I sped home—and so you find me."

Father came up from behind, adjusting his spectacles to the tip of his nose and peering down at her. "It would have eased all of our minds, my girl, had you told me where you were going to begin with."

"I know, Father." She reached for his sleeve. "And for that I beg your pardon. Yours too, Mother." She glanced back to the sofa.

"As well you should!" Her mother snorted a most unladylike *humph* as she pushed up on the cushions. "Where did you spend the night?"

This was it. The moment she'd known would come at her like a broken-braked locomotive. She sank to her mother's side and collected one of her hands between hers. "The only choice I had, Mother, was to weather the storm out in the wild or accept the hospitality of Sir James. I chose the latter, as I suspect you would have too. He was ever the gentleman, putting me up in one of the manor's guest rooms."

"But—but—" Mother spluttered, her small eyes bulging to the size of ripe acorns. "You were unchaperoned! In the house of a known vampire. Oh! The pains. They are coming again."

Ripping her hand from Rosa's, she once again collapsed against the cushions, signaling with one finger for Lucy to resume her fanning.

Her sister speared Rosa with a daggered look, sharp and glinting as steel. "You see? This is what comes of refusing to settle into nuptial bliss." She waved her kerchief double time. "There now, Mother. Calm yourself."

Rosa's heart sank. This was all her fault. But how to fix it? "I was not wholly unchaperoned." The concession sounded weak even in her own ears. "Sir James's mother was there, as was the maid, the cook, and the butler, so surely my reputation is not ruined."

"Is that so?" Father rubbed his chin. "I haven't seen the dowager in years. We all assumed she'd passed on."

"She has not. I—I saw her myself." And she had, but still it tasted like sour deception. It took all her willpower to push her lips into a smile and lighten her tone. "So you see, Mother, all is well. What might have been a calamity turned into a lovely evening in a very nice home. You may tell your friends how kindly the Morgans treated me."

"I can do nothing of the sort!" Mother bunched her hands into fists on her hips. "Everyone will look all the more askance at you—at all of us—now that you've fallen prey to a creature of the night. No man in his right mind will have you after this. And I can only hope your indiscretion will not affect your father's business."

Rosa hung her head, the truth of her mother's words yet ringing in the room. She could live with no more flowers from fawning men, but what she couldn't stomach was the possibility that she'd attached some sort of stigma to the library—which was her father's sole means of income.

NINETEEN

A brave man's blood is the best thing on this earth when a woman is in trouble.

Sunshine. At last. Holding her hat with one hand, Rosa paused on the street corner and tipped her face to the sky. After being Mother's prisoner for the rest of the day yesterday—and for part of this morning—she welcomed the fresh air and warmth on her cheeks. Mother had insisted she stay out of the public eye to give any gossip time to fizzle out. But a mere twenty-four hours wasn't time enough. On the way to the library, Rosa had encountered several women who'd immediately crossed themselves when passing and suffered a particularly off-colour remark by a man wearing orange stockings. Orange! As if he had any right to comment on others.

"There she be. Can tha' see has th' lass any pricks on her neck?"

"Don't appear so, tho' she do be pale as a lily."

The whispers came from behind. For a wicked moment, Rosa was sorely tempted to whirl about and bare her teeth just to see the rumour-mongers flee, but that would be the same behaviour James said his mother had given in to.

And that had not ended well at all.

She did whirl, but with a pleasant smile. "Good morning, ladies. Can I help you with anything?"

Two pairs of wide eyes blinked. The older woman slapped a hand to her chest, the hideous feather attached to her hat bobbing and dancing.

"No, miss. Nary a thing."

"Then I bid you good day." Rosa resumed her route to the library, now understanding—at least in part—what James suffered every time he visited town.

The bell jing-jangled as she pushed open the front door. "I am here, Father. Sorry I am late." She glanced around the rows of shelves. No bespectacled man flitted about. Hmm. The back room, then. She advanced, upping her volume so he'd hear. "Mother asked me to help her move a load of chamomile she had been drying for one of her tinctures, and then the whole thing dumped and—"

Words dropped off her tongue as she took in the sight of her father, hair ruffled as if he'd been pulling at it, pacing the length of the office with a reddened face.

"Father, what has happened? What is wrong?"

"It's been a dreadful morning. Dreadful! Two cancellations for your mother's medicines and five—*five!*—subscriptions terminated." He plopped into his chair, the wood complaining as loudly as he. "Then there's the whole matter of the bicycle. It's gone. Stolen! And what is to be next? Scathing epithets painted on the walls? Egg on our windows? Or maybe mutilated livestock thrown onto our front stoop? We are marked, just as your mother feared." He slapped the desk with an open palm, the sharp report making Rosa flinch. "I never should have allowed you to go to Morgrave Manor in the first place."

"This is all my fault." She pressed her hands to her belly, dreadfully sorry about everything. Oh, what a tangled web! "Perhaps I ought to stay away from the library for a while until things settle."

"No, no. There is no need for such drastic measures." A long sigh deflated his chest. "While it's easy to blame your night at Morgrave, it's probably just that times are tough for people right now, what with last season's lacking herring harvest. Add the bout of bad weather rotting the crops and the fire that destroyed Spinson's Warehouse, putting so many out of work—people are just being careful with their coins, I suppose."

His words were balm, even if wholly unjustified.

"As for the bicycle"—he shrugged—"someone must have nicked it."

If only it were so. She bit her lip, knowing full well she should have told him last night about the bicycle and the book. She retrieved a ball of twine from off the corner of his desk and fiddled with the string, giving her hands—and her eyes—something to do. "I am afraid I have an explanation for that."

"Such as?"

She unwound the string for several lengths then slowly rewrapped it as she spoke. "I told you the bridge over Spital Beck collapsed, but I may have neglected to mention I was actually riding across it when the thing went down."

"What!"

She dropped the ball, twine unraveling just like her explanation. Rosa snatched the thing up before it rolled all the way to the front door. "I—em. . .well, you see," she mumbled as she began rewinding, "Sir James happened by and was able to get me safely onto solid ground, but in the meantime, the bicycle washed away."

"Rosa!" her father boomed. "Why did you not tell me this yesterday?"

She cringed. He was more than right. She should have spoken up as soon as she'd arrived home. Resetting the string on the desk, she circled back to crouch beside him, taking both his hands in hers. "You and Mother were so upset by my disappearance I did not want to distress you any further."

"It *does* distress me—very much. You could have been seriously injured instead of only a scuff." His gaze roamed to the scrape above her eye, his own brow sagging as he did so.

"I was never in any real danger because Sir James was nearby. Despite what others say, he is an honorable man. He would not let harm come to me."

"Maybe so, yet it is ultimately God who put him there for such a moment."

Rosa pulled back, the thought a little too big to hold. Conceding that God had sent James out for a walk at the precise moment she'd needed help smacked of the supernatural. Granted, there were tales much more spectacular accounted for in Scripture, but that was during biblical times, not now. It must have been a coincidence. . .wasn't it?

Father rose, once again taking to ruffling his hair, his face reheating to the shade of corned beef. "Still, the fact remains that the bicycle is lost, and it was our sole means of delivering books."

"I know." She hung her head. If he was this distraught about the bicycle, he'd suffer an apoplexy when he learned of the rare book she'd destroyed. What had she been thinking when she'd taken it? Surely she had told herself a faery tale as fictional as those spouted by the fishwives. But as much as she wanted to confess her failings, shame held her words in check so that she could only mutter, "I never meant for any of this to happen."

"I know, child." He patted her cheek. "And I suppose there's naught to be done for it now. We'll limp along somehow. Though at the rate our funds are dwindling, I may have to take up Preston Mallow's offer to buy us out."

"No, Father! Never. This town needs the library, not a larger shipbuilding enterprise."

"I would like to think so." Heaving another great sigh, he resumed his seat and reached for a pen. "But no matter what the future holds, at present we shall have to send out notes to let our customers know there will be no more deliveries for the time being."

"Nonsense. I have two good feet."

"A solution for those in town, but we shall have to put a pause on bringing books to the country folk. And you are definitely done with Morgrave Manor."

She reached for the back of the chair and squeezed. "But I promised the baronet I would be there this morning as usual."

Father licked the tip of his pen before setting it to paper. "Sir James will understand, I am sure. He has the means to come get his own books if he likes. I'll pen his note first."

Just the thought of no more mornings with James made her grip the chair all the harder. How dismal life would be without their daily conversations, his quick wit, those haunting dark eyes. "I will deliver the note straightaway, then, and retrieve the books I left with him."

Father set down his pen and, after sanding the ink, held out the freshly written card. Far too much knowing twinkled in his eyes. "The lady doth protest too much, methinks. We both know it is not the books you care about."

She pinched the paper from his fingers and whirled away, her cheeks aflame.

Warm hands cupped her shoulders, easing her back around. Concern soaked Father's eyes behind his round glasses. "Please rethink your relationship with this man. I don't want you to get hurt, Daughter."

She forced a smile. "You worry too much."

"Even so, this is your last visit to the manor. I will not have you walking so far alone. There's still someone—or something—out there killing livestock. The farmers are all being extra vigilant."

A protest rose on her lips, then died at the concern wrinkling his brow. She'd seen what her disappearance had done to him. What would a more serious injury—or worse—do? "I understand." She brushed a kiss on his cheek. "And I will be back by the time you finish writing the rest of those notes and deliver them as well."

"Or sooner, for if there is any hint of those planks over Spital Beck being wobbly, you shall turn right around, and I'll send a boy instead. No more risk-taking!"

"I promise."

She whirled to the door—just as her father said under his breath, "I am too lenient with that girl."

Frowning, she tucked the note into her pocket and stepped out into the glorious day. Somehow she had to make things up to Father, and replacing the bicycle would be the best way to do it. But where to get the funds? Her savings wouldn't be enough unless, perhaps, she sold her typewriter as well. But how sad to part with such a kind gift from James. A sigh leaked out of her as she left Whitby behind and wound her way up towards the abbey. Yesterday's blister reminded her she ought to have added some cotton batting to her stocking.

She continued on, though, puzzling over how to purchase another bicycle all the way to Spital Beck, where she stopped. Slowly, a smile broke through her gloom, stretching until her cheeks hurt. A rope railing had been added, staked into the ground on either side of the banks. The planks had been increased, four now instead of two, and lashed at intervals to keep them together. Even the ground itself had been fortified at each end. This crossing would be safer than all her previous treks across the old rickety bridge, and all because of a certain brown-eyed man.

She made it to the other side without even having to hold on to the rope, so wide and sturdy was the wood. That problem was more than solved, but the blister on her foot grew and grew. Though she was close enough to see Morgrave, by the time she reached the door, the back of her heel would be a bloody mess. . .and she couldn't very well go shoeless on this gravel road. She'd ruin her stockings for sure.

Bother. Shading her eyes, she scanned for a shortcut across the neighbour's field and—there. That grassy path would cut off at least a quarter of the length from her trek, and there was a gate as well. Perfect.

In no time, she traipsed across the lush field, drawing so close to Morgrave she could practically see the pattern on the draperies through the windows. Off to her left were two adorable calves. One romped. The other huddled near a few mama cows, shying away as she passed. Her heart warmed at the scene—

Then instantly chilled when an ungodly snort drowned out the whirr of insects.

Rosa whirled.

Stepping out from behind the only tree in the field, a bull lowered his head, then gave it a quick shake like that of a freakish dog.

Rosa's breath balled up in her throat as sunlight glinted off the brute's sharpened white horns. She backed away a step, heart fighting to get out of her chest.

"There now," she cooed, remembering the way James had gently urged his horse across the bridge yesterday. "You stay there, and I will just be leaving."

She chanced another two steps, never pulling her eyes from the thing.

The bull blew out another hideous snort, pawing the ground with a great hoof. A divot of earth flew over its back. Several more followed. How sharp would the pain be if that nightmare gored her right through the stomach?

"Please, Mr. Bull. Do not do this." Her soothing words turned garbled as she continued padding backwards. How far was that ridiculous fence anyway? She didn't dare look behind her.

The animal's eyeballs bulged, the whites glistening grotesquely in the sunshine. The bristles on its back stood up like bayonets. Sweat trickled between Rosa's shoulder blades.

Don't scream. Don't scream. Don't—

Too late. James's name ripped past her lips, completely unstoppable. And again.

"James. James!"

The bull backed up a step and froze, nothing moving but its big sides heaving in and out like a macabre bellows. Sweet, beautiful mercy! Had shouting been the thing to do all along? She continued her careful retreat, and surprisingly, the bull didn't move. Perhaps making lots of noise had stunned the thing.

"Go bull! Shoo!" She waved her shoes, emboldened now to start trotting backwards. Surely her back would hit the fence any moment.

A low growl rumbled out from the beast, shocking her. She had no idea bulls could snarl so menacingly. More hoofing, then. Flinging clods. The animal scraped its horns into the dirt, gouging the field, more enraged than ever.

Rosa swallowed. Perhaps hollering hadn't been such a brilliant idea.

The bull charged.

But she didn't scream. She fled.

James reached for his shirt, cracking his neck as he fumbled with the buttons. The eleven chimes of the mantel clock condemned him for being a sluggard. Likely he'd already missed Rosa's visit, which was a punch to the gut, but he'd sat the night at his mother's side, breath by breath wondering which one would be her last. Yet she'd held, thank God, rallying as the sun had risen and allowing him a few precious hours of sleep.

Yawning, he pulled his waistcoat off the hanger, then froze as his name shivered on the air. His waistcoat plummeted to the floor.

Rosa.

He dashed to the window and yanked open the drapes. In the nearby field, Rosa faced off with a bull. His heart stopped.

And then he burst into action.

He grabbed the fire poker on his way out, running like the wind. If that animal charged, she'd be tossed into the air like a rag doll and break her neck when she landed. Unless she were gored to death first.

God, please no!

By the time he neared the fence, the creature charged.

James vaulted over the gate. "Rosa, get out of here. Now!"

She flew past him as he ripped off his shirt and waved it like a lunatic. "Here, you bloody beast. Over here!"

For all its girth, the bull pivoted at lightning speed, snorting like a daemon.

"That's it, you brute. I am your man." He whipped the fabric in the air, snapping it like broken bones.

The animal tucked his head, then ran straight for him.

James zigzagged, cutting back and forth across the field towards the gate where Rosa scrambled to get over. If he led the bull there now, the animal would go for the easier prey. Her.

So he dodged sideways, leading the fuming monster away from her. The bull lunged. Sweat stung his eyes as he stood still, waiting. Timing was everything.

The ground reverberated beneath his feet as the animal thundered closer. And closer. James crouched. Three, two—

He swung the poker with all his might, cracking the animal on the muzzle and taking a gash on the arm as the thing veered away.

"I am safe! I am over," Rosa hollered.

He bolted for the gate.

"Watch out! He is coming again."

The earth shook at his back. Again he took a crooked route, praying to God to break the animal's momentum. The next snort sprayed against his back.

He threw his shirt, hoping against hope that the flying white fabric would be a distraction.

And then he leapt. Flew. Arced over the gate just as the bull crashed into the thick wood.

Dazed, James rolled to a stop, gasping for air.

Blue skirts billowed beside him. Worried brown eyes peered into his. "Oh James, I fear I shall be the death of you."

"Perhaps." He sucked in another great breath then smiled. "But it is well worth it to hear my name on your lips."

Frowning, she pressed her fingers to his cheek. "Are you all right?"

Ahh, but he could lie here forever, basking in the care and concern of this woman. Lose himself in her touch. Live in her sweet lilac scent.

Instead, he pushed up to sit, wincing at the sting on his arm. "Not much the worse for wear after tangling with that hellion."

"Liar." She stared pointedly at the blood oozing down his forearm. Pulling out a handkerchief, she pressed it to the wound while arching a brow. "It seems our roles have reversed, hmm?"

"I should hope so. Here, let me do that." Gently he nudged away her fingers and applied more pressure than she'd dared. He scanned her for any hint of scrape or scratch as she slipped on her shoes. Other than torn stockings and a ripped hem, she appeared to be unscathed. "What about you? Were you harmed in any way?"

"I think I shall be forever skittish to cross a field in the future, but other than that I am fine. Thank you for taking the brunt of that bull. Had you not come, I would not have. . .I mean I—I was so frightened." She pressed her lips flat, shaking her head.

"What is done is done. Come. I think we have both had enough of outdoor adventures." He turned towards the house, too late remembering his shirt lay in the dirt, baring his skin to sunlight and the sharp gasp of Rosa.

"Your back!"

He froze, unable to face the horror surely written upon her lovely face. Or worse, the pity swimming in her gaze. Both sickened him, yet both were inevitable. Scar upon scar marred his flesh from previous sun exposures as a young man. And even now he could feel the burning prickles of blisters growing like a cancer on his unprotected skin.

"You should go home now," he murmured without turning around. Then louder, "And stay on the road this time."

He strode off, hating his own nakedness, hating more that Rosa witnessed his shame. He could bear all the scorn and more from others, but not from her. Never from her. And yet somehow God had seen fit for him to endure that very thing.

Oh God, have mercy.

Footsteps shooshed through grass, but not fleeing away—growing louder at his back.

Rosa caught up to his side, staying him with a touch to his arm. Her brown gaze met his directly. "If you think to be rid of me so handily, sir, you are quite mistaken. What is it you suffer?"

A fair question. One he didn't wish to answer. He'd rather go head-to-head with that bull than explain to Rosa about his family's curse. But those blasted brown eyes of hers would not let him go.

He inhaled until his lungs burned, then slowly let it all out. "Allow me to get a fresh shirt and I will meet you in the sitting room."

She jutted her jaw, the dimple on her chin tempting him to trace it with his finger. But despite the show of defiance, she gave in with a nod.

Silence linked arms with them the entire way back to the manor, him trying to figure out how much to tell her. And what of her? Only God knew what went through the woman's mind as she kept pace at his side. The flesh on his back looked like a gargoyle's scales. It was a wonder she hadn't tucked tail and run at the sight of it.

He held open the side door. "Do you know the way to the sitting room from here?"

She peered down the darkened passageway to their right before facing him. "I do."

"Then I'll meet you there shortly." He strode the opposite direction, taking the rear stairs. All the while as he donned his shirt, waistcoat, and suitcoat, a furious battle waged in his mind. He didn't have to share his family's secret, yet part of him yearned to unmask himself as never before. To be known—and to know all of Rosa in return.

My, what a sentimental fool he was becoming. A smirk twisted his lips as he wove his way back to the sitting room, his mind finally made up. He'd take the middle road, telling Rosa only so much as would satisfy without revealing every sordid detail of his malady.

She stood near the sofa table, paging through a book and looking lovely despite her muddy gown and loosened hair.

He drew near, speaking quietly so as not to startle her. "I see you have found the books to return."

She turned, the smile on her lips fading as her gaze drifted from his chin to his hairline. "There are red patches on your cheeks and brow. What is happening to you? How far will this"—she circled her free hand inches from his face—"progress?"

"Hopefully not much farther. I was not out there that long." He took the book from her and stacked it neatly on the small pile. "As you know, my mother fails from a disease that neither doctors—nor I—am able to stop."

"What is it?"

"An ailment called porphyria." He leaned against the table, remembering the first time he'd heard that detestable diagnosis. The doctor's words haunted him still.

"Porphyria is in the blood. There is nothing to be done to rid the body of such a malignancy save for draining the veins, which in and of itself is a death sentence."

James folded his arms, feeling more than helpless. "I expect my mother will die any day."

"How awful!" Rosa cried, her fingers light against his sleeve. "I am so sorry, truly, but what has that to do with you, unless. . ."

Her eyes widened. Immediately she pulled back and bit her knuckle, stifling a small cry.

If nothing else, the woman was perceptive, but indeed, she was so much more. "My mother's ailment is hereditary. So now you know. . .and I trust you will keep this to yourself."

She lowered her hand, and he didn't miss the tremor in her fingers. "Of course I shall, but I can scarce believe it. You seem so healthy. So vigorous."

"I am." He rubbed the back of his neck, wincing at the itch and resultant sting. "That is until sunlight hits my skin."

Rosa slowly shook her head, her brow folding. "My father was right. What a dreadful day."

"Hear, now." He lifted her chin with the crook of his finger. "Do not fret for me. I still have time to find a remedy. It is my mother who is beyond hope, unless by some great miracle you have got a new book tucked into your pocket with the key to my dilemma?"

"The only thing I have in my pocket is a note from my father." She retrieved a small slip of paper and handed it over. "I am afraid that without a bicycle, my daily visits must end."

Saddened, he scanned the tight handwriting, then balled the missive into a wad and chucked it into the hearth. "In truth"—he straightened—"I am surprised your father allowed your visits to begin with, bicycle or not. You know as well as I what everyone says about me."

"Nonsense! Nothing but superstitious gibberish." She padded across the carpet, her doe eyes large as she pressed her palm lightly to his cheek. "Does it hurt much?"

He smiled, the curving of his mouth becoming quite the habit in this woman's company. "Do not worry on my account."

"I. . ." She bit her lower lip, her teeth white against the red swell of her mouth. Whatever she wished to say would apparently cost her much. "I shall miss you, James. More than you know."

"But I do know." He stepped closer. "For you see, if you miss me half as much as I you, then your heart will bleed drip by drip until there is nothing left." He kissed the inside of her wrist, relishing the softness of her skin. "I have come to cherish our time together."

"As have I," she whispered.

He rubbed a light circle where he'd kissed, imprinting the silkiness in his memory. "Remember when I declared I was your beau?"

"I shall never forget."

"Would to God it were true."

"Then make it so." Her gaze burned into his, so pure, so innocent, it ached in his chest.

And he could stand it no more. He grabbed the back of her head, bringing his mouth down against hers, so much passion flaring he burned. She was star fire, this woman. A beacon in his night. The only softness in his life.

And sweet heavens, but she *was* soft, her body molding perfectly against his. Her hair silky between his fingers. The side of her neck an unbearable sort of velvet as his lips trailed along her skin. She tasted of rosewater and promise, an intoxicating honey he'd never get enough of.

"James," she murmured as her lips sought his, and when her kiss landed hard and hungry, full on his mouth, a jolt shot through him.

He jerked away, breathing hard and shaking his head. "We cannot do this. It is not right. I sail for Transylvania the moment my mother is laid to rest."

"Then take me with you."

He stared down at her fingers entwined with his, marveling at how they seamlessly fit together—and sorrowing at the rift he knew he must create. "It is not possible." His voice was flat even to his own ears.

"But I. . ." She angled her head, peering up at him with so much affection it hurt the soul. "I love you."

He closed his eyes, his jaw clenching. Such a profession! One he'd never expected to hear in his lifetime, not from a woman such as this. Everything inside yearned to pull her to him, vow his unfailing devotion, kiss her again and again and again. But it wouldn't be fair. He was six years her senior. Old enough to know that allowing full rein to the wild emotions they shared would only bring her heartache. No woman ought to be bound to a stigmatized man who would eventually go mad.

Though it killed him in a thousand different ways, he slipped from her grasp and hardened his tone. "I am sorry, Rosa. I am not the man for you."

TWENTY

Do you not think that there are things which
you cannot understand, and yet which are;
that some people see things that others cannot?

Her father had cautioned Rosa not to get hurt, and yet here she was, trekking the road from Morgrave Manor at breakneck pace, with a broken heart, a blistered foot, and Albin Mallow's warning trilling shrilly in her ears.

"All I ask from you, as your friend, is to be careful around him. Very careful."

She kicked a rock, stubbing her toe and welcoming the pain. Just the thought of admitting Albin was right turned her stomach. Yet what else was she to believe? Granted, James had played the part of a gentleman, saving her from danger several times over now. But had he not also preyed upon her sympathies, spinning her such a tale of woe about his mother and himself, looking so handsome she could think of none other? Oh, why did she tell him she loved him? What a naive goose, blurting her feelings like that. There was no possible happy ending for a simple librarian and a baronet. She flattened the cool of her palms against her cheeks, soothing the burn somewhat.

Then completely unbidden, her fingers drifted to her mouth. Her step faltered as she touched her lips that had been so shamelessly and thoroughly kissed. The taste of him—slightly cinnamon, mostly exotic—would have driven her to her knees had he not held her so tightly. Even now she trembled at the memory. She'd never felt so whole in all her life.

Had he been using her for his own physical enjoyment as Albin had said he would? Or. . .

Had she been using him? After all, she was the one who'd approached the man in the first place, who'd laid her palm against his cheek.

She jerked her hand from her face, mortified. She'd practically thrown her body against his. What a Jezebel! She'd asked for that kiss as surely as if she had extended Sir James a written invitation. No wonder he'd rejected her. No man wanted such a brazen woman.

By the time she returned to the library, her blister was forgotten in the angst torturing her conscience. She half stomped, half limped through the door, thoroughly disgusted with herself.

Father looked up from the counter, lowering his spectacles to the tip of his nose. "Don't tell me you've had another mishap."

"No." She jutted her jaw. "I am perfectly fine. Have you the notes for me to deliver? I fancy a brisk walk."

"But I was going to have a delivery boy. . ." He narrowed his eyes, studying her like a bug beneath a magnifying glass, then pushed a stack of folded papers and two books across the countertop. "Well, if that's the case, then you may as well stop by Mrs. Hawkins's on your return to town and drop off the titles she requested. I expect you could use some girl talk other than what your mother might provide."

She tucked the notes into her pocket and scooped up the books with a wry twist to her lips. That her father understood her so well was a comfort and a bane. She fled out the door before he deduced what she'd been up to at the manor.

It took the entire afternoon to traipse around the countryside, which considerably thinned the padding she'd slipped between her shoe and her blister. Much more of this and the thing would be rubbed even rawer. By the time she reached Mrs. Hawkins's, she was weary of hearing everyone's superstitious theory about who—or more likely what—was responsible for draining the blood of sheep and goats alike in the area. Apparently the sun had tired of all the foolishness as well, for it sank rapidly towards the horizon. . .a good reminder not to overstay her visit this time.

She rapped on the door of the small cottage, the weathered wood rattling beneath the assault, and smiled the moment the woman swung it open. "Good afternoon, Mrs. Hawkins. I have brought your books."

It was hard to say exactly how old the woman was, for despite the crinkles at the corners of her eyes and the increasing lag in her step, a timelessness hung about her. If Rosa believed in such things, she'd swear Mrs. Hawkins was some sort of immortal, called into being by a mage—or perhaps was one herself. Which was ridiculous, for though the old dear still clung to faery stories, she was a godly woman, attending church prayers every morning and three times on Sunday.

"Come in, Rosa lass, 'n sit ye down. I've a spot o' tea jes waitin'." Mrs. Hawkins stepped aside, her faded blue skirt swaying with the movement.

Rosa hesitated, but her father had said she should take time to talk with Mrs. Hawkins. As long as she didn't dawdle overlong, she should easily be home by supper. "How lovely, but only one cup." Rosa smiled as she entered the tiny sitting room. The space might seem bigger were it not for stack upon stack of old tabloids and broadsheets lining the walls. The oily scent of ink and dust tickled her nose as she set Mrs. Hawkins's books on the small side table next to the woman's threadbare chair. It worried her, this obsession with newspapers, for the woman's other vice was oil lamps, and they were all lit. All the time. Should one of those papers take fire, there'd be no saving the old dear.

Rosa perched on the footstool, the only other place available to sit. "How are you faring, Mrs. Hawkins?"

"Betta than ah should be, by God's good grace." She took a pot of tea sitting on the windowsill and poured two cups of steaming liquid. "An what o' thou? Ah've not seen ye much o' late. Flittin' in. Flittin' out. Ah've bin worried for thou, what wi' t' livestock killings an a vampire in t' area. Wha's kept thou so occupied?"

Wasting my time with that so-called vampire, that's what.

Face heating, Rosa bit back the retort while accepting a cup of watery tea. "Library business, nothing more."

"Ach! T'aint books what colours a lass's cheeks so. Yer in love, ah can tell. Ah've bin prayin', thou know, that tha good Lord would fetch thee a godly man into thy life." Mrs. Hawkins sank into her chair with a wink. "Looks like He 'as."

Rosa sipped her tea, glad she'd not asked for sugar. The bitterness of the brew suited her mood.

"I am sorry, Rosa. I am not the man for you."

The tea barely made it past the lump in her throat. Even now she could hear the finality in James's voice, in the words that would haunt her for the rest of her life. She adjusted her seat on the footstool. "I am afraid you are mistaken, Mrs. Hawkins. As it turns out, the man I thought I loved apparently does not love me, so clearly he is not the one God has in mind."

"Don't be ta sure." The old woman clucked her tongue. "God moves in mysterious ways, thou knows."

"Well, I wish He would make Himself more plain!" Instant remorse squeezed her heart, and she set her cup on the chipped saucer. "I beg your pardon. Such an outburst was totally uncalled for. It is just that, well. . .I admit sometimes I do not understand God's ways at all."

"Oh, bairn." Leaning forward, Mrs. Hawkins patted her knee. "If God wor so small tha' thou could understan' 'im, 'e would not be good enuff ta stand wi' thou in all that ye face. Every one of us needs a God who is bigger than we credit, else 'e 'ood not be God."

Rosa nodded absently. "I suppose it is rather arrogant of me to expect God to answer on my own terms."

"I'll tell thou what ta expect." She squeezed Rosa's knee then settled back against a rather flattened cushion. "Expect the good Lord ta give thou a glass o' water when yer parched, ta grant thou rest when weary, ta gi' miracles 'n mercy 'n a regular dose o' comfort when thou needs. But the one thin' thou shouldn't expect—ever—is for 'im ta show up lookin' like thou might imagine."

Rosa breathed in the woman's words. Truly, Mrs. Hawkins ought to be in the pulpit on Sunday mornings instead of in the pews. "You give me much to think on."

"Then think on this, bairn. 'Tis the moment thou lets go of thy expectations tha' God can fettle wi' ye. 'Til then, ye've not surrendered, thou see?"

"I think so." She smiled. "But I suspect it is not as easy as you make it sound."

"Din't say t'were easy. Just necessary. Now, let me tell thou all abaht ol' Mrs. Godalming 'n 'er tussle wi' Kingsley's goat. Who came out tha victor may surprise thou."

Rosa glanced at her watch brooch as Mrs. Hawkins talked, then sucked in a breath. Almost seven o'clock!

Before Mrs. Hawkins could start another story, she shot to her feet, leaving the old footstool wobbling. "I have had a merry time visiting with you, Mrs. Hawkins, but I must return home or Mother will have the vapors."

"Well, we can't 'ave that now, aye?" Mrs. Hawkins scooted forward in her chair. "Ahl just be seein' thou off, then."

"Pray do not trouble yourself." Bending, Rosa hugged the woman about her shoulders. "I can see myself to the door quite nicely. You enjoy those books I have brought you. I will bring more next week."

Mrs. Hawkins smiled up at her. "God bless thou, Rosa dear."

"You as well."

As she ventured outside, whisps of fog coiled around her, leeching much of the lingering daylight from the air. She shivered. No wonder all the superstitious stories involved fog. The speed with which it could move was almost unnatural. She hurried down the path, despite the aggravation to her blister. It would not be wise to be caught out when the full bank rolled in. Such a sea fog was known for making a full-moon night lightless.

But the fog thickened faster than she could walk, and it soon became clear it would be near to impossible to remain on the path. If she veered too far astray, a tumble down the cliffside would end in a broken neck—and there'd be no gallant baronet to help her this time. As much as she hated to worry her parents again, she'd best stay the night with Mrs. Hawkins. Mother would suffer another fit, but at least this time Father knew where she was.

She whirled, only to see nothing but a grey wall of cloud. Not so much as a hint of gold glowed from one of the many lamps burning inside Mrs. Hawkins's cottage. Cold sweat beaded on Rosa's brow. How could the lights have disappeared so thoroughly in such a short amount of time and space?

For an eternity she stood still, lost in shadow and mist, debating the lesser of two evils—try to find her way back to the cottage or press on towards home. No matter which one she chose, the distinct possibility of plummeting over the cliffs taunted like a daemon. She could hunker down here, brave the dark of night and nip of sea, but dampness already seeped into her gown, and she shivered. She'd take a chill for sure. *Oh God, what have I done? And now, what do I do?*

She waited for an answer, recalling every verse and Scripture she'd memorized since girlhood. None of them told her which direction to go save for *a wise man's heart is at his right hand; but a fool's heart at his left.* Did that mean she ought to go to the left because she'd been so foolish? Or ought she go right in the hope that God would give her wisdom?

La. What a dilemma.

Eventually she settled upon tentatively putting one foot in front of the other, toeing about before she put her full weight on the next step. She'd gone ten, perhaps twelve yards when in the distance a yellow dot of light appeared. A lantern, perhaps?

God, please.

The closer she drew, the more the tightness in her shoulders loosened. Ahead was the dark shape of a huge man with a lamp in hand. Thank God! It must be Mr. Klausenburg, the town's gentle giant, on his way for a pint at the Pelican and Child. The ancient pub hunkered at the outskirt of Whitby was one of his favorite haunts.

Rosa followed him, relieved when her feet reached the cobbled streets of town. Then she picked up her pace, hoping to thank him for his guidance. He paused by the golden light spilling out from the pub's bay window.

"Mr. Klausenburg!" she called.

But the dark shape didn't turn towards her. Nor did he enter the public house.

He vanished.

Rosa stumbled to a stop on the very cobblestone where she'd last seen the man. Wrapping her arms about herself, she turned in a full circle. Clearly whoever had led her wasn't here now. But there was no possible way anyone of that size could disappear in the blink of an eye. So, where had he gone? Who had it been. . .or *what* had it been?

Gooseflesh lifted on her arms.

He was a monster. A miscreant. Less honorable than a maggot feasting on rotted flesh. James clutched his lantern so tightly his knuckles cracked. Eerie beams of light reached out into the mist, snagging on tombstones. It wasn't dark yet, but it might as well be, so thickly did the fog coat St. Mary's graveyard. He belonged here, among the dead, for the way he'd hurt Rosa had cleaved his heart in two. He could still see the tears that'd welled in her big brown eyes when he'd rejected her. The image was branded on his soul. He never should have allowed her to become so attached to him, and he most definitely should not have kissed her.

So he stalked amongst the graves, regret his companion, grief his very breath. And as for pain, Lord have mercy. Though he'd bound the worst of the blisters on his back and chest, his shirt still irritated the raw skin. Thankfully the welts on his face hadn't developed into sores, a small consolation. He deserved this agony and more for having entangled himself with a woman to whom he could offer nothing more than a cursed life, shut away in a castle married to a madman rumoured to be a vampire.

His toe hit a raised tuft of grass, and he stumbled. Fitting, really. Everything seemed off-kilter at the moment. He never should have come to Whitby in the first place. He'd been no help to his mother, so what was the point? Tomorrow he'd purchase some valerian root and combine it with the remaining dregs of the wolfsbane in a last effort to cure her. And then. . .

Well, only God knew what then.

"Is someone there? Help!" A man's voice bled through the mist, making it hard to pinpoint its origin.

James held his lantern higher and squinted into the fog. "Where are you?"

"Over here. On the ground."

His gaze shot to the grave nearest him, then drifted on to the next—where a lump of black cloth leaned against a tombstone. The rector, by the looks of him, clutching his ankle. This rescuing of people from trips and topples was turning into quite the career. He strode over to the man—Mr. Austen if he remembered correctly.

"Praise be!" The rector's teeth shown white in the gloom. "You're a gift from God, man."

"Many would say otherwise. Allow me to help you inside." James wove his arm beneath the clergyman's and hefted him up, hiding a wince as the man's weight pressed on his blisters. "I believe we are not far from the church. Care to tell me what happened?"

"Haha! Now there's a story." The man hobbled along, bumping against James's side every other step. "I always put out a dish of milk on Mrs. Spencelagh's grave for her cat. It was her dying wish, you see, that her tabby shouldn't go without. Downright eerie how the cat never fails to show up in the dark of night to lap the bowl clean. Then again, the good book is full of stranger stuff than a cat who visits a grave."

James steered them around a toppled stone covered in moss. "And your ankle?"

"Afraid I stepped wrong after I set down the dish. Must have sprained it, and it's not the first time. Weak bones, you see. At any rate, I was afraid I was either going to have to crawl back to the church or spend the night with Mrs. Spencelagh. Haha! Wouldn't that make the old spinster roll over a time or two?"

James arched his brow at the irreverent reverend.

"Say, don't I know you?" Austen's bushy eyebrows lowered as he peered at him, and then he snapped his fingers. "Yes! Now I remember. The man whose *soul is at peace with the Lord*, or so you told me. I've been praying for you, my son, though it would be helpful to have a name to go along with that prayer."

"Sir James Morgan, at your service. And here we are." He shoved open the church door with his shoulder, once again clenching his jaw against a shot of pain.

But that was nothing compared to the burning memories rising from the dead as he glanced around the sanctuary. It was here—in this house of worship—the first accusations of black magic had been flung against his family. No nine-year-old should have to wipe the spittle off his cheek from the very people who professed to love one and all. The scorn of that day still bit deep.

He cut a sideways glance at the rector. "Is anyone here to help you?"

"No, I like to be alone in the quiet of the night before I retire to the rectory. It's easier to hear God if nobody's nattering in your ear. If you could just help me hobble back to the vestry, I'll stay here till morning. There's a comfortable chair and I've plenty of books to keep me company. Besides, I'd just made a pot of tea, so neither will I perish for want of nourishment. Not that that's a danger, mind. Haha!" He patted his potbelly, the slap of it jarring in such a holy place. "The vestry's just down the aisle over there."

James followed the sweep of the rector's hand, then readjusted his grip and helped the man down the aisle. By the time they reached the smaller room, sweat trickled down Austen's clean-shaven face. James helped him lower into a high back that was as well upholstered as the man himself.

Settling against the cushions, the reverend pulled out a handkerchief and dabbed his brow. "Mmm. Much better."

James eased the injured ankle atop a footstool, then frowned at the height. The thing was way too low to prevent more swelling. He grabbed a few books off a shelf and propped the reverend's foot higher.

Austen cocked his head. "You've done this a time or two?"

"You could say that. Of late, it seems God has seen fit to bring all sorts of ailments and calamities across my path."

"Haha! You see? People need you and you need people. That's the way of humankind."

Was it, though? Because were that true, then he was the most wretched of men. The only ones he could count on were a decrepit butler, a nurse who with every breath threatened to leave, and a steward who lived thousands of miles from here. Worse, no one needed a failure like him. Removing his hat, he scraped his fingers through his hair. Even his mother would gladly trade him for someone who could actually cure her disease.

"You are troubled, I think." The rector reached for the teapot on the small table next to his chair. "Take a cup and sit yourself down, Sir James. I have plenty of time to listen."

Telling God his troubles was one thing, but exposing his hardships to a stranger was not only a risk, it was downright dangerous. He shook his head. "I ought to be getting back to the manor."

"Oh? Must be quite the pressing engagement, especially since I found you rambling about the graves in a fog—or more like you found me. Haha!" He paused in pouring his tea, his cat-like eyes glowing in the lamplight. "Sit and let us speak for just a few minutes of the burden you carry, for it is a heavy load you're not meant to bear alone."

Reluctantly, James perched on the edge of a wooden stool near the hearth, unsure if he ought to censure or admire the man's insight and tenacity. "I will humour you for the time, but only because I fear it will be a long night for you here alone."

"But I am never alone. And neither are you." He reached for another cup and wiggled it in the air. "Will you take some?"

"No, thank you. I am the sort of heathen who prefers coffee."

"It's not what goes into the body that makes one an infidel, but what comes out of the heart." He chuckled as he set the cup down.

What an odd fellow. Perhaps living cliffside, at the mercy of a wild sea was getting to him. James held his hands out to the fire, thinking aloud. "How long have you served here?"

"Nigh on fifteen years now." He sipped his tea then smacked his lips before setting the cup aside. "I find I quite enjoy this congregation. They're a colourful lot, which is exactly how I like it. You might too, should you give the people a chance."

He snorted. "I lost hope in religious people a long time ago."

"Bravo!" The rector clapped his hands, the loud report shocking in the small room. "I salute you, Sir James. For you see, man is not meant to find hope in anything of this world, but rather to lose hope in all things worldly."

"Well, there you have it. There is no need for me to attend services, then."

"But that's not at all what I said, nor what God has to say about the matter, either. If the foot shall say, because I am not the hand, I am not of the body; is it therefore not of the body?" He speared a finger towards him. "You are a foot, Sir James. And like it or not, you are needed. You have a role in society, one you've been avoiding."

His lips twisted—as did his gut. "You hardly know me, sir."

The clergyman's eyes twinkled. "Am I wrong?"

James shot to his feet, hating how this man of God could so easily lift the rock covering his life and expose the disgusting creepy-crawlies lurking in his soul. "If there is naught else I can do for you, then I think I should be going."

"Haha! Hit too close to the truth, did I?" He slapped his thigh, then *oofed* when the movement jiggled his sore ankle.

James stifled a small smile. "The truth is, I have a mother who needs me."

"Do you? Then by all means, don't let me keep you from her. But please take what I said to heart. Shutting yourself away doesn't solve your problems. It only magnifies them. God brings people into our lives to walk beside us through our troubles, yet we are the ones who must open the door and let them in."

He nodded then wheeled about. If what the man said was true, had he been wrong to turn Rosa away so harshly?

TWENTY-ONE

There is this peculiarity in criminals.

A freak in a sideshow at least made a living from pity and contempt. Perhaps James ought to sell tickets next time he came to town. Scowling, he flicked egg off his brow from a well-aimed projectile that had hit just between his hat brim and sunglasses. It wasn't the slurs that irritated so much as the sunshine burning his nose. He ought to have sent the stable boy to manage his errands, but the fellow had taken off earlier to help with a difficult foaling at the neighbour's farm.

Another set of insults and a few rocks hurtled through the air as he trotted past a gathering of boys.

"Git thee back to Beelzebub where thou belongs."

"A pox on thou, ye bloody daemon!"

Little criminals. James leaned low over Belle's neck, settling her with an "Easy, girl," whispered into her ear and a reassuring pat. Thankfully, the apothecary was now in view. He upped his mount's pace, slid off, and tethered her before the boys caught up to him. He had no wish for a confrontation here on the street. That would only garner more attention and possibly a few more bruises.

The moment he walked through the door, a successive round of sharp yaps split his eardrums. Most shops used a bell to announce a customer. Not Rawling's Apothecary and Notary Services. Mr. Rawling stationed his beloved Yorkshire terrier atop a red velvet cushion on a stool at the end of the counter.

James bypassed the little dog, making sure to keep his hands in his pockets. He'd already learnt that the furball had a penchant for nipping at gloves—and the leather on his right hand had the teeth marks to prove it.

"What can I do for you today, Sir James?" Mr. Rawling wiped his hands on his apron as he strode from a back room. He was a giraffe of a man, long-necked and with excessively extended legs, the only man in town James had to look up to. His red hair was slicked back with an oil that smelled suspiciously like horseradish, adding to the plethora of scents from all the herbs and ointments lining the shelves.

"Valerian root, if you please, Mr. Rawling." Pulling out his handkerchief, James wiped away the crusty remains of the egg white that'd dried on his cheek. "Oh, and some wolfsbane as well."

"Wolfsbane?" The apothecary's pencil-thin moustache twitched. "You do realize that is poisonous?"

"I am well aware." James held the man's gaze.

"Very good." The apothecary pulled down several jars, then removed the lids and began measuring out a tea-coloured powder. "I cannot help but notice you have made some interesting purchases over the past month. Perhaps if you'd tell me what you're about, I might be able to recommend something to accomplish your purposes."

Outside, the boys rapped on the window. James turned his back to them, mulling over Mr. Rawling's offer. Just last night Mr. Austen had charged him with allowing others into his life. Coincidence?

He glanced at the ceiling, thoughts churning. *Is this your way, Lord, of nudging me to heed the rector's words?*

Inhaling deeply, he gave in to the sensation of free-falling, conflicted by the choice set before him. "Perhaps you might be of some help," he murmured, then faced Rawling. "Though I must require that whatever is spoken here is not repeated to anyone."

"Nor will it be." Mr. Rawling tapped a funnel with his long finger, coaxing the last powdery remnants of valerian into a small paper pouch. "I don't routinely share personal information with others."

James rubbed the back of his neck. Rawling had never given him cause to think him anything other than a man of integrity. Perhaps this was a risk worth taking. "Then I thank you for the offer and would appreciate any insight you might have. I came here because my mother suffers from a bloodborne disease. Acute porphyria, to be exact. Have you heard of it?"

"Hmm. Not per se." The apothecary picked up a pencil and a pad of paper, then penned the words *Lady Dorina* and *acute porphyria* in large, loopy letters before looking up. "I assume you've sought Dr. Seward's counsel?"

"I have, but he has withdrawn his services, which leaves her care to me."

"I see. What are the symptoms you're trying to manage?"

James stifled a snort. He may as well be looking down a gun barrel, so loaded was that question. He daren't say anything about the mad bouts his mother suffered. His family had enough of a false reputation without adding any truth to it. He shifted his weight as he sifted through what to say and, more importantly, what not to say.

"My mother suffers a distinct sensitivity to light, has an accelerated heart rate, and experiences occasional seizures along with severe abdominal pain. Also, of late there have been uncontrollable nosebleeds, which I suspect is something completely unrelated."

Mr. Rawling wrote each symptom on his notepad followed by *near death*, then dutifully jotted down all the ingredients James had tried thus far, marking the most toxic with a check mark. For a while he tapped his pencil against the page, leaving faint dots in the margin.

"That is a quandary," he mumbled. "I confess I am at a loss as to what to suggest further other than a mix of laudanum and ginger for the abdominal pain. But about that nosebleed, I agree it might very well be unrelated. As I recall, you purchased some skullcap root, did you not?"

James sucked air through his teeth. Thunderation! Rawlings was right. Why had he not thought of that? Perhaps the rector had been correct, and he *did* need people, for with his lack of sleep and all else, he'd overlooked such a simple side effect. "Very astute, Mr. Rawling. I shall stop administering it at once."

"I wish I could be of more help." The tall man shrugged as a volley of catcalls leached through the front window, setting off a succession of warning yaps from the Yorkshire.

James absently rubbed his arm where a sharp piece of gravel had nicked him. The little criminals had added to their number, a few women and some men. Shouldering his way through that lot would be a trick.

"That will be four shillings, Sir James."

He fished out the coins. "Tell me, Mr. Rawling, are you not concerned for your business by serving me? Those people out there would harass you for merely giving me the time of day."

"I'm not in the least worried." He tipped his head towards the ruffians outside. "They need me and my goods, so it matters naught."

"You are not at all anxious they might be right about me?" He arched a brow. "That I am a vampire?"

Rawlings dropped the coins into the cash register drawer and slammed it shut, his thin moustache riding the wave of a smirk. "I'm a businessman, Sir James, and money is money. I'd as soon take a coin from a vampire as from a king."

James grunted as he tucked the small bag into his pocket. "If you do not mind my saying, you are quite the anomaly."

"So my wife informs me daily. Now then, why don't you slip out back through there." He pointed to a wooden door at the corner of the rear wall. "I'll send John to see your horse is brought 'round. John!" He hollered towards the workroom before James could refuse.

Not that he would have, anyway, so stunning was the offer. Other than Rosa, he'd not witnessed such a kindness.

Moments later, a boy no more than nine years old skittered out sideways from a backroom so quickly he nearly tripped over his feet. "Aye, Mr. Rawlings?"

"Lead Sir James's horse to the delivery entrance and be smart about it."

The boy nodded as he raced to the door, startling the little dog into yet another round of shrill yips. Apparently the lad had only one speed—breakneck—which suited James just fine. The sooner he left town, the sooner that crowd would find something else to do.

"I appreciate the effort." He nodded at the apothecary. "Thank you, Mr. Rawling."

Resetting his hat lower on his brow, James stalked off, marveling that the rector's words had been true.

Perhaps people—some of them, anyway—could be trusted.

Usually, a ride through town in his ralli cart was as soothing as a fine glass of port. Not today. Two things were bothering Albin, and he wasn't quite sure which one annoyed him the most. . .the horsefly that wouldn't stop buzzing about his face or his uncle's continual pressure that he wed Rosa Edwards. Uncle had lobbed some particularly sharp barbs at the breakfast table this morn, questioning his courage, his intelligence, and ultimately his manhood. What tripe!

Albin swatted at the fly humming near his ear. Not that he didn't wish to make the feisty little librarian his own, for just like his uncle, the more he was denied a desire, the more he wanted it. A Mallow trait to be proud of, for it screamed of spirit and determination. But it seemed no matter how many flowers he delivered, how sweet his words or fine his appearance, Rosa simply would have nothing to do with him.

It had to be the baronet keeping her from him. Vampire or not, he had cast some spell over her. It was the only explanation possible for why Rosa continued to snub him when he had done everything right, played his role to perfection.

He squeezed the reins until they shook, confusing the horse, but so be it. It was only a matter of time until he found the right moment to strike at the baronet with that manuscript he'd found. Would that it might be today!

Ahead, a cluster of people huddled around the apothecary's shop. Boys mostly, but several women and some men. He slowed the horse as he neared, scanning the gathering for the sweet face of Rosa. No amber-haired pixie grabbed his attention, but the mention of Sir James did.

He tapped a lad in a flat cap on the shoulder with his horsewhip. "You, boy. What is this about?"

"Th' baronet's in Rawling's." He hitched his thumb towards the shop. "Got my rocks ready right 'ere fer when 'e shows his face." Up shot a filthy fist clutching a handful of gravel.

Well, well. Albin smiled. Perhaps his moment had arrived.

He set the brake and climbed down, reading the crowd like a penny dreadful. After several horrid beatings by school bullies, he'd learned at a young age how to calculate who to sidle up to and who to stay away from. In this case, he might make the best headway by inciting the women first. They were generally weaker brained, easier to influence. As a bonus, ruffled skirts meant the men's protective instincts would be heightened. And once animal instinct was unleashed, there'd be no stopping a rampage.

He sidled up to a plump hen in a brown skirt standing at the edge of the crowd. "Terrible business, I say. Who can feel safe when such a terror is free to roam our streets?"

The woman swiveled her head, the nostrils in her pug nose flaring. "I've not felt safe since that monster set foot in this town. Why, these boys said nary a drop o' Sir James's blood spilled though they pelted him right cruel with gravel. T'aint natural."

A man with a square jaw bobbed his head. "I agree. I seen them boys chase that creature in 'ere. No blood on 'im a'tall."

Albin hid a smile. This was going better than he'd expected. "Well," he drawled, "we all know vampires don't bleed."

"Mercy!" A woman with fake ringlets fanned herself, the pasted curls hardly moving.

The woman next to her craned her neck, peering through the window. "But what's a vampire doing out in the daylight?"

Albin upped his volume, making sure all the gathering might hear. "Criminals always track their prey by light of day, then strike in the dark of night. There is no doubt in my mind the baronet is probing for his next victim."

One woman shrieked. The pug-nosed lady swayed on her feet, tilting his way. Albin righted her lest she knock him over and the dirty pavement sully his suit. The ruckus, however, was working. A few more men crossed the street, adding to the numbers.

"Filthy cur." The man near Albin's elbow spat on the cobbles. "Near to wiped out Widow Andrews' goats. Them animals were like babes to her, and her sole source of income."

"Aye!" Another man chimed in. "Old Mr. Arthur's sheep have been culled as well, and he can't afford to replace the loss. Something must be done."

"Goats. Sheep." A horse-faced fellow shook his head. "What's to be next?"

There it was. Uncle always said once a customer asked a question, his coin was as good as in your pocket.

Albin skimmed through the gathering, taking up a post front and center. "Good citizens of Whitby, I can tell you what's to be next, for I've researched the matter of vampires extensively. This villain will not stick with livestock, not for much longer. His appetite, his very need for blood, will drive him until he can no longer restrain himself. Mark my words, friends. Though it pains me to say it"—he ran his index finger from one person to the next, singling out each onlooker—"he'll be coming for your daughters next, for that is the way of a vampire."

Fists shot into the air. Faces bloomed with a murderous red. Pug-nosed lady really did swoon this time.

Albin spread his arms, relishing the power surging through his veins. "Sir James must be stopped, I tell you. Are you with me?"

A chorus of ayes rumbled.

Albin shouted all the louder. "I say again, are you with me?"

"I am!" A burly man shoved past him.

The rest of the crowd swelled at his heels. Albin teetered sideways, caught in an eddy of swirling skirts and broad shoulders. He grabbed for his hat before the thing fell to the ground, then entered the fray himself. Too late, though, judging by the comments fluttering around like bats in the night.

"He's not here!"

"I swear I saw him through the window."

"Just like a daemon to vanish like that."

"Where is he, Rawling? Hand 'im over!"

Albin crept behind the counter, seeking the best vantage point to watch without actually getting involved should fisticuffs start flying.

For his part, Mr. Rawling didn't appear to be frightened in the least, even though the men now had him cornered against the shelving. "Unless you have business here, gentlemen, I must ask that you leave. I will not serve such an unruly mob."

One man pulled out a pistol, the cock of the hammer sharp in the air. "Where'd that hellion go?"

"Put that thing away!" Rawling bellowed. "I have no idea what you're talking about."

Oh yes he did. Clearly he was covering for the baronet, but why? Had he fallen under the same spell as Rosa?

The raised voices continued, women's nattering mixed in. It didn't take long before his ears started ringing. What a flop this turned out to be. He angled to leave, then narrowed his eyes on a pad of paper sticking out halfway from a shelf beneath the counter. Large, loopy handwriting covered the top sheet, with Sir James and Lady Dorina clearly written alongside a list of. . .he leaned closer. Ingredients—purchased by Sir James. Used for treating his mother, apparently. But he was no doctor. What was the baronet up to?

He snatched the paper and scurried outside, devouring the rest of the contents as if his life depended upon it. Which it didn't. No, more like the Lady Dorina's life—and possibly Rosa's—depended upon the words written in Mr. Rawling's hand, especially the most incriminating one. . .

Deadly.

Tucking the note into his pocket, Albin hoisted himself up to the carriage seat, worry pinching his brow. If Sir James was administering those ingredients to his mother, he was more devious than Albin had credited. And if the man was capable of harming his own flesh and blood, then what of Rosa?

He clicked his tongue, setting the horses off at a trot. If Lady Dorina died, the baronet could rightfully be accused as a murderer. He wouldn't need to use Stoker's manuscript to indict the man, for this would be far more condemning.

TWENTY-TWO

If only I knew! If only I knew!

For two days now, Rosa had forced a smile and told the world she was fine when on the inside everything was a disaster, ever since the kiss she shared with James. She could still taste it. Taste him. Hear his deep voice say he wasn't the man for her. Which was she to believe? The passion she'd felt in his embrace or the cold words that'd slipped from his lips moments later? Sighing, she set down her pen and pinched the bridge of her nose. Not even Father's steady presence working alongside her at the library counter eased the heartsick ache in her chest.

Midway through "Haul Away for Rosie," he quit whistling. "Of all the crimes in the world. Look at this!"

Startled from her melancholy, Rosa blinked at the pile of ragged paper sitting in a heap in front of her father. A thin slice of spine clung for dear life to the stack, along with a cover so mangled the thing looked as if it'd been run through a sausage grinder.

"What an abomination." Her father's voice shook. "What an outrage!"

Rosa laid a soft touch on his arm, hoping to soothe. There was no sense in both of them fretting about things out of their control. "Maybe we could rebind it with some new pasteboard?"

"Half the pages are chewed." He slapped the countertop with a flattened palm. "I ought to send the constable after Mr. Braithwaite, or more like his dog. Of all the carelessness. Probably left the book sitting on the floor. The floor! You'd better believe I'll be charging old Braithwaite a pretty penny for this disgrace."

Rosa's belly tightened. If Father was this worked up about the ruination of a circulating book, what would he say when she finally told him of the rare one she'd lost? She must do so sooner or later, and the thought of it swung like a noose in the wind.

But now was not the time, not with his ire already enflamed. She slid the derelict book to her side of the counter. "Do not worry, Father. I will see what I can do to fix it up."

He snorted but his scowl lessened. "I fear it shall never be the same, but I suppose it's better than the sacrilege of throwing a book into the dust bin." He rose from his stool, shaking his head. "If only people would treat books as the valuables they truly are."

He was right. She never should have been so careless with such a treasure. Guilt bubbled up her throat—and nearly choked her as Father grabbed the bookcase key and strode towards the rarities.

She jumped to her feet, her stool teetering precariously as she dashed to block her father's path. "Can I get something for you? I was just. . .erm. . .going to pull a title from here myself. I would be happy to bring you whatever book you need as well."

His eyes narrowed behind the shine of his spectacles. "I thought you were going to fix that book Braithwaite ruined."

"Yes, I am." She bobbed her head vigorously—perhaps too much so, judging by the arch of his brow. "I merely thought I would get a bit of inspiration from some of the beauties on these shelves. I know. . .how about you go make a pot of tea and we will settle in back for some reading. It has been so long since we have done that, and we have not been busy today. What do you say, Father? For old time's sake?"

"Hmm." His lips pursed as he stroked his chin. "I suppose we haven't read together for quite some time." He nodded, then handed her the key. "Very well. I should like to look over *The Memoirs of Reverend David Stoner*. The vicar's sermon last Sunday touched on a theological point I wish to delve into further. You should find it on the top shelf, fifth book from the left."

"I shall retrieve it in a trice."

Blessed relief filled her lungs as he strode away. That had been a close call, one she didn't wish to repeat. She must tell him tonight after dinner when his belly would be full and he would be relaxed.

That decided, she opened the glass case and ran her finger along the spines, counting from the left. One. Two. Three. Four. Then squinted at the next one. Clearly her father had made a mistake, for Stoner's memoirs were the sixth book over. Even so, she pulled down the fifth. Inexplicably drawn to the ancient leather cover, she ran her finger over the title.

Perturbationes Sanguinem, a Dissertationem de Sanguine.

Hmm. Whatever that meant. Curious, she flipped it open and glanced at the contents. More Latin, none she could understand, but two words in particular stole her breath.

Mortiferum Porphyria.

Pulse quickening, she paged through to that chapter. She had no idea what mortiferum meant, but hadn't James said porphyria was the disease afflicting him and his mother? She could barely understand the contents of the next few pages, but James might. She hugged the book to her chest. He should see this.

But there was no way she'd risk another rarity being lost.

Darting to a nearby table, she pulled a pen from the ink stand, retrieved a blank sheet of paper from the drawer, and began dutifully copying the words. She couldn't be certain this was the same malady he'd mentioned, but even if it wasn't, perhaps the information might spur him on to other ideas. She hoped so, for his sake and his mother's.

By the time she reached the second-to-last paragraph, Father's voice drifted out from the back room. "The tea is ready."

She pushed her pen all the faster, praying she didn't make any egregious errors. The result was very sloppy handwriting, but by the time her father called her again, she'd finished and returned the book to the shelf.

"Coming!" Quickly, she pulled out the memoirs for Father and grabbed a perennial favorite of hers, a first edition of *Melmoth the Wanderer*, then sped to the back room.

Her father was just setting the tea tray on the desk, the porcelain lid of the pot rattling as it landed. "That took you long enough."

"Sorry, I—"

A rapping at the back door drew her gaze.

Father stepped away from the desk. "I wasn't expecting any more deliveries today, were you?"

"No." Rosa shook her head. "But go on, I will pour the tea."

Humid air curled through the door as her father tended to the matter. Men's voices—her father's and another—wandered in as well, though too indistinct to decipher. The tangy scent of bergamot steamed up from the teapot as Rosa filled their cups and wondered what on earth the discussion might be about. Generally, a signature was the only requirement, not a full-blown conversation.

By the time she settled in a chair with her cup and book, Father peeked his head around the door. "Rosa, you'll want to see this, I think."

Intrigued by the twinkle in his eye, she ventured outside where her father stood next to a shiny black bicycle. This time a genuine smile lifted her lips. "Oh Father!" She ran her hand along the back fender. "Where did it come from?"

"The delivery receipt listed the buyer as anonymous, but we both know there are only two men in this town wealthy enough for such an extravagant donation. And I'm fairly certain Mr. Mallow would have delivered it himself."

Mother was dying. That much was certain. In minutes or hours. At worst, a painful lingering for another day. But she wouldn't last longer than that. James sat quietly by her bedside, helpless to stop her moaning and writhing. It was a horrifying sight, watching the bones grind beneath her translucent skin. Though he'd never had a close relationship with the woman—and in truth, as a young lad had longed for a normal mother who would love him more than herself—still. . .he would trade every penny of his family's wealth if only he knew how to cure her. And himself. God knew he did not look forward to suffering the same ignoble end—a dread he liked to think the great and blessed Saviour understood, for did He not sweat great drops of blood the night before being nailed to a cross?

Renfield's shuffling steps approached the door, drawing his attention. "Begging your pardon, sir, but Miss Edwards is here to see you."

James's lips twitched with a ghost of a smile. Rosa's quick mind had wasted no time in figuring out who *anonymous* was and putting that new bicycle to good use. He'd purchased it but this morning, just before the egg-and-rock pelting on the way to the apothecary.

Rising, he speared Nurse Agatha with a sharp gaze where she sat on the other side of Mother's bed. "Under no circumstances are you to leave Lady Dorina unattended. Is that quite clear?"

"It is." She lifted her nose, her wrinkly jowls swinging above her starched collar. "Though I cannot vouch the same for tomorrow. I'll most likely be leaving for my sister's at Robin Hood's Bay."

He didn't roll his eyes at her bluff—because it wasn't one. She would indeed be packing up her steel grey gown and white apron. Mother would have no more use of an attendant.

An odd mix of grief and relief weighted his steps as he strode to the sitting room. It seemed wrong to feel such a strong sense of respite to leave his mother's side, to look forward to seeing Rosa's beautiful face. And yet warring with that sense was a burning need to be in his mother's bedchamber for her final breath—which won out and upped his pace. Like it or not, he'd have to cut this meeting short.

"Miss. . ." Rosa's name languished on his tongue as he scanned the empty sitting room. Surely she hadn't already left. He glanced back out into the hall, but what was he thinking? She wouldn't be there. She loathed Mother's gargoyle, though she'd never admit it aloud.

"Renfield!" he called, but who knew if the old fellow would hear him? Bah! He didn't have time for this. He rang the bell next to the sitting room hearth. The old fellow needed to leave service yet also needed some kind of gainful employ to keep busy. James took to pacing the rug, mulling over just how to bring that about before setting sail on the next ship to Transylvania.

"You rang, sir?"

Renfield's voice put an end to his route on the rug. "Where is Miss Edwards?"

The old butler's wiry eyebrows welded into a solid line. "Miss. . . ? Oh! I neglected to say she would be waiting for you outside, sir."

"Yes, you did," he snapped, then immediately repented. Renfield didn't deserve such harshness for a simple mistake. Lord knows he made enough. "Pardon me, Renfield. It has been a trying day."

Renfield's shoulders hunched. "No offense taken, sir."

Bypassing the man, James stalked to the front door, pleased to see clouds covering the late afternoon sky. At least he'd not have to waste minutes retrieving his hat, sunglasses, gloves and the like.

Off to the side of the walkway, Rosa sat on a bench with the new bicycle leaning against the wrought-iron arm. Even without sunshine, her burnished hair gleamed beneath her bonnet. Her lavender gown followed every curve, creating a vision so lovely it actually pained him, but as he'd told her at their last meeting, he was not—*could* not—be the man for her.

And that hit him like a hammer to the gut.

A sheepish smile curved her lips. "Sir James, I. . .I know you weren't expecting me, but my father and I felt I should come at once to thank you for your kindness." Her grin grew as she ran her finger along the handlebars. "I thought you might like to see the new bicycle."

He stopped just short of the bench. "What makes you so certain I am deserving of such gratitude?"

"Are you not?"

Clever sprite. He wiped a flake of mud off the back fender. "Does it suit you?"

"It does." She grinned "Very much."

"Good. Then I suggest you try to keep this one out of the river."

She pressed her hand to her heart. "I vow to do my utmost to prevent another such catastrophe."

Stars above! But she was adorable with that fierce gleam in her eyes and the little upturn to her nose. He clenched his hands lest he lose all control and loosen her bonnet ribbon, take the pins from her hair, and pull her close. It would be no effort at all to get lost in her scent, fresh as an April morning, and kiss her until neither of them could breathe.

A shriek—albeit muffled—jerked him back to reality.

Rosa's gaze lifted to his mother's window. "Was that. . . ?

"Indeed." He sighed. "My mother shall not live much longer, I am afraid. Today. Tonight. Tomorrow at the latest."

"Oh James, I am so sorry," she whispered, then faced him with a surprising determination in the set of her jaw. "But I might have something to help you, I mean to help your mother, that is." She pulled some folded pages from her pocket and handed them over.

He glanced at the words, too stunned to actually digest them. "You read Latin?"

"No. But one of the words looked like something you had said. I thought it might be information about the disease your family suffers. Is it?"

He scanned the text. The material on the first page was nothing new to him, but that last paragraph on the second—now that might be something he could use. He snapped his gaze to Rosa. "Where did you find this?"

"In one of the library's rare books, one I had never noticed before or I would have copied it down sooner. I hope you can read my abysmal writing." She clenched her hands in front of her. "I would have done it in shorthand, but even if I understood Latin, I am newly proficient at transcribing English let alone a foreign language."

"You did a fine job. It appears I am the one who owes you some gratitude. Thank you."

"No need. I am far more in your debt than you are in mine. I pray those notes are beneficial. So go." She waved her fingers towards the house. "Work your magic."

With a quick dip of his head, he dashed towards the door. There was no time to waste.

TWENTY-THREE

Then, as he is criminal, he is selfish; and as his intellect is small and his action is based on selfishness, he confines himself to one purpose. That purpose is remorseless.

Outside the library window, the morning call of a skylark trilled loud enough to be heard through the glass. The sweet sound usually brightened Rosa's spirits. Today, however, she frowned as she pulled the last book from a shelf to finish Mr. Holmwood's order. The pained look in James's eyes yesterday still haunted her, and once again she peered out the window, gaze drawn to the hulking manor on the hill. Her heart ached for him, for the grief that had thickened his voice when he'd spoken of his mother. For the grief that was yet to come. Had the notes helped him find something to relieve her suffering or—God willing—to even cure her?

Or was Lady Dorina even now drawing her final breath?

Returning to the counter, Rosa added the book to the small stack, inadvertently bumping the service bell with her elbow. A shrill ding-clunk cut through the air as the thing crashed to the floor, blending with the jingle of the door chimes—neither of which drew so much as a glance from her father. He bent over the newest publishing catalogue as if it were a shrine and he a faithful saint.

Rosa scooped up the bell then inwardly cringed as she faced the primped peacock strutting through the door in a perfectly tailored suit.

Albin Mallow homed in on her like a falcon to the kill, stopping close enough that breathing would be difficult, so thick was his cologne. "You look exceedingly lovely today, Rosa."

Her name on his lips was a defilement. Retreating a step, she forced a smile, though it likely looked more of a grimace. "How may I help you, Mr. Mallow?"

"By calling me Albin and taking a stroll with me." He proffered his arm with a flourish.

She ground her teeth. Would the man never give up?

"I am sorry, but Mr. Holmwood is expecting this load of books." She patted the stack then raised her voice loud enough to wake the dead. "I dare not disappoint a patron, right, Father?"

"Hmm?" He didn't look up, but at least he'd answered.

"I was telling Mr. Mallow about these books." She picked up the stack several inches then dropped it with a loud thwunk against the counter. "You know, Mr. Holmwood's delivery?"

"Holmwood?" He finally glanced at her over the rim of his spectacles. "Oh yes. I completely forgot to tell you he cancelled his order. His daughter gave birth, and he went to see his new grandson over in Sneaton. He won't be back for at least a week."

"There you have it. Problem solved." Albin wiggled his arm.

She gestured to a large bin. "But I really should see to the reshelves, is that not so, Father?"

Too late. He already refocused on his blessed catalogue so that he couldn't see the pleading in her eyes.

"Reshelves are finished," he murmured.

Drat. She bit her lip, thinking hard. "The old titles, then. If you are expecting to purchase new books, I ought to weed out those we plan on retiring to free up shelving space."

"I did it yesterday."

Albin arched one of his thin brows at her. "Out of excuses yet?"

She glowered. "Father, about that book cover I was regluing, do you not think—"

"Rosa, please." Her father glared at her from the opposite end of the counter. "All your nattering is distracting. Could you and Mr. Mallow take your conversation outside?"

"But—"

"Now."

Albin angled his head, his arm practically touching hers.

Well. That hadn't gone as planned. Thoroughly annoyed, she bypassed Albin and marched to the door. "This will be a short stroll, Mr. Mallow," she called over her shoulder. "*Very* short."

He caught up to her on the pavement. "Then allow me to come quickly to my point."

"Please do."

The morning air did nothing to diminish the overpowering waft of his sickening cologne. She faced away from him, breathing through her mouth.

He cleared his throat. "I have been courting you for over a month now, my dear, and thought you should know that these days have been the happiest of my life."

She snapped her gaze back to him. What sort of delusional world did the man live in? "I would not call it courting, Mr. Mallow. I would not call it anything other than you trying to coerce me into some sort of relationship by sending me flowers and chocolates."

"Oh, but there you are wrong." He planted her hand firmly on his sleeve. "Do not forget the poems I have written."

She nearly tripped on a cobblestone. How could she possibly forget the embarrassing lines he had delivered on a regular basis? Just thinking of the syrupy words set her teeth on edge.

"The truth is, Rosa"—his voice dipped to a husky tone—"you have come to mean the world to me."

She yanked back her hand, itching to stop up her ears. "I have given you no cause to say such a thing, sir."

"Your very being gives me cause. Everything about you is perfection." Leaning close, he sniffed her hair.

This was getting ridiculous. Across the lane, two women craned their necks, clearly interested in the spectacle of Albin's making. Rosa pivoted, ending the stroll before it had hardly begun. "I will not listen to such things, Mr. Mallow. Please excuse me."

He pulled her back. "I do not think you fully grasp how marvelous we could be together. Unstoppable, really. We could own this town."

"I do not wish to own this town or any other, nor do I give a fig about your wealth." She wriggled.

He held tight. "But you do have wishes, I know you do, and I am the one who can give you that happily-ever-after. You would never know need or want again as my wife. So, what do you say?" His touch grazed down her arm, his fingers entwining with hers as he dropped to one knee. The overlarge ring on his pinky cut into her flesh. "Will you marry me, Rosa?"

The women across the lane tittered. This would be all over town in a matter of minutes.

Instant heat flamed in Rosa's belly. She tried to yank away, but he held on all the tighter.

"Get up, Mr. Mallow. Get up this instant."

"I will not." The mole at the side of his mouth taunted her as he pursed his lips. "Not until I have your answer, my love."

"I refuse to answer unless you get up this very minute!"

He gasped. "Truly?" A huge grin spread across his face as he shot to his feet and pulled her into an embrace. "You have made me the happiest man in all of Whitby." His lips sought hers.

Spectators or not, Rosa wrenched away and slapped him with an open palm. "How dare you!"

Albin rubbed his jaw, murder in his eyes. No longer a loving suitor, he transformed into a scarlet-faced dragon, his breath coming in hot puffs. "You little vixen."

His fingers dug into the soft flesh of her arms as he manhandled her around the side of a building and shoved her into the crevice between the shoemaker and the bakery.

"You are hurting me." Her heart beat hard against her ribs. Until now, she'd never realized just how much bigger he was than her, with his body pinning hers against a brick wall. Nor had she imagined the strength in those soft hands of his.

"Pish! You have no idea what it means to hurt." His face twisted into an ugly scowl, though mercifully his grip on her eased. "To face over and over again bullies who wouldn't stop kicking, punching, grinding your face into the dirt. To receive jeering laughter because you cried out for mercy. To feel the strike of a hot poker because you were a disappointment. That's *real* pain."

Rosa swallowed hard as horror—then pity—eclipsed her fear and fury. What had Albin endured growing up? What evils yet drew blood from this man-boy? Suddenly many things made sense about him, even his unrelenting pursuit of her. She lifted her chin. "I am sorry to hear you were treated so horribly. Truly, such abuse is unconscionable. Yet despite your awful past, that gives you no leave to behave so cruelly in the present."

Tears shimmered in his eyes. "I swear I mean no harm to you, but do you not see? This is the one thing I can't fail at. You are meant for me. We were meant to be together." He rubbed his cheek against hers, the stubble of his side whiskers scraping her skin. "I need you, Rosa. Please say yes."

She wrenched her head aside, a momentary relief but not permanent. There was no escaping this. He outweighed her and blocked the exit. She'd have to try a different tactic, but what? So much fear choked her she could barely breathe.

Wait a minute.

Fear?

She could use that. *Albin's* fear.

"You do not need me. What you need is to reconsider your actions. How long do you think it will be before those women come peering around that corner?" She tipped her head towards the opening, desperately trying to still her trembling. "They have got more than enough fodder to spread this scene around town, but if you do not leave me at once, I will scream and give them even more to laugh about. Yes, that is right. Laugh! About you, the man who gave his heart publicly to a woman who would not have him."

A momentary panic flared in his eyes. Then an abnormal calm eased the lines on his face. "You've been bewitched, Rosa, by a man who is not all he seems to be. But not for much longer, I will see to that."

A man who is not all he seems to be—James? Rosa's breath caught in her throat. "Leave him be, Albin. The poor man suffers enough with his mother about to die. He may even be grieving this very moment."

"Is that so?" Tipping his chin, Albin looked down his nose at her. "Perfect timing, then."

He pivoted, striding away with as much speed as he'd employed when hauling her into this alcove. His shoes kicked up gravel, leaving her alone in a cloud of dust and nauseating cologne. A sickening feeling grew in her belly.

Just what did he intend?

Death eventually comes for all, but even in the knowing, it was still a shock when the grim reaper stalked through the door and grabbed Mother by the hand. With a heavy heart, James tucked her cold grey arm beneath the white sheet, trying to be thankful she was finally at peace. But was she really? Of all her cries before her last breath, not one of them had been for God to help her. He could only hope she'd done so inwardly. But judging by the gaping, twisted mouth and look of horror frozen on her face, that hope was small indeed.

On the other side of the bed, Nurse Agatha brushed her fingers against his mother's eyes, closing the lids, then straightened. "She's gone." Her voice was hollow, completely devoid of her usual mannish confidence.

"It appears so." A surprising coldness settled into his bones with the finality of it all. He scrubbed his hand over his face, stubble rasping audibly. When was the last time he'd shaved? And why the deuce did he think of such a trivial thing now?

He dropped his hand and peered over at Nurse. "You will find an envelope with your name written on the front atop the bureau in the hall. I trust the payment for your services will be more than sufficient. And with that, you are free to leave."

"I…em…" She wrung her hands—a sight as stunning as the lifeless shell on the bed. "I am sorry for your loss, Sir James. Your mother were a hard woman but… Well, she were still your mother." Tears glistened in her eyes.

James swallowed a sudden swell of emotion, and it took him several tries simply to eke out a thank you.

The nurse smoothed her palms along her white apron—or what had been white, soiled now with stains of bodily fluids from last night's battle against death.

"I'll be off to my sister's, I suppose. God bless ye, Sir James." She nodded, then hurried out of the room, skirts swirling as if a hound of hell nipped at her heels.

And just like that, he was alone with nothing but the steady *tick-tock* of the mantel clock and the sound of his own beating heart. Both seemed a mockery of the death in front of him. He really ought to straighten his mother's body before rigor mortis set in and froze her in the claw-handed, twisted leg position from which she'd drawn her last breath. She looked like a monster lying there, but no wonder. What a fight it had been. Inhuman, really, the way she'd gasped for air during her final moments, desperate to fill lungs that had already stopped working.

He scowled at the nightstand, at the suctioning bulb, the syringes, the bottles of remedies he'd thrown together in a frenzy to save her. They'd all failed.

He'd failed!

With a mighty roar, he backhanded the lot of it. Glass crashed. Liquid splashed. So be it. It was an aberrant pleasure watching the amber liquids drip, drip, drip down the wall and soak into the rug. He stood there a good long time, strangely mesmerized by the mess, until, weary beyond measure, he collapsed into his chair and dropped his head into his hands. So much for trying to play God. He should have known better than to tamper with days that were sovereignly numbered. His were already counting down and there was nothing he could do to stop them. He knew that now. Oh, how well he knew it.

God, grant Your pardon and mercy. Whatever is to become of me, I fully surrender to You.

Footsteps shuffled outside the door, stopping at the threshold. "Sorry to bother you, sir, but there is someone to see you in the sitting room."

"Not now, Renfield. I am not fit company." He blew out a long breath. "Tell Miss Edwards I am no longer in need of any books. I am no longer in need of anything."

"It is not Miss Edwards, sir. There are several men...several lawmen, I should say."

"Police? Did they say why they are here?"

Renfield shook his head. "I asked their business, sir, but they are insistent they will only speak with you."

Thunderation. Of all the worst timing. Sala had written in his most recent letter that the baron had filed a lawsuit against him, but how could his greedy neighbour possibly have managed to bring the law in England against him as well? Vindictive jackanapes!

James shot to his feet and marched down the corridor, fury rising. He'd lost his mother. He would not lose her land, not without a fight.

"Officers." He nodded at the three heads in blue caps that turned his way as he strode through the sitting room door. "What is this about?"

A leather-faced constable stepped away from the other two, approaching him with a swagger that announced he was in charge—and James didn't like it one bit, not under his own roof.

"Sir James Morgan, I presume?"

"Yes," James clipped. "I am Sir James Morgan."

"Very good. I am Officer Murray. These"—he swept his hand towards the other two—"are Officers Thomas and Canon. We are here on official business and should like to see your mother. Immediately."

"My mother?" James repeated Murray's words, but they still made no sense. His mother had received no callers these past fifteen years, so it was more than ludicrous to entertain some now—and constables at that. He cocked his head. "What sort of cruel jest is this?"

"No jest at all, sir." Murray tapped the truncheon hanging from his belt, his sausage-like fingers making a point. "I merely need to confirm your mother is alive and well."

James folded his arms, refusing to be bullied by the man. "She is not."

Murray narrowed his eyes. "She is not alive, or she is not well?"

"If you must know, my mother died within the past hour, and I will thank you to leave me to my grief." He reached for the bell pull. "And now if you will excuse me, my butler will be here shortly to see you out."

Officer Murray sidestepped, blocking his escape from the room. "I'm afraid it's not as simple as all that, Sir James. While I am sorry to hear of Lady Dorina's passing, if that is truly the case, I still need to corroborate the information. It is a delicate situation, I realize, but I must insist you take me and my colleagues to her at once."

"I will not." James's hands curled into fists. "And furthermore, I should like you to leave my house immediately."

"You are not above the law, sir. I was hoping we could conduct this matter in a civilized fashion."

He clenched his fists so hard his arms shook. "Do you presume to threaten me beneath my own roof, Officer Murray?"

"No threat at all, sir. The thing is we will see Lady Dorina with or without your cooperation." He tipped his head at the other two officers, who immediately stepped up to flank James. "So, what is it to be?"

Bah!

"Fine. This way." He shoved past Murray, setting a breakneck speed. It was perverse, taking such pleasure in pounding his heels, desecrating the sanctity of what should be a time of solemn quiet. He made it to his mother's room before the officers cleared the landing.

Pushing open the door, he stood silently, waiting for the men to file past him, then followed.

The shortest officer gasped the moment he faced the bed. "Lord, have mercy."

"It's true." The other officer faced Murray, disgust carved into the lines of his face. "He killed her all right. Jus' look at 'er face."

James frowned. What was this? "Someone had better tell me what is going on."

Murray nodded sharply at the other two. Canon pulled out his truncheon, Thomas a pair of handcuffs.

Officer Murray stared down his nose at James. "You, Sir James Morgan, are under arrest for the premeditated and willful murder of your mother, the Lady Dorina."

TWENTY-FOUR

Oh, how we are beset! How are all the powers of the devils against us!

Of all the grisly ways James imagined dying, never once had he considered a fast drop from a short rope. Yet were he to be found guilty of the absurd accusation made against him, he would hang. . . that is, unless the mob pelting the prison cart with rocks and all manner of refuse got ahold of him first. Then he'd be ripped to shreds.

"Tol' ye he'd move from livestock ta humans," a gruff voice hollered outside. " 'Twas only a matter o' time once the taste o' blood takes hold."

James gritted his teeth as a fist banged against the wall near his head.

"I heard he turn't on 'is own mother, the devil!"

A rock flew through the bars on the back door. He jerked his head aside, the projectile whizzing past his ear and nicking the wood with a crack.

"Heard 'e drained her dry. Not a lick o' blood left in the ol' witch."

The entire carriage rocked as something heavy slammed against the side. James teetered on the rough wooden bench, struggling for balance. With his wrists shackled behind his back, the best he could do was wedge himself into the corner and plant his feet wide.

"Back it off, now!" Officer Murray's voice melded with the snap of a whip. "Justice will be done."

"The only justice that monster deserves is a stake thru 'is black heart!"

James closed his eyes, wishing he could as easily stop up his ears. Was his accuser amongst that mob? And who was he? Unless it wasn't a he but a she.

He grimaced. No. That couldn't be.

The cart made a sharp left turn and shortly thereafter lurched to a stop. A man's bearded face appeared in the window, his arms stretching through the bars, his face twisted with hatred. "Git o'er here, ye daemon! I'll choke th' life right out o' ye."

Boots thudded on the cobbles. The whip cracked again. The bearded man's face contorted with a howl, and he dropped away.

"Get yourselves to the other side of the street or I'll have you all arrested!" Murray bellowed.

The slurs continued, but at least they quieted somewhat as the crowd shuffled away. The shorter officer—Thomas—jingled some keys and eventually swung open the door. "Out," he ordered.

James ducked through the door, pausing to scan the situation. Across the lane, twenty or so men shook fists at him. Several more rocks flew. If he jumped now and that mob rushed the three officers to get at him, there'd be no way he could fight back.

"Hurry it up." Officer Canon yanked him down.

He landed wrong. His knee buckled. James plummeted forward, unable to break his fall. His chin hit first, his chest next, knocking the wind from him. The mob roared jubilantly.

Canon hauled him up as he fought for air, and once he could finally breathe, he turned aside and spat blood. His teeth had punctured his tongue.

"Lookie that!" one man yelled. "He's full as a tick after 'is last feeding! Why, that's 'is mother's blood, no doubt."

Murray nudged him in the shoulder with the butt of the whip. "They won't hold for long. Move it, now."

Officer Thomas led the way to the front door of the redbrick police station. Once inside, they bypassed a frosted glass door with the word *Superintendent* painted in gold ink and stopped at a big desk with a tall man sitting behind it. The sergeant stripes on the officer's arm didn't even make it halfway around his bicep. He was a blob of fat and muscle, all folds and layers, his flesh in need of a good ironing. His dark eyes skimmed over James, then his gaze shot to Murray. "He give you any trouble?"

Murray opened his mouth.

James beat him to the punch. "Tell me, Sergeant, what sort of trouble would you expect me to give trussed up like a Christmas goose? I demand these cuffs be taken off. Furthermore, I demand to know my accuser and the grounds for the basis of my arrest. And I demand a solicitor at once!"

"Well, well." The sergeant sucked his teeth, his tongue making a hump in his cheek as if searching for a leftover piece of pork from his lunch. "You're just full of demands, eh baronet? But you're not in your fine manor home up on the hill now, are you, Sir James?" His thick brows pulled into a severe line. "And I am not your servant."

Though it hurt, James lifted his chin, furious beyond measure. "You are a public *servant*, are you not, sworn to carry out your duties? As a citizen of England, you owe me an explanation for dragging me down here."

The sergeant cast his gaze sidelong at Thomas and Canon. "Listen to that, boys. This gent is telling me how to do my job." A great belly laugh rumbled out of him, the other officers joining in to make it quite an ear-ringing chorus in the small room.

Their mockery dug in with claws. Though he was innocent, well did he know the malice of men, how injustices happened every minute of every day.

The sergeant's grin faded as he leaned back in his chair, the wood creaking ominously beneath his great girth. "Citizen or not, I owe a murderer nothing but room and board until execution, and that is what you shall have."

James shook his head. "I am no murderer."

"There's a body in his manor that says otherwise, Sergeant Carfax." Murray tipped his head towards the other officers. "We saw it, did we not, fellows?"

"Aye," Canon agreed. "And it were a god-awful sight."

"We got there just in time too," Thomas chimed in. "Tried to destroy the evidence, he did. Broken bottles. Needles on the floor. He poisoned her, all right."

Idiots. James clenched his jaw, then grimaced from the resulting sharp pain in his chin. "What you saw were medications. I was trying to help my mother, not harm her. Anyone who says otherwise is a liar."

"That's what they all say." The sergeant snorted like a bull, little flecks of moisture hitting the paperwork on the desk. "And I haven't the time nor inclination to listen to a criminal's flimsy alibi. You, Sir James Morgan, are accused of murdering your mother, the Lady Dorina, the details of which will come to light at the assizes. Empty his pockets, boys."

"No!" He wrenched from Canon's grip—only to crash into Murray, who immediately drove a fist to his gut.

Once again fighting for breath, James doubled over as fingers dug into his arms, holding him in place. Another set of fingers groped his pockets, pulling out naught but a fob watch.

Carfax humphed as he jotted down James's full name and single possession into a ledger. "I've seen drunkards with more trinkets than this. Lock him up, Thomas."

James struggled as Thomas frog-marched him around the desk and through a door behind it into the cell block. More like hell, really, so thick were the shadows and putrid the stench. They passed one cell where curses flew out like bats from a cave. The next was empty with its door closed, and the last gaped open like the maw of an abyss, which is where they stopped.

"Hold on." Behind him keys jingled again. The cuffs fell away, but before he could relish the blessed relief, Thomas shoved him in.

James pitched forward as the door slammed shut, the sharp clank of it like a cleaver to the skull. He barely regained his footing before smashing into the opposite wall. And no wonder. The space was only five—maybe six—paces one way and the other. A bench lined one wall and a bucket sat in the corner. This place wasn't fit for a dog let alone a man. Rubbing the raw skin on his wrists, he scowled, suddenly understanding how a caged lion felt. He didn't belong here! He'd done nothing but try to save a woman who never loved him.

Wheeling about, he faced Thomas. "Who claimed I killed my mother? Who put me in here?"

"I can't rightly say. I didn't take the report, but I thought I heard it were a woman." He turned the key in the lock.

His blood ran cold. Only Nurse Agatha or Rosa knew about his mother.

"A name." He gripped the bars. "Did you hear a name as well?"

"Some sort o' flowery name," Thomas mumbled as he secured the key ring to his belt. "Lily? Marigold? Nah, that ain't right. I dunno. Like I said, I weren't part of the conversation. I reckon you'll find out soon enough, though, when you face the judge."

Thomas strode away, keys jingling at his side, completely oblivious to the white-hot fury igniting in James's gut.

With a wild cry, he slammed his fists against the wall, over and over, barely registering the flesh tearing from his knuckles until blood stained the bricks. With a last primal growl, he sank to the cold floor and dropped his head back against the damp wall.

Thoroughly spent.

Thoroughly gutted.

Surprisingly numb.

Just like all those years ago when he'd naively trusted a crippled daughter and her father, here he was, betrayed.

Again.

She was a fraud of the worst sort. It was that simple. Rosa smoothed out wrinkles in the cloth thick with paste water as she tried to fix the cover ruined by Mr. Braithwaite's dog. Here she was, trying to restore an ordinary title ruined by someone else when she'd done worse by losing a rare one. But it was better to anguish over how to tell Father about her blunder than give in to the fury that simmered under her skin from her earlier encounter with Albin. Bewitched indeed. Should she even now fly out the door to pedal as fast as she could to warn James that Albin might be up to no good?

"Say, Rosa." Father swung into the back room, book in hand. "You don't by any chance have the first edition of *The Accounts of Principalities of Wallachia and Moldavia* with you, do you? I'm looking for a cross-reference to verify some of the information in this one." He waved a book in the air.

Stepping away from the worktable, she smoothed her palms along her apron. This was it. The moment of her disgrace. "No, I. . ." Her tongue quit working, the traitor.

"That's strange." Father rubbed the nape of his neck, lips pursing. "I can't seem to find it. Must've gotten reshelved in the wrong place, I suppose." Shoving his spectacles up the bridge of his nose, he turned to go.

Rosa pressed a hand to her belly, fighting a sudden queasiness. It was now or never. "Um, about that book, Father."

He glanced back. "Yes?"

"I. . .well. I have been meaning to tell you that I am afraid I lost it."

He wheeled about, yanking his spectacles completely off his face. He blinked a few times as if blinded by her confession. "You what?"

She swallowed. Hard. "I lost it."

His knuckles whitened on the book in his hand, the fabric on his sleeve shaking. "How did you manage to lose a book that's not to ever leave these walls?"

She gripped the table behind her, seeking support. "I took it out of the building, Father. I know I should not have, but I did."

"Well, then retrace your steps immediately and get it back!" he boomed.

"I cannot." Her voice sounded impossibly small even to her own ears. "I had it in the bicycle basket, the one that I also unfortunately lost."

Dark red spread up his neck like a thermometer about to burst. "Do not tell me that book has been washed out to sea."

Oh, how she wished with all her heart she didn't have to tell him any such thing. Why had she been so reckless?

"I cannot be sure that is where it has gone, but in all likelihood. . .yes." Ever so gently, she placed her hand on his sleeve. "Father, I swear I will repay the loss. You can dock my pay until the full amount has been reimbursed."

He stared at her fingers, refusing to make eye contact—and that cut more deeply than anything he could possibly say. "It's not just about the money, Rosa. You know as well as I that it was a rare book and, as such, cannot be replaced. I am deeply disappointed with you. You should have known better."

He vanished into the big room, leaving her behind with a regret so powerful she yanked out her handkerchief and dabbed her eyes. It hurt to let down a loved one. It hurt even more to know she'd damaged his trust in her. Sniffling, she stood there for a long while, cataloguing her many shortcomings over the past month and resolving to make wiser choices in the future, to be less reckless, and above all to be less deceitful.

Oh, how easy it had been to stray from the narrow path.

The doorbell jingled, putting a pause to her time of remorse.

She shoved her handkerchief into her pocket, drew in a last shaky breath, then marched into the front room with a confidence she didn't feel. "I will see to the customer, Father."

She didn't dare look over at the rare book section, but even so, she could see from the corner of her eye the way her father stood in front of the shelves, shoulders slumped.

A man swooped in, jittery as a sand martin, rubbing his shoulder like a broken wing.

Stepping behind the counter, Rosa forced a pleasant smile. "How may I help you, sir?"

"I've a note here for Mr. Edwards." He winced as he pulled a folded paper from the satchel strapped across his chest. Was the thing so heavy that it pained him?

"Thank you." Rosa reached for the note. "I shall see that he gets it."

He snatched it back. "Sorry, miss. I was told to put it in his own hand."

"Very well." She retraced her route, her heart breaking as Father glanced at her coldly. Of course he was angry. He had every right to be.

But that didn't make it any easier to bear.

She dipped her head. "There is a man here with a note for you, Father."

A long sigh heaved out of him. "Very well." He pivoted away from the bookshelf. "I am Mr. Edwards," he said as he approached the man.

"Then this is for you, sir." He held out the paper.

"Thank you." Father plucked the note from his fingers and sank onto the stool.

Mission accomplished, the man went back to rubbing his shoulder and darted a glance at Rosa. "Would ye have a liniment for sale that might ease a body's achin'?"

"Yes, third bottle on the left at the bottom, just over there." She pointed at her mother's medicinals on the shelves near the window. "Shall I get one for you?"

"No need. It's not my feet what are hurtin'." He winked and darted across the room.

"Blast it!" Father grumbled from his perch, then speared her with a sharp look. "What on earth did you say to young Mallow?"

"What?" She scrunched her nose. "Why?"

"Preston Mallow's pulled his patronage." He shook the paper at her. "First the loss of an expensive book. Now this. Do you have any idea how much money you've cost my business today?"

Her stomach sank. Apparently Albin had gone home crying to his uncle. "I am sorry, Father. The thing is that Mr. Mallow treated me very poorly, in word and in deed."

"Did he hurt you?" A murderous undertone ran deep in her father's voice, one that spoke volumes of his love for her despite his anger about the loss of the rare book.

"No, thankfully." Which was good, for there was no telling what her father would have done had the man actually harmed her.

"Still, I am of a mind to go have a word with the young man." He slammed the paper onto the counter with a huff.

"Father, please." She touched his sleeve. "Do not trouble yourself. If we leave the situation alone, it will fade. Albin Mallow will move on to some other woman, and that will be the end of it."

"We can hope, but that man—those Mallows—don't tend to let things go so easily." He stood, his mouth pulling into a tight line. "I'll go look at the accounts and see what—if anything—can be done to right this loss."

She watched him walk away, the drag of his step an awful sight. What a perfectly horrible day.

"This the one, miss?" The messenger tapped the bottle on the counter.

"Yes." She pulled back her shoulders, hopefully looking more like the shopkeeper she ought to be. "That will be twelve pence, please."

"Hope this helps." He fished out the coins then once again rubbed his shoulder, grimacing as he tried to work out the sore muscle. "I din't realize throwin' a few rocks could tear up a body so."

"Perhaps you ought to take up reading instead," she murmured as she put the coins into the register.

The messenger laughed. "I'll leave that to my wife. Don't expect to have to toss any more stones now that the hubbub's died down."

"What hubbub?" She closed the drawer and looked up.

"Oh, din't hear, eh?" His face lit up. "I s'pose not, tucked away on this side o' town as you are. It were quite the ruckus, that mob a'followin' the Black Maria all the way from town's edge to the gaol."

"Hmm. Usually a criminal does not attract that much attention unless. . .aha. Did they finally catch who's been killing the livestock?"

He retrieved the bottle and tucked it into his bag, buckling it shut with a nod. "That they did, miss."

"Who is it?" She angled her head, eager to know who'd been responsible for kindling the vampire gossip into a wildfire. "Who was responsible?"

"Just as I suspected all along." He patted his bag as if the answer were sealed inside. "It were that blackguard livin' like a king atop the hill."

She gaped. "Surely you do not mean. . . ?" She couldn't even finish the sentence, so repulsive was the question.

"But I do mean, miss. It were the baronet, and ye'll be glad to know they got that vampire locked up tight. Why, I expect he'll be swinging from a rope in no time a'tall."

Rosa's heart stopped, the library suddenly quiet as a tomb.

No. God, no!

TWENTY-FIVE

The whole of life seems gone from me all at once,
and there is nothing in the wide world for me to live for.

Rosa had never stepped foot inside the Whitby jail before—or any other, for that matter—but it was much as she expected. A distinct air of degradation and body odour permeated the receiving room, and the stink wasn't helped much by the big officer sitting behind the desk eating what smelled to be a limburger sandwich. If her father knew she was here, he'd have her head.

Sergeant Carfax—were his nameplate to be trusted—pounded on his chest, his lips bulging with a held-in belch before asking, "Can I help you, miss?"

She folded her hands at her midriff, straightening to full height. "I should like to see Sir James Morgan, please."

He shook his head, loosening a freefall of crumbs from his beard. "I don't think that's advisable for a lady such as yourself. Wouldn't want you fallin' under his spell. I hear a vampire can suck you dry in a matter of minutes."

She gritted her teeth. "Sir James is not a vampire."

"Ahh." The sergeant narrowed his eyes. "Already bewitched you, has he?"

Bah! He'd never let her see James if he thought as much. She pulled a small book from her pocket, glad now she'd brought it along. Maybe this battle could be won with Scripture.

She set the book on the desk and flashed the officer her most beguiling smile. "I merely came to offer the poor soul a book from the library. You know, something to keep him occupied during his stay. I am certain you do not wish his mind to be concocting ways of escape. And who knows? This little psalter"—she tapped the cover—"may work a miracle."

"You're going to give a vampire God's Word?" He slapped his thigh. "That's a good one, that is. Well, go on, then, give it a go. Kingstead!" he hollered over his shoulder.

A man in a constable's uniform poked his head out of a door behind him. "Aye, Sergeant?"

"Escort this lady to the cell block and see that no harm befalls her."

"Aye, sir. This way, miss." He tipped his head towards the very door from which he'd appeared.

Rosa snatched up the book then followed Kingstead, stopping just inside a poorly lit area with cells lining each side.

He peered at her. "Which prisoner do you wish to see, miss?"

"Sir James Morgan, please."

His eyes widened. "I won't be opening that door, but yer welcome to speak to him through the bars. If he'll speak to ye, that is. He hasn't said a word since I locked him up yesterday. He's the last cell on the left."

"Thank you, Officer Kingstead. I should not be long." She gathered the hem of her skirt as she traversed the short passage. Something puddled on the floor, and she shuddered to think what the yellow liquid might be. The flicker of overhead lamps cast macabre shadows, making everything larger than life in a ghastly fashion.

She passed by the first cell, where an animalistic snore ripped out. She could only imagine what the brute inside sounded like when he was awake. Quietly, she hurried on and didn't stop until she reached the last cell.

Where her world tipped on its axis.

"Oh James," she whispered, grabbing hold of the bars.

The man who could command her world with a flash of his eyes now sat alone on a blistered bench, elbows on his long legs, hands hanging between. His dark hair fell forward, hiding his face as he stared at the floor, shoulders bowed by the weight of a despair he ought not be forced to carry. He was a husk. A shell. The mere outline of the space where once the magnificent baronet had lived and breathed.

Merciful heavens! This man did not belong here, locked away like a common criminal.

"What happened?" she said louder.

He didn't look, didn't move. Didn't breathe a word. He sat as immobile as the horrid gargoyle in his front hall, his silence as sharp as a smashed pane of glass. Was he even breathing?

"James, please. Talk to me." She gripped the bars until her knuckles whitened. "How can I help you?"

"You have already done enough, have you not?"

The coldness in his voice burrowed under her skin. Never before had he used such a frigid tone with her, and she was hard-pressed to figure out why he'd do so now. "But I have done nothing."

Despite her defense, he still wouldn't look at her. "Go away, Rosa."

His words were gravestones, each one marking the death of whatever fragile affection had been between them. She pressed her forehead against the cold iron, desperate to stop the tears flooding her eyes.

"I know this is hard." She swallowed against the tightness in her throat. "You are upset, which is to be expected. I. . .I have brought you something to read that will hopefully be of comfort." She poked the psalter through the bars, a gesture that garnered no reaction whatsoever.

So she crouched, about to push her offering beneath the cell door, then thought better of it. Sliding it through the nastiness on the stone floor would only ruin yet another library book. She wrapped the psalter in her handkerchief and shoved it under.

"I. . ." She frowned. What else was there to say? Clearly he didn't wish to speak to her. "I will pray for you, Sir James."

"Pray? For what?" Bitter laughter rumbled out, ugly in its mockery. "For me to burn in hell?"

He shot to his feet and flew to the bars, grabbing so tightly to the iron that the skin on his knuckles was practically translucent. "Why!" he shouted, his voice primal. "Why did you betray me?"

She couldn't breathe. Think. Move. Losing her father's trust was one thing, but this? This was unjustified and deadly, piercing her in ways from which she'd never recover.

"Back it off now, mate." Officer Kingstead struck fast and hard, the tip of his truncheon plunging through the bars and cracking against James's skull with a sickening thwack.

James stumbled back, the heel of his hand to the wound on his head.

Kingstead grabbed her arm. "Best we leave, miss."

"But I—no!" She wrenched away. "I am not finished." She glared at the man until he retreated several steps.

"Fine, but I'll be right here with my club. You hear that, Morgan?" He smacked the tip of it against the bars.

Rosa turned to James while the crack still reverberated. "I did not betray you. How could you think such a thing? I would never do anything to harm you."

With the back of his hand, he swiped away the trickle of blood oozing from his hairline, then flung it aside. "I have it on good authority that someone with the name of a flower put me in here, *Rosa*."

"But it was not me. I swear it!"

"Do you?" He stepped close again, one eye on the officer, the other on her.

"I know people have let you down in the past, but I have not—and will not—ever turn against you. I meant it, you know, when I told you I lo—" She clamped her lips tight lest she embarrass herself yet again. Could she never rein in her passions?

"Time's nearly up, miss," the officer threatened behind her.

Rosa stiffened. There was still so much to say and know. Who'd told him she'd betrayed him? How had he gotten the awful scrape on his chin? Was he hungry? Cold? How did his mother fare? A hundred other questions heaped atop that pile, but she shoved them aside, opting instead to put his mind at ease. "I am your friend, James. You can trust me."

"You have no idea how much I want to believe that." His gaze burned into hers, so forlorn her heart wrenched. "How much I *need* to believe."

"Then do."

Behind her, Officer Kingstead shuffled his feet. "All right. You've had your say, miss. Time to go."

No! How could she leave the only man she'd ever loved in this pit of despair? She grabbed the bars. "I will get you out of here. I do not know how, but I will—and then you shall know you can trust me."

James huffed a ragged sigh. "Whether you put me in here or not, I am a tainted man. Stay away, Rosa. Stay away from anything to do with me."

"None of that matters. I would do anything for you."

"Then let me go." His voice dropped an octave. "I will not be your ruination."

"You should listen to him, miss." Officer Kingstead grabbed her arm. "Now off we go."

Rosa stumbled after him, looking over her shoulder, unwilling to lose sight of James. How forsaken he was, standing there alone, trapped behind bars. Tears welled, and she dabbed them with her sleeve.

Officer Kingstead opened the heavy cell block door. "After you, miss."

She sniffled as she exited, leaving part of her heart locked away with James.

Sergeant Carfax eyed her approach, one of his big brows lifting. "Get brutish with you, did he, miss? I warned you I didn't think a visit would be advisable. Thank you, Kingstead. That will be all." He dismissed the man with a nod.

Drawing in a final shaky breath, Rosa straightened her shoulders. Now was not the time to play the part of a wilting flower. "What are the charges against Sir James?"

The sergeant reached for a stack of papers. "The baronet is accused—and confirmed—of murder. Now if that will be all, miss." He tapped the papers into order on his desk. "I've a mound of reports to get through."

Rosa held her ground. "But he did not kill any livestock. Sir James has nothing to do with sheep or goats."

"Didn't say he did." The sergeant met her gaze. "The baronet is indicted for murdering his mother."

"That is absurd! He was trying to cure her. I can vouch for that. I *will* vouch for that!"

"And my officers can vouch for the dead body of Lady Dorina."

Rosa pressed her hand to her mouth. Oh dear. His mother had died, then. Poor James. He ought to be home grieving in private, not locked in that stinking hole of a jail cell. No wonder he'd been so volatile. He must be half out of his mind. Why on earth would anyone think he'd killed her?

Then again, why wouldn't they? Everyone believed him to be a prince of darkness, even the sergeant reaching for a pencil in front of her, and sadly enough, it seemed now James believed so as well.

She stepped closer. "Lady Dorina was ill, Sergeant Carfax, struggling against a disease that Sir James was desperately trying to remedy. He did not murder her."

The big man tapped his pencil lead against the desktop a few times, then aimed it at her like a gun. "You'll swear to that?"

"I will."

He clicked his tongue. "Even so, won't do the blackguard any good. It's your word against the accuser's. You'd need another witness to swear the same as you."

Never one to back down from a challenge, she lifted her chin. "Well then, I shall find one. Good day, Sergeant Carfax."

She turned, then immediately whirled back. "I nearly forgot. The accuser. It is Albin Mallow, is it not?"

The sergeant lifted his pencil with a scowl, clearly annoyed she was still here. "I cannot say, miss. The person wishes to remain anonymous until the trial."

"And when might that be?"

"The assizes are in two days, though the judge ought to arrive tomorrow evening. It won't be soon enough for my liking, though. Housing a shape-shifting monster isn't what I signed up for. And with that I bid you good day." His big head dropped back to his pile of paperwork.

The information sank like bricks to her stomach as she made her way outside. She inhaled a lungful of fresh air the moment the door shut behind her. How awful for James to be stuck in that fetid place, not knowing whom to trust or even if he should trust. She had to help him, or at least try. After all, how many times had he come to her rescue? Surely his old butler Renfield could confirm her word or. . .no. She knew exactly who would be most believable!

Grabbing her hat with one hand, she hurried down the pavement, retracing her route to the library. A quick trip on the bicycle ought to put an end to this fiasco.

She sailed into the library at full speed, only to be stopped by two skirts. Lucy and Mother turned to the sound of the jingling bell, her sister immediately rushing over and hooking her arm through Rosa's. "Here you are, Sister. We were just about to tell Father the news, but you may as well hear too since it involves you."

"Me?" This couldn't be good.

Apparently Father didn't think so either. He sat behind the counter, arms folded. "Well, you'd better get on with your storytelling so Rosa and I can close the library in peace."

Mother fanned herself, her face flushed. It must be some news for her to endure such exertion. "As you know, Sir James Morgan, the man of whom we once entertained thoughts of a possible match for our own dear Rosa, has been arrested, but I have found out why. He is accused of murdering his own mother!" In two steps, she cupped Rosa's face with her gloved hands, the lace pressing into her cheeks. "Imagine if we'd allowed you to go through with an engagement to that man. Why, we'd all have been ruined."

Rosa wrenched away. "But it is not true! He did not kill his mother. He did not kill anyone."

Mother flailed her arms. "Regardless, you couldn't have possibly married a vampire, let alone one who is in jail. I've told you all along Albin Mallow is the man for you."

Lucy bobbed her head, her auburn curls bouncing her agreement. "Mother and I have discussed this thoroughly. We believe Mr. Mallow is your faery-tale match, Sister."

"Yes, well, she may have burned that bridge," Father said under his breath.

Mother jerked her head towards him. "What's that?"

"This is ridiculous." Rosa rounded the counter, choosing the safer side, where her father sat. "I do not love Albin Mallow. He is not a good man, and I will not have him. I told him as much yesterday."

Mother's small eyes popped two sizes larger. "You didn't!"

"Oh Rosa." Her sister shook her head. "How could you?"

"I am afraid this is all my fault," said Father.

They all turned to him, voices melding in a unified, "What?"

Huffing a long breath, her father rose and rested his hand on her shoulder. Sadness rippled in his eyes. "I should have confronted the man when you told me of his rough handling of you. Not only that, it is I who has done you a disservice by allowing you to work here, Daughter. The truth is your mother and sister are right. It is high time you marry. Settle down. Have children of your own. But that will never happen if you're tucked away amongst these bookshelves day in and day out. Though it pains me to say this, I must terminate your employment."

"Father, no! How can you say such a thing?"

"It's for your own good, Rosa."

She whirled away, biting her knuckle to keep from crying aloud. Not only had she lost the man she loved, she'd lost her wages, putting an end to all she'd worked for, an end to all her dreams.

And undeniably an end to any chance of a happy ending for her.

God is our refuge and strength,
A very present help in trouble.
Therefore we will not fear,
Even though the earth be removed,
And though the mountains be carried into the midst
of the sea;
Though its waters roar and be troubled,
Though the mountains shake with its swelling. . .

. . .though he sit in a stinking cage awaiting death. James slammed the cover shut on the psalter and leaned back against the wall, a disgusted sigh leaking out of him. It surely didn't seem as if God was present. And yet it probably didn't seem so to Paul the many times he'd been imprisoned, either, and that man still managed to sing praises when locked up.

James scrubbed his face with both hands as he paced. He didn't feel like singing, and God knew he was no saint like Paul. Still, what good was faith if it didn't get him through the hard times?

And this was definitely one of those.

He dropped his hands and lifted his face. *Very well, God. Have I not already learned You alone are the One to number my days? I will trust You in this, even if it kills me. Which it might. Be my strength, for I have none of my own.*

He pulled his collar tighter at the neck, which did no good. The chill of the damp space had long since seeped through the fabric and into his bones. It was a fruitless effort, but at least it gave him something to do other than recount the bricks in the wall, all one hundred seventy-two of them.

Or think of Rosa.

Blast! Too late. His mind fell into the well-worn groove of how lovely she'd looked in this forsaken abyss. Even now her sweet lilac scent lingered like a summer morn. How fierce had been the fire in her eyes and strength of her voice when she'd vowed she'd not been the one to betray him. And—God help him—he believed her. That left only one other woman who knew enough to have made the accusation that landed him here. Nurse Agatha. But there was nothing flowery about that name.

He sank onto the unforgiving bench, saddle-sore from having sat on the hard wood all day. Picking up the psalter, he rubbed his thumb over the embossing on the cover, a soothing action that did little to quell the throbbing in his temple. It didn't make sense that the nurse had turned him in. Oh, she'd blustered and blown about leaving her position every blessed day for the past two years, but never once had she threatened anything otherwise. Why would she wish to see him hang for a disease she knew very well he'd done nothing but try to remedy?

Unless. . .the officer hadn't heard correctly or been full of hogwash.

The heavy cell block door thwunked open, and even before bootsteps entered, the man two cells over shouted, "Get me outta here, Carfax. Ye can't leave me alone with a vampire. It's inhuman!"

"Is that so?" The sergeant's gruff voice bounced against the brick walls. "Finally figured out who your neighbour is, eh, Cheyne?"

"I heard you and Kingstead talkin'. It's my blood ye'll have on yer hands!"

Deep laughter rumbled. "Not if he drains you dry first."

Cheyne spat out a mouthful of curses, calling down all sorts of wrath upon the sergeant, his mother, and his dog. "Yer a heartless snake, ye know that? A pox on you, I say."

"Don't pin this on me. You're the one who should have thought twice before dipping your hand into old man Chatham's till. You've no one but yourself to blame for your predicament." Metal scraped against stone.

"There's your plate, so eat up. I hear a vampire likes a fat kill."

The bootsteps headed his way, and soon Sergeant Carfax came into view with a tin plate in hand and a noxious stench of garlic hanging about him like a thick fog.

"I've brought your supper, baronet, though it's likely not the fare you're used to." He slid the plate under the door with a smirk. "No blood."

James glanced at the plate. A grey mound heaped in the middle with lumpy brown gravy oozing down its sides. His stomach turned. He'd rather eat rat meat than force that thick slop down his throat.

"No thank you." He shoved it back with the toe of his shoe. "How long do you intend to hold me here?"

The sergeant whipped out his truncheon. "Step it back, Morgan. You're too close to the door."

The bump on his head from earlier throbbed, and he retreated several steps. "You did not answer my question."

"You shouldn't be here long. The assizes are in two days, so you ought to meet a quick end. Quite the blessing for a monster such as you." He yanked out a white lump from his pocket and began rubbing it along the length of the bars. Garlic. The stink of which infused the small area with eye-watering strength.

James snorted. "Do you really think that would stop a vampire?"

Fear flashed in the sergeant's eyes, then as quickly, confidence hardened his jaw. "Guess we'll find out now, eh? Leastwise Cheyne will."

"I heard that!" Cheyne yelled.

James rolled his eyes. "Listen, Carfax. If I am to go before a judge in two days, it is my legal right to meet with a solicitor beforehand."

"I'm working on it. It's not easy finding someone to represent a fiend." He pocketed the leftover remains of the smashed garlic. "But don't worry, I'm sure one will be found eventually."

Sickened, James turned away. Indeed, one might be found, but no one of repute. What sort of dullard or greedy goblin would it be? No one trustworthy—he could bet on that—which left his only hope in Rosa's promise to find a way to free him. But could he trust her to do so, especially after how he'd treated her, warning her away like a snarling dog?

He collapsed onto the bench. Either he trusted Rosa or God would have to perform a miracle. . .and the two might very well be one and the same.

TWENTY-SIX

I am afraid to think of what may happen to us. We are truly in the hands of God.

It wasn't fair that the life of a man could hinge on the ankle of a carriage horse. Rosa ground her heels into the gravel on the road to Robin Hood's Bay. It seemed everything was against her today. Against James. Against all that was good and right and true.

Then again, she hadn't been very right and true. Guilt nipped her conscience as she paced the wheel rut. Maybe she should have told her mother she wasn't merely going to spend the afternoon with Mrs. Hawkins but had planned all along to take the older lady along with her to find Nurse Agatha Bilder. Was a lame horse a sign of God's retribution? She glanced at the guileless sky.

Oh God, do not turn your face away from James on account of my rash behaviour. Help him. Help me to help him. Work a miracle, Lord.

Mrs. Hawkins fanned herself on a rock next to the horseless carriage, eyeing her with pity. "Yer goin' ta go lame yerself, love, you keep workin' that ground like y' are."

Rosa flailed her hands. "What's taking that driver so long? He should have been back with a fresh horse by now."

"Frothin' yerself into a frenzy won't bring the man any faster." She patted the empty space on the boulder beside her.

"I know, I just wish. . ." The words languished on her tongue. Mrs. Hawkins simply didn't understand the enormity of it all or she'd be pacing too. Rosa had used the last of her funds—money that should have gone to finishing her correspondence course—to hire this claptrap of a carriage, and that after having wasted yesterday afternoon trekking up to Morgrave Manor only to find the nurse had departed the day before. And even now the sun mocked her, inching its way towards the western horizon. Time was running out. Oh, she simply must get to that nurse!

"Come now, Rosa dear. Rest yerself."

Rest? No, not until James was freed. Even so, she sank onto the rock next to the older lady.

"Good girl." Mrs. Hawkins patted her leg. "It will all work out, lass."

Rosa was tempted to push her hand away, resentful beyond reason at the haunting image of James standing forlorn in that damp, dark cell. "You cannot know that."

Her wizened face softened with a smile. "True, but I know the One who does know."

"There is a man's life on the line here, Mrs. Hawkins." She jumped back to her feet, one hand fisted on her hip and the other swinging wildly towards Robin Hood's Bay. "It is of the utmost importance we find that nurse to testify with me as soon as the judge arrives in town—and he arrives at seven o'clock tonight."

"I know yer fearful, child, but fear or not, all will be accomplished in God's timing, not yours. His will—and His goodness—cannot be thwarted."

"Well, I wish He would make haste." She dropped her hands, her head, her defenses. She sounded like a petulant tot. "Forgive my runaway tongue. It is just so hard to understand why a good man like James Morgan must suffer so much."

Mrs. Hawkins patted her arm. "Perhaps 'tis the sufferin' what's made him so good."

Rosa narrowed her eyes at the older lady. "That seems a cruel way to refine someone's character."

"Ach!" Mrs. Hawkins chuckled as she brushed some loose grey hairs away from her eyes. "Are you in the business of telling God how to manage His creatures, then?"

"No, but there ought to be a better way."

"You think you know better than God, lass?"

Once again conviction bit—harder this time. She plopped onto the rock and picked at a thread on her sleeve. "I suppose that does sound rather arrogant of me."

"Rosa, dear." Her gnarled hand pulled Rosa's from her nervous picking. "It is a mystery why some live life seemingly untouched by troubles while others can barely lift their head beneath the weight o' their sorrows. Not everything can be explained—nor should it be—else we would be like God, and that was Eve's downfall, was it not? Wanting to be like Him?"

Rosa looked out absently at the grassy tufts poking up in a nearby farmer's field. She'd tried so hard to get everyone else to believe there was a reason for everything. Yet could she really explain how James happened to be walking along the cliff when the bridge collapsed under her? Or how he distracted a raging bull with naught but a shirt? Much less the lantern-carrying man that guided her through the mist—for despite all her discreet inquiries, she had yet to discover anyone who had been out that way that night. Maybe, just maybe, not everything could be explained—leastwise on this side of heaven. But now that she thought on it. . .

She sucked in a sharp breath. Explainable or not, each of those occasions turned out to be for her good. What if all along it wasn't the circumstances she couldn't understand but God's all-encompassing goodness towards her and those that love Him?

Mrs. Hawkins squeezed her hand. "Ye can trust that God will grow each of His true children into His likeness in His own time *and* in His own way."

Rosa offered her a weak smile. "I suspect, Mrs. Hawkins, it will take a very long time before I ever resemble Him."

"Hah! Yer not as old as I am, lass. Apparently the good Lord is working overlong on me." She chuckled.

"I do not think that is the reason at all." Rosa leaned her head onto the older woman's shoulder. "I think you are an angel in disguise sent here to guide me."

"Stars and garters! Wouldn't ol' Mrs. Godalming take issue wi' that.

Callin' the likes o' me an angel." She hooted—just as the sound of hooves drew near.

Rosa stood, thankful to see the driver she'd hired arriving on a fresh horse.

He tipped his hat as he dismounted. "I'll have this one hooked up in no time, ladies. And I brought you a little something to tide you over."

"Thank you." Rosa peeked inside the small sack he offered, then smiled as she pulled out a piece of taffy and handed it to Mrs. Hawkins. "Looks like our sweet tooth will be very happy for the rest of the trip."

True to his word, the driver had them back on the road in a trice. Even so, it was teatime as they descended the steep drop into Robin Hood's Bay. The tiny town nestled amongst the cliffs, looking as if the houses wished to take a dive into the vast stretch of sea lapping at its edges. Dark history ran rich here, with its tales of wreckers and smugglers, and Rosa believed it. Amongst all the nooks and crannies of the crooked lanes, it was the perfect place to duck away from a revenue man hot on your heels.

The carriage stopped in front of an off-shooting road too narrow to enter.

"Out you go, ladies." The driver helped them down. "Here's Sunny Place. You should find number seventeen just a few doors up this passage. I'll be waiting down at the pub when yer ready to return to Whitby."

"Thank you." Rosa guided Mrs. Hawkins onto Sunny Place, which was a ridiculous misnomer the way the tall buildings leaned over one another. The only time sunlight could ever grace this thin throat of a passageway was at noon, and then likely only for a few minutes.

Rosa stopped in front of an ivy-covered home with a whitewashed door and banged the knocker.

Moments later, a mouse of a woman appeared. Her mobcap was as ruffly as the lace at her neck, both outdated by several decades but clearly prized by Mrs. Hawkins, whose eyes lit with admiration.

"Pardon us," Rosa began, "but I am looking for a Nurse Agatha Bilder. Is she here?"

The mousy woman scrunched her nose. Had she whiskers, they would have twitched. "She is not."

Rosa frowned. "But this is number seventeen Sunny Place?"

"It is."

"I have it on good authority that this is where she's come to stay."

"She has, but she's not here right now." The woman's small eyes darted between her and Mrs. Hawkins. "And you are?"

"I am Rosa Edwards, and this is my friend and companion, Mrs. Hawkins. Please madam"—she pleaded with her eyes—"it is of the utmost importance I speak to Nurse Bilder at once. Where might I find her?"

"I'm afraid my sister has gone to buy some new chickens from Farsyde Farm, but she should be back in an hour. Unless she gets to taking tea with Mrs. Farsyde. Then it'll be near to dark before she returns. Shall I tell her you called, or would you like to come in and wait for her? I was just about to take some tea myself, and you're welcome to join me."

Rosa bit her lip. What to do? Haul Mrs. Hawkins about to find this Farsyde Farm? Explain to Nurse Bilder's sister the dire situation and leave it to her to tell the woman once she returned home? Or ought she wait to plead in person? Every way would take time. . .time she didn't have. Time James didn't have. And yet perhaps now more than ever, it was time to put her own faith to the test. Trust God for wisdom, guidance, and most of all, rely on His goodness.

Even if she couldn't understand it.

Was this it, then? His last night on earth? James pressed his forehead against the cold bars of his jail cell, the metal unforgiving against his skin. He had no doubts whatsoever about how the trial would go in the morning, and his neck ached with the thought of the rough rope that would choke off his breath. At least he wouldn't suffer for months on end as his mother had. A small consolation, that.

He pushed against the iron until his head throbbed. Though he knew now that every beat of a heart was in God's hands alone—sweet-blessed mercy!—he wasn't ready to die. Not yet. He did not fear meeting his Maker, but what of Sala? Of Renfield? They'd never known a life without being in service to his family. How were they to manage? Oh, Sala would get by somehow, he supposed, but old Renfield was too advanced in age.

He'd end up in a poorhouse if he were lucky, the streets if he weren't. An ignoble end to such a faithful servant.

James closed his eyes, unwilling to face head-on the thought of the only other person he loved. Rosa. How quick he'd been to assume she'd betrayed him on naught but the hearsay of a constable. He'd lashed out blindly, fueled by ignorance and mistrust. . .just like the people of Whitby acted against him. He was no better. What a hypocrite he'd been!

Wheeling about, he stomped over to the hard bench. How pitiful that in all his thirty-two years, he had only three people who'd ever cared for him. And what did he expect? He'd been the one to cut himself off from the world, from the church, from life. He deserved no better. But what if. . . ? Ah, what if, indeed. Rosa had proven herself trustworthy and reliable in the past—even consistently defying his pleas to disassociate with him. So, what *if*, by the grace of God, she succeeded? He was freed?

Stretching out on the wood, he laced his fingers behind his head. He might not have been able to cure his mother and he might never find a cure for himself, but perhaps—just perhaps—God didn't mean for him to use the knowledge he'd gained only for himself. Maybe all along God had meant it to be of use to others. Maybe even the megrim powders he'd created and the salve he'd crafted for Renfield's knuckles were intended to be shared with the world. Perhaps, as the rector had said, he was an integral part of the body of Christ and ought to stop locking himself away from others. True, more often than not those in the church were quick to mistrust him without cause, yet had he not done the very same to Rosa?

He shifted on the unforgiving bench, eyes locking on the black iron bars. Deep down he suspected by withdrawing from church he'd missed out on much more than liturgies and sermons. He'd missed out on communion with his fellow man, the chance to love and be loved, the chance to forgive and be forgiven. Yes, indeed, if he ever had the opportunity, he would accept the rector's invitation and walk through St. Mary's doors.

A good resolve, but would he ever get the chance to act upon it?

It was to be expected a taproom would smell of ale and unwashed men, but the stench inside Black Horse Inn ought to win a trophy for its strength. Rosa tried not to breathe too deeply as she and the entourage she'd brought along—a motley crew of Nurse Bilder; the apothecary, Mr. Rawlings; and Renfield—approached the counter.

"Pardon me, but could you tell me where we might find Judge Westenra?"

The innkeeper—a squat little man with a purple nose—narrowed his eyes. "Is he expecting you?"

"No, but this is important."

The man sucked his teeth as he dried out the inside of a mug with a towel. "He don't like to be disturbed the night before a session."

"It cannot be helped. Please"—she pressed her palms on the countertop—"which room is he in?"

"I am not accustomed to give out such confidential information." He slammed down the mug, the accompanying scowl on his face fierce enough to wither wild heather.

"Listen here, Varna." Mr. Rawlings joined her side, his voice low and menacing. "Neither am I prone to revealing private matters such as your wife's recent purchases to manage a particular medical situation from which you may be suffering, but that would be personal information, unlike a room number."

"So, it's to be blackmail, is it?" The innkeeper—Varna, apparently—threw down his towel. "All right. Room number four, but don't go blaming me if the judge locks you all up for trespassing."

Despite the glower on the man's face, Rosa grinned. "Thank you!" She turned to Mr. Rawlings. "And thank you as well."

Indeed. She owed them all gratitude for leaving their homes at such a late hour, made all the later by first having to see Mrs. Hawkins safely home. Each one of them had willingly answered her plea, which in and of itself was a miracle. Why they'd do so merely because she'd asked them to was beyond explaining. It appeared there were a great deal of things, when inspected closer, that could not truly be explained, despite whatever rational reasons could be provided.

Heart hopeful—yet anxious—she wove her way among the mostly empty tables in the taproom and climbed the stairs, then strode the length of the corridor to number four. She hesitated before knocking.

"Are we all here?"

"Renfield needs a moment more." Nurse Bilder said from behind Mr. Rawlings. The man was so tall he all but blocked the woman from sight.

"Would you like me to greet the judge first in case he's in a sour mood?" he asked.

"How kind." She smiled. "But no. I got you into this situation, so it is only fair I bear the brunt of whatever mood the judge may be in."

Renfield shuffled down the passageway, waving his hand. "I'm here, Miss Edwards."

"Very good." She nodded. "And once again, I thank you all for showing your support for the baronet. Let us pray for a favorable meeting."

Heart hammering, she rapped on the door. For James's sake, this had to work. "Judge Westenra?"

The door opened to a mulish man with enormously large ears. "Yes?"

Rosa squared her shoulders. "Pardon me, Your Honour. I know it is quite unseemly for us to appear on your doorstep like this, and were the matter not urgent, we would not have dared impose."

"Do you know what time it is, Miss. . . ?"

"Edwards. Rosa Edwards, and yes, I realize the hour is late, but a man's life depends upon this meeting—depends upon you."

"It usually does," he snapped, but then with a sigh, he stepped aside. "Come in, then, but make it quick."

Rosa, Nurse Bilder and Mr. Rawlings made short work of passing the threshold. Renfield shambled behind. It was a large room sparsely furnished, smelling of comfrey liniment and socks that'd been worn one time too many.

Judge Westenra indicated the two high-back chairs near a hearth that was barren of coal. "I am afraid I cannot offer you all a seat, but ladies, if you please."

She and Nurse Bilder sat while the judge dragged over a wooden chair from the desk.

"Thank you, Your Honour," Rosa said as she smoothed her skirts. "We will be brief. We have come here to testify on behalf of Sir James Morgan."

"Hmm. . . The man accused of murdering his mother." The judge rubbed his hand over the stubble on his head. "Why did you not wait until the session tomorrow and speak your piece then?"

Rosa clasped her hands earnestly. "I fear we would not have had the chance. You see, Your Honour, there will be no peace in your courtroom tomorrow. Through no fault of his own, the citizens of Whitby are enflamed against Sir James."

"I affirm that summation." Mr. Rawlings stepped beside her chair. "My shop was nearly destroyed by a fearful mob the last time the baronet made a purchase. If you try Sir James publicly in the morning, there's no telling what chaos will ensue."

The judge's salt-and-pepper brows rose to his hairline. "So, you're saying that keeping me from my bed is for my benefit?"

"We're saying the baronet is innocent." Nurse Bilder swept her hand towards them all. "We are here to testify to that fact."

The judge leaned back in his seat, folding his arms with a scowl. "This is highly irregular."

Oh dear. Rosa shifted in her chair uncomfortably. Given the sour look on his face, this wasn't going well.

A longsuffering breath whistled from the judge's nose. "I suppose it is a moot point to deny your testimony now, though, being that I let you in. Let's have it and be quick about it. You." He pointed to Renfield. "Who are you and what have you to say?"

"I am Joseph Renfield, Your Honour." The old fellow's voice came from directly behind her chair. "I've worked for the Morgan household since before Lady Dorina became a member of the family. She suffered from a debilitating disease, one that Sir James was trying to cure."

The judge's brows lowered. "Why did he not seek out a medical professional?"

"He did, sir, but Dr. Seward said there was no more to be done. Sir James would not give up, though. Through extensive study and at great cost to himself, he sought a cure up until the Lady Dorina's very last day. You'll not find a man with more determination or integrity than the baronet in all the land."

"You cannot possibly know that unless you are intimately acquainted with all the men in the land."

Humour? Rosa's hopes lifted.

But then, with a flip of his hand, the judge dismissed the old butler and speared Mr. Rawlings with a direct stare. "I assume you are the aforementioned doctor?"

"No, Your Honour. I am Mr. Rawlings, the apothecary. Dr. Seward is out on a call tonight but said he will be happy to supply a written affidavit confirming Mr. Renfield's information."

The judge pursed his lips. "Then what have you to do with the matter?"

"I am the one who sold Sir James the ingredients he used to try to create a remedy for Lady Dorina. He was well informed on toxicity and the like and is an accomplished chemist. It is my firm conviction he used his knowledge and the items I sold him to try to cure his mother, not murder her."

"Yet you were not in the house." He leaned forward in his seat, skepticism thick in his tone. "If this baronet is so well-versed in poisons, how can you be sure he did his work for good and not ill?"

Rosa tensed.

"*I'm* sure, Your Honour," Nurse Bilder cut in.

His gaze settled on her, firm and measuring. "You are. . . ?" The question dangled like a hook in the water, just waiting to snag a name.

"Miss Agatha Bilder, nurse to Lady Dorina these past two years." The no-nonsense woman hadn't been happy when she'd first discovered Rosa at her sister's home, yet when she'd been told the details of the baronet's arrest, she'd grabbed her bonnet and practically dragged Rosa—and Mrs. Hawkins—from the house.

The nurse straightened her spine. "I never left the lady's side, not once. The medications Sir James administered to his mother were the very same he first tested on rabbits and—when need be—on himself. His remedies were safe."

"And completely ineffective *if* what you say is true." His unnerving gaze swung to Rosa. "What is your part in this, Miss Edwards?"

She inhaled deeply, praying for words that would persuade this man of granite. "I work in the library, Judge Westenra, and daily delivered medical texts that Sir James used to make informed decisions on what might work to help his mother. He was trying to help her, and we will all swear to that. The way I see it, that gives you four reliable testimonies in favour of the baronet against the one malicious lie that put him in jail in the first place."

"You are very outspoken, young lady."

She quelled a shiver at the ice in his tone. "I speak earnestly, Your Honour, for a man who is innocent of the crime of which he is accused." Her voice broke as tears closed her throat. She'd meant to make things better for James, but so severe were the hard lines on the judge's face, she feared she'd only angered him.

Without a word, the judge crossed to the door and yanked it open. "I've heard enough, and I will thank you to leave now while I think on it."

Rosa dashed over to him, pressing her palm against his sleeve. "But surely you see there is no evidence other than hearsay to convict Sir James."

"I said I've heard enough." He plucked her hand from his arm. "And with that, I bid you all goodnight."

"But—"

Mr. Rawlings grabbed her arm. "Thank you for your time, Judge Westenra. You've been most generous."

Generous? Hardly! Rosa fumed as the apothecary led her from the room.

Why was the judge not donning his hat and rushing down to the jail to release James?

James was no stranger to being alone, a condition he'd thought he'd mastered. Until now. It was cruel being locked up like an animal, crueler still to know he might never again feel the breeze on his skin, breathe the sweet sea air. . .gaze upon Rosa's lovely face. He buried his own face in his hands, for once grateful for the rock-hard bench keeping him from lying prostrate on the cold floor.

Minutes—maybe hours—later, the cellblock door scraped open, birthing a whole new round of caterwauling complaints from the prisoner two cells down.

"Pipe down, Cheyne!" The sergeant banged his truncheon against the man's bars.

James rose as Sergeant Carfax lumbered into view. No one accompanied him. Apparently he was to be deprived of a lawyer until he was hauled into a courtroom. Was this it, then? A final escort to a courtroom filled with hecklers. He cracked his neck, working out a kink. If nothing else, at least he'd go out of this world facing his accuser.

Without a word, the sergeant opened the door. The scowl on his face was enough to make a lion cower. It wouldn't take much to provoke him. James held out his wrists, unwilling to be manhandled into a pair of shackles. If this was to be his lot, so be it. He'd take it all with as much dignity as he could muster.

Surprisingly, though, Carfax merely handed him his pocket watch and stepped aside. "You're free to leave, Sir James."

"I am—what?" He gripped the watch tightly, the metal cool against his palm. Was this some sort of trick? If he walked out that door, would he be accused of escaping and take a bullet to the back?

"He's what?" the prisoner Cheyne hollered.

"Shut your gob, Cheyne." Storm clouds darkened the sergeant's eyes. "You heard me, Sir James. As misguided as it might be, I've got my orders to let you go."

"I do not understand."

He pursed his thick lips. "Neither do I, but that's how it is."

Well, then. Better confusion out in the fresh air than trying to extract information from a man who clearly didn't wish to see him walk free. James strode past him and Cheyne, who backed away the instant they locked gazes, then through the cell block door. He pocketed the watch as he rounded the front desk, and with brisk steps, escaped into the night. Pausing on the pavement, he inhaled until his lungs could hold no more. What glorious freedom.

"James!"

He spun to Rosa's voice. She stood at the corner, the streetlamp painting her in a soft glow. He took off at once—as did she. They met in a heartbeat.

"Thank God you are free." She smiled up at him.

"I do thank Him." He tipped her chin to study her face. "And I suspect I might owe you thanks as well. Are you the reason I was released?"

"Not just me. Renfield, Mr. Rawlings, and Nurse Bilder all testified that you had nothing to do with your mother's death, and in fact had been trying to help her. Based on our testimony, the judge ruled there wasn't enough evidence to support the charge, so he dismissed the case."

He shook his head. "I can hardly believe it."

"Nor can I." She beamed. "But it is true. I had nearly lost hope, but I am coming to learn that some things simply cannot be anticipated or explained."

He rubbed the back of his neck. "But then who accused me? None but the four of you and Dr. Seward knew anything about my mother."

Her lovely smiled faded, replaced by a fierce set to her jaw. "I suspect I might know who, and I intend to find out tomorrow."

"No." Dropping his hand, he shook his head. "Leave it alone. It does not matter anymore."

Her brow crumpled. "Whyever not?"

"Whoever desired me gone shall soon have his way. I will leave for Transylvania at once. With my mother gone, there is nothing more to keep me here."

"Nothing?"

Hurt pooled in her eyes, piercing him straight through the heart. Though he'd resolved to interact with humanity more often, and as much as he dearly wanted Rosa by his side as he did so, he could not—*would* not—saddle her with watching him make a slow and ugly decline into death.

"Rosa." Her name came out husky. "Please try to understand."

"You did not answer my question. Is there nothing at all to keep you here?" She stepped so close he could feel the heat of her. "Tell me the truth. Tell me you do not love me, and I will walk away."

She stood there so bravely, a soldier in a gown facing a firing squad of an answer—an answer he couldn't give, because the truth was he did love her. Agonizingly so. His gaze drifted to her lips.

"James," she whispered, leaning into him.

Though it killed him in a thousand different ways, he set her from him. "Goodbye, Rosa."

He walked away without looking back, for if he did, he'd swing her up in his arms and never let her go.

TWENTY-SEVEN

But his child-mind only saw so far; and it may be that, as ever is in God's Providence, the very thing that the evil-doer most reckoned on for his selfish good, turns out to be his chiefest harm.

Goodbye. How was she to live with that word? Would she be doomed to drag it around for the rest of her life like a millstone tied to her heart? Rosa sucked in a shaky breath, desperately trying to pull herself together as she approached the Mallow mansion and rang the bell. She hadn't slept a wink last night, though she could also blame her tossing and turning on the hurricane she'd faced upon arriving home so late. Mother wouldn't get over that for days, nor would she let Rosa forget about it.

La. She might never sleep again.

Stifling a yawn, she squared her shoulders as soon as a pasty-faced butler answered. "I should like to speak with Mr. Albin Mallow, please."

The words tasted like spoiled milk. She'd never dreamed she'd be calling on the man she'd been trying to avoid for the past month.

The butler sniffed, nose in the air, every bit as self-important as his master. "Very good. This way, miss." He stepped aside until she entered, then shut the door behind her. "Whom may I say is calling?"

"Rosa Edwards."

He dipped his head then led her through an ornate hall and into a large parlour. "I'll let him know at once, Miss Edwards."

"Thank you."

As soon as he disappeared, she strolled around the room, wondering if she'd entered a museum instead of a house. Egyptian artifacts graced a curio cabinet that took up nearly an entire wall. From amulets to flint knives with jewel-encrusted hilts, the wealth displayed here could feed all the fisherfolk of Whitby for a year. Apparently Albin hadn't been jesting when he'd claimed he could provide amply for her.

"Rosa! What a delightful surprise so early in the morning." Though the words were cheery enough, a shadow of uncertainty clouded Albin's face as he entered. His flowery cologne reached her before he did. He was dressed in a dark blue suit, matching waistcoat with golden-threaded embroidery, and a crisp white cravat spilling in a ruffly waterfall at his neck. Just how early did he rise to dress so impeccably for the day?

"Yes, well." She retreated a step. "I was hoping to catch you before you left the house."

"And so you have. Come." He reached to place his hand on her back, then suddenly withdrew, a flush of crimson crawling up his face. Could he possibly be feeling some guilt over how he'd manhandled her the last time they met? She would have never thought it possible, but then Albin had never physically withdrawn from her like that either. Instead, he gestured to a velvet-covered sofa. "Take a seat. Be at ease. What can I get for you?"

She sat with a frown. "An explanation, sir."

For the briefest of moments, he glanced at the door, almost as if he wanted to make a run for it. So, he was guilty, then, as she'd suspected.

But run he didn't, though he perched on the sofa as though ready to do so—and as far away from her as possible. Another first.

"I suppose I owe you an explanation after my beastly treatment the last time we were together." His gaze fixed on some place over her shoulder. "I should have known better than to approach you the way I did, with everyone so tense about these animal killings. And being operating manager of a big shipyard, well, it has turned out to be more taxing than I realized, especially of late. Uncle Preston can be quite particular. As a result, I wasn't thinking as clearly as I should have been. Not that any of this excuses my behaviour, mind, and I know I don't deserve it, but"—his throat actually bobbed as if he believed his own words—"I hope that you might somehow look beyond my actions of that day."

He met her eyes with something akin to real agony, stopping her snort short. Could it be that James wasn't the only misguided one in Whitby? Discomfited by the thought, Rosa studied her hands, clenched in her lap. "Though I have every right to bring charges of assault against you, I will be merciful and not do so. But that was not the explanation I came for."

Albin shifted towards her, his body relaxing into his normal pompous mien. "Then what shall I explain for you, my sweet? How it is that your smile lights up the world? How fondly my heart beats for you alone? How your brilliance shames the sun and moon and stars?"

She edged back on the cushion, any momentary sympathy vanishing. Squaring her chin, she looked him straight in the eyes. "Are you the one who accused Sir James of murdering his mother?"

His nostrils flared, her question clearly catching him off guard. "I—" His mouth snapped shut, and he abruptly strode to the small cart in the corner to pour a glass of water.

He didn't admit, but neither did he deny it. Her stomach turned. That meant she'd been right all along. "How could you do such a thing? You accused a man who is blameless."

"That is a moot point now. I received word not long ago that the case was dismissed." He stood with his back towards her, the coward. "But besides that, how was I to know Sir James wasn't to blame? It was an honest mistake."

"Your mistake nearly cost the baronet his life. You do realize he could charge you with slander for such an affront?"

"I—" He shuddered, and his shoulders hunched as if he expected her to physically strike him. "I only did it to protect you." His words were barely a whisper.

This time Rosa did snort. "From what? My association with a vampire?"

"No." Albin wheeled about, driving her back. In the short time he had been turned away, the pampered puffball had deflated to a pale shell of a man. "The fact is I came across some information that the baronet had been using dangerous substances in treating his mother. If he could so easily harm a loved one, then how much more peril would *you* be in? So when you turned down my proposal, refused to let me protect you. . .what else could I do?"

Had he really been that misguided, or was this a ruse? "You should have gone to Sir James with your questions, not to the police."

"I realize that now." A kicked puppy couldn't look more contrite. "Say you'll forgive me?"

She blew out a long breath. Naturally she must forgive him, seventy-times seven and all that, but this one—this *one*—was like swallowing nails. "Very well, but if you really care for me, Mr. Mallow—"

"I do!" He held his arms wide. "I most emphatically and ardently do care for you. You have but to say the word and I shall show you just how much."

If he thought for one second she'd run into that embrace, then he belonged in an asylum. Lifting her chin, she held her ground. "All I ask is that you please stop trying to ruin the baronet's life."

He blinked. "Sir James need have nothing to do with us. Surely you know that."

Though it made her belly clench, she gathered his hands in hers. His eyes widened at her touch. "Please, Albin." She softened her tone. "Sir James has suffered enough, and I cannot bear to see him shoulder any more griefs. If for no other reason, leave Sir James alone for my sake, and I will speak to him on your behalf that he will not press charges against you."

He stared at her fingers, then slowly lifted his face to hers. "You would do that for me?"

"Consider it done."

"Then for you, Rosa, I vow I will have nothing more to do with the baronet. Nothing at all."

She gasped softly. For once he looked like a man of integrity instead of a conniving little boy. "Thank you." Releasing him, she turned to leave. "Goodbye."

She walked away, surprisingly lighter of step than when she'd arrived. There might be hope for Albin. He could change. Not that she'd hold her breath on the matter, but still.

God had shown her that miracles still happen.

Albin stared at the crack in the draperies where the last of day's light crept in like a thief. Oh, how he welcomed the oncoming darkness. As far as he was concerned, it couldn't come soon enough to ease the pounding in his head. Ever since his encounter with Rosa that morning, he'd been battling a beast of a megrim—one he deserved. Nay, he deserved far worse. Not because he had failed, but because he had nearly succeeded. He had almost cost an innocent man his life because of his drive to win Rosa. Why had he ever thought that removing Sir James would win her favor? He'd been a fool. All he had done was wound her and drive her ever closer to the baronet. And yet somehow, miraculously, she'd acquitted him of all offense—something his uncle never would have done. What a wonder. What a mind-boggling marvel.

And he wasn't quite sure what to do with that.

Pinching the edge of the drapery between his thumb and forefinger, he ran his hand up and down, up and down, the velvet soft between his fingers, a soothing habit he'd picked up as a small boy when Uncle locked him in his room after every little infraction. Rosa's grace towards him baffled like nothing else. He simply didn't have a category for kindness in the face of failure.

Footsteps pounded in the corridor, and he barely had time to turn before the door burst open. The silhouette of Uncle Preston stood on the threshold like a monster on a rampage.

"Where were you today?" his uncle boomed.

Albin winced, the volume banging around in his head like a loose steel ball. He pressed his fingers against his temple. "I've been here all day, Uncle. I am not well."

"Not well," he growled. "Not fit for anything, more like it. You should have been at the office this afternoon. That delivery of hemp you were in charge of didn't arrive. Do you know what that means?" He stomped over to the dresser and poured a glass of sherry, then slugged it back, every little sound magnified a hundredfold.

Albin sank onto the edge of his mattress. "Please, try to keep it down. My head—"

"Your head is what I'll have if you cost me any more money on this."

He slammed down the glass. "Without that shipment, we are now further behind on the Galatz order—and you know what a short fuse Henry Galatz has. If we lose his business because of you, there will be the devil to pay, and you can consider me your personal daemon."

Hah! How well he knew that. The man had been sinking his fangs into him since he was a child. Though it pained him, he faced his uncle with a bowed head. Better to appease a dragon with a show of humility than lift the face to a killing blast of fire. "I will put my full attention on the matter first thing in the morning when I am recovered from my megrim."

"No. You will get yourself down to the office right now and quit whining about your blasted headache." He grabbed Albin's waistcoat off the wooden valet and threw it at him.

Albin caught it before the ball of fabric hit him in the head, flinching from the sudden attack and the hammering in his skull.

"Quit looking like such a wounded weasel." Uncle sneered, his upper lip curling. "You have no one to blame for this mess but yourself. None of this would be an issue if you hadn't botched things up with that Edwards skirt."

Albin smoothed the wrinkles in the green satin before carefully pulling on his waistcoat. "I fail to see how a missed delivery has anything to do with Miss Edwards."

"That's because all you know how to do is spend money, not make it, so let me put it to you plainly." He kicked Albin's shoes towards him. "We cannot afford to be slack on our production, and in fact, must increase our pace—which is impossible unless we expand. We need that piece of land the library sits on, and we need it now."

Albin grabbed one shoe and buffed out a scuff, fighting against a fierce glower. To do so would only enrage his uncle all the more. "There must be some other way."

"There is no other way! I will have that property no matter what it takes."

A chill ran down his spine as he grabbed the other shoe and sat to put them on. His uncle had ruined many a good man in his time, one of them even rumoured to have been murdered.

"I never should have trusted you with a task that was meant for a man." Voice dangerously calm, Uncle Preston grabbed Albin's frock coat from off the stand and held it out like a sack of drowned kittens.

Carefully, Albin took the fabric, fearing—yet required—to meet the man's icy gaze. "What do you intend?"

"I think you know what I am capable of." Sniffing, his uncle looked down his nose. "Even now I have set watch on the Edwards man and his daughter, so it shouldn't be long before the perfect opportunity arises. With those two out of the way, the Edwards matriarch will sell in a heartbeat."

Unheeding of the garden of creases he'd create, Albin clutched great fistfuls of his frock coat to his chest. "No. You cannot harm Rosa."

"Can I not?" Frigid blue eyes stared into his soul. "Why nephew, I believe you really care for the chit. Too bad you failed so spectacularly at bringing her to your bed."

Uncle Preston seized him by the collar and hustled him out the door. "Now get you gone and fix that delivery."

Albin stumbled as his uncle gave him a shove, his coat falling to the floor and tangling his step all the more. He slapped out his hand to balance against the wall, wishing beyond reason he was instead slapping the life out of his uncle. He had to find a way to stop the man from harming Rosa and her father.

But how?

TWENTY-EIGHT

Well, the Devil may work against us for all he's worth, but God sends us men when we want them.

There was something about a graveyard that instantly sobered one to the core. James unlatched the gate to the family plot at the back of the manor and entered circumspectly. It was a grey day, but even if the sun were out, beneath the overhang of an enormous chestnut, this garden of the dead was always gloomy. Headstones of past Morgans popped up from the ground like so many ghosts, some of them weathered beyond reading. Fingering the dark crimson rose he carried, he stopped at the one with the crispest engraving.

His father's.

James frowned. He hadn't been here to pay his respects in at least fifteen years. Did that make him a bad son? A wry smile twisted his lips. No worse than a bad father, he supposed. Sir Jonathan Morgan had been a phantom. A flash of suitcoat and hat caught from the corner of a little boy's eyes as he strode out the door. The man never had the time of day for his young son, was too busy gadding off on another gambling spree, too occupied to care that he left his own flesh and blood in the custody of a mother who had proven herself incapable of uttering a kind word.

Crouching, James ran his finger along the epitaph his father had wished etched for eternity.

Remember as thou walkest by
As ye are now, so once was I
As I am now, shall ye surely be,
Prepare thyself to follow me.

James curled his hands into fists. He had no intention of following the legacy that man had left, no plan to lie forgotten on a wind-blown stretch of land above the sea. But how was he to change the course of a lonely life doomed for a dishonorable death? To act upon the resolve he'd made to bring his knowledge to others? The questions sank to his gut like a cold, thick porridge. He had no idea. For now, the best he could do was to see Renfield properly set up in comfort before he left for Transylvania. At least someone would have happy days until his last breath.

James stepped to the freshly dug grave next to his father's, the unearthly screech of a gull splitting the sky. The earthworm muskiness of the upturned soil raised his own mortality to the surface. God alone held his soul. In that knowledge there was inexplicable peace, yet as he laid the rose atop his mother's final resting place, he couldn't help but wonder. . .

Was she at rest?

"I thought I might find you here." God entered the fenced plot—or at least His dark-suited representative did.

James tipped his head at the rector, Mr. Austen.

The man stopped at his side, mimicking his stance with hands clasped behind his back as he too gazed at Lady Dorina's grave. "My condolences for your grief, Sir James."

Is that what this was? This coldness in his chest? This numbness in his heart? The churning and burning of not knowing where his mother now dwelled? Question after question spread like a rash, but even so, he settled for a simple, "Thank you."

The rector shuffled his feet, the grass heavy with dew that seeped into the hem of his trousers. "Death never comes easy, even when it is expected. And we may all expect it."

How well he knew that. James nodded. "I admit it was no surprise that my mother died, and in truth, it was a welcome relief from her physical suffering."

"Yet I detect you do not find solace in that."

"No." James clenched his jaw. "I do not."

"May I ask why?"

Lifting his face, he gazed at the maze of chestnut leaves and beyond to the patches of sullen sky, speaking more to God than to the clergyman beside him. "As far as I know, my mother was not saved from damnation, so where is she? Cast into eternal darkness? Burning in the flames of hell?" Flailing his arms, he faced the bushy-browed man. "Tell me, Mr. Austen, is my mother even now weeping and gnashing her teeth?"

"Well," he chuckled, "there you have it."

James's jaw unhinged. What sort of answer was that? "There I have what?"

"You said, and I quote, 'As far as I know.'" A Cheshire smile spread across his face. "Therein lies your hope."

Frustrated beyond measure, James shook his head. "I am sorry, sir, but I have no idea what you are talking about."

"Though you may have never witnessed your mother's outward cry for God's help, there is no way you can know what went on in her mind. There might have been a flurry of repentance and submission to our great and gracious Lord."

The rector paused as another gull screeched overhead, his eyes following its flight. Once it passed, he faced James and stared into his soul. "It is my firm belief that if the thief on the cross had merely thought the words *Remember me when you come into your kingdom*, Jesus still would have promised the man he'd be with Him in glory that very day, for He alone discerns our thoughts. He alone is the defender of our soul. I suggest, Sir James, that instead of focusing on what happened if your mother didn't cry out to God, that you turn your thoughts towards what happened if she did and cling to that."

James raked his hand through his hair, surprised by a sudden rush of hope upping his pulse. "I. . .I would like to think such a thing might be true."

"Then do so." The rector clapped him on the shoulder. "Ultimately your hope is in a good and gracious God who may be trusted to do with your mother as He willed. After all, He loves her more than you ever could."

Instant guilt tasted sour in his mouth. If God did see his thoughts, then He knew all the many times James had wished for a different mother.

"I am afraid I did not love her very well," he murmured.

"Your actions speak otherwise. Did you not travel all this way to care for her during her final days?"

"I did, but—"

"But nothing. You did. And even if you hadn't"—he gestured towards the mound of dirt—"you are here now, standing in front of her grave, a dutiful son come to say goodbye."

James narrowed his eyes at the fellow. "I think you are determined to see the best in me, sir."

"I am." He grinned. "As is God."

James clasped the man's arm. "Thank you, Mr. Austen. Your words have given me hope."

"God alone is the giver of hope." He rested his hand atop James's fingers and squeezed. "Now then, does that mean I can expect to see you at services this Sunday?"

Pulling away, James shook his head. "I am afraid not. I sail tomorrow on the next ship to Transylvania and, in truth, ought to hurry off now to prepare."

"Then Godspeed, Sir James. It has been a pleasure getting to know you."

"The pleasure, Mr. Austen, has been mine." He gave the man a bow, then strode down the gravel path and around to the front of the house, amazed at the lightness of his step. He felt as if a great burden had been lifted. Simply sharing his heart with the clergyman had buoyed his spirit—for now, anyway.

The grind of wheels rolled up the drive as he was about to mount the stairs. Instead of going inside, he waited until the grim-faced driver of a freight wagon reined in the big draft horses.

"You be Sir James?" His voice boomed.

"I am."

The two men sitting beside the driver craned their necks, the ruddier of the pair asking, "Where's the crates?"

James slapped at a fly, the insect as annoying as the question. Where did the man think the crates would be? "They are just inside the hall, and take care, for a fair number of them hold glass."

The driver spat off the side of the wagon, then swiped a meat hook of a hand across his mouth. "Best have 'em brought out then, and we'll be on our way."

James glowered. "You were hired to transport my goods, which includes hauling them from the house and loading them."

"We'll not be steppin' foot inside that house. Not enough money in the world to take a risk such as that. Yer lucky we agreed to come in the first place. I daresay no one else would."

Of all the superstitious claptrap. James gritted his teeth, which didn't make it easy for his words to grind out. "If I were truly a vampire, I could as easily drain your blood out here on the lawn as in my home."

The big driver exchanged a look with the other two, their brows wrinkling. Seriously? Hadn't the thought occurred to one of them?

Eventually the driver nodded at his companions as if ending some sort of wordless conversation, then faced James with a superior tilt of his head. "Even so, we stand firm."

James blew out a disgusted sigh. Misguided half-wits. Wheeling about, he ground his heels into the gravel path towards the stables to get his boy to help haul crates. Though the sky was clouded over, already sweat trickled between his shoulder blades. He shrugged out of his coat and cast it over his shoulder as he stomped onward. It wouldn't be too soon to leave behind all the mistrust and slander of these people. But as for leaving a certain brown-eyed, amber-haired woman. . . His step hitched.

Now that would rip the heart right out of him.

Dried glue flakes on her sleeves and ink stains on her fingers. Was this what life was now to be? Slumping on her stool, Rosa shoved back a loose curl hanging in front of her eyes. Ever since returning home from Albin's house yesterday, she'd been slaving away for her mother, writing labels and slapping them on bottle after bottle. She huffed a long breath and stretched a crick from her neck. If only Mother would let her type the contents, but no amount of debate had moved her to change the look of her medicinals. Rosa suspected it was more of a punishment than an unwillingness to update the bottles. Her mother was still cross about her escapade of the other night.

And Rosa was still cross with James for telling her goodbye.

Aimlessly, she picked up the brush and slathered glue onto another label. Better to put her mind on work than on the ache in her heart.

A semi-accurate execution of "God Save the King" whistled down the corridor, and moments later her father swung through the door.

Rosa set the brush in the wooden tray, stifling a sigh when once again her sleeve unrolled and dragged through a big glop. She reached for a rag while eyeing her father. "I have not finished filling the last box yet. I thought you wouldn't be here until lunch break."

"I wasn't supposed to be, but I need to talk with you, Daughter." He pulled off his spectacles and speared her with a direct look. "I cannot stop thinking on what you did the other day."

She tucked her chin. Apparently her father was still cross with her too. "I know it was wrong of me to tell Mother I'd be with Mrs. Hawkins yet not tell her exactly where Mrs. Hawkins and I would be. I have since apologized and explained everything." She peered up at him. "But you know all this."

"I do. Neither am I here to rebuke you any further on the matter." He cornered the worktable and stopped at her side. "I am here to offer back your old job."

"You—what?" She grabbed the edge of the table. Had she heard correctly?

"What you did, Rosa." He shook his head. "Why, I can hardly believe it. To your own detriment, you saved a man from execution. You spent your life savings to see that justice done, taking it upon yourself to gather those who would speak of the baronet's innocence. I am ashamed to wonder if I would have done half as much for a man rumoured to be a vampire. Yet you did it all with your usual determination and efficiency. That is no small thing, my girl, and I am proud of you." Leaning close, he pressed a kiss to the crown of her head.

The world turned watery, and it took her several blinks to bring it back into focus. "Thank you, Father," she whispered.

He tapped the rim of his glasses on the table. "You must really love him."

She swallowed, fighting back another rush of tears. Love was too small a word. How to describe the wholeness she felt in that man's arms? How she lived for one of his rare smiles? How she would never again laugh or love the way she had when they were together? Yet James had made it very clear he did not feel the same way about her—and that gutted her like nothing else.

"Rosa?" her father prompted.

Slowly, she nodded. "I do love him." She did. She always would, whether he returned her affection or not.

Father cupped her cheek with his hand. "Then why do you look so sad?"

A single, traitorous tear broke loose, burning down her cheek and over his fingers. "He will not have me."

"Posh! What's this?" With one swipe, her father wiped away the tear then flourished his hand in the air. "Of course he will. You have only to tell him of your feelings. No man could resist that."

"I did—and he still said goodbye. He told me so in no uncertain terms."

Red crept up her father's neck. "Then I think I must have a word with the man."

"No, Father, you cannot." She grabbed his arm, the thought of her father confronting James sickening her. "I would be mortified."

"I can—and I will." He tucked her hand into the crook of his arm. "Come along, Daughter. We'll just see about this."

TWENTY-NINE

They, an' all grims an' signs an' warnin's, be all invented by parsons an' illsome beuk-bodies an' railway touters to skeer an' scunner hafflin's, an' to get folks to do sometin' that they don't other incline to.

James flicked sweat off his brow as he glowered at the crew he'd hired to transport his goods down to the docks. He and his stable boy had single-handedly lugged out crate upon crate and stacked them near the dray. Only half of the wooden boxes had made it onto the wagon bed thus far. At this rate, he'd make it to Transylvania long before his belongings ever did.

A hack entered the front gate, snagging his attention. The black carriage lumbered along, listing to one side, a wonder the thing didn't tip over. Either the occupants had rented the broken-springed transport, or they didn't have the funds to keep up their carriage. James rolled down his sleeves as he strode to meet his callers, woefully aware he'd left his suit coat in the house. Hopefully he wouldn't be meeting trouble in naught but his shirt and waistcoat.

The bespectacled Mr. Edwards exited first, then assisted Rosa to alight after him. Well. This was a surprise—and a torture. He thought he'd said his goodbyes to her, but apparently now they were both to suffer more salt on that wound.

"Mr. Edwards, Miss Edwards." He dipped his head towards them. "Pardon my appearance. I was not expecting anyone."

Rosa kept her gaze on her skirt hem, seeming rather subdued. Alarm prickled over his scalp. She usually faced the world head-on.

"Good day, Sir James. I would like to have a word with you." Mr. Edwards pressed his fist into the small of his back, arching somewhat, and no wonder. After a ride in that dilapidated carriage, a lot more than a stiff spine likely pained him.

Though James had no idea what the man might have to say to him, he nodded. "Very well." He glanced at the men who were supposed to be loading his goods. Every last one of them looked his way, watching as if this were some sort of theatre production. He turned back to Rosa and her father. "Let us take this inside, shall we?"

He led them without a word past the sluggards. No sense giving them anything to gossip about, and perhaps they'd work harder now that they didn't have anything to do other than load his crates.

Once inside, Mr. Edwards sucked in an audible breath as they passed the gargoyle. Like father, like daughter. James couldn't help but smile as he ushered them into the sitting room.

Mr. Edwards stayed by the door. "It might be easier on Rosa if we first speak alone."

James glanced between the two of them, and still Rosa would not make eye contact. What could the man possibly have to say that he wouldn't want his daughter to hear? Why bring her along in the first place?

"As you wish." He tipped his head towards Rosa. "Please make yourself comfortable. I am sure we will not be long."

She nodded, looking so small and desolate it took all his willpower not to pull her into his arms.

Which obviously would not do. He swept past Mr. Edwards, indicating for him to follow. "My study is just this way, though you must excuse the disarray."

He strode down the corridor, clear now of the crates he and the stable boy had hauled outside, and directed Rosa's father into his study. The room was mostly empty shelves, his desk absent of papers and beakers and the rest of his medical paraphernalia. He offered Mr. Edwards the wingback while he retrieved his suitcoat from the back of his desk chair where he'd laid it earlier. "I apologize for the lack of creature comforts. I will be quitting the country tomorrow, and as you saw outside, am even now in the midst of packing."

Rosa's father took the chair and lowered his glasses to the tip of his nose. "Running away, are you?"

Taken aback, he shoved his arms into his coat, debating how to answer the accusation. "Not per se. I have pressing business to attend that affects my family's estate. But even if that were not the case, I think it is best for everyone if I remove myself from England."

"Best for everyone or for yourself?"

So, this was where Rosa got her spunk. He scraped his wooden chair across the floor and set it squarely in front of the man. "You are quite harsh, sir."

"And you are quite a coward."

James arched a brow. "You do not know me."

"No, I do not." Mr. Edwards pulled out a pipe and a small tobacco bag from an inside pocket. "But I do know my own daughter. Do you mind?" He waved the pipe in the air.

"Not at all." Rising, he retrieved a match from the box on the mantel and offered it over.

Rosa's father methodically tamped tobacco into the bowl, the rich scent filling the room even before he lit it. He paused, though, before striking the match, his pale brown eyes locking onto James. "Are you aware, Sir James, that Rosa is in love with you?"

His heart missed a beat. Had he deduced such a conclusion, or had she told him? Either way, there was no denying it. "Yes, she has made that clear."

"Hmm," Edwards murmured, then lit the pipe. After a few draws, he settled back in the chair and blew out a stream of smoke. "Then explain to me how leaving her with a broken heart is a good thing."

James's jaw clenched. Nothing about this was good. Couldn't the man understand that?

"Do you really want your daughter marked by stigma, scorned in public, treated like an outcast? All that and more would be her life if I claimed her as my own."

"Do you love her?"

A fierce scowl pulled his brow. "That is beside the point."

Mr. Edwards aimed the stem of his pipe at him like a bayonet. "Do you?"

Blast! The man was a dog with a bone. James rose, unable to sit another second beneath Mr. Edwards's probing gaze. He stalked to the window and stared out, unseeing. "The truth is, sir, that there will never be anyone else for me."

"I am happy to hear it. So, simply take Rosa somewhere else and start a new life."

Would to God that he could. James closed his eyes, sickened by the thought of his own disease. "It is not that simple, Mr. Edwards."

Footsteps thudded behind him. A hand rested on his shoulder. "Then explain it to me, son."

He stiffened even as his heart softened. Not once had his father taken the time to ask him to explain anything, least of all with an accompanying loving touch. Ought he take a chance on being transparent with this man, or would sharing his personal details only come back to haunt him? But he'd be an ocean away starting tomorrow. And if Rosa's father understood his motives, then perhaps the man would be better able to comfort his daughter.

Oh, how he hated to be the one to cause her pain.

Sighing, he turned back. "I must ask you to keep what I say confidential."

Rosa's father nodded. "Undoubtedly." He took another draw on his pipe. "I desire to hurt neither Rosa nor you. I merely seek to unravel this snarly mess in which you both seem to find yourselves entangled."

"Very well." James inhaled deeply then began before he changed his mind. "I admit it is not just the contempt of the people of Whitby or any other people that keeps me from wedding your daughter. To be plain, I suffer from a disease called porphyria." The very word tasted like death in his mouth, and unbidden, his voice dropped. "The same ailment that recently killed my mother."

He blew out a long breath, years of anguish and denial leaking out of him. "It is hereditary, carried in the blood, and ends in madness and death." James clamped his mouth shut, repulsed by his own confession.

"Porphyria." Mr. Edwards's pipe hovered in the air as he repeated the word. "Is that so?"

"It is." He swiped his hand over his face, uneasy with this whole conversation, and yet it was necessary. "Rosa does not deserve to watch me degrade into a monster."

Her father set down his pipe and leaned forward in his seat. "Should it not be her choice?"

"No." James shook his head violently, so abhorrent was the thought. "She could never understand how horrific a life like that would be, not as I do. With every arch of my mother's back as she writhed in pain, I felt it in my own spine. When I close my eyes at night, I swear I can still hear her ragged cries, her moaning. It turns my stomach to think of the anguish my mother suffered. I would not have Rosa witness such. To the denial of my own desire for your daughter, I would spare her that hell. Nor would I wish this disease to be passed on to any future generation."

Mr. Edwards let out a long breath. "It appears I was wrong about my earlier assumption." He pushed his glasses to the bridge of his nose, his eyes narrowing. "You are no coward, sir."

The praise went down so deep that James bowed his head. How different might life have been if his own father had commended him with as much fervor? He could barely speak for the tightening in his throat, yet he managed to push out, "Thank you, sir."

Heels thudded in the corridor, and James tensed when Renfield entered at a good clip. The old fellow never did anything at a good clip, nor did he ever enter without a knock.

"Excuse me, sir, but there is a situation outside."

James frowned at the unprecedented behavior. "What sort of situation?"

"One that involves pitchforks and torches."

Oh Lord. Will this nightmare never end?

"Pardon me, Mr. Edwards." He stalked from the room, but evidently Rosa's father did not pardon him a whit. He followed.

Prepared to once again spar with a few farmers intent on blaming him for their dead livestock, James flung open the front door. Then froze. This was no mere gathering of three or four disgruntled men.

This was a mob.

"There he is!" a big man in the front bellowed, shaking a torch at him. "There's the blackguard who's killed all our livestock."

James glowered. "I have done no such—"

The mob roared, coming at him like a tidal wave.

He barely had time to slam the door shut before they struck. Mr. Edwards stared at him, eyes wide as the crowd rammed against the oak. The door would hold for now, but it wouldn't take long before they—

Glass broke.

Rosa screamed.

James's blood ran cold.

A ferocious growl filled the small office. Albin pressed his fist to his gut as he glanced at the wall clock. Nearly noon. No wonder his stomach complained. He'd not had a bite since lunch yesterday.

Yawning, he set down his pen and pinched the bridge of his nose. At least his headache had abated sometime during the long night as he'd worked on righting the wrong of the hemp delivery and ensuring the Galatz order would be fulfilled. It had been a challenging maze of paperwork and a tedious recounting of inventory, but he'd done it. Uncle could have nothing to say against him if he went home for some well-deserved sleep.

He glanced in the mirror as he donned his frock coat. What an unsightly wreck. Dark crescents hung beneath his bloodshot eyes, his hair was rumpled, and his cologne had worn off hours ago. Hopefully he wouldn't run into anyone of import.

Collecting his hat, he traipsed from the office, ducking his head as he passed by the burly guard Uncle kept at the front door. The man was only a commoner, but all the same, Albin had no wish for his unkempt appearance to be the talk of the shipyard. As soon as he rounded the corner of the building, a hand grabbed him by the collar.

"I'll see that uncle o' yers, an' I'll see 'im now." The words traveled on a waft of fish breath.

Albin wrenched away and frowned at the thug who'd grabbed him. He'd seen better dressed scarecrows than this raggedy stick man snarling at him through yellowed teeth. Blood stained his sleeves and the backs of his hands, though he didn't appear to be injured. Albin wasn't sure if he ought to be frightened or disgusted.

"I should think my uncle is in his office. Go see him for yourself." He turned on his heel.

The man yanked him back. "No doubt he is, but that sack o' meat at the front door"—he hitched his thumb over his shoulder—"won't let me in."

"Write him a note, then. Correspondence will be answered in a timely fashion, I assure you."

"A note." The man spat on the ground. "I'm the one what's owed a note—a five-pound note! Ye tell that scupper if I don't have my money in my hands by tonight, I'll go to the law. I will, and don't ye think I won't."

Albin studied the man, mind whirring. "You're not employed here. I've never seen you before. Why would my uncle be indebted to you?"

"I been doin' his dirty work these past weeks. Oh, he's quick to send the word to slice some necks, to blame it all on that high and mighty lord up there in his fancy manor, but yer uncle ain't as timely to pay for what work he hired."

Albin cocked his head. "Are you saying you're the one responsible for killing the sheep and goats in the area?"

"Not me. Yer uncle's the one what told me to do it." He poked Albin in the chest. "And I demand to be paid."

Albin shoved the man's hand away. His uncle was more than capable of it, but why? Just because of some old grudge he bore against the baronet's father? No, there had to be something more to it than that.

"Wait here." He brushed at the wrinkle the man's finger had bunched in his waistcoat. "I shall see about this at once."

He backtracked into the building and climbed the steps to his uncle's office. Bypassing the clerk with a tip of his head, he strode into Uncle Preston's lair unannounced.

"A word please, Uncle."

From behind a massive desk, the man himself looked up from a ledger, his blue eyes a January wind. "This had better be good or I'll throw you out of here myself."

Albin stayed near the door, preferring to duck out rather than suffer a boot to the backside. "There's a man outside who says you paid him to kill livestock and blame it on Sir James."

A cloudburst of curses filled the room. "Idiot!" His uncle slapped the desktop. "Can't hire any good help nowadays. I suppose I'll have to have him taken care of as well."

"So, it's true?"

"I told you I'd remove Morgan from the picture, and so I have." He closed the ledger and folded his hands atop it, appearing as concerned about his admission as he might be about a hangnail.

Albin tugged down his waistcoat. "Don't be so sure whatever you've planned won't backfire on you. The man is threatening to go to the law."

"Let him." Uncle laced fingers behind his head. "A few banknotes slipped into the right hands will put him away instead of me. Besides, he's the one who actually committed the crime. I merely made it worth his while. There's no record of our arrangement. It will be his word against mine."

Disgust churned the juices in Albin's empty gut. Uncle Preston didn't appear the least perturbed about the damages he'd caused. The people he'd hurt. No wonder the man had no friends. He'd die a lonely old cuss with no one to mourn his loss but Albin. . .yet would he *really* grieve once his uncle was gone? He feared the man, yes, but did he truly love him? Did anyone?

Albin sucked in a breath. Great heavens. If he continued on in Uncle's footsteps, the very same fate would happen to him, and he didn't even have a nephew. He didn't want this! He didn't want to be like this cold and calculating old devil, grinding and grabbing and greedy. No wonder Rosa had turned him away.

"You're despicable." Albin curled his lip.

His uncle's eyes hardened to cold marble, then he fluttered his fingers in the air. "This whole affair is nothing to trouble yourself with, Nephew. It will all be over in an hour or so anyway, if it's not already."

A wave of foreboding washed over him. "What do you mean?"

"The townfolk are so enraged after last night's killing spree, they're likely even now burning the manor home down around the baronet's ears, along with that uppity Mr. Edwards and his persnickety daughter. It paid to have them watched, and it's quite the bargain if you ask me, ridding the world of two roadblocks and one vampire. Very convenient."

Albin swung towards the door.

"Not if I can help it," he muttered under his breath.

THIRTY

Is this all a nightmare, or what is it?

It was an inferno. Or soon would be. Rosa beat a pillow against the flames licking up the legs of the tea table, the acrid smoke of the burning rug stinging her eyes. At least four—possibly five—torches had sailed through Morgrave Manor's windows, shattering the glass and her opinion of the men outside, most of whom she'd known all her life.

James charged into the room. "Rosa! Are you hurt?"

"I am fine, but—"

Her father skidded into the room on James's heels. "Great heavens!"

"Rip down the draperies." In two strides, James grabbed hold of the red brocade and yanked at the nearest window coverings.

Her father followed suit. As they worked to smother the fires, more shouts launched in from outside, as did two more torches, one of them landing dangerously close to Rosa's skirt. How dare they? Fury blazed in her heart. These were their neighbours. Their friends. How could good men commit such a heinous act? She struck the rag-wrapped branch soaked with kerosene again and again, until the pillow she used burst and feathers rained out along with a sob.

God, please. . .help!

They did need help, divine help.

James grabbed her by the arm, leading her away. "We have got to get out of here. If we hurry, the route to the stable ought to be clear before the mob tries to burn that down as well."

"But this is your home, James." She pulled from his touch, brow pinching. "If we do not fight this, you will have nothing left but ashes."

"I will fight it." Wrath flashed in his eyes. "But first I will see you to safety."

"He's right, Daughter." With a final whack, her father put out the last flames—leastwise for now. "This is no place for a woman. Go. I'll stay and put out any more fires that spring up."

"But Father—"

"Stop! What you're doing is wrong." Outside, a man's voice crested louder than the mob. "Put those torches down!"

Rosa sucked in a breath, hardly believing her ears. Could it be? She whipped around, staring out through the broken glass, as did her father and James.

Sure enough, the splotch of a bright yellow carriage sat at the edge of the crowd. She had never seen Albin look anything but impeccable in his appearance, yet there he stood, hair rumpled and clothing wrinkled. And it didn't seem to bother him in the least as he squared his shoulders like a knight braced for battle.

"The baronet is not to blame," he shouted. "Listen to this man!"

He tugged up the fellow cowering next to him—a collection of blood-stained bones, really—and forced him to face the crowd. The horse tossed its head at the sudden movement. Several men in the mob turned towards the commotion.

"Now's our time," James hissed in her ear and once again wrapped his fingers around her arm.

"Wait. Please." She planted her feet, unwilling to pull her gaze from the spectacle outside. If this was the divine intervention she'd wished for, it was nothing like she expected or imagined, just as Mrs. Hawkins had warned her. Yet what other explanation could there be?

"Rosa, it is not safe. I have got to get you and your father out of here while I have the chance." There was steel in his voice.

Even so, Rosa would not budge. "Listen for just a moment more. Running away might not be needed."

"Tell them why Sir James is not to blame!" Albin bellowed.

Nearly all the crowd now gawked at the yellow carriage, their backs towards the manor. Even James stopped and stared at the sight.

Over the heads of the mob, the thin man next to Albin slowly nodded. Rosa didn't recognize him, but someone in the gathering did, cursing him like a dog who'd stolen a chicken.

After a shake from Albin, the man opened his mouth. "Mallow's right, lads. Morgan had no hand in all the dead livestock. It were Preston Mallow what ordered those killings. There ain't no vampire a'foot other than that bloodsucking shipyard owner. I'll swear to that in a court o' law."

"Aye?" One man raised a fist. "Prove it!"

Another fellow bobbed his torch in the air. "We oughtta burn this mongrel too!"

The man paled, shrinking back to the seat.

Albin hauled him right up again, this time whispering something into his ear—which turned the man's complexion to a deathly shade of grey.

"Fie!" the man spat out, then louder, "It were I what did the deed, and there ya have it."

The throng roared.

"But I had no choice!" He flapped his arms. "I had no say! Preston Mallow said he'd slice me own throat if I did not do as he said. And the money he were to pay me were too good to walk away from. Ye'd all do it to keep yer family fed and don't say ye wouldn't!"

Rosa pressed her fingers to her lips. Was this true?

The mob advanced on the carriage.

"Hold it right there!" Albin shot out his hand. "Yes, this wastrel cost you money and lots of it, but harming him is like pulling off a single leaf from a weed, only for the thing to keep growing and consuming. It is my uncle who is the root. He is the one responsible. You have a witness, and I heard it from my uncle's own lips. So take your fight to the law and see that justice is enacted on Preston Mallow. It is the court who will order my uncle to compensate those who were wronged. And I will see that justice is meted out to this man." He gave the skinny fellow another shake.

Rosa blinked as a foreign surge of admiration welled for Albin.

"I'll tell ye where we'll take our fight—to the shipyard," a burly fellow in front of the crowd bellowed. "We'll destroy Mallow's livelihood as he's destroyed ours!"

Albin shook his head, eyes widening. "That's not what I mean, and you'll get nothing that way. This is a matter for the law!"

"We're the law now." The burly man took off at a run.

So did the others, bypassing the carriage and swarming down the gravel road like a mad pack of dogs.

"Wait. Stop!" Albin shouted as he plummeted to his seat and took the reins. The skinny man beside him nearly toppled out headfirst as Albin wheeled the carriage in a tight roundabout then gave the horses lead to tear after them.

Rosa sagged against James, his shoulder a solid beam holding her steady. That had been a close call. . .yet the danger hadn't ended. It had only flown towards the town. She peered up at him. "We have got to help Albin warn those at the shipyard, or someone could get hurt."

He nodded. "I will go."

"And I will go with you."

"No. As you have witnessed, a mob is unpredictable." A muscle jumped on his neck. "I would not have you in danger."

"Nor would I you, but it must be done, and you cannot confront those men alone. It was only minutes ago they were after you." She lifted her chin, resolute on the matter.

"I know that look, Sir James." Father yanked off his glasses and cleaned them with the hem of his shirt. "Either you take her with you, or she'll find another way to get there herself, and I'm sure you have a horse that's faster than that broken-springed cab I hired."

For a long moment, James's gaze bounced between Rosa and her father. Eventually he held out his hand. "Are you ready for a hard ride?"

She answered by entwining her fingers in his.

It took longer than she would have liked for him to saddle Belle, and as much as she admired the strong move of his muscles as he worked, she couldn't help but fret. It was not just one life that could be lost at the shipyard. Once set afire, that blaze would spread from building to building—potentially consuming the entire town.

They were going to need yet another miracle.

Smoke violated the air. Thick and white and menacing. An ill portent that promised heartbreak and death. James's gut hardened to a rock as he dismounted Belle far from the crowd thronging near the shipyard's gate. Even at this distance, safety wasn't a guarantee, not with this unpredictable grouping. He tied Belle's lead loosely around a fence post. God sure picked a strange way for him to start interacting with his fellow man again.

"Stay here," he ordered.

Rosa frowned down at him. "I should come with you. These people know me. Their wives know me. If I could speak to them, maybe they would listen."

He set his jaw as he shot her an I-will-not-be-trifled-with stare. "I will do what I can, but I shall not endanger you. And if trouble heads this way, get out of here as fast as Belle will carry you. Understood?"

"Understood." Her jaw jutted. "But I do not like it."

"Neither do I." He stalked towards the mob. Curses spread like a cancer, as did the raised fists and fury. James shouldered his way through the zealous pack, morbidly grateful not to be the center of attention for once.

As he neared the front of the crowd, he spied Preston Mallow shouting angrily from atop a stack of crates. Sweat glistened on his bald head and dripped down his brow.

Albin Mallow held the ground in front of him, arms spread wide as if he could keep the throng from surging against his uncle. "Take this to the constable!"

"What, and give him time to escape? None of it!" The mob roared. "Burn it down, boys. Burn Mallow down!"

Several men dodged past the thin line of guards stationed around the Mallows. Torches arced through the air, landing on shingles, on lumber, on barrels of tar. Smoke rose like an unholy prayer.

"After all I've done for you people?" Blue veins popped out on Preston Mallow's neck. "I'm the one who keeps this town afloat."

"Yer the one who nearly ruined us!" One man threw a rock, nicking the shipyard owner on the cheek.

Mallow narrowed his eyes, not even bothering to swipe away the blood. "Keep this up and I will ruin you."

"You already have!"

More rocks flew, pelting him so hard, he hunched over, blood oozing through his fingers as he tried to protect his face. The crowd surged, lusty for a fight. Albin stumbled, his back against the crates. If something weren't done now, they'd both die beneath the crush of the horde.

James ducked between two guards, the harried men too preoccupied with holding back the masses to stop a lone sprinter. As he passed Albin, he spoke low, for his ears alone. "I will create a distraction. You get your uncle out of here however you can."

Albin's jaw dropped, then firmed with determination as he nodded.

James swung around to the back of the crate stack and climbed up. Thankfully the boxes were full, so it was a rather sturdy little platform. The instant he reached Mallow, he shoved the man behind him. "Go."

Mallow scowled, a ghoulish sight with the blood dripping down his face. "This is my business, not yours."

"You will not have a business if you do not leave immediately." He shoved the man closer to the edge.

Albin hesitated a second more, then grabbed for Preston. "Come, Uncle."

Leaving them both behind, James faced the crowd, arms spread wide. "People of Whitby, hear me!"

Some looked.

A few muttered, "It's the baronet. What's he doin' here?"

Most continued pressing against the line of guards.

"Listen!" James roared. "What you are doing is no more right than trying to burn down my home. Leave now before you do something you will regret."

A particularly large man eased to the front and swung a club. "Only thing we'll regret is listening to you. Come on, boys!"

James ducked away from a broken bottle flying through the air. "Albin Mallow is right. This matter belongs in the courts, not in your hands."

"What do you know?" a rail of a man yelled. "You don't even live here. Yer not one of us."

A demented cheer rose to the heavens. The rioters swelled ahead. One man caught in the middle fell sideways, his cries and body completely obliterated by the stamping of feet.

James gritted his teeth. There'd be no stopping this frenzied pack. He had to get out of here—and more importantly, get Rosa as far away from this deadly chaos as possible.

THIRTY-ONE

There was nothing further to be said, and we parted.

It was a melee. A wild free-for-all. And the man she loved was caught in the middle. Rosa slid from Belle at the sound of the rioters roaring against James, heart stuck in her throat. Yes, he'd told her to stay put, and she had.

Until now.

Hiking her skirts, she dashed towards the shipyard gates, lifting a prayer for protection as she ran—then prayed even harder for James when she caught sight of him. He stood alone on a stack of crates, the writhing mass swarming towards him. If he fell, he'd be crushed.

Not only that, but thick smoke billowed into the air now, spreading fast. In no time, it would break its lead to terrorize the town. The library would be one of the first buildings to go. The thought of losing all those books sickened her. Someone had to stop this, and though James tried, no one listened to him.

Well, then.

She charged ahead, slipping past the rear edge of the mob. An empty wagon stood opposite James, and she hefted herself up onto the bed. Once she looked out over the boiling chaos, fear began chipping away at her bravery. She'd been trying to stamp out superstitions for years, but no one had listened to her then, even when heads were calm and tempers cool. There was no logical reason this mob, inflamed as they were, would listen to her now. Yet inexplicably God had somehow used Albin Mallow to turn the mob away from the manor, so could He not use her here now?

Please let it be so. . .

Clenching handfuls of her skirt for courage, she lifted her face. "Friends, neighbours, listen to me!"

As she feared, the mob paid her no mind, a single voice—and a woman's voice, at that. James snapped her a look of fierce determination. "Rosa, leave!"

She should and she would. But before she did, she had to give it one last shot. Determined to make her final words count, she scanned the crowd, searching for inspiration. "Mr. Danvers, Mr. Elliot!" She bellowed so loudly it ached in her throat. "Mr. Carpenter and Brougham. A word for all of you, my neighbours, my friends."

The men she'd named turned and eyed her. Mr. Danvers even nudged Mr. Brougham with his elbow, recognition lighting his face. "It's the Edwards girl."

She sucked air in sharply. Could it be that simple? Perhaps if she singled out more by name, a measure of humanity might be restored. She identified as many as she could, shouting loud, shouting fast. "All of you must turn around and go home. You were wrong about Sir James. Do not be in the wrong again."

James clambered down from his perch and shouldered his way towards her. The mob murmured and shuffled, perched on the edge of indecision. One brute she didn't know flung her an obscene gesture. "We're not wrong, woman. Get yourself gone."

"You tell her, Wolf!" the man next to him shouted. Others glanced between the gates and the growing flames licking at the shipyard buildings.

"Rosa!" James pushed through the throng like a freight train.

But she wasn't leaving now. Couldn't. Because though she might not be able to reason with this mob, God could. *Please, God, let it be!*

"Listen, men! What you are doing here is no better than what Preston Mallow did to you."

Wolf hurled a few curses. "He and Grafton killed our animals!"

"And you are destroying much more than that. By burning down this shipyard, you are putting countless people out of work, maybe even taking lives in the process."

That stopped a few of them, the older ones, those with a tender conscience.

But others merely scowled. "Mallow ruined our livelihoods. It's time that Lucifer pay in kind."

"Rosa, come down." James shot up his hand.

She glanced away from it. As much as she appreciated his protection, this was too important. "What Mr. Mallow did was despicable, but so is burning down the shipyard. This is not how you conquer wickedness. You are only spreading the devastation, ruining the livelihoods of others, your own fellows."

James swiped for her, but she retreated a step as more and more men lowered their torches to listen.

Not Wolf, though. His face darkened to a deep purple, spittle flying as he yelled, "It's better to let the town burn to get rid of such an evil!"

"Is it?" Rosa popped her fists onto her hips. "Is your thirst for vengeance so strong that you would destroy your homes? Your families? Yourselves? Do not let honour die here this day, for I believe you are all men of honour." She slid her gaze from one sweaty face to the next. "I implore you not to let truth and justice burn to ashes. I know your wives, your children. Do not risk their lives by letting this fire go beyond the shipyard. Put it out now!"

Mumbles began, then grew in strength.

"She might be right. That wind changes, there'll be no stopping it."

"My wife's abed with our newest. I can't have this spreadin'."

"There's no might about it. The Edwards' girl *is* right. We are better than this. We ne'er shoulda listened to them fishwife tales anyway."

Hope flared in Rosa's chest. "Let us put behind us all the rumours and superstitions that have divided us for so long and work together to put this fire out."

As if on cue, clanging firetruck bells grew louder.

"Well done," James's voice warmed her ear, and she turned to him, startled. She'd not noticed him climb up on the wagon bed. He tucked her behind him and faced the crowd. "We can do this, men. Find a bucket. Heave a rain barrel. Do whatever you can to help the firemen put out these flames."

Firemen poured in through the gates, and thankfully the mob not only allowed them passage, some of them even helped guide the hoses.

James grinned at her. "You were brilliant. Now, take Belle and go home. I have a fire to put out."

He jumped down then held up his hands to guide her.

She accepted his aid, but even so, arched a brow the moment her feet hit the dirt. "You mean *we* have a fire to put out."

"Rosa," he grumbled, the cut of his jaw stern.

She merely laughed. Such a look might frighten those who didn't know him, but not her. Not now. "You are wasting your time, you know."

"Indeed, you are." Her father joined their side, clapping James on the back. "So, are the two of you going to help put this fire out or stand here arguing about it?"

James rolled his eyes. "The pair of you are incorrigible."

Rosa smiled at her father. "How many times have we heard the same from Mother?"

"Too many to count." Her father snatched a bucket from a lad passing them out and handed it to James.

He took it while frowning at her. "I can see I will not win this battle, but even so, I insist you stay by my side the entire time. I will not have you—"

"I know." She flashed him a mischievous grin. "You will not have me in danger, nor will I be, for I trust you will allow nothing to harm so much as a hair on my head."

"As I said, incorrigible." He looked down his nose, yet there was a distinct twinkle in his eyes.

"To work, then!" Her father dashed into the fray.

Armed with buckets, they set to work, and work it was. Grueling, actually. In no time her arms ached and her legs shook, weighted down by sodden skirts. But oh, how it warmed her heart to see the men of Whitby treat James as one of their own. Shoulder to shoulder they laboured beside him, not one of them flinching to stand so near a so-called vampire.

By the time nightfall threatened on the horizon, no more bursts of orange or red flamed from any of the buildings. They'd done it, mostly. One man said the damage had spread beyond the back gate to the next-door brewery and jumped across the lane to the smithy, but other than that, the fire had been contained.

Rosa straightened, arching her back against an ache as man by man passed by, filthy with soot and ash. No doubt she looked as bad.

Mr. Danvers approached, buffing James on the arm with a playful swat. "Well done, sir." His gaze slid to hers. "And well done to you too, Miss Edwards. We were a mite out o' control."

"Perhaps." With the back of her hand, she swiped hair from her eyes. "But the important thing is that you did not let the fire get out of control."

"This one, anyway." Beside her, Father chuckled. "I suspect we've one more blaze to tamp down at home. We'd best make haste to put your mother's mind at ease."

James tipped his head at her father. "May I have a word with your daughter before you leave?"

"By all means." Father swept out his hand, indicating a quiet corner near the very wagon she'd stood on hours ago. "That may be your only spot for privacy, though, such as it is."

James gave him a nod, then tucked her hand into his arm. "Shall we?"

At her assent, he set off, his long legs steady and sure, hers jittery. Could be from the toil of fighting fires all afternoon, but more likely it was from the uncertainty of what he might say to her. Was this it? Would he finally declare his love for her? Maybe even ask her to be his wife? Her heart soared.

Oh God, make it so!

He stopped with his back to the wagon, facing the passing men, and warmth filled her chest. Even now that the danger of fire was past, he was still protecting her by keeping watch.

Then his gaze sought hers, the whites of his eyes a startling contrast against the blackened smudges on his face. "You did a good thing today."

"As did you."

Pulling out his handkerchief, he wiped her brow, the heat of his body still warming the cloth. His own brows lowered, weighted by a sorrow she couldn't name. "I shall treasure my memories of you always."

Her breath caught. That didn't sound like a proposal. "Why do I feel you are saying goodbye again?"

He tucked his cloth into his pocket. "Because I am. You know I sail tomorrow."

"I know. I was just hoping. . ." She swallowed, forcing down a swell of disappointment. Perhaps she had been wrong about his kisses, that they'd meant nothing more than a sweet stolen moment to him. What a fool she'd been to give him her heart, but there was no taking it back now.

For a long while, he stood there saying nothing, looking past her, his big chest rising and falling with deep breaths. His dark hair curled at his temples, dampened by perspiration. Ash coated his head and shoulders. He smelled like he'd just conquered hell. Even like this, unkempt and weary to the bone, she loved him—and loved him fiercely.

Without warning, his gaze shot to hers like a lightning bolt, his eyes blazing as bright as the flames they'd put out. "I love you, Rosa Edwards. I have loved you since the day you tumbled off your bicycle. And because of that love, I must let you go."

She shook her head violently. "That does not make sense." None of this did. First he said "goodbye" and now "I love you"? What sort of man did that? Tears burned in her eyes.

"Rosa." He cupped her cheek with his hand. "Please try to understand. I cannot give you the life you deserve. You saw what happened to my mother. The same fate awaits me. There can be no happy ending for us."

A sob rose in her throat. "I do not need a happy ending. I just need you." Her voice broke. So did a tear.

James wiped it with his finger, grief etched into the sooty lines on his face. "Come, now. Say you will see me off tomorrow with a smile, for I would have my last sight of England be your beautiful face."

"But I do not want you to leave. I cannot bear the thought of not being with you."

"I know, love. I know." He pressed a kiss to the top of her head. "This is not easy for me either."

So much pain rattled in his husky tone, it cut straight to her heart. Instinctively she knew her objections hurt him, and she felt horrible about it—she truly did—but the agony inside overshadowed it all. She burst into tears.

Instantly his arms wrapped around her, and she wept into his waistcoat, already damp from the bucket brigade and heat of his own labour. This would be the last time she breathed in the scent of him, the strength of him, and the thought made her cry all the harder.

He held her while her body shook and heart raged, his big hand rubbing little circles on her back as he whispered, "Shhh. All will be made right, for we serve a good and gracious God."

It was a hard truth, but a truth all the same. God had shown her His goodness in ways she'd never expected.

When at last exhaustion draped over her and her shoulders sagged, he set her from him, the love in his eyes so pure it hurt to look at him. "You're weary, and your father is waiting. I will see you on the wharf tomorrow at ten, yes?"

Somehow she managed to nod. It was the best she could do, for she might never speak again, so thick was the sorrow clogging her throat. She'd never cry again, either. Never weep. Never sob. She couldn't.

She had no tears left.

Albin slammed the lid on his suitcase then stomped over to the bell pull and gave the thing a good yank. The sooner he was out of his uncle's house, the better. He hadn't a clue of where he'd settle, but for now, just leaving Whitby would suffice.

Snatching his hat off the bureau, Albin strode to the mirror. It was hard to predict just how long this newfound courage might last, but one thing he knew for certain: he liked the feel of independence surging through his veins.

As he set his hat just so atop his head, a servant entered. "You rang, sir?"

He gave his hat a final tap. "Please see my bag to my carriage immediately."

"Very good, sir." The man hefted the suitcase with a stifled grunt—a good reminder to hitch up two horses instead of one. So many garments had been shoved into the traveling bag, not only was it inordinately heavy, but Albin wondered how he'd ever get the wrinkles out of the fabric.

Another problem for another time, though. For now, he grabbed a leather messenger bag and shouldered it. Indeed, this problem must be settled first. He adjusted the strap then patted the bag.

"What do you think you're doing?" A gravelly voice hit him between the shoulders.

Albin turned, then recoiled as he gazed upon his uncle's mangled face. One of his eyes was swollen shut, purple as a turnip from a fist he'd taken when Albin had ushered him away from the shipyard. The edge of a jagged cut peeked out from a bandage that'd gone askew, and the lump on his nose testified to the broken cartilage underneath. If a faithful foreman hadn't stepped in to help, Uncle Preston would no doubt be lying in a heap, crushed beneath the boots of the mob.

Albin grabbed his gloves off the table near the door, a surprising amount of pity mixing with his anger. "I'm leaving."

Uncle Preston narrowed his eyes. "Where to?"

"I don't know."

"Typical." Uncle snorted. "Stop this nonsense and get some sleep. We've an inordinate amount of work to do tomorrow."

To his surprise, his resolve did not weaken before his uncle's disdain. Albin lifted his chin. "No."

"What did you say?" A cougar couldn't have growled more menacingly.

Even so, Albin tugged off the big gold ring on his pinky and threw it at him. Uncle caught it with one swift reach, surprise flashing silver in his eyes. "You'll have to find someone else to manage your business affairs. I am not your puppet anymore."

Uncle Preston reared back his head. "You're mad."

"Correction. I *was* mad. Not anymore. I'm done with this. I'm done with you." He was—and how freeing it felt. Albin stalked past him, only to be yanked back by one arm.

"If you walk through that door," he said, the words puffing out on hot breaths, "there will be no turning back. I took you in once. I'll not do it again."

Albin wrenched away, astonished his uncle's threat didn't paralyze him with fear. "You think I don't know why you housed me? It was for no great love of family or kindness of heart. You tolerated me for the sole purpose of gaining and spending my inheritance, as small as it was. Mine!"

Uncle Preston spat out a curse. "You're no victim. You didn't have to stay."

Though he hated to admit it, his uncle was right again. He hadn't needed to stay, but—God help him—he'd enjoyed all the benefits of his uncle's money and status. No, it was more than that. So much more.

He shook his head sadly, knowing his uncle wouldn't understand, but needing to speak the words anyway. "You were all I had left in this world. The only link to my mother and father."

His uncle's thin lips pulled tight over a sharp-toothed sneer. "They were no saints. Your father married a tavern wench."

Albin grabbed his uncle by the collar and gave him a shake. "My mother was an innkeeper's daughter, a respectable woman, and you will not speak of her so. My father loved her, loved me!" He released Uncle Preston with a shove. "But I guess love is something you'll never understand."

He wheeled about and strode to the door, his steps surprisingly light. He should have stood up to the man years ago.

"You'd better bloody well get back here," his uncle raged. "You can't walk away like this."

Pressing the messenger bag tight against his side, Albin upped his pace. "Goodbye, Uncle."

"You'll never make it out there on your own, not without me. You're in for a rude awakening!"

His uncle's voice faded as Albin trotted down the grand stairway, the eyes of countless dead relatives on the wall watching his bold departure. Let them. Let them all witness that Albin Mallow was finally his own man.

Outside, he climbed into his carriage and urged the horses onward, passing by a police cart headed towards his uncle's house. He couldn't help but smirk. It appeared Uncle Preston was the one who would experience the rude awakening.

Streetlights glowed eerily in a mist settling over the town. Not many people were about so late, which suited him. The fewer witnesses, the better.

Despite the lack of foot or horse traffic, he guided his carriage down one back lane, then another, and finally pulled to a stop in front of the library. Setting the brake, he cast a glance around before hopping down to the cobbles. He unlooped the messenger bag as he strode to the after-hours depository. It was a small atonement for his sins against Rosa, for he had treated her brutishly at times. Hopefully, though, this offering would suffice.

He shoved the whole bag into the book depository, then walked away without a backwards glance, ready to be a new man in a new place.

THIRTY-TWO

Some have seen sorrow; but there are fair days yet in store.

It would be easier to mourn a lover who died at sea. A man who kissed you breathless then set sail, only to be dashed against the rocks because of a squall was a morbid truth, yet one a heart could understand, for there was cause and effect. Simple as that. Rosa opened the last window shade, allowing weak morning light to seep into the library. She'd never understand why James was leaving. Oh, she could comprehend the mechanics of his words well enough, the syntax, the syllables, even the sentiment of his motivation, but she'd never grasp how he could profess to love her and then leave her behind.

Listlessly, she wandered over to the medicinals and began restocking the little brown bottles on the shelves. Saying goodbye to James today would be the hardest thing she'd ever have to do, for it would be permanent. Like a pot of indelible ink tipped over on a white counterpane, her heart would be forever stained.

She put the box of Mother's elixirs away and unlocked the front door, wishing she could walk right out of this town. The need to leave Whitby burned hotter than ever in her chest. As much as she denied the supernatural—at least the superstitious kind—too many ghosts would haunt her here. Too many bittersweet memories of the moments she'd shared with James.

From sheer muscle memory alone, she shuffled to the book depository and opened the lid to retrieve the overnight returns. Reaching in, she fingered the smooth leather of a bag, not a book cover. Odd, that. She pulled out a messenger satchel, a very fine one by the look and feel of it. Who in the world would have left this along with their books? Hopefully there would be some identification inside.

She unbuckled the strap and pulled out two items. One was nothing but a collection of bound papers and the other was a beautiful—

Little tingles skittered over her scalp as she stared at the rare book and the manuscript she'd lost. How could this be? Who had found them? Where and when? And why drop them in the depository like a thief in the night instead of returning them for some sort of reward?

She dug back into the satchel, feeling about for any sort of documentation that might give a clue as to whom this belonged. Nothing. Frustrated, she turned it upside down and shook the thing properly, hoping for something to fall out.

Nothing did.

Carefully, she went back to examining the lost items. Except for a faint smudge on the cover of Mr. Stoker's manuscript, both appeared to be just fine.

"Thank You, God," she whispered, then set aside the manuscript and clutched the rare book. Bypassing the front counter, she hurried to where her father bent over one of the new arrivals, the same position he'd been in since they'd arrived. He'd not even whistled once, so engrossed was he.

"Father, look! I can scarce believe it."

"Hmm?" he asked without looking.

She slid the book atop the journal that engaged him. "It is the title I lost. The rare one. Someone returned it in the depository along with Mr. Stoker's manuscript, and both are unscathed."

Brow wrinkling, he hunched closer. He lifted the cover and paged through, then reverently closed it. Even though he wasn't squinting anymore, there were still little creases at the sides of his eyes. "You're right. This title is no worse for the wear. Are you certain this went down with the bicycle?"

She bobbed her head. "More than certain."

"Who returned it?"

"I wish I knew. I should like to properly thank them."

"As would I." Father's gaze drifted back to the book, and he murmured as he ran a finger over it, "Amazing."

Rosa gripped the back of her father's chair, peering past him to search the cover once again for any dings or mars. He was wrong. This was more than amazing. This was a flat-out miracle. That rushing water should have completely ruined such a perishable collection of paper and glue. How on earth had a book survived a river that'd completely destroyed a heavy metal bicycle?

She glanced towards the heavens, a small smile twitching her lips at God's goodness. "I guess some things cannot be explained," she breathed.

"And some things can." He set the newly returned title aside and handed her the book he'd been reading, holding it open to a particular page. "Read this."

At first she scrunched her nose, thoroughly confused with all the medical jargon and Latin comprising most of the text. But the more she read, the more her pulse took off at a gallop. This was about porphyria—*two* kinds of porphyria. Never once had James mentioned there was more than one.

She handed him back the journal. "What does this mean?"

"It means, Daughter"—a slow smile spread on his face—"that Sir James might not be facing the same fate as his mother. If I am to understand this correctly, there is an acute variation that affects the nervous system, which—as in the case of Lady Dorina—can lead to madness and death. If he has not yet suffered any of her symptoms other than the skin lesions, then this study claims his affliction is not fatal."

She clapped her hands. "But that is wonderful news!"

"News that should be shared, don't you think?" He winked.

"Oh Father, I shall tell him at once!" She whirled.

He tugged her back. "Here, take this." He held up the journal.

"But this is a new arrival not even yet registered." She gaped, hardly daring to touch it again. "It ought not leave the library."

He pressed the journal into her hands and wrapped his fingers around her own. "You are more important to me than a book. Take it with my blessing, Daughter."

Holding back a sheer white curtain with one finger, James peered out at the manicured lawn of Seward's Home for the Aged and Infirm. Outside, two grey-headed men shuffled along a pea-gravel pathway, deep in conversation. Beyond them, another pair of sloop-shouldered gentlemen played a game of draughts at a wrought-iron table. Late summer flowers bloomed in abundance all around, and on the horizon, a strip of steel-grey sea blended into the overcast sky. He might almost be gazing upon a painting, so picturesque was the scene. James smiled. It would do.

"I trust you shall be comfortable here." Dropping the curtain, he faced Renfield. "And if not, send word and I will arrange for something else."

The old butler stood wide-eyed near the doorway of his new bedchamber, almost as if he were afraid the room might disappear if he entered too far. "Oh sir, a man could ask for nothing more. Gardens. Companionship. Three meals a day and snug accommodations." Renfield shook his head. "It is all too much, really."

"It's all too late, more like. I should have insisted you retire here long ago. You have been faithful to my family for many years." He rested his hand on Renfield's shoulder. "You deserve this, Joseph."

The old fellow's pale blue eyes misted, from hearing his Christian name spoken by his employer or from gratefulness? Hard to say. "It has been my honour, sir. And don't you worry about the manor. I'll keep my eye on it. A daily constitutional will do me good."

"I appreciate that." He squeezed Renfield's shoulder then donned his hat. "Once I have finished with the threat to my family estate in Transylvania, I shall more than likely sell Morgrave. I will keep you posted. But at least now that you and Belle are both taken care of, I can travel with a lighter heart. Oh, and I nearly forgot." He pulled out an amber jar from his pocket. "More salve for your knuckles to hold you over until I can send a shipment."

"Thank you, sir, and Godspeed." The old man's Adam's apple bobbed, his voice thick with emotion. "God bless as well."

"Thank you, my friend. Goodbye." Dipping his head, James strode from the room.

The retirement home was situated close to town, so the ride to the dock was a short affair, which was a blessing. The cab he'd rented smelled of sausage gone bad. Worse, the morose thoughts he'd been holding at bay all morning threatened to billow in on him now that he was alone. He couldn't wait to shake the dust of Whitby from his feet, and yet at the same time, he had no desire to go, not when it meant leaving behind a certain brown-eyed woman. How could he possibly feel two such conflicting emotions simultaneously? To dissect one meant he'd have to abandon the other, and yet he wasn't quite sure which one he ought to let go of first.

He exited the cab and flipped the driver a coin, glad for a waft of briny air and the bustle of the wharf. Better to put his mind on keeping out of the way of burly stevedores as he searched for the correct berth than to brood upon the goodbye he must give Rosa.

As he neared the fourth slip—the one assigned to the merchant ship that would carry him home—he spied a green skirt. Rosa paced with quick steps in front of the gangplank, brow pinched, clutching a thin book, possibly two. Alarm tightened his chest. He knew this parting wouldn't be easy, but such agitation didn't bode well.

"Rosa?" Sidestepping a pile of rope, he closed the distance between them, nearly dropping to his knees when he caught her lilac scent. This would be the last time he inhaled her sweetness. "You are troubled. What is wrong?"

Whirling, she beamed at him, her smile bright enough to shame a July sun. "Nothing that a pair of dark glasses and a wide hat brim cannot fix."

Her words, her buoyancy were in such complete opposition to her former pacing, he could only frown. "I suppose you are making some kind of point, but I fail to understand what it is."

"Oh James! It is wonderful, that is what it is." She hugged the books as if they were puppies to be nuzzled.

"Hmm." A gust of wind clanked through the ship's riggings and nearly snagged the hat off his head. "Not exactly the sort of goodbye I was expecting, but I am glad to see you have finally accepted my medical condition and my need to bid you farewell."

"I most emphatically do and do not." She lifted her pert little nose.

"You are very cryptic." And very adorable with the way she kept batting her bonnet ribbon away from her cheek. He'd never tire of gazing upon that beautiful face—a face he would miss dearly.

Behind them, the ship's bell clanged, setting off a squawk of seabirds. "All aboard!" a sailor bellowed.

This was it, then. The moment he'd dreaded. The last time he'd speak to the woman who captivated him like none other.

He shifted his weight, his heel scuffing against the worn boards of the dock. "As much as I enjoy bantering with you, I am afraid it is time to say goodbye. Thank you for coming to see me off. You have no idea how much that means to me."

"I have something to show you that will mean a great deal more." A mischievous smile curved her mouth as she handed him what she'd been carrying. "The first folder is Mr. Stoker's manuscript, which I thought I had lost, and the other is something I would like you to read now. Page one hundred five."

A strange gesture, to be sure, but perhaps this was her odd way of saying farewell. A poem of a sweet parting, perhaps? Even stranger was that she'd found the manuscript. He eyed her. "Where did you find—"

"I shall tell you later." She tapped the thin book, a newer edition medical journal he'd not yet seen. "Page one hundred five, straightaway, please."

He couldn't help but smile at her little-girl excitement and flipped to the page she suggested. After reading only a few sentences, the world around him faded. He devoured the rest like a starving man.

> *. . .this group study of the blood borne disease relating to hemato porphyrin definitively resolves that there is a distinct separation between two very different strains, that being acute intermittent porphyria and cutanea tardea. The acute mainly affects the nervous system, causing severe neurological attacks including but not limited to seizures, trances, and hallucinations which may persist over days, weeks, or even years. In this form, the mortality rate is nearly one hundred percent. Cutanea tardea, however, affects the skin upon any exposure to light, namely, in welts and blisters. It is an unsightly affliction, but rarely—if ever—is it fatal.*

He re-read it. Again and again. *Two* types of porphyria? Why had he never heard of this before? Why had the world never heard it? Surely he was not the only one who believed the lie that he could expect nothing less than a horrible death. This information should be blasted from a mountaintop! *If* it were true.

And that was a pretty big *if.*

"Is this not good news?" Rosa bounced on her toes, giddy as a schoolgirl who'd won an award. "Your disease is not fatal. You are not going to die like your mother."

"But. . ." Could it be? He stared at the page, unsure if he could—or should—quell the rising hope this one obscure study ignited in his heart. He'd hunt down the author, the participants, and question each and every one. And if it proved to be true?

Oh God, please let it be so.

He dragged his gaze from the page to the brown-eyed beauty in front of him. For the first time in his life, he dared to think of a happy future, one he might share with someone else instead of suffering alone.

Slowly, he shook his head. "This could change everything."

"It *does* change everything." She grinned. "I could not be more pleased that you no longer have to face a horrific death."

"That is not at all what I am talking about."

Her brow wrinkled. "Now you are the one making a point I fail to understand."

"Then allow me to be perfectly clear."

Heedless of the sailors and fisherfolk around them, he dropped to one knee and, setting down the journal and manuscript, took her hands in his. It was reckless, this display, opening them both up to ridicule and scorn, and yet freeing in a way he never imagined. He'd not waste a minute more without making this woman his own. "If this study proves to be legitimate, then will you, Rosa Edwards, do me the honour of becoming my wife?"

"Would ye look at that?" A nearby fisherman gawked, elbowing a man in a ratty jumper next to him. "The baronet's pledgin' his troth to the Edwards girl!"

"She won't marry a vampire," the other fellow grumbled.

"Hush yer gob!" the fisherman barked. "He's no bleedin' vampire. He's one o' us now."

The kind words went down deep. He'd never belonged to any people. Not that it really mattered. The only one he wanted to belong to was the woman who held his entire world in her hands.

Rosa pressed her fingers to her mouth, eyes shining like stars. Her head bobbed as she choked out, "Yes! Yes, I will."

James pressed a kiss to her palm, then rose and brushed away her tears—happy tears for once.

"Boarding!" the sailor at his back called again.

James gave him a sharp nod over his shoulder, then pulled Rosa into his arms. "I still must go," he whispered against her ear, "but you can be sure I will return for you."

"Oh James"—she pressed her fingers against his cheek—"I love you so."

"No more than I love you."

"Kiss the girl already!" The fishermen joined in a chorus of belly laughs.

Embarrassing—but a good suggestion. He claimed Rosa's lips with a foreign surge of happiness.

"Now tha's more like it," the men heckled.

Despite the catcalls for such a public exhibition, Rosa kissed him right back. When he pulled away, he couldn't help but grin so wide, it ached in his jaw. "Next time I sail, you will be at my side. Never again shall we part. I vow it."

"Last call!" the sailor hollered.

Rosa handed him the manuscript, then scooped up the journal and pressed it into his hands. "Take this, for then you will have to return soon." A rogue smile curved her lips. "The overdue fines would be exorbitant."

"I will return posthaste, yet it has nothing to do with fines. Be ready, for I will marry you the moment my feet hit English soil."

And with that, he wheeled about and sailed away.

THIRTY-THREE

You are nearest and dearest and all the world to me;
our souls are knit into one, for all life and time.

One Year Later, Worcester, England

No wonder women didn't come here. The stuffy auditorium of the British Medical Association was a man's world, filled with the funk of one too many hair pomades. Being the only skirt in the gallery—nay, in the whole room—Rosa was extremely grateful for the two familiar faces on each side of her, though she still found Sala's perpetual scowl to be intimidating. He hadn't smiled once since arriving in England last week, though to be fair, he didn't grin at home in Umbră Castle, either. She'd thought once the foul business with the land dispute had been decided in James's favour, the man would have brightened up somewhat.

The loud drone of men's voices buzzed around her, and she twisted the golden band on her third finger, anxious for the noise to end and the lecture to begin. Had she typed the notes properly? What if she'd made an error, fouled up the medical jargon or put something in the wrong order? She'd be mortified.

And James would be shamed.

She spun the ring round and round. This was more nerve-wracking than all those long days she'd waited for her beloved to return from Transylvania.

Renfield patted her hand with his gnarled fingers, stilling her nervous movement. "There now, don't fret, Lady Morgan. Sir James knows how to handle himself."

She glanced at the dear old man. As far as she was concerned, they didn't see him often enough and had even suggested he travel with them as they straddled lives between Whitby and Transylvania. But Father would have none of it. Renfield had become a permanent fixture in the library now that she no longer worked there, and the two men had struck up quite a friendship.

She gave his fingers a little squeeze. "I am not worried so much about my husband as I am about the notes he is to read."

"No doubt they are impeccable, else you'd not have graduated with honours from your secretarial course."

Her lips parted. "How would you know that?"

"Oh, my dear, he's very proud of you, you know."

Warmth filled her chest. She'd never tire of witnessing the many ways James showed his abiding love for her. Her! Not the picture her family painted of her but her true self. Even her mother and sister had finally admitted there could never be another man who would cherish her more than James did.

A gavel cracked on wood, and after three strikes, the bass hum in the room diminished somewhat.

"Gentlemen, doctors, esteemed guests." A man in a blue suit and striped cravat banged on the podium once more, fully quieting the auditorium. "Tonight, the British Medical Association is honoured to present a speaker who has devoted years of exhaustive research into the different types, symptoms, and treatments for porphyria, a malady that up to this point has been misunderstood at best and ignored at worst. Shrouded in superstition and stigma, this disease affects a sizable portion of the population, encompassing rich and poor alike, and is even rumoured to have been the cause of our own King George III's progression into madness. It is of the utmost importance that this ailment is brought to the forefront of medical attention, which is what we are about this evening. And so, without further ado, I give to you Sir James Morgan."

Applause thundered around the room as James shook hands with the man then took command on stage. Indeed. He could rule the world with those dark eyes.

"Gentlemen"—his gaze shot up to hers, one brow arched—"and lady, I come to you with material that is life-changing for those who suffer from a dreaded disease that not only afflicts the victim bodily, but mentally as well. I should know, for it has been the bane of my existence."

As he went on to explain the intricacies of porphyria in its various forms, Rosa leaned forward in her seat, not so much enthralled with the speech but with the man. He was resplendent in his black suit, choosing not to hide behind the lectern but to stride about, his long legs traveling the stage. He was a beautiful creature, a lion among these learned doctors, garnering not only her attention but that of every man in the room as he shared possible treatments.

By the time he ended with a call for more research, Rosa shot to her feet and clapped so hard her palms stung. And she wasn't the only one. Applause reached to the rafters.

But even before it died down, Sala wrapped his fingers around her arm and spoke into her ear. "Come. He'll be waiting."

She frowned. "But will he not wish to meet with the doctors and—"

"He wishes to be with his wife on this auspicious occasion, for so he directed me." Without a word more, he led her and Renfield out to the lobby, just as James slipped through a side door.

Rosa rushed over to him. "You were wonderful!"

"Because I have a wonderful secretary." He brushed his lips against her brow then offered his arm. "Now, shall we? It will not be long before those men file out here, and our carriage awaits."

She hesitated. "This seems highly irregular. Are you certain you do not want to stay? I have no doubt many will wish to shake your hand and congratulate you."

"Your praise is all I need. Besides, crowds make me nervous." He winked, then tucking her hand into the crook of his arm, tipped his head at Sala and Renfield, indicating for them to get moving.

Their little group hardly made it several steps outside the door before a man in black advanced through the shadow and mist of the night. "Sir James, Lady Morgan, a word, if you please."

Rosa's eyes widened as she peered up at a familiar stoat-like face.

"Mr. Stoker! What a surprise!"

"Not really. I planned to ambush the both of you here tonight." He wagged his eyebrows.

"Sounds ominous," James rumbled beside her.

"Nothing of the sort. I had heard you were to be in Worcester the same time as I and wished to deliver this in person before I travel to America on another production tour for the Lyceum." He offered her a green velvet box that fit neatly against her palm.

Rosa lifted the lid to reveal a small silver crucifix.

James peeked inside as well, then arched a brow at Mr. Stoker. "Are we to ward off vampires with this?"

Mr. Stoker laughed, his barrel chest bouncing. "Nothing of the sort. It is merely a token of my appreciation for your notes on my manuscript, and for you, Lady Morgan, for providing me with a rare book I could find nowhere else. Because of you two, I am closer to capturing the essence of my story."

"I am sure my wife would agree it was our pleasure to help. You are always welcome to visit our home in Transylvania and see the countryside for yourself."

"My husband speaks truth. Though folktales will always paint the land in a shade of superstition, there is no lovelier place."

"No doubt, Lady Morgan, but I wouldn't want to shatter the image of Dracula's castle I've painted in my mind. And so, with a grateful heart for the invitation and the help you've given me, I bid you both goodnight." He dipped his head.

"To you as well," James replied.

Rosa turned to him as Mr. Stoker disappeared into the night. "Well, that was a surprise."

"So is this." He removed the box from her hand and pressed a folded paper against her palm.

She opened it, curious beyond measure, but after she scanned what appeared to be a bill of sale, she scrunched her nose up at James. "What is this?"

"You will be happy to know that when we return to Morgrave manor, there will be no gargoyle in the hall to greet you."

Her jaw dropped. "You sold it?"

He grinned, so boyish yet manly her heart skipped a beat. "I did."

"But why?" She shook her head. "Your mother loved that piece."

"Yes, but you did not, and you are my wife. No, more than that. You are my life." Bending, he kissed her warmly, then pulled back. "There, happy?"

"Deliriously so." She ran her finger down his chest, relishing the feel of him, the scent, the fact that forevermore he was hers alone.

"You know," she murmured, "I always wished for a happy ending, but I have discovered that was a fruitless desire. True love can never end that way."

His brows pulled into a line. "That seems a contradiction."

"No, my sweet." She smiled up at him. "You see, a love like ours never ends."

HISTORICAL NOTES

All chapter quotes are taken directly from Bram Stoker's Dracula.

Bram Stoker

The celebrated author of *Dracula* was forty-five years old when he visited the subscription library in Whitby and asked for *The Accounts of Principalities of Wallachia and Moldavia*. The librarian wasn't even aware this rare book was part of their collection but did locate it, and Stoker paged through it while under supervision. He also visited the Whitby Museum and perused the tombstones at St. Mary's (where he did indeed get the name of Swales). Stoker wrote fifteen novels, but he wasn't only an author. He also managed the Lyceum Theater for Henry Irving. I took a bit of license in saying that his publisher was interested in his manuscript, because this story is set in 1890 (when he really did visit Whitby), but *Dracula* wasn't published until 1897.

Circulating/Subscription Libraries

Before libraries went public and made their books free for all to use, people had to pay for the privilege of borrowing books. Fortunately, most of these institutions kept their prices reasonable and as a result brought reading to the masses. . .namely, the middle class. The poor often didn't have time to read or funds to do so, while the wealthy had their own private collections. These libraries made it possible for women to further their education and indulge their imaginations. In large part, it was the rise of circulating libraries that popularized the gothic novel. And believe it or not, there are still a few subscription libraries in operation in the United Kingdom.

Porphyria

Both James and his mother suffer from an ailment that was notoriously misunderstood, often stigmatizing the sufferer, for it was known as the *vampyre disease*. Look at this list of symptoms and you'll understand why: sensitivity to sunlight, receding gums that make it look as if you have fangs, urine that is blood red, an aversion to garlic because the sulfur content could lead to acute pain, and facial disfigurement, which naturally would lead one to avoid mirrors. There are several different strains of porphyria, but most can be divided into one of two categories, acute or cutaneous. All are hereditary.

Bargheust Hound

A creature of folklore, the bargheust hound—or Yorkshire bargheust—is said to haunt the coastal regions of North Yorkshire. It's a huge beast, standing between six and nine feet tall at the shoulder and is reported to have glaring red saucer-sized eyes. Naturally the brute has lots of sharp teeth and foams at the mouth. Definitely not something you'd want to meet up with in the dark of night. Is it real? Who knows. You be the judge.

The *Demeter*

Besides being the ship that James Morgan arrives in, the *Demeter* is a fictional ship that is based on the real-life wreck of a Russian schooner, the *Dmitry*. Surprisingly, the ship made it safely to port during a "storm of great violence." But the next day, the sea was just as wicked and beat over the poor schooner. Her masts were destroyed with a huge crash, and the crew abandoned her. The ship was reported to have been ballasted with silver sand. When Bram Stoker heard the tale, it gave him the inspiration to rename the ship and fill it with dirt from Dracula's homeland.

Fat Rascals

When Rosa and her mother pass the bakery, Rosa's mother comments on bringing home some fat rascals. So, what exactly is that? Pure deliciousness, that's what! This tasty treat is a form of tea cake that was popular in the Yorkshire region during the nineteenth century. It's loaded with butter and cream, so you know it has to be good. Look up a recipe and give it a try. . .you won't be sorry.

Sea Shanties

Rosa's father has a quirky habit of whistling sea shanties. A shanty is a work song that's sung to a rhythm that would help to while away hours of hard labour. They are catchy little tunes with often repeating refrains. Here are some of the songs he whistled, and you can look them up on YouTube to hear what they sound like: "Spanish Ladies," "Ben Backstay," "Boney Was a Warrior," and "Haul Away for Rosie."

Yorkshire Pudding

To American ears, Yorkshire pudding sounds like it ought to be a delectable dessert. . .but it's not. Actually, it's more like a popover. A recipe was first published in 1747 in *The Art of Cookery Made Plain and Simple* by Hannah Glasse, distinguishing the Yorkshire pudding as lighter and crispier than in other parts of the country. Puddings were originally a meat-based food, like sausage, but over time it came to mean a bread dish or dessert.

Assizes

It was a blessing in disguise when James was thrown into jail, because the timing couldn't have been better for the assizes that was to meet in Whitby in two days. Held only twice a year (March/April and July/August), the assizes was a regional court circuit that dealt with more serious offenses such as murder, rape, robbery, and the like. Prisoners accused of such were held until one of the state-appointed judges made his rounds to the area. Judges traveled the circuit to hear cases all over England.

Rector George Austen

The clergyman who befriends James and imparts solid biblical truths was actually not a fictional character. George Austen, M.A. Canon of York, served at St. Mary's from 1875 until 1920. Though I don't mention any, he would have had several curates working with him as well. And no, I don't believe he was related to the famed author Jane Austen.

BIBLIOGRAPHY

Browne, James J. *The Original Ghost Walk of Whitby*. Ashford: Florun House Press, 2014.

Cook, Robin. *Whitby History Tour.* Gloucestershire: Amberley Publishing, 2018.

Skal, David J. *Something in the Blood: The Untold Story of Bram Stoker, the Man Who Wrote Dracula*. New York: Liveright Publishing Corporation, 2016.

Skinner, Julia. *Did You Know? Whitby, A Miscellany*. Salisbury: The Francis Frith Collection, 2010.

Stoker, Bram. *Dracula*. New York: Barnes & Noble, 2012.

Stoker, Bram with a foreword by Wynne, Dr. Catherine. *Bram Stoker Horror Stories, An Anthology of Classic Tales*. London: Flame Tree Publishing, 2018.

Thompson, Ian and Frost, Roger. *Secret Whitby.* Gloucestershire: Amberley Publishing, 2016.

ACKNOWLEDGMENTS

A novel is not written by a single author. It is the culmination of lots of the people who pour into an author's life. My gratitude goes out to too many to name, and yet here are a few.

Experts

Some facts are simply not to be found in books, leastwise some I cannot get my hands on. That's where those-in-the-know come in handy. I owe my gratitude to Sara Johnson, library supervisor at the Whitby Library, and Barbara Cowie, library volunteer at the Whitby Literary and Philosophical Society, for answering my questions about clergy members at St. Mary's Church during the 1890s.

Hand Holders

Thanks to my editors extraordinaire, Annie Tipton and Reagen Reed, and the entire team at Barbour.

Shout out to Wendy Lawton, my agent over at Books & Such Literary Agency.

Pants Kickers

Critique buddies who slashed and burned through this story with a pointy-tipped red pen are: Sharon Hinck, Tara Johnson, Julie Klassen, Elizabeth Ludwig, Shannon McNear, Ane Mulligan, Chawna Schroeder, MaryLu Tyndall, and first reader Dani Snyder.

Encouragers

There are those special people in this world who have a way of keeping an author smiling even when it feels like the plot has derailed, so kudos to Cheryl Higgins, Stephanie Gustafson, Maria Nelson, and Erica Vetsch.

Inspirers

You, my readers, inspire me to keep penning tales of hope. To name just a few: Aubrey Ann DeBaar, Vicki Jones, Charity Henico, Liz Vander Lee, and Marcia Brown.

And as always, I couldn't do any of this without the love and support of my husband, Mark, the hero of my life story.

OTHER BOOKS BY MICHELLE

The Bride of Blackfriars Lane
The Thief of Blackfriars Lane

Lost in Darkness

The House at the End of the Moor

Brentwood's Ward
The Innkeeper's Daughter
The Noble Guardian

The Captive Heart

The Captured Bride

Once Upon a Dickens Christmas

HIGH ADVENTURE AND INTRIGUE FROM MICHELLE GRIEP

The Thief of Blackfriars Lane

Newly commissioned officer Jackson Forge intends to clean up the crime-ridden streets of Victorian London even if it kills him, and it just might when he crosses paths with the notorious swindler Kit Turner—but Kit's just trying to survive, which is a full-time occupation for a woman on her own.

Paperback / 978-1-64352-715-4

The Bride of Blackfriars Lane

Detective Jackson Forge can hardly wait to marry the street-sly swindler who's turned his life upside down. But as Kit digs into the mystery of what happened to Jackson's brother, she unwittingly tumbles into her own history and endangers her future happiness with Jackson.

Paperback / 978-1-63609-268-3

ABOUT THE AUTHOR

Michelle Griep's been writing since she first discovered blank wall space and Crayolas. She is the Christy Award-winning author of historical romances that both intrigue and evoke a smile. An Anglophile at heart, you'll most often find her partaking of a proper cream tea while scheming up her next novel. . .but it's probably easier to find her at www.michellegriep.com or on Facebook, Instagram, and Pinterest.

And guess what? She loves to hear from readers!
Feel free to drop her a note at michellegriep@gmail.com.